JUL 9 1992

SAN FRANCISCO PUBLIC LIBRARY

3 1223 02558 1092

SO-BRF-196

The House of Ulloa

The House of Ulloa

A novel by Emilia Pardo Bazán

Translated by Roser Caminals-Heath

University of Georgia Press   Athens and London

F
Pardo Bazan, Emilia.
    The House of Ulloa.

© 1992 by the University of Georgia Press
Athens, Georgia 30602
All rights reserved

Set in 10 on 14 Galliard by Tseng Information Systems
Printed and bound by Thomson-Shore
The paper in this book meets the guidelines for permanence
and durability of the Committee on Production Guidelines for
Book Longevity of the Council on Library Resources.

Printed in the United States of America
96 95 94 93 92   C   5 4 3 2 1

Library of Congress Cataloging in Publication Data

Pardo Bazán, Emilia, condesa de, 1852–1921.
[Pazos de Ulloa. English]
The House of Ulloa : a novel / by Emilia Pardo Bazán;
translated [with critical introduction] by Roser Caminals-Heath.
p. cm.
ISBN 0-8203-1372-6 (alk. paper)
I. Caminals-Heath, Roser. II. Title.
PQ6629.A7P313 1992
863'.5—dc20   91-12757
                                                CIP

British Library Cataloging in Publication Data available

This translation was supported by a grant from the
Dirección General del Libro y Bibliotecas of the
Spanish Ministry of Culture.

3 1223 02558 1092

S.F. PUBLIC LIBRARY

Contents

Acknowledgments

A project of this nature and length is always teamwork. I must and wish to thank my husband, Bill, who first suggested the idea of this translation and has closely seen it through; my mother, María Antonia, for sharing its joys and agonies; and my father, Josep, whose knowledge of country life accounts for some of my notes to the novel; my friend Janice Cole, who with proverbial generosity gave me her time and advice; my colleagues at the Hood College Library, for going well beyond the call of duty; the Board of Associates of Hood College, from whom I received a grant in the early stages of my work; Karen Orchard, associate director of the University of Georgia Press; the readers for the press, for believing in *The House of Ulloa*, and Janis Bolster, copyeditor; and finally, the Spanish Ministry of Culture, for its financial support. I warmly extend my gratitude to all those who have contributed to this publication anonymously but no less effectively.

Excerpts from this translation of *The House of Ulloa* have previously appeared in the *Monocacy Valley Review*.

A Note on the Translation

Los pazos de Ulloa was published in Spain in 1886; a slightly revised edition appeared in 1892. I have followed the first edition, which Pardo Bazán scholars prefer for two reasons: it is doubtful whether the changes introduced in the second edition were made by the author's hand, and in any case, they do not always constitute an improvement. The existing English translation by Ethel Harriet Hearn, *Son of the Bondwoman* (London, 1908), out of print for sev-eral years, has a marked Victorian flavor. *The House of Ulloa* is an American English version that attempts to preserve the character of nineteenth-century prose—long-winded sentences, slightly archaic and Latinate words—and the traits of Pardo Bazán's style discussed in the Introduction. It is my belief that both are too essential for the translator to ignore and that a translation must be faithful, if not to the letter, to the spirit of the original. Aware of the limitations inherent in my task, I have done my best to make the author's prose palatable in English; but to tone down all her sharp notes, to reduce all her linguistic adventures to conventional exercises, to tame, in sum, her aesthetic instinct, would be an act of cowardice and a betrayal. In *The House of Ulloa* the reader will perhaps be surprised at certain phrases, certain forms of dialogue; so is the reader of the novel in Spanish. This translation prefers the risks of Pardo Bazán's originality to the safety of an English version that did not attempt to reflect it.

There is no denying that for the native English speaker the word *Ulloa* defies pronunciation. A simple phonetic analogy may help.

In Spanish, *u* sounds very much like *-oe* in *canoe;* the double *l* is actually a single sound not unlike the English *y;* and the last two letters, *-oa,* may be pronounced as in *Samoa.* The stress is on the second syllable: *U-lló-a.*

The *Autobiographical Sketches* are replete with allusions to international literary works. I found it nearly impossible to adopt a satisfactory system for these titles. When they are well-known classics I simply give them in English; but many are obscure and have never been translated. Rather than attach a translation to every title, I have opted for a compromise: when the main words are cognates that the reader can identify (i.e., *Historia universal*), I have left them in the original; when they are not, I have supplied either the existing or my own English translation in parentheses the first time a work is mentioned.

Introduction

The reader who is not well versed in the literature of Spain will pause over this volume and wonder: among all the Spanish works unavailable in English, why *The House of Ulloa*? Hispanists and the Spanish public, on the other hand, would not hesitate to answer that, from the days of the gaslight to the days of the neon light, in the classroom and in the living room, one generation after another has read *The House of Ulloa*; that Spaniards, from the scholar to the housewife, consider it part of the timeless cultural legacy that defines them as a people; that *The House of Ulloa* is, beyond question, a classic. It has remained in print since it first appeared in 1886; today several scholarly and popular editions are available in Spain and Latin America. As for its repercussions abroad, we know of translations into English (1908), French (1910), German (1946), and Italian (1925, 1961). It is high time that a work of this importance should be brought to the English-speaking reader in a fresh, updated version. That the author happens to be a woman adds to its interest, but is hardly a necessary argument for the translation. The novel speaks for itself.

Although *The House of Ulloa* is Pardo Bazán's masterpiece, it is by no means the only significant work of her career. Pardo Bazán, known familiarly as Doña Emilia in Spanish literary circles, nourished an early omnivorous curiosity about every intellectual mode of her age, true to her dictum that "it is better to understand than to be shocked, because in aesthetics being shocked does not prove anything." As a scholar, her main goals were to raise awareness of world literature and to stimulate debate on subjects as diverse as Galician poetry and German philosophy. In 1887 she published *La revolución y la novela en Rusia* (Revolution and the novel in Russia), a milestone in the study of Russian fiction and the chief reason for the contemporary popularity of this fiction in Spain. Between 1891 and 1893 she financed her own literary magazine, *El nuevo teatro crítico* (New critical forum), with a small family inheritance. But perhaps her major contribution as a critic was *La cuestión palpitante* (The burning issue, 1883), the most articulate and polemic of the numerous Spanish reactions to French naturalism. Both as a critic and as an artist, Pardo Bazán maintained close contacts with the major figures of her time, and she stood firmly at the apex of Spanish intellectual life.

Her feminist views constitute another chapter of her thought. Her collected articles, *La mujer española y otros artículos* (The Spanish woman and other articles), continue to be of great interest. Despite the stubborn opposition that met her advocacy of women's rights and her personal ambitions, in 1906 she was elected the first woman president of the Literary Section of the Ateneo, the leading learned society of Madrid. In 1916 she became the first female professor of Romance languages, although she did little teaching because few students were willing to take courses from a woman.

Her fictional output included numerous short stories, a genre in which she excelled, and nineteen novels. Reflecting the movements of her time, her writings progressed through realistic, naturalistic, and spiritualistic, fin-de-siècle stages; given Pardo Bazán's marked personality, however, we must apply these categories loosely. Although the first period produced a courageous and unprecedented study of working-class women, *La tribuna* (The orator, 1883), only in the second did Pardo Bazán develop her full potential as a novelist. In *The House of Ulloa* (1886) and its sequel, *La madre naturaleza*

(Mother Nature, 1887), she achieved perfect narrative structure and an extraordinary moral complexity. These two novels balance naturalistic techniques, social and psychological realism, and spiritual speculation as her later works do not; for this reason they are the strongest of her fictions.

The House of Ulloa, Los pazos de Ulloa, came out amid the greatest flowering of Spanish fiction since Cervantes. Together with the works of Benito Pérez Galdós, the father of nineteenth-century Spanish realism, and of Leopoldo Alas ("Clarín"), it takes a place of honor in the renaissance that followed the decline of romantic prose. These writers, casting aside quaint locale and sentimentalized characters, drew inspiration from the history and geography of Spain.

The second half of the nineteenth century, with its political upheavals and social changes, offered a rich background for their modern epics. The significant events that took place in Spain throughout Pardo Bazán's lifetime punctuate the action of her novel: the revolution of 1868, whose ultimate failure shattered the hopes of liberals such as Máximo Juncal, the feisty spokesman of modern science and radical politics in The House of Ulloa; the First Republic in 1873; and the restoration of the Bourbon monarchy a year later. The history of these decades can be summarized as a fitful attempt to make a transition to liberalism that ended in a parliamentary monarchy controlled by oligarches. One of the armed groups that opposed the liberals, the Carlists, presented its own candidate for the throne: Don Carlos. Carlos, brother of King Ferdinand VII, who reigned between 1814 and 1833 and was succeeded by his daughter Isabella II, was a figurehead of reaction and fanatical Catholicism. As we see in The House of Ulloa, Carlism found its staunchest supporters in the ultraconservative sectors of rural areas: the clergy and the landed aristocracy.

Galicia was Pardo Bazán's native region and the setting of much of her fiction, including *The House of Ulloa*. Located in the north-western corner of the peninsula, with a rainy climate and lush vegetation evocative of England, it is one of the most distinctive areas of Spain; it has its own language, a culture of Celtic origins in contrast to the classical and Arab influence predominant in Spain, and a history of poverty and abuse by a reactionary feudalism that has over the years driven many of its inhabitants to emigrate to the Americas. *The House of Ulloa* is the definitive novel of Gali-cia. Faithful to the tenets of realism, it offers an accurate portrait of a rural aristocratic family, not only in decline but in regres-sion to a barbaric state. The author's firsthand knowledge of the subject is evident. Born in the ranks of the nobility herself, Count-ess Pardo Bazán spent her summers in a family mansion in the province of Orense, in which her novel is set. Crumbling estates neglected by idle gentlemen, who often had moved to the local capital or to Madrid, were a familiar sight to her. Equally familiar were the characteristics of such gentlemen, typified in the novel by the lord of Ulloa, the Marquis Don Pedro Moscoso, who, unlike his eighteenth-century ancestors, shows no interest in the arts and the humanities and is hardly educated.

While the bourgeoisie was taking control of the industrial cities, as the urban fiction of Alas and Galdós reflects, in the backward Galician countryside the peasantry displaced the aristocracy. Pardo Bazán's Don Pedro divides his plentiful energy between hunting—the passion of the scions of his class—and his maid Sabel, by whom he has a child. The management of his property is in the hands of Sabel's father, Primitivo. In order to improve this state of af-fairs, Don Pedro brings into his household a wife from the city—his cousin Nucha Pardo—and a new administrator—the young priest Julián Alvarez. But his halfhearted attempts crash against the powers that rule over the house of Ulloa.

Primitivo, the barely literate but cunning steward of Ulloa, contrasts sharply with the idealized peasants that populated romantic novels. This quiet Iago slowly but firmly secures his status as true master of the house, to the point of betraying the marquis in the political elections and causing his defeat. That Primitivo's position proves to be the decisive factor in the election indicates his social and political influence. Sabel, although a victim of her father's tyranny and the marquis's abuse, is appropriately portrayed in the kitchen, surrounded by sly old women, as a queen in her court. In the sequel to *The House of Ulloa*, *La madre naturaleza*, Primitivo's dynasty has inherited the future: Sabel and her peasant husband run the property. The foreshadowing that closes the first novel, the image of the marquis's legitimate daughter in rags and his son by Sabel in fine clothes, is fulfilled in the second, in which Perucho, Sabel's boy, prevails as heir. Pardo Bazán makes clear that Ulloa is the rule rather than the exception: the other noble mansion portrayed in *The House of Ulloa*, the house of Limioso, is practically a ruin. As a document of social history, therefore, *The House of Ulloa* records the sunset of a social class and the dawn of another.

A main theme underlying the novel is the tension between nature and civilization, between the country and the city. It has been said that the real protagonist of *The House of Ulloa* is the house itself and its wild surroundings. In the end, these two entities win the struggle against the intruding civilized world and force out its timid messengers. The house constantly takes center stage, and its garden, more like a jungle than a work of human artistry, is a fitting symbol of the regression to barbarism that the narrative traces. The stone-carved coat of arms buried under the weeds, the muddy pond, and the granite balls that had once decorated the garden, now scattered on the ground "like gigantic projectiles on a deserted battlefield," are not only vestiges of the epic past of the Ulloas but proofs of their physical and moral degeneration. The vicious vegetation of the Ulloa cemetery is a disquieting reminder that only the earth lives on, thriving at the expense of our bodies once they no longer feed on its fruits. In compliance with a basic dogma of naturalism, Pardo Bazán accepts the supremacy of the environment over the taming and moralizing efforts of civilized mankind.

Nature, however, is not merely hostile and destructive; it is also alluring and splendid. The countryside that surrounds the house of Ulloa appears alternatively ominous and bucolic, and this oscillation lends a peculiar rhythm to Pardo Bazán's descriptive prose. Few novels have celebrated the beauty of nature more eloquently, and few have been more wary of its threat. The sensitive Julián is constantly torn by this tension. The morning after his troubling first evening in the house, he opens the window and the sight of the meadows fills him with bliss; just when he is deciding to leave the house of Ulloa, his attention is drawn to the peace of the countryside in a balmy night; the next morning, while he plans a hasty departure, he gazes sadly at the garden, the fields, and the mountain, and realizes that he would like to spend the rest of his life there. Nature remains an ambivalent source of horror and aesthetic pleasure, of attraction and repulsion, an amoral goddess that bestows life and death.

A key to the novel's artistic success is that it combines a close study of the environment with a dramatic plot in which the actors are not mere marionettes. The characters group themselves around the two polarities discussed above: the marquis, Primitivo, Sabel, and Perucho are children of nature; Julián, Nucha, and her family belong to civilization. The inhabitants of the coarse world of Ulloa are animalistic and bound by the laws of matter. Julián whispers to himself, "What a country of wolves!" as he enters for the first time the forbidding boundaries of the Ulloa estate; his remark might well apply to the group of people that he is about to meet. Primitivo is often likened to a fox, the abbot of Ulloa to a bear, and the wet nurse who eventually feeds Don Pedro's little daughter to a cow. The house, in contrast to the comfortable urban residence of Nucha's family, is a "den." When the marquis goes to the town of Santiago de Compostela in search of a wife, he chases his cousin Rita as if she were hunting prey. On the other hand, human eroticism is used to dramatize the hunt in chapter 22: the hare is the "shy maiden," the "Dulcinea" courted by numerous suitors who would rather die of a bullet than give up their amorous pursuit. Julián's first taste of social life in his new home is the sight of the four-year-old Perucho crawling among the dogs to get a share of their food, and then later inebriated by his grandfather, Primitivo. Another social event, the gargantuan meal on the patron saint's day at Naya, offers a counterpoint to the restraint and gloom of Nucha's wedding feast.

Not surprisingly, these animalized human beings—with the exception of Primitivo, who, being the most calculating and intelligent, is driven by greed—are at the mercy of their physical appetites; Don Pedro, the abbot, Sabel, and Perucho live to a greater or lesser extent on an instinctive level, concerned mainly with the satisfaction of their sensual desires. The most developed of these characters, Don Pedro, illustrates Pardo Bazán's gift for masculine portraits. For all his coarseness and brutality, she highlights his sexual magnetism and gives us glimpses of his charm and good judgment of character. But ultimately, the marquis is like the house and grounds of Ulloa: uncultivated, gone to seed. He lacks even a basic education to curb his desires. In Santiago, a university town where, as Pardo Bazán says, no one wants to pass for ignorant, Don Pedro feels constricted and humiliated like a caged animal. After the first months back at home with his wife, he resumes his relations with Sabel. Nucha's father, on the other hand, provides an alternative to the unevolved rural aristocrat. Although physically he is portrayed in hyperbolic terms, as if he were an epic warrior, his colossal proportions somehow fit in the frame of civilized life; continuous contact with fellow beings and the subduing influence of his wife and daughters have rubbed off his awkward edges. Don Manuel Pardo proves the same point as Don Pedro Moscoso, the power of the environment; but in his case the environment is cosmopolitan.

Pardo Bazán draws her hero, Julián Alvarez, as a foil to Don Pedro. Julián comes not only from Santiago de Compostela but from an institution of the civilized world, the Catholic church. He lacks the physical skills that the marquis possesses to such a high degree: in the opening scene, he cuts a rather poor figure riding a horse that escapes his control; later, in the hunt, he earns himself the contempt of all those present, even the hound. He is light, beardless, and given to fainting. The temptations of the flesh are—at least at the beginning—practically unknown to him, to the point where his virginity is more a natural state than a triumph of his will. Like Nucha, the young priest represents the values that are absent in the house of Ulloa: spirituality, culture, and on the negative side, faintheartedness.

Julián is the agent of change in the marquis's household. In his position as inexperienced administrator, he has the task of pruning the things that Hamlet would call "rank and gross," starting with the archives. Their paper jungle, on which insects feast undisturbed, is no less chaotic than the vegetation of the garden. But he extends his civilizing zeal to the human inhabitants of Ulloa when he undertakes the education of Perucho and the moral reformation of the marquis. It is Julián who conceives the plan of salvation by marriage and suggests Nucha as the perfect wife for Don Pedro.

We follow the narrative through Julián's point of view, except in chapter 28, where the author temporarily shifts to Perucho's. It is through the priest's eyes that we first see the gloomy walls of Ulloa and its dwellers and watch events unfold. Whereas we have only a few lines from Primitivo, whose actions are revealed indirectly, and an external knowledge of the marquis, we are allowed into Julián's thoughts by means of interior monologues, and into his subconscious by means of his dreams. His privileged position within the narrative framework, together with his values, which are in consonance with Pardo Bazán's Catholicism, lead some critics to argue that she identifies with her character and makes him her spokesman. Furthermore, it is a common opinion that the urban characters in general, who stand for culture, spirituality, and civilization, are morally superior to their rural counterparts and, therefore, enjoy the author's favor.

This argument presents some problems. It is safe to say that Julián and Nucha are the most admirable people in the house of Ulloa, but no one escapes Pardo Bazán's satirical eye. A case in point is Nucha's family in Santiago. The eldest sister, Rita, to whom the marquis is originally attracted, behaves with petty vindictiveness when he turns to the self-effacing Nucha; not only does Rita refuse to speak to her, but she contrives to deprive Nucha of her small inheritance and secure it for herself. Manolita, the second sister, in love with an indecisive gentleman that Pardo Bazán openly ridicules, goes as far as to send unsigned insidious notes to a rival for his love. The father, Don Manuel Pardo de la Lage, is not capable of drunken bouts—although he has no qualms about crude jokes—or physical violence, like the marquis or Primitivo, but he runs his daughters' lives like a tyrant, and not always to their benefit: he would never give their hands to middle-class men, but he gladly delivers Nucha to as unpromising a husband as his nephew Don Pedro. For all Pardo Bazán's aristocratic outlook and indulgence toward her class, there is no question that the pages on the Pardo de la Lages are spiced with irony. The city of Santiago itself, appealing for its art and history, seems to be a hotbed of malicious gossip. We have to conclude that Pardo Bazán exposes the evils—and the rewards—of both nature and civilization.

Is Julián exempted from this ironic treatment? Are we to take

him always seriously as the author's mouthpiece? Even a superficial reading reveals that Pardo Bazán delights in making fun of
him. As mentioned earlier, his presentation in the first chapter is
far from flattering; his obsession with cleanliness and his prudishness prompt a comparison with an untouched maiden and a nun;
his naiveté and inexperience in worldly matters often make him an
object of derision for others.

A closer look at his role in the events of the novel points to
the conclusion that Pardo Bazán's criticism goes beyond gentle
mockery. No one would dispute Julián's honesty and good intentions, but his good intentions pave the way to Nucha's hell. He
plots her marriage to Don Pedro and, with her father's complicity,
shares responsibility for Nucha's misfortune. Critics tend to blame
exclusively the marquis and Primitivo, the rural characters that fall
on the side of nature and immorality; we certainly must not ex-
onerate them, but the initial architects of her demise are in the
headquarters of civilization. Nucha would like to enter a convent,
but marries the marquis to please her father. As for Don Pedro,
whose instinct leans toward the voluptuous Rita, it is the priest
who urges on him the merits and excellence of Nucha. That she is a
mystic girl of frail health, temperamentally incompatible with her
cousin, never occurs to Julián as an obstacle to their union. Lacking the slightest knowledge of human love, he seals Nucha's fate
without hesitation. If Don Pedro and Primitivo sin against religion and morality, we have to wonder whether Julián sins against
nature by simply ignoring it.

And yet, for all his inadequacy and incompetence in practical
things, the young priest engages our sympathy and rises from his
status of semicomic figure to become an almost tragic one. His
growth from an angelic, sexless being to the mature manhood of
the last chapters is one of the greatest achievements of the novel.
The most revealing moment in this respect is his visit to Nucha's

grave on his return to Ulloa, after a ten-year hiatus. While Nucha lived, Julián did not admit—perhaps did not even know—that he was in love with her. He regarded her as an incarnation of the Virgin Mary of whom Don Pedro was unworthy, but never dreamed of claiming her for himself; even when he heard of her death in his exile, the thought of her happiness in the afterlife kept him surprisingly calm. But Pardo Bazán soon destroys the illusion of his Christian resignation, reminding us that not even Julián is wholly spiritual, and that moral and natural laws wage their war within us as much as without. When Julián is confronted with the physical reality of Nucha's grave, he kisses and claws at it; this gesture of rebellion is an admission of his feelings not as a priest but as a man. Julián understands now things that he had not understood before, and for the first time sees himself. Suffering has cured him of his blindness and awakened his consciousness.

The female characters illustrate Pardo Bazán's views on women in contemporary society. These views may have been partly inspired by her liberal father, who rejected double standards for the sexes. In a similar vein, she declared once: "I am a radical feminist. I believe that women should have all the rights that men have." Although a century ago the words "radical feminist" did not imply what they do today, they suggest her position on the issue. Pardo Bazán denounced the fact that the middle-class Spanish woman, except in some privileged regions, was discouraged from engaging her mind in anything but trivialities; the more superficial she was, the more admired. As long as the system refused to educate women and prepare them for a meaningful existence, she saw little hope for the progress of Spain as a nation. These ideas, formulated in her articles and lectures, are dramatized in her fiction.

In *The House of Ulloa* the Pardo girls are hothouse flowers, cultivated to capture the fancy of prospective husbands. Their father regards them as so many financial burdens that marriage will take from his shoulders. Nucha, the victim rather than the heroine, is an example of the well-to-do, helpless city lady whose situation the author deplored. Her good qualities exempt her from the shallowness of her sisters and make her more sympathetic; but society does not grant her a say in her future, which is decided by the men in her life—her father, her husband, and her spiritual mentor. Nucha dutifully submits to their designs and realizes, much too late, that she is being punished for her obedience. Her gentle rebuke at this stage is meant not only to give Julián pangs of conscience but to indict a system that imposes its unjust laws on her and then makes her a scapegoat: "Don't you agree that this marriage had to fail? My sister Rita was almost engaged to Pedro when he asked my hand. Through no fault of mine, Rita and I haven't spoken since then. I don't know how that happened; God knows that I did nothing to attract his attention. Papa advised me to marry my cousin anyway. I followed his advice. I made a resolution to be good, love him dearly, obey him, see after my children . . . Tell me, Julián, what did I do wrong?"

Similarly, Sabel has no will of her own. Her father forces her to stay in the house of Ulloa as the marquis's mistress, even though she prefers men of her own class; when she attempts to free herself of this bondage, her master beats her brutally, with Primitivo's consent. In Pardo Bazán's fiction, upper-class women resign themselves to unwanted marriages and lower-class ones accept seduction with equal passivity. Of course, neither group has any choice, but at the same time we must keep in mind an important peculiarity of Galician society: among the peasantry of this era there was little or no stigma attached to the seduced girl; her peers regarded her relations with the landlord—or with any other man—as a matter of fact, which did not diminish her matrimonial prospects. In *La madre naturaleza* we learn that Sabel has married the bagpiper who courts her in *The House of Ulloa*, and that, furthermore, he is proud of his wife's son by the marquis.

Female virginity, which seems meaningless amid the stark reali-
ties of peasant life, is sacred to the aristocracy and the bourgeoisie
of Santiago. As Pardo Bazán comments slyly, in these circles "a girl
often loses her reputation before her virtue." This may well be the
case of Rita, whose flirtatiousness marks her as "fair game" and
induces the marquis to sacrifice his inclinations to his prejudice.
It goes without saying that Pardo Bazán takes a dim view of Don
Pedro's notion of conjugal honor, "extremely indulgent in the case
of the husband and implacable in that of the wife." It is in light of
this principle that he finally proposes to Nucha: there is no question of her virtue up to the present, and no apparent reason to
worry about it in the future.

Aside from the character study and the dramatization of the
milieu, the novelistic craft of *The House of Ulloa* is remarkable.
Pardo Bazán has a scenic sense of chapter; each of the thirty that
compose the novel is a complete dramatic unit without cracks and
without filling. Their endings climax, as the reader will notice, with
subtle, unsettling foreshadowings, instead of the clear heightening
of suspense typical of the nineteenth-century novel in installments.
Internal coherence results from the inclusion of every necessary
detail and exclusion of the superfluous. To appreciate this point,
we must observe how Pardo Bazán's sensual prose reveals plot developments visually more than verbally. Let us take the accusation
of adultery that looms over Julián and Nucha through the last
section of the novel. We guess Primitivo's design to arouse Don
Pedro's suspicion from his cold, scrutinizing glance at the priest
and the lady in the chapel. Later, the priest of Naya gossips with
the archpriest of Loiro in the midst of a raging windstorm; Pardo
Bazán chooses to reproduce the storm rather than the dialogue,
drowned out by the wind, but we infer that they are talking about
Nucha and Julián. When the slander reaches the marquis, his confrontation with the supposed lovers is conveyed through Perucho's
eyes, which once again give us the gestures instead of the words.

There are other examples of this technique. Julián discovers dark rings around Nucha's wrists, and we fear correctly that the marquis has been subjecting her to the same treatment as Sabel. We do not hear the political leader Barbacana and his hired killer plot Primitivo's murder; but we see them talking in a dark room behind drawn curtains, and we know. Not surprisingly, some of these dramatic visual sequences coincide with the ends of chapters.

Pardo Bazán's style is one of the richest and most original in Spanish fiction. For this very reason, it is also one of the most difficult to capture in another language. *Los pazos de Ulloa* displays a staggering lexical range, from Galician colloquialisms to terms of pathology that illustrate the naturalistic novelist's endeavor to introduce science in literature. The physical and psychological descriptions of the characters obey the scientific laws then in vogue: Julián and Nucha are lymphatic and nervous, the marquis sanguine and muscular. Doctor Máximo Juncal, an advocate of modern hygienics, gives Pardo Bazán an opportunity to satirize and also to indulge in the jargon of contemporary medicine. This scientific zeal extends to the realm of plants, to the point that Pardo Bazán has been accused, not without some reason, of pedantry and of writing "botanical" novels. As the critic Carmen Bravo Villasante says, she "names things by name because she knows the things and loves the names."[1] This is true not only of the animal and vegetal kingdoms but also of kitchen utensils, horseback-riding gear, clothes, liturgical objects, writing implements, and every other humble instrument of everyday life. Furthermore, the prose does not follow the familiar paths of convention, but deliberately seeks the unexpected word. The pantry of the priest of Naya is not full or stuffed, it is "insatiable"; Don Pedro's opinions are not conservative or old-fashioned, they are "rancid." The unusual application of adjectives like these lends her writing a piquant, sensual flavor.

1. *Vida y obra de Emilia Pardo Bazán* (Madrid: Revista de Occidente, 1962), 72.

But perhaps the trademark of her style is her frankness and directness, her contempt for decorum. Anything that stands in the way of expressiveness—the chief objective of her language— is mercilessly dismissed. By the standards of the period, she wrote like a man, and an uninhibited man at that. From the first chapter, the presence of the marquis "in his manly dishevelment" exudes primary sexuality, and his language is vulgar; Sabel is brutally appraised as "a good piece of luxuriant flesh," and her beauty depicted as through the eyes of a man; at the pastoral scene of the banquet at Naya, Pardo Bazán describes one of the peasant men as "stupid with a vengeance," and further refers to him as "the village idiot." The rugged effect of her prose is exacerbated by the presence of wordy and angular sentences. On these occasions Pardo Bazán lingers on the fringes of what is formally acceptable, but she also achieves unusual strength. In the words of Maurice Hemingway, hers is "a knotty and deliberately unflowing style, which, through the very awkwardness of the reading process, gives the reader a sense of the density of the world being described."[2]

Her sensitivity to masculine beauty, her alarming sincerity, and the boldness of her language earned her a reputation as a pornographic and heterodox writer in her lifetime. From our present perspective, we can barely suppress a smile of condescension at the first adjective, but we must accept the second as a compliment to the author. Heterodoxy in itself may not be an artistic asset, but her individual departure from orthodoxy is. Emilia Pardo Bazán wrote unlike anyone else and wrote well. If she exhibited a frankness not expected from a woman, it was not in a spirit of imitation of male novelists. On the contrary, her work mirrors her personality. Fond of her social status, she maintained the appearance of an impeccable private life that, in truth, was less irreproachable

2. *Emilia Pardo Bazán: The Making of a Novelist* (Cambridge: Cambridge University Press, 1983), 12.

than she led her contemporaries to believe; her separation from her husband and her sporadic love affairs were well-kept secrets. But as a public figure, she refused to behave like a "lady writer." Other literary women in Spain, like Concepción Arenal, Fernán Caballero, or Rosalía de Castro, purged with their puritanical lives the "dishonor" of their profession. Pardo Bazán, on the other hand, did not renounce worldly pleasures or the ambitions traditionally reserved to men. Her outspoken and opinionated manner irritated some male intellectuals, who half critically, half admiringly, said of her: "Quite a man, this woman." Even in our decade Nelly Clémessy qualifies her in a positive way as a "woman of letters with definitely masculine attitudes."[3] The notion of the feminine and the masculine may vary with time; what has not changed is the validity of Pardo Bazán's self-portrait: "Curious, uninhibited, and open."

Like every strong individualist, Pardo Bazán appears contradictory. A moderate liberal in politics and a conservative in religion, she severed her early ties with the Carlist party because of its fanaticism and intolerance toward certain liberal positions; on the other hand, she upheld her aristocratic views and loyalty to the throne, rejecting the revolutionary tactics of the Republicans. To the traditionalists she was a scandal; to the liberals, a reactionary. Her attacks against both are evident in the negative portrayals of the two rival leaders in *The House of Ulloa*. In truth, Pardo Bazán chronicles local politics accurately. Her rendition of the grotesque electoral process is no caricature. Historical documentation testifies to the use of corruption and manipulation of the electorate as common practices in rural Galicia.

The literary judgments of this unusual woman also baffled her

3. *Emilia Pardo Bazán como novelista* (Madrid: Fundación Universitaria española, 1981), 827.

contemporaries. The burning issue of the 1880s in Spain was the naturalistic school of Emile Zola. Zola's concept of the novel as a scientific experiment, designed to prove that genetic and environmental factors rather than free will determine human conduct, outraged the conservative wing of Spanish Catholicism. Pardo Bazán's book *La cuestión palpitante* made a dispassionate analysis of the movement and assessed its leading figure as an artist. Although, on the whole, she rejected the philosophical tenets of naturalism, her receptiveness to some of its techniques aroused the hostility of tradition-minded critics and novelists. The controversy on naturalism was one of the bitterest in Spain throughout the nineteenth century, and Pardo Bazán was at the center of it. Once again, her ability to evaluate an ideology from a multiple viewpoint caused her to be misinterpreted. Conservative intellectuals lashed out at this Catholic wife and mother who prodded into so sordid a business as naturalism; Zola was flattered, but could not understand how a Catholic could find anything positive in his thought. Typically, Pardo Bazán could not—would not—follow any prescribed line.

As usual, the most enlightening contemporary analysis is her own. She pronounced herself neither an idealist, nor a realist, nor a naturalist, but an eclectic; to formulate the same conclusion in different words: not an ideologue, but an artist. From romanticism, she borrowed a Gothic ambience and an animistic treatment of nature reminiscent of Emily Brontë's *Wuthering Heights*; from naturalism, the strong—but not irreversible—influence of the milieu. Ultimately, it was her broad-minded realism that enabled her to encompass the basic truths of science and the mysteries of the spirit. As she put it to a hostile Catholic scholar: "I incline toward mysticism in the supernatural order and toward positivism in the natural one."

Despite the controversy around the author's personality and

views, *The House of Ulloa* was an instant success. A highly positive review by Leopoldo Alas, the most prestigious and feared Spanish critic of the period, drowned out a few disgruntled voices. If praise seems logical from a liberal and an advocate of naturalism, it is more surprising that Juan Valera, a classicist opposed to the excesses of the modern school, should say: "Devil of a woman! She has a peculiar and rare talent . . . I think that, for all her perversion of taste, morality, and theodicy,[4] Doña Emilia is quite a novelist."[5] Perhaps Don Juan agreed that in aesthetics being shocked does not prove anything.

The *Autobiographical Sketches* that follow the novel were written as a preface to *The House of Ulloa*, as Hawthorne's *Custom House* was to *The Scarlet Letter*. Strangely enough, they have never been reprinted after the first edition of 1886 or translated into English. As the author's only autobiographical account—Pardo Bazán disliked discussing her private life—they are too valuable to be forgotten. The reader may be disappointed to find that, like Hawthorne, she promises to be forthright and in truth is elusive. The style, convoluted and sometimes flowery in the nineteenth-century fashion, may seem in itself a barrier. But if these pages throw little light on Pardo Bazán's intimate life, they do illuminate her novel, by expounding her ideas on the art of fiction. Through them, we follow the basic stages in the making of the artist and the evolution of her literary thought. In this sense, the *Autobiographical Sketches* help us to understand the author of *The House of Ulloa* and how her masterpiece came to be.

Welcome to *The House of Ulloa*.

---

4. From the Greek *theos,* god, and *dike,* justice: the belief that evil exists in order for divine justice to be vindicated.

5. Quoted by Carmen Bravo Villasante in *Vida y obra de Emilia Pardo Bazán*, 127.

The House of Ulloa

Chapter 1

Although the rider pulled the rein with all his might and whispered soft and soothing words, the shaggy horse continued its descent at a trot so clumsy that it would have unsettled anyone's insides, breaking from time to time into a headlong, crazy gallop. That slope in the highway from Santiago to Orense was very steep— much steeper than the law allowed, travelers used to mumble, shaking their heads; and they added that the engineers knew what they were up to when they designed that road: no doubt the property of some political figure or someone with strong electoral influence was nearby.

The horseman's face was flushed not red but pink, as befits lymphatic temperaments. His youth, delicate frame, and smooth skin gave him the appearance of a boy, an impression belied by his priestly garb. Under the yellow dust beaten by the nag one could see the lad's plain black suit, with the loose and clumsy cut that marks all lay clothes worn by churchmen.

His gloves, already worn through by the coarse bridle, were as black and new as the bowler that he had pressed down to his eyebrows, for fear that the jolting might fling it to the ground— which would have been most embarrassing. An inch of bead-embroidered stock showed under the collar of the graceless overcoat. The horseman displayed little riding skill: as he leaned over the saddlebow with his knees bent, ready to be ejected over the horse's ears, his face revealed as much terror as if the nag were a wild steed bursting with fierceness and vigor.

At the end of the slope the horse resumed its usual calm pace, and the rider straightened himself up on the round saddle, so wide that it had disjointed every one of his sacroiliac bones. He sighed, removed his hat, and felt the cool evening air on his sweaty forehead. The sunbeams slanted down on brambles and hedges, and a road laborer in shirtsleeves, his jacket set aside on a granite milestone, was languidly hoeing weeds by the ditch. The rider pulled the halter of his horse, which, weary of trotting downhill, stopped immediately. The worker raised his head and the gold plate on his hat flashed for a second.

"Will you kindly tell me how far is the marquis of Ulloa's house?"

"The house of Ulloa?" the worker replied, repeating the question.

"That is correct."

"The house of Ulloa is over there," he murmured, pointing at the horizon. "If the beast makes good time the road ahead of you goes fast. But mind you, first you have to continue to that pine forest, see it? Then you need to go left, and then you need to turn right, down the shortcut to the crossroads. Once you're at the crossroads you can't miss it; you'll see the house, a huge building."

"But, how far do you reckon it still is from here?"

The worker shook his sunburned head. "A little morsel, just a little morsel . . ."

And with no further explanation he resumed his listless job, lifting the hoe as if it weighed a hundred pounds.

The traveler, resigned to going on without knowing how many miles make "a little morsel," spurred his nag. The pine forest was not very distant; horse and horseman began to follow a very narrow path that meandered through the thick shade. Buried in the darkness of the woods, the trail was almost impassable; but the nag, confirming the ability of Galician horses to handle rough terrain, plodded on with great caution. Head down, it felt its way with its hooves to avoid cart tracks, stones, and pine logs lying in the most inconvenient places. They progressed slowly, until they came out onto a wider path amid young pine trees and hills covered with furze, without stumbling upon a single estate, a single cabbage field that might suggest human existence. Suddenly the horse's hooves ceased to echo and plunged into a soft carpet: a blanket of green manure spread, according to the local custom, in front of a peasant's shack. At the doorstep a woman nursed a baby. The horseman stopped.

"Madam, is this the way to the marquis of Ulloa's house?"

"It is, it is . . ."

"Is it still far?"

Arched eyebrows, apathetic and curious look in her eyes, ambiguous reply in dialect. "Just a dog's run . . ."

"I'm done for!" the traveler thought. He did not know the distance covered in a dog's run, but he feared that for a horse it must be considerable. Well, whenever he reached the crossroads he would see the Ulloa estate. Finding the shortcut to the right proved to be no easy task. There was no sign of it. The trail broadened as it went into a mountain scattered with oaks and a few chestnuts still loaded with fruit; dark heather spread to the right and to the left. The rider experienced an unsettling discomfort, justifiable in anyone who, born and bred in a quiet dreamy town, faces for the first time the majestic loneliness of nature and recalls tales of plundered travelers and people murdered in deserted places.

"What a country of wolves!" he mumbled to himself, gloomily impressed.

His spirits rose at the sight of the narrow and steep shortcut on his right, descending between twin stone fences that divided two hills. He was riding down, trusting the nag's skill to elude obstacles, when almost at an arm's length he discerned something that made him shudder: a black wooden cross with white streaks, half fallen on a wall that supported it. The horseman knew that these crosses mark the spot where a man has met a violent death; he crossed himself and whispered the Lord's Prayer while the horse, which no doubt sniffed the scent of a fox, shivered slightly, pricked up its ears, and initiated a timid trot that shortly took them to an intersection. A stone cross emerged amid the branches of a superb chestnut.

The stone was ordinary and so crudely carved that at first glance the cross looked like a Romanesque monument, although in reality it was only a century old, the work of some stonecutter with am-bitions as a sculptor; at that time and place, under the canopy of the magnificent tree, the cross was poetic and beautiful. The horseman, soothed and filled with devotion, bared his head and muttered: "We worship you, Jesus Christ, and we bless you, for by your holy cross you redeemed the world." And as he prayed, his eyes strayed far away to the house of Ulloa, which had to be that massive, square building with towers down in the depths of the valley. This moment of contemplation was brief, for the horse made a speedy escape, mad with terror, its ears pricked up, and the priest came near kissing the ground. The situation called for such a retreat—two shots had just resounded alarmingly near.

Afraid to search the underbrush for his hidden aggressors, the rider froze and held onto the saddlebow; but his anxiety did not last long: down the slope behind the cross he saw three men pre-ceded by as many hounds, whose presence proved that their mas-ters' guns posed no threat except to wild creatures.

The leading hunter appeared to be twenty-eight or thirty years old. Tall and well bearded, he had a sunburned neck and face; but his open shirt and bare head revealed the fair skin of his chest and forehead, usually protected from the weather. The broad torso, with a tiny island of curly hair between the nipples, suggested a vigorous constitution. Leather boots buckled up to his thighs protected sturdy legs; a well-stuffed hunting bag covered with a linen net hung over his groin; and a modern, two-barrel gun rested on his shoulder. The second hunter seemed a mature man of lowly condition, perhaps a servant or a tenant: no buckles on his boots and no bag other than a coarse sack; his hair cut very short; his old-fashioned gun, which used percussion caps, held together by twine; and on his face, clean-shaven, stolid, with sharp and energetic features, an expression of concealed cunning and savage astuteness more characteristic of the red Indian than the European.

As for the third hunter, the horseman was shocked to realize that it was a priest. How did he know? Certainly not by the tonsure, erased by a bush of thick gray hair, or by his shaving, for the bristles of his bluish beard were at least a month old; even less by the stock, which he did not wear at all; nor by his outfit, which resembled that of his hunting friends, with the addition of a pair of worn-out and deeply cracked leather riding boots. And yet he had the smack of clergy and bore that intimidating stamp of ordination that not even hellfire can obliterate in the indefinable expression of his face, in his air and posture, his eyes, his walk, in everything about him. There was no doubt: he was a priest.

The rider approached the group and repeated the proverbial question: "Would you kindly tell me if this is the way to the marquis of Ulloa's house?"

The tall hunter turned around toward the others with familiarity and self-assurance. "What a coincidence! Here's the stranger. Primitivo, you're in luck; I was planning to send you to Cebre for the gentleman tomorrow. And you, abbot of Ulloa, here's the man who'll help you set your parish in order!"

As the horseman seemed to hesitate, the hunter added: "I assume you're the person recommended by my uncle, Señor de la Lage?"

"Your servant and chaplain," the churchman answered eagerly as he tried to get off his horse, an arduous task in which the abbot assisted him. "And is your lordship the marquis?" he exclaimed, facing the party.

"How's my uncle? You rode all the way from Cebre, didn't you?" replied the marquis elusively, while the chaplain eyed him with keen interest that bordered on curiosity.

There was no question that the marquis, in his manly dishevelment, his skin a bit damp with perspiration and the gun on his shoulder, cut a fine figure; and yet his arrogant person had a wild and rustic air and his hard glance contrasted with his warm, unceremonious welcome.

The chaplain explained himself obsequiously. "Yes, sir, exactly. In Cebre I got off the stagecoach and took this horse. The riding gear is something, I must say . . . Señor de la Lage is just as nice as ever, with his usual sense of humor—he makes the stones themselves laugh—and still handsome for his age. I was just thinking that if he were your father you couldn't resemble him more. The young ladies are fine, happy and in good health; from the young gentleman, who is in Segovia, I only hear good news. Before I forget . . ."

He fumbled in the pocket of his overcoat and produced a handkerchief neatly pressed and folded, a little prayer book, and a black morocco folder fastened with an elastic band, out of which he took a letter for the marquis. The hounds, footsore and exhausted, had sat down at the foot of the cross; the abbot was taking apart a bad cigar in order to make a cigarette, having stuck the edge of the paper on his lip; Primitivo, resting the butt of the gun on the ground and his chin on the barrel, scrutinized the newcomer with his little dark eyes. The sun sank slowly amid the quiet autumn landscape. All of a sudden the marquis laughed loudly. His laughter was vigorous and powerful like himself, and rather than contagious, despotic.

"My uncle," he remarked, folding the letter, "is always so funny and mischievous. He says he sends me a saint to preach and convert me . . . as if I was a great sinner, isn't that right, abbot? Isn't it true that I haven't committed a single sin?"

"Of course, of course," the abbot mumbled hoarsely. "We all keep our baptismal innocence around here."

As he spoke he glanced at the newcomer under his bushy eyebrows, the way a veteran might look at an inexperienced recruit. Inwardly he felt only contempt for the beardless priest, with his girlish face in which the only priestly traces were the sternness of the fair brow and the ascetic features.

"Is your name Julián Alvarez?" the marquis inquired.

"At your service."

"And you couldn't find my property?"

"I had some difficulty. The country folks around here wouldn't clear my doubts or give me an accurate sense of distances, so . . ."

"You won't get lost again. Would you like to walk the rest of the way?"

"Gladly, sir."

"Primitivo," the marquis ordered, "take this halter." And he started to walk, conversing at the same time with the chaplain. Primitivo obediently stayed behind with the abbot, who was lighting his cigarette with a match. The hunter approached the priest. "Tell me, what do you think of the lad? He doesn't command much respect, does he?"

"Bah! It's common practice now to ordain jackanapes who show off their fancy stock and neat gloves. Fiddlesticks! If I was an archbishop I'd give the damn gloves to the devil!"

Chapter 2

When they reached the grove in front of the imposing mansion of Ulloa the moonless night had fallen. Darkness engulfed the lines of the structure, revealing only its massive dimensions. No lights shone in the large building, and the front gate seemed to be locked. The marquis went to a small side wicket, where a strong woman with a lighted candle instantly appeared. After passing through several somber corridors, they entered a dirt-floor basement with a stone dome, which, to judge from the rows of barrels along the walls, must have been the wine cellar. From there they soon reached the roomy kitchen. A fire, or what is archaically known as a fair pile of logs, burned in the hearth. It consisted simply of a few oak boughs and some broom added from time to time.

Strings of red and black sausage, as well as an occasional ham, were displayed on the tall chimney; a bench on each side invited one to sit down comfortably and warm up by the bubbling black pot that hung on a chain and offered its insensitive iron belly to the kiss of the flames.

When the party stepped into the kitchen an old woman was huddled by the pot. Julián caught barely a glimpse of her: strands of coarse white hair fell over her eyes, and her flushed face glowed by the firelight. As soon as she noticed people coming into the room, she rose faster than her age permitted and mumbled in a whining voice: "God be with you, good night!" And she vanished like a shadow, nobody knew how. The marquis faced the maid: "Didn't I tell you I don't want old hags around here?"

She hung the candle on the pilaster of the chimney and answered quietly: "She was doing no harm, just helping me peel chestnuts."

The marquis might have gone into a rage if Primitivo, still angrier and more commanding than his master, had not cut in to scold the girl: "What are you babbling about? You'd better fix us some food right now! Come on, move!"

An oak table, blackened by use and covered with a coarse cloth smeared with wine and grease, stood in a corner of the kitchen. Primitivo, who had left his gun in the corner, took out of his bag two partridges and a dead hare, its eyes dim and its fur caked with blood. The girl pushed the booty aside and placed on the table pewter plates, knives and forks of solid old silver, a huge loaf of bread, and a jug of wine to go with it; then she hurriedly stirred and uncovered a few baking pans and took a monumental soup tureen down from the shelf.

Once again the marquis addressed her with irritation: "And the dogs? What about the dogs?"

As if they understood their right to be tended to before anyone else, the dogs emerged from the darkest corner and, forgetting their weariness, began to yawn hungrily, wag their tails, and sniff around with their cleft noses. At first Julián thought that they had multiplied from three before to four now; but when they came into the bright firelight he realized that what he had mistaken for another hound was no less than a three- or four-year-old ragamuffin. His dress, a brownish coat and cotton drawers, blended in the distance with the bicolored fur of the dogs, with whom he seemed to live in the closest intimacy. Primitivo and the maid arranged the animals' meal, which was carefully chosen from the best in the pot, in wooden bowls; and the marquis, who supervised these activities and was not completely satisfied, dragged the depths of the stew with an iron spoon until he extracted three fat pork slabs, which he then distributed among the three bowls.

The dogs howled periodically, inquisitive and anxious, not daring yet to set their teeth in the prize; at Primitivo's command they buried their noses in it at once, chewing and smacking noisily. Maddened by unmitigated hunger, they looked askance at the child crawling under their feet, bared their teeth, and growled in a threatening way. Suddenly the boy, tempted by the slab left in the bowl of the female Chula, stretched out his hand; the dog turned her head and snapped at him ferociously, but fortunately she caught only his sleeve. Frightened and tearful, the boy rushed to hide behind the petticoat of the young woman, who was serving broth to the rational group. Julián, pulling off his gloves, took pity on the child and stooped down to pick him up in his arms. Despite the grease, filth, fear, and tears, he realized that the boy was the most beautiful wild angel in the world.

"Poor thing!" he muttered affectionately. "Did the dog really bite you? Is it bleeding? You'll tell me where it hurts, won't you? Wait and see how we fix the dog, yes sir, we will. You naughty, bad dog!"

The chaplain noticed that his words had a peculiar effect on the marquis. His features hardened; he frowned and, snatching the child from Julián's arms, sat him roughly on his knee and felt his hands for bites and injuries. Reassured that only the jacket had suffered, he laughed.

"You rascal!" he shouted. "Why, Chula didn't even touch you. Can't you leave her alone, eh? Any day she'll chew off your cheeks and you'll have a good cry. Quiet! Let's see that smile right now! Are we or aren't we a brave boy?"

And as he talked he filled a glass with wine and offered it to the boy, who took it without hesitation and drank it up in the twinkling of an eye. The marquis applauded. "Long live the brave!"

"The little brat is really something," the abbot of Ulloa mumbled.

"Won't all this wine make him sick?" Julián objected, incapable of getting it down himself.

"Sick? Heavens, no!" the marquis replied with a touch of pride in his voice. "Give him two, three more glasses and watch him. Would you like to try?"

"He'll soak them up like a sponge," the abbot stated.

"No sir, no. The boy might even die. I've heard that wine is poison to children. He must be hungry, though."

"Sabel, feed the boy," the marquis ordered, turning to the maid.

Sabel, who had sat throughout the previous exchange without comment, came with a bowl full of broth. The child sat down by the hearth to sip it calmly.

At the table the men ate with a hearty appetite. A heavy stew with plenty of pork followed the rich broth. On hunting days the basic pot stew, which could not be carried to the mountains, was served at home in the evening. The eggs and sausage revived the thirst awakened by the salted pork. The marquis jostled Primitivo. "Bring a couple of bottles . . . of 1859."

And, turning to Julián, he added unctuously: "You shall sample the best dessert wine brewed in this area. It comes from the house of Molende: rumor has it that there is a secret to make it taste like the best sherry, not too sweet but retaining the raisin flavor. It gets better all the time, unlike the wine from other cellars, which only turns to sugar!"

"It is worth trying," the abbot declared as he cleaned the remaining egg yolk from his plate with a piece of bread.

"I know very little about wine," Julián said timidly. "I drink hardly anything but water."

Catching a look under the abbot's bushy eyebrows so contemptuous that it was almost commiserative, he corrected himself: "That is to say . . . on special days I don't mind a few drops of anisette in my coffee."

"Wine warms the heart. He who doesn't drink is not a man," the abbot pronounced.

Primitivo was already back from his little excursion, in each hand a bottle wrapped in dust and cobwebs. Lacking a corkscrew, they opened the bottles with a knife and at once filled the small glasses brought for the occasion. Primitivo tipped his merrily, while he joked with the abbot and the host. Sabel, on her part, as the banquet progressed and the liquor raised spirits, served with greater familiarity, leaning on the table to giggle at some joke that made Julián, inexperienced in the after-dinner conversation of hunters, lower his eyes. The truth is that Julián averted his eyes not so much on account of what he heard as to avoid the sight of Sabel, whose looks had strangely displeased him from the first moment, in spite or because of the fact that Sabel was a good piece of luxuriant flesh. Her moist, submissive blue eyes, her fresh complexion, her chestnut brown hair, curled in two shells and braided down below her waist, greatly embellished the girl and concealed her imperfections: cheekbones that were too high, a stubborn, low forehead, and a wide and sensual turned-up nose. In order not to look at Sabel, Julián concentrated his attention on the urchin, who, encouraged by his sympathetic glances, slipped gradually into his lap. Once settled in, he lifted his impudent, smiling face and, tugging at Julián's vest, begged: "Can I have it?"

Everyone laughed loudly; the chaplain did not understand.

"What does he want?" he asked.

"What do you think? The wine, of course!" the marquis replied in a festive tone. "What else? Your glass of wine!"

"Mamma!" the abbot screamed.

Before Julián could decide whether to give the child his nearly full glass, the marquis lifted the ragamuffin, who would have been extraordinarily handsome had he not been so unkempt. He resembled Sabel, but surpassed her in the brightness of his eyes, his abundant curly hair, and, most of all, the correct design of his features. His plump brown hands stretched toward the wine, the color of topaz; the marquis raised the glass to his lips and amused himself for a while by taking it back when the boy thought it already in his power. Finally the child seized the glass and in a trice transferred its contents into his mouth, licking his lips.

"He certainly isn't finicky!" the abbot said loudly.

"Not him," the marquis concurred. "He's a real veteran! I bet you can put down another glass, Perucho?"

The cherub's pupils flashed; his cheeks were burning, and the nostrils of his classical little nose swelled with the innocent concupiscence of an infant Bacchus. The abbot winked maliciously and served him a second glass, which the boy held in both hands and drank to the last drop. Immediately he burst out laughing. Before the echo of his Bacchic laughter faded, he grew very pale and his head dropped on the marquis's chest.

"Don't you see?" Julián protested anxiously. "He's very young to drink like that and he can get very sick. Such things are not for children."

"Bah!" Primitivo cut in. "Do you think that's too much for the little brat? He can handle twice as much. Watch this!"

He took the child in his arms, dipped his fingers in cool water, and ran them over his temples. Perucho opened his eyes, looked around with surprise, and regained his rosy color.

"How are we doing?" Primitivo asked him. "Do you feel up to another drop of wine?"

Perucho turned to the bottle, and then almost instinctively shook his curly head. Primitivo was not the kind of man that gives up so easily. He thrust his hand in his pocket and took out a copper coin.

"Well, if it comes to that . . ." the abbot rumbled.

"Don't be such a brute, Primitivo!" the marquis whispered, partly complacent and partly grave.

"Good Lord and Holy Mary!" Julián beseeched. "You are going to kill this child! My good man, don't insist on making him drunk; it's a sin as bad as any! One can't just sit and watch certain things!"

Julián rose as he protested, burning with indignation and casting aside his natural submissiveness and timidity. Primitivo, also on his feet but without releasing Perucho, stared at the chaplain coldly and slyly, with the contempt of the persevering for those who lose their temper for the moment. He closed the boy's hand around the coin and his lips around the open bottle, still half full of wine, tipped the bottle, and held it up until all its contents had gone into Perucho's stomach. Once the bottle was withdrawn the child's eyes shut, his arms fell listlessly, and not only pale but livid like death itself, he would have collapsed on the table had Primitivo not held him. The marquis, looking rather serious, began to pour cold water on his forehead and wrists; Sabel approached and helped with the sprinkling. It was useless: this time Perucho was really "out."

"Like a wineskin," the abbot blurted out.

"Like a barrel," the marquis mumbled. "To bed with him at once. Let him sleep and tomorrow he'll be as fresh as a cucumber. This is nothing."

Sabel walked out carrying the boy, whose legs swung lifelessly at each of his mother's movements. Dinner ended less merrily than it had begun: Primitivo hardly spoke and Julián had fallen completely silent. When the feast finished and everyone was ready to retire, Sabel came back holding a three-burner oil lamp, with which she lit the wide stone stairway that led to the second floor and then wound up to the tower.

Julián's room was spacious. The lamp's glimmer dispelled little of the gloom, revealing only the whiteness of the bed. As the marquis bid him good night at the doorstep, he added with gruff cordiality: "You'll have your luggage tomorrow; I'll send to Cebre for it. So, rest well while I get rid of the abbot of Ulloa. He's a little . . . do you know what I mean? I'll be surprised if he doesn't fall on his way back and have to spend the night by a fence!"

As soon as he was alone, Julián took out a print of the Virgin of

Carmen in a spangled frame and set it up on the table where Sabel had just left the lamp. He knelt down and started the rosary, counting every ten prayers with his fingers; but because he felt so tired that he craved the cool sheets, he omitted the Litany, the Creeds, and the Lord's Prayer. He undressed modestly, laying his clothes on a chair as he removed them, and turned off the light before he lay down. Then the events of the day began to dance in his imagination: the little horse that nearly made him kiss the ground; the black cross that sent a shudder down his spine; and most of all, the dinner, the noise, and the drunken child.

Evoking the people he had met in the last few hours, he found Sabel provocative, Primitivo insolent, the abbot of Ulloa a heavy drinker too interested in hunting, the dogs spoiled, and as for the marquis . . . Julián was reminded of certain words used by Señor de la Lage: "You'll find my nephew fairly vulgar. The village stupefies, impoverishes, and degrades those who stay in it forever."

As he recalled this severe statement, the chaplain felt remorse and a painful anxiety. Who had given him the right to make rushed judgments? He had come here to say mass and help the marquis to manage his property, not to formulate opinions about his character and conduct. Better to go to sleep now . . .

Chapter 3

When Julián awoke a gentle, golden autumn sun was shining into the room. As he dressed, he scrutinized the chamber carefully. It was very spacious and had a slanted ceiling. The light came in through three windows flanked by broad benches; most of the panes were missing and had been replaced with paper patches taped together.

The furniture was neither sumptuous nor abundant, and in every corner there were obvious signs of the last occupant, the abbot of Ulloa, former chaplain to the marquis: cigar butts stuck on the floor, two pairs of worn-out boots in a corner, a box of gunpowder on the table, and on one of the benches, several cynegetic implements: partridge cages, dog collars, and an ill-tanned and worse-smelling rabbit fur. Aside from these relics, pale cobwebs hung between the beams, and the dust had settled comfortably everywhere, as if it had ruled the place since the dawn of time.

Julián gazed at the traces of his predecessor's negligence. As much as he tried not to accuse him of being a pig, all this filth and crudity stirred in him a great longing for order and cleanliness, a wish for neatness in life as well as purity of the soul. Julián belonged to the army of the meek, with a shy virtue, the scruples of a nun, and the prudishness of an untouched maiden. Having clung to his mother's skirts until he attended classes in the seminary, he knew of life only what books of piety teach. His fellow seminarians called him "Saint Julián," and added that the only thing he lacked was the little white dove in his hand. He was not aware how his religious call had originated; maybe his mother, the housekeeper of the house of de la Lage, considered a devout woman, had pushed him gently into the church since his earliest days. And he had gladly consented. The truth of the matter is that as a boy he played at saying mass and as a man he was determined to say it in earnest. Continence came easily, almost imperceptibly, to him; for this reason he kept himself unpolluted, confirming the moralists' dictum that it is easier not to sin at all than to sin only once. In his triumph Julián was assisted not only by the grace of God, for which he fervently prayed, but by a weak, nervous, purely feminine temperament free of excitement and rebelliousness. Gently inclined, sweet and mild as a lamb, he was not exempt from those occasional upsurges of energy common in women, the feeblest creatures in normal circumstances but the strongest in a nervous crisis. For his composure and hygienic habits—learned from his mother, who perfumed his clothes with lavender and put a sweet apple between each of his pairs of socks—Julián earned a reputation as a chic seminarian, particularly when his fellows got hold of the idea that he often washed his hands and face. Indeed, they were correct, and had it not been for certain notions of scrupulous prudery, he would have extended his regular ablutions to the rest of his body, which he kept as tidy as possible.

On his first day at the house of Ulloa he felt the need to refresh himself a bit and shake off the dust of the road that still clung to his skin; but the present abbot of Ulloa undoubtedly regarded all toiletries as superfluous, because Julián saw nothing except a tin basin standing on a bench. No water jar, towel, soap, or bucket. He stood in front of the basin in his shirtsleeves wondering what to do next until, convinced that it was impossible to bathe in water, he decided to open the window and bathe in air instead.

What he beheld delighted him. The valley sloped gently upward, displaying in front of the mansion all the exuberance of its most fertile side. Vineyards, chestnut groves, cornfields—some tall, some already harvested—and dense oak woods grew up a little hill, whose gray slope glimmered in the sun in a hazy whiteness. At the very foot of the tower the garden looked like a yellow-rimmed green carpet with a great mirror in the middle: the surface of the pond. The air, cool and invigorating, filled Julián's lungs and dispelled immediately the vague terror that the house and its dwellers instilled in him. However, the muffled sound of cautious footsteps behind him renewed it; he turned around and saw Sabel with a cup and a saucer in one hand, and in the other a pewter tray and a large glass of fresh water, with a heavy, folded napkin on top. The girl's arms were bare to the elbows and her tousled hair dry and in disorder, no doubt from the warmth of her bed; by daylight the freshness of her complexion, very pale and as if infiltrated with blood, was more apparent. Julián put on his overcoat in a hurry, mumbling: "Next time kindly knock twice on the door before you come in. I happen to be already up, but I might well have been still in bed or . . . getting dressed."

Sabel eyed him up and down without embarrassment and replied: "Forgive me, sir. I didn't know. The one who doesn't know is like the one who can't see."

"All right, all right. I'd like to say mass before I have my chocolate."

"You can't do that today; the abbot of Ulloa has the key to the chapel, and God knows how long he'll sleep or if anyone will go to get it."

Julián held his breath. Two days without mass already! His religious fervor had dutifully redoubled since he had become a priest, and he still felt the youthful enthusiasm of the new officiant under the impression of his august investiture; consequently, when he performed communion he strove to highlight every detail of the ceremony, trembling when he raised the host, humbling himself when he consumed it, always with unspeakable devotion. Well, if there was nothing he could do . . .

"Leave the chocolate there," he said to Sabel.

As the maid obeyed his order, Julián looked up at the ceiling and down at the floor and coughed, searching for a formula, a tactful way to express himself. "When did the abbot last sleep in this room?"

"It wasn't too long ago. It's been about two months since he went down to the parish."

"I see. That's why it's a little . . . dirty, don't you think? It would be a good idea to sweep it . . . and sweep in between the beams, too."

Sabel shrugged her shoulders. "His lordship the abbot never told me to sweep the room."

"Frankly, everybody likes cleanliness."

"Yes, sir, of course. Don't you worry, I'll fix it nice and clean."

She uttered these words so submissively that Julián, in turn, wished to show a little kindly interest. "And the boy?" he asked. "Was he sick yesterday?"

"No, sir. He slept like a little saint, and now he's running around the garden. See? There he is."

Julián, looking out of the window and shading his eyes with his hand, spotted Perucho. He was throwing pebbles into the pond with his head bare in the sun.

"What doesn't happen in a year may happen in a day, Sabel," the chaplain admonished sternly. "You must not tolerate those who try to make your son drunk; it's an ugly vice even in adults, not to speak of an innocent child like that. Why do you allow Primitivo to give him so much to drink? It's your duty to prevent it."

Sabel stared at Julián with her blue eyes, which did not indicate the slightest gleam of understanding or conviction. At last she said quietly: "What can I do about it? I can't turn against my own father."

Julián, astonished, remained silent for a moment. So the man who had inebriated the child was his own grandfather! He could not find the right words to answer or even convey his disapproval. In order to hide his confusion he raised the cup to his lips. Sabel, assuming that the conversation was over, had begun to withdraw slowly when the chaplain asked her a final question: "Is your master up?"

"Yes, sir. He must be around the garden or in the shed."

"Please take me there," Julián said. He rose and wiped his lips hurriedly, without unfolding the napkin.

The chaplain and his guide scouted the whole garden before they found the marquis. The large piece of land must once have been primly cultivated and decorated in the symmetrical and geometric fashion that came to us from France. Of all that, hardly anything remained: the family coat of arms drawn on the ground with myrtle was now a tangle of boxwood, where the sharpest eye could not detect a trace of the wolves, pine trees, crenelated turrets, roundels, and other emblems that shone in the illustrious heraldry of the Ulloas; and yet an indefinable air of artistic and purposeful design persisted amid that confusion. The stone edge of the pond was half fallen, and the plump granite balls that had decorated it were rolling on the grass, green with moss, scattered here and there like gigantic projectiles on a deserted battlefield. The pond, clogged by slime, seemed now a muddy puddle that contributed to the garden's appearance of neglect and decay. The summerhouses and quaint benches of yesterday were overgrown with weeds; the terraced vegetable garden had become a cornfield, bordered by thorny, straggling, widespread rosebushes of a choice variety—like a stubborn reminiscence of the past—whose tallest branches kissed the plum or pear trees in front of them.

Amid these remains of former splendors the last scion of the Ulloas wandered with his hands in his pockets, whistling distractedly, like someone who does not know how to kill time. Julián's arrival solved this problem. Master and chaplain walked together and, as they celebrated the beauty of the day, completed a close scrutiny of the garden and strolled as far as the thicket and the oak woods that marked the northern limit of the marquis's vast property.

Julián opened his eyes wide, as if to absorb all rural science through them, so that he might understand at once the explanations about the quality of the soil and the growth of the trees; but accustomed to the cloistered existence of the seminary and the urban life of Compostela, he found that nature seemed too difficult to comprehend, and he was almost frightened by the vital impetus that he felt beating in it: in the thick of the bushes, in the harsh vigor of the trunks, in the fertility of the fruit trees, in the pungent purity of the air. He sighed with sheer hopelessness: "I confess the truth, sir . . . I don't know a word about country affairs."

"Let's go in and see the house," the lord of Ulloa suggested. "It's the largest in the area," he added proudly.

They now directed their steps toward the enormous building, which they entered through the garden door. Having paced the cloister of ashlar masonry arches, they went past several rooms filled with decrepit furniture. There was no glass in the windows; humidity had faded the paint on the frames; and the moths had been no more merciful with the wooden floors. They stopped in a relatively small room with a lattice window. The black beams seemed very high, and the large, unpolished chestnut bookcases caught the eye because they had thick lattice instead of glass doors.

This gloomy place was decorated with a desk on top of which stood a horn inkwell, an old leather tablet, God knows how many goose feathers, and an empty pillbox.

Numerous bundles of paper and protocols peeped from the open shelves. More papers, more yellowish, decrepit, worm-eaten, wrinkled, torn files, lay scattered on the floor, on the two leather chairs, on the table, even on the sill of the lattice window. All this paper spread a humid, sour smell that tickled the throat unpleasantly.

The marquis stopped at the doorstep with a somewhat solemn expression and announced: "The house archives."

At once he cleared the leather chairs and explained excitedly that everything in the room was topsy-turvy—an altogether unnecessary remark—and that such disorder was due to the negligence of Brother Venancio, his father's administrator, and of the current abbot of Ulloa, in whose sinful hands the archives had become what Julián now saw.

"We can't go on like this," the chaplain replied. "Important papers treated in this manner! Some of them could even get lost."

"Of course! Heaven knows the damage they've already done me and in what state everything must be! I don't even want to look at it. Things are just as you see them: disastrous, beyond hope! Look, look what's under your feet! Under your boot!"

Julián, very frightened, lifted his foot, while the marquis stooped down to pick up from the floor a small book bound in green felt with a lead seal. As Julián opened it respectfully, he was struck by a superb heraldic miniature, fresh and lively in color despite its age, on the first parchment sheet.

"A patent of nobility!" the master declared in a grave voice.

Julián, fingering the document delicately, removed the mold with his folded handkerchief. Since he was a boy his mother had taught him to revere aristocratic blood; so that miniature golden parchment written in red ink seemed to him a venerable object, worthy of compassion for having been trampled and soiled under his boot. As the master remained serious, with his elbows on the table and his hands folded under his chin, a few more of Señor de la Lage's words came to the chaplain's memory: "Everything in my nephew's house must be in disarray. You'd perform a work of charity if you set it in order." The truth was that he knew little of paperwork; but with patience and willingness . . . "Sir," he murmured, "why don't we try to organize this properly? Between the two of us we can hardly fail. Look here: first we shall separate the modern from the old; we could make copies of everything that's damaged. Whatever is torn can be carefully pasted together with strips of transparent paper . . ."

The master deemed the project perfect. They agreed to start work the next morning. Unfortunately, that day Primitivo found a whole flock of partridge leisurely pecking at the ripe ears of the nearby cornfield. And the marquis shouldered his gun and left the chaplain alone to struggle with the documents from then on for ever and ever, amen.

Chapter 4

And struggle he did, relentlessly and without respite, three or four hours every morning. First he cleaned, shook, pressed with the palm of his hand; then he joined the torn shreds of some writing or other with cigarette paper. He felt as if he were dusting, gluing together, and setting in order the house of Ulloa itself, so that it would come out of his hands as clean as a silver cup. Although the task appeared to be easy, it was in fact quite trying for the fastidious priest. He suffocated in an atmosphere heavy with mold and humidity. Sometimes, when he picked up an armful of papers that had lain on the ground from time immemorial, half of them fell apart, eaten away by the mice's slight but untiring teeth. Moths that looked like organized flying dust beat their wings and sneaked into his clothes. Cockroaches flushed from their most secret hideaways came out mad with fury or fear, forcing him, despite his repugnance, to squash them under his heels and cover his ears to shut out the frightful *squish!* from the insect's crushed body. Spiders, swinging their hydropic bellies on their monstrous stilts and following their mysterious strategic instinct, were usually quicker to take refuge in dark corners. Of all these revolting bugs, Julián perhaps found most repulsive a kind of cold, black, humid earthworm, which remained curled up and motionless under the papers and felt like a soft, sticky piece of ice to the touch.

With a great deal of patience and determination Julián won his battle against these impertinent creatures. Once he cleared the shelves, he gradually lined them with documents, which by a miracle of good order took only half the former space and fit in where they never had before. Three or four patents of nobility with their hanging lead seals were set apart and wrapped in clean cloths. Now everything was organized, except a shelf on which Julián glimpsed the gold-rimmed dark spines of some old books. They belonged to the library of an Ulloa of the early century. Julián reached out, picked up a volume at random, opened it, and read the cover: "*The Henriad*, a French poem versified in Spanish. Its author, Monsieur Voltaire . . ." He restored it to its place, pursing his lips and lowering his eyes as he always did when something hurt or shocked him. He was not extremely intolerant, but when it came to Voltaire he would gladly do what he had done with the cockroaches. He limited himself, however, to condemning the library by not dusting the books even with a wretched rag; so moths, worms, and spiders driven out from everywhere found shelter by the ironic Arouet and his rival, the sentimental Jean Jacques, who had also slept there quietly since 1816.

Cleaning the archives was not child's play, but the real Herculean task was classifying them. "Let's see how you handle this one!" the old papers seemed to say, as soon as Julián tried to sort them out. A mess, a hopeless tangle, a labyrinth with no leading thread. There was no lighthouse to guide him through that unfathomable sea: no books detailing property rights, no accounts, nothing. The only documents he found were two greasy books reeking of tobacco in which his old predecessor, the abbot of Ulloa, wrote down the names of the house renters and, on the margin, with a sign comprehensible only to himself or in even more enigmatic words, the balance of their payments. A cross appeared next to some names; next to others, scribbles or an exclamation mark; and next to a few, the phrases "no payments," "payments to come," "payments coming," "paid off." What, then, did the scribble and the cross mean? It was a perplexing mystery. Income and expenses

mingled on the same page: here was Señor So-and-So as an insol-
vent debtor, and two lines further as one who had paid his debts
in daily labor. The abbot's book gave Julián an excruciating head-
ache. He blessed the memory of Brother Venancio for having been
more radical and not having left a trace of his accounting or the
slightest voucher of his lengthy term.

Julián had tackled his job with great zeal, in the belief that it
would be possible to find his way among the chaotic paperwork.
He wore out his eyes trying to understand the ancient handwriting
and elaborate signatures on the documents. He wanted at least to
sort out the benefits of the property's three or four main income
sources. He was amazed that such a hodgepodge of papers, so
much indigestible documentation, was necessary to draw so little
money, such insignificant amounts of rye and corn. He lost himself
in a maze of leaseholds, apportionments, rents, pensions, entail-
ments, endowments, tithes, thirds, minor lawsuits about overdue
payments and major ones about partitions. At every step Julián became more confused with all this embroiled paperwork. Whereas
the restoration work, like putting sturdy white paper covers on
the disintegrating documents, he did easily by now, anyone not
extremely intelligent and experienced would have found it difficult to decipher the confounded papers accurately. At that point
he confessed his discouragement to the marquis: "I can't handle it,
sir. What we need is a lawyer, an expert."

"Yes, yes; I've been considering it for a long time. It's imperative
that we do something about it, because the documents must be in
shambles. How did you find them? In bad shape, I'm sure."

The marquis said this in that vehement and gloomy tone that
he assumed for dealing with his own affairs, no matter how insignificant they might be; and while he talked, he busied himself
fastening the collar around Chula's neck, ready to go quail hunting.

"Yes, sir," Julián whispered. "They aren't exactly in good shape.

But somebody accustomed to this kind of work would straighten things out in no time. And whoever it may be, he's got to come soon, for things aren't getting any better."

The truth is that the archives made the same impression on Julián as the rest of the house: that of a ruin, a vast, threatening ruin, which stood for past greatness but was now crumbling down at an alarming rate. This irrational apprehension of Julián's would have developed into a conviction had he known in detail some of the history of the marquis's family.

Don Pedro Moscoso de Cabreira y Pardo de la Lage lost his father when he was still very young. Had this misfortune not befallen him, he might have pursued a university education: since the days of the Francophile, encyclopedic, Masonic grandfather who allowed himself to read "Monsieur Voltaire," the Moscosos had retained an aged cultural tradition, now half extinguished but still sufficiently powerful to push a Moscoso into the classroom. The Pardos de la Lage, on the other hand, upheld the axiom that a living ass is worth more than a dead doctor. At the time the Pardos lived in their manor, not far from the Ulloas. When Don Pedro's mother became a widow, the de la Lage heir married a distinguished lady in Santiago and moved his household to the city; Don Gabriel, the second son, came to the house of Ulloa to escort his sister—so he said—and be her protector. Actually, slanderers remarked, he came to enjoy at his leisure the income of his dead brother-in-law. What is certain is that after a short period Don Gabriel took over the administration of the property: it was he who discovered and appointed that blessed, secularized Brother Venancio—half senile since secularization, half-witted since birth—in whose shadow he was able to manage his nephew's estate as he pleased while serving as the boy's tutor. One of Don Gabriel's abilities was that of dividing property with his sister so artfully as to take away from her nearly all of her inheritance. The lady, inept in business, consented to this plunder; her only talent was saving money, which she hoarded and foolishly converted into old-fashioned gold ounces. There was little revenue of the Moscoso wealth that did not slide between Brother Venancio's shaky fingers into the tutor's hard palms; but if by any chance it passed to Doña Micaela's, it was transformed into gold doubloons destined for a mysterious hideout, around which a local legend began to form. While the mother accumulated wealth, Don Gabriel educated his nephew after his own image, taking him to fairs, hunts, rural feasts, and perhaps less innocuous pastimes, and teaching him, as they say hereabouts, "to shoot the white partridge." The boy worshiped that jovial, vigorous, resolute uncle skilled in physical exercises and coarsely humorous at the table, like all the de la Lages; the kind of landlord revered in the country, who pragmatically instilled in the heir of the Ulloas contempt for mankind and abuse of power.

One afternoon at four o'clock uncle and nephew were entertaining themselves as usual four or five leagues away from the house. They had left the doors of the mansion open and had taken the servant and the stableboy with them. A bunch of twenty men whose faces were smeared with coal broke in, tied and gagged the maid, forced Brother Venancio to lie down on the floor, and, seizing Doña Micaela, tried to persuade her to show them the coins' hiding place. When the lady refused, they slapped her and started to cut her with a jackknife, while some suggested heating up oil and frying her feet. As soon as they began to slash her arm and breast, she begged for mercy and disclosed the notorious hideout, under a huge trunk, by lifting a trap door that looked identical to the other floorboards. The thieves took the beautiful medals and all the hand-carved silver they could find and left the house at six, before dark. A couple of farmers and laborers saw them come out, but what could they do? There were twenty of them, well armed with guns, pistols, and blunderbusses.

Brother Venancio, who had suffered only an occasional kick or a contemptuous punch, needed no further passport to leave this world in a week, from sheer fright. The lady was not in such a hurry, but as we usually say, she was never herself again; a few months later a serous apoplexy put an end to her scraping together any more gold ounces destined for a new, safer place. For a long time there was talk in the area about the theft, and strange rumors circulated: it was said that the criminals were not professional bandits but well-known and well-to-do people, some of whom held public offices, including individuals who had long-standing family ties with the Ulloas; therefore, they were familiar with their habits and knew on which days the men left the house, and how insatiably and regularly Doña Micaela hoarded up the most valuable gold coins. Whatever it was, the police did not identify the culprits, and Don Pedro was soon left with no other relative than his uncle Gabriel. Brother Venancio was replaced by a rough priest, a great hunter who would never die of fear facing a gang of thieves. Primitivo had long been helping them in their hunting expeditions; he was the best furtive gun in the area, the surest shot, and the father of the prettiest girl ten leagues around. Doña Micaela's death enabled father and daughter to move into the property, she as a maid and he as a . . . hunt master, we would have called it centuries ago; nowadays there is no suitable term for the job. Don Gabriel kept them both at bay, detecting in Primitivo a serious threat to his own power; but three or four years after his sister's death, Don Gabriel was plagued by attacks of gout that jeopardized his life, and at that time rumors began to spread about his secret wedding to the daughter of the jailer of Cebre. The gentleman went to live—or rather, to rage—in the little village and made his will, in which he left his property and wealth to his three children, and to his nephew Don Pedro not even a watch in his memory. When the gout reached his heart he reluctantly delivered his soul to God, and the last of the Moscosos became entirely his own master.

Because of all these misadventures, swindles, and fragmentations, the house of Ulloa, despite two or three fair sources of income, was disorganized and decimated; it was what Julián presumed: a ruin. Given a tangle like this and the atomic subdivision typical of Galician properties, the slightest negligence or mismanagement suffices to undermine the foundations of the most substantial country estate. Certain overdue rents and the interest on them had made it necessary to mortgage the house; but a mortgage is like a cancer: it begins by attacking one spot in a living organism and ends up by invading it all. Under the pressure of these expenditures, the Ulloa heir searched persistently for the gold ounces in his mother's latest hiding place. It was a waste of time: either the lady had not accumulated any more after the theft or she had hidden them so safely that the devil himself could never find them. The discovery of the mortgage depressed Julián, for the good priest was beginning to feel that peculiar fondness of chaplains for the noble homes that they serve; he was even more surprised to find among the paperwork documents pertaining to a petty lawsuit on partitions between Don Alberto Moscoso, Don Pedro's father, and . . . the marquis of Ulloa.

The time has come to say that the legal, authentic marquis of Ulloa, the one listed in the *Peerage*, was riding in his buggy down La Castellana[1] at leisure in the winter of 1866–67, while Julián exterminated the cockroaches in the archives of the house of Ulloa. Little did he realize that his title, for which he had religiously paid his fees to the crown, was being enjoyed at no charge by one of his relatives in a corner of Galicia. Granted that the legitimate marquis

1. One of the main avenues of Madrid.

of Ulloa, a first-class grandee of Spain, duke of something or other, three times a marquis and at least twice a count, was unknown to everyone in Madrid except as a duke; this title simply outshone the rest, even though the name of Ulloa, rooted in the illustrious Portuguese lineage of Cabreira, might supersede all of them in age and value. When the Ulloa estate passed to a lateral branch of the family, the marquisate fell on whomever it belonged to by strict succession; but the villagers, who knew nothing of succession and had always associated the mansion with the title, continued to call its owner "marquis." The landlords did not object: they were marquises by customary right. And when a farmer in a ditch respectfully bared his head to Don Pedro and muttered, "God be with your lordship the marquis," Don Pedro felt a warm tingling on the skin of his vanity and replied in a resounding voice: "Good evening."

Chapter 5

Julián emerged from the notorious purging of the archives with cold feet and a hot head. As much as he wanted to cheer up and put into practice the notions he had acquired about the state of the house, so that he could begin to perform his administrative duties intelligently, he did not know how to begin: he could not do it. His inexperience in rural and judicial matters was apparent at every step. He tried to study the inner mechanisms of the property; he took the time to go to the stables and the barn, to follow the farming, to visit the granaries, the oven, the yards, the cellars, the sheds, every piece and every corner; he asked what was the purpose of this, that, and the other, how much it cost and how much it sold for; a useless task because, although he suspected abuses and irregularities everywhere, his lack of malice and shrewdness never allowed him to expose and remedy them. The master did not accompany him on these rounds: he had enough to do with his fairs, his hunting, and his visits to the people of Cebre or to the mountain gentry; so Primitivo was Julián's guide. And a most pessimistic one, at that. Every reform Julián suggested he, shrugging his shoulders, deemed impossible; everything that struck the chaplain as superfluous and that he tried to eliminate, the hunter pronounced indispensable for the good functioning of the house. A myriad of minute difficulties confronted Julián's zeal and prevented any useful innovation. Most alarming was to realize Primitivo's covert but real omnipotence. Servants, renters, laborers, even the cattle in the stables, seemed to be under his thumb. The flattering respect they showed toward their master and the half-contemptuous, half-indifferent greeting with which they received the chaplain turned into absolute submission to Primitivo. Rather than by outer signs, they expressed their servility by instant compliance with his will, which sometimes was indicated by a single hard cold glance of his tiny, lashless eyes.

Julián felt humiliated in the presence of this man, who from his ambiguous position of servant with an air of steward ruled there as an undisputed autocrat. Primitivo's scrutinizing stare lay heavy on his soul, analyzing his most insignificant actions and studying his face to find the weak spot in this sober and disinterested priest who averted his eyes from pretty farm girls. Perhaps Primitivo's belief was that no man is free of vice and that Julián was no exception.

Meanwhile, winter went on and the chaplain began to get used to country life. The pure, lively air whetted his appetite. He no longer felt the waves of piety of the early days, but a kind of human charity instead that awakened his interest in whatever he saw around him, especially children and animals, on whom he poured his natural tenderness. His compassion for Perucho, the urchin inebriated by his own grandfather, grew; it grieved him to see the child always wallowing in the slime of the yard or the manure of the barn, playing with the calves, suckling warm milk from the udders of the cows, or sleeping in the donkey's hay. And he decided to devote a few hours of the long winter nights to teaching him the alphabet, some Christian doctrine, and mathematics. He settled by the large table, not far from the hearth that Sabel fed with heavy logs. By the light of the oil lamp, he sat the child on his knees and patiently led his little finger through the ABCs as he repeated the monotonous psalmody where all human knowledge begins: "b-a, *ba;* b-e, *bii* . . ." The boy yawned, made funny grimaces, pouted, and shrilled like a caged starling; he fortified and defended himself against science in every imaginable way, kicking, grumbling, hiding his face, slipping away at the slightest negligence of his teacher to hide in a corner or in the warmth of the stable.

In cold weather the kitchen served almost exclusively as a meeting place for the women. Some would come in barefoot and careful to step sideways, their heads covered with a kind of woolen cloth; many groaned with pleasure as they approached the delightful flames; others, taking the spindle and a linen ball, warmed up their hands and wove, or took chestnuts out of their pockets and roasted them by the smoldering coals; and all of them mumbled softly at first and ended up chatting like magpies. Sabel was the queen of that little court. Flushed by the fire, her arms bare and her eyes moist, she received the incense of flattery; and as she dipped the large iron spoon into the pot and filled the bowls with broth, a woman would disappear from the circle and withdraw to a corner or a bench, from which she could be heard as she munched avidly, blew into the boiling concoction, and flicked her tongue around the spoon. There were nights when Sabel never stopped filling cups while women kept coming in, eating, and leaving to make room for others. No doubt, the whole parish passed through that kitchen as through a cheap inn. On their way out they took Sabel aside, and if the chaplain had not been so distracted with his rebellious pupil, he would have seen an occasional slab of bacon, bread, or pork shoulder quickly smuggled into a jacket; or a red sausage promptly cut down from the strings hanging on the chimney and thrust into a pocket. The last guest to leave, the one who whispered the longest and most intimately to Sabel, was the old woman with coarse hair Julián had glimpsed on the night of his arrival. The witch's ugliness was imposing: her white eyebrows stood out from her profile, as did the bristles of a mole; the fire highlighted the whiteness of her hair, her darkened face, and the huge double chin that disfigured her neck in the most repulsive way.

As she talked with the buxom Sabel, an artist's fancy might have recalled the paintings of Saint Anthony's temptations, in which a loathsome sorcerer and a beautiful sensuous woman with cloven hooves appear together.

Julián, though he did not know why, began to feel annoyed by Sabel's chat and familiarities. She constantly came close to him under the pretext of searching the drawer for a knife, a cup, or any other item. When she fastened her blue eyes, drowned in warm moisture, on him, the chaplain experienced an intense discomfort comparable only to what he felt whenever he caught Primitivo's stare stealthily riveted on his face. Unaware of any grounds for his suspicion, Julián thought, nonetheless, that they were plotting something. Except for sporadic outbursts of wild happiness, Primitivo was a somber man whose bronze face rarely revealed emotion. And yet Julián believed himself to be the object of a concealed hostility on the hunter's part. In all fairness, it should not even be called hostility; it was rather watching and spying, the quiet stalking of a beast that, without hatred, one simply wishes to shoot down as soon as possible. This attitude could hardly be defined or conveyed. Julián withdrew to his room and dragged the reluctant boy with him for his habitual lesson. Before they knew it, winter was gone and the warmth of the hearth had lost its appeal.

In his room the chaplain noticed more than in the kitchen how filthy the wild angel was. Half an inch of crust covered his skin, and several geological layers slept in his hair—stratifications in which soil, tiny pebbles, and all sorts of strange bodies resided. Julián picked up the child by force and dragged him to the washstand, which was well provided with jugs, towels, and soap. He started to rub. Holy Mary, he could not believe how that devilish little face had muddied the first rinse! It was like the thickest, most turbid bleach water. As for the hair, he had to use oil, ointment, plenty of water, and a coarse comb to clear that virgin jungle. As this

work progressed, exquisite features colored with a patina of sun
and air, worthy of an ancient chisel, gradually came to light; the
unimpaired curls arranged themselves artistically as on a Cupid's
head and took on a golden chestnut hue in perfect harmony with
the rest of the figure. God had made the little fellow incredibly
beautiful!

Every day before class Julián scrubbed him like this, whether he
yelled or submitted. Because of his respect for human flesh, he did
not dare to wash the boy's body, as necessary as such an operation
was. But with these ablutions and Julián's sweet temper, the little
rogue began to take too many liberties and wreck everything in
the room. His increased laziness exhausted the priest's patience.
Perucho used the ink bottle by pushing his whole hand into it and
then pressing it on the primer; the pen, by pulling its feathers off
and breaking its point chasing flies on the windowpanes; paper,
by shredding it and making cones with it; the sand, by spilling
it on the table and shaping small mountains and hills readily destroyed by a cataclysmic push of his little finger. Moreover, he went
through Julián's dresser, upset the bed by jumping on top of it,
and one day went as far as to set his teacher's boots on fire by filling
them with lighted matches.

Julián would gladly have put up with this mischief, in the hope
that he might find some good in such a heretic; but a far more serious complication turned up: Sabel's comings and goings in and
out of the room. She always found some pretext to go up: she had
forgotten to pick up the chocolate cup; she needed to change the
towel. Gradually she grew bolder and took her time about depart-
ing; she lingered to arrange things that needed no arrangement or
rested her upper body on the window, all sweetness and smiles,
and boasted a familiarity that Julián, more reserved every day, did
not allow at all.

One morning at the usual time Sabel walked in with the water jugs for the chaplain's ablutions. The priest could not help but notice that the girl wore only her bodice and underskirt; that her blouse was open, her hair loose, and her pale legs and feet bare. For Sabel, who always wore shoes and did only the cooking—and that with plenty of help from farm girls and gossips—had neither a rough skin nor deformed limbs. Julián stepped back and the jug shook in his hand, so that a thread of water spilled on the floor.

"Cover yourself, my good woman," he murmured in a voice choked with embarrassment. "Don't ever bring me the water when you're in this state. This is no way to appear before people."

"I was doing my hair and I thought I heard you call," she replied coolly, without as much as putting her hand across her bosom.

"Even if I had, it isn't right to come in these clothes. The next time you're combing your hair tell Cristobo to bring my water up here, or tell the girl who looks after the cows, or anybody."

As he spoke he turned away from Sabel, who withdrew slowly.

From that point Julián avoided the girl as he would a brazen and harmful animal. However, he still found it uncharitable to attribute her indecorous carelessness to evil motives, preferring to think it ignorance or rusticity. But she was determined to prove just the opposite. One evening shortly after that stern rebuke, Julián was quietly reading the *Guide for Sinners* when he heard Sabel sneak in and, without raising his head, realized that she had begun to arrange something in the room. Suddenly he heard a thud like the fall of a human body on a piece of furniture and saw the girl stretched on the bed. She moaned and sighed painfully and complained of a sudden "affliction." Julián, confused but sympathetic, rushed to soak a towel in water and apply it to her temples. No sooner had he approached the distressed woman than, despite his inexperience and simplicity, he realized that the alleged attack was but the most roguish and shameless of all acts. A wave of blood swept Julián's face up to the roots of his hair. He felt that sudden, blind anger that only rarely aroused his lymphatic temper, and pointing to the door, he shouted: "You'd better leave at once or I'll put you out! Do you hear me? Don't walk through this door again. Everything, absolutely everything I need, Cristobo shall bring me. Get out of here!"

The young woman, crestfallen and contrite, like somebody who has been deeply humiliated, withdrew. Julián, on his part, stood there shaken, unhappy with himself, as peaceful people are apt to be when they lose their temper: he even felt physical pain, in his epigastrium. Undoubtedly, he had taken it too far. He should have addressed the girl with a fervent exhortation instead of contemptuous words. His duty as a priest was to teach, to straighten, to forgive, not to tread on people as on the bugs in the archives. After all, Sabel had a soul redeemed by the blood of Christ, like everyone else. But who stops to think? Who can control himself in the face of such impudence? There is a kind of impulse that scholastics call *primo primis:* it is fatal and inevitable. This is how the chaplain comforted himself. Still, it was a bad thing to live near that artful female, no more modest than the cows. How could women like that exist? Julián recalled his mother, so decorous, with her eyes always down, her voice sweet and soft, and her jacket buttoned up to her chin; and on top of it, to be even chaster, she wore a well-pressed black silk shawl. And those women! The women one encounters in this world!

After that ill-fated incident Julián had to sweep his bedroom and carry his own water upstairs, for neither Cristobo nor the maids paid the least attention to his orders; as for Sabel, he could not stand the sight of her. What surprised and frightened him most was that after this episode Primitivo did not even bother to hide his furious glare, sizing him up with a look that amounted to a declaration of war. Julián could not doubt that he was not welcome

in the house. Why? Sometimes he interrupted his readings of Friar
Luis de Granada and Saint Juan Crisóstomo's six books on priesthood to ponder over it. But discouraged by so much adversity, in
despair that he would ever be useful in the house of Ulloa, he soon
plunged again into the mystical pages.

Chapter 6

With none of the neighboring parish priests did Julián get along as well as with Don Eugenio of Naya. Although he saw the abbot of Ulloa more often, he did not like the abbot's incorrigible fondness for the bottle and the gun. Julián, in turn, irritated the abbot, who dubbed him "Sissy," because in the abbot's opinion it was the ultimate degradation in a man to drink water, wash with scented soap, and clip his fingernails. In the case of a priest, the abbot ranked these crimes with simony. "Effeminacy, pure effeminacy," he grumbled between his teeth, convinced that priestly virtue, to be legitimate, must appear coarse, rustic, and wild. Besides, a churchman does not ipso facto lose his privileges as a man, and a man must smack of fierceness from miles away. With the other priests from the surrounding parishes Julián did not associate much either; so whenever he was invited to take part in religious services he withdrew at the end of the ceremony and declined its indispensable complement, a meal. But when Don Eugenio invited him, with his cheerful amiability, to spend the local patron's day in Naya, he consented gladly and promised to attend.

As they had agreed, he hiked up to Naya, after he had refused the horse offered by Don Pedro. It was hardly a league and a half, and such a splendid afternoon! Leaning on a staff, taking his time to enjoy the twilight, and resting now and then to contemplate the landscape, he reached the hill that surrounds the hamlet of Naya. He arrived at an opportune moment, in the middle of the dances that, to the music of the bagpipe, the drum, and the timbrel, and by the light of the gently swinging straw lanterns, were a prelude to the joyful festival. Soon the dancers came down from the parsonage, singing and prancing wildly. Julián descended with them.

The priest of Naya was waiting right at the gate. With his sleeves rolled up, he carried a wine jar aloft, and the maid held a tray with glasses. The group halted. The exhausted bagpiper in blue corduroy wiped his sweaty forehead with a silk handkerchief. He allowed his instrument to deflate, with the pipe resting on the red fringe of the drone. The glare of the straw lanterns and the lights from the priest's house revealed the impeccable features of his handsome face, framed in a pair of arrogant chestnut whiskers. When they served him wine, the peasant musician said graciously: "To the health of your lordship the abbot and all the attendants!"

And after drinking it up, he ran his hand over his mouth and added tactfully: "To your health twenty years from now, Sir Abbot!"

The libations that followed were not accompanied by such courteous toasts.

The parson of Naya, who enjoyed a roomy house that now bubbled with preparations for the feast, watched unflinchingly the preliminaries to the sacking and ruin of his pantry, cellar, woodshed, and garden. Don Eugenio was young and as happy as a lark, playing the role of a naughty, sly little scamp rather than a father of souls. His boyish facade, however, concealed a good deal of worldliness and practical knowledge. Sociable and tolerant, he had not made a single enemy among his fellow priests, who regarded him as a harmless lad.

He gave Julián his best bedroom after a cup of chocolate, and woke him up when the bagpipe was serenading the dawn, which had begun to brighten the skies. The two clergymen went together to inspect the decoration of the altar for the solemn mass.

Julián supervised it with special devotion, for Naya's patron was also his own: the blessed Saint Julián, who stood above the main altar with his innocent face and ecstatic grin, in his frock and short breeches, holding the white dove in his right hand and delicately resting the left on the ruffle of his shirt. The modest image, the bare church with no ornaments other than a few rippled candles and wild flowers in coarse earthen pots, stirred in Julián a tender pity, an effusion that, softening and relaxing his spirit, did him much good. The neighboring priests began to arrive, and from the grass-carpeted atrium they heard the bagpiper fine tune the instrument. Inside the church, the fennel spread on the floor tiles and trodden by those who streamed in released the freshest country scent. The procession began to form. Saint Julián had stepped down from the main altar. The cross and banners swung over the swirling crowd in the narrow aisle, and the young men, who wore silk bands on their heads and were dressed for the occasion, offered to carry the holy emblems. After circling the atrium twice and stopping briefly in front of the cross, the saint returned to the church and was lifted in his litter onto a table by the main altar, richly adorned and covered with an antique cloth of crimson damask.

Mass started joyfully and rustically, in tune with the other festivities. More than a dozen priests sang at the top of their lungs; the rickety incense burner swung back and forth, its old chains tinkling, and blew a thick aromatic smoke that kindly smothered the dissonance of the Introit and the hoarseness of the ecclesiastical larynxes. The piper, displaying all his artistic devices, released the pipe from the bag and played it as a clarinet. When the orchestra joined in, he reinserted the pipe in the leather bag, in order to follow the elevation of the host with a solemn royal march; the post-communion he accompanied with one of the most recent and cheerful *muñeiras*, [1] and after mass he repeated it in the hall,

---

1. A Galician folk dance.

where boys and girls danced at their leisure to make up for the
composure they had observed through an hour in church. And the
dancing in the atrium, bathed in light; the temple, strewn with fennel and cattail leaves pressed by footsteps, and lighted less by the
candles than by the sun pouring in through windows and doors;
the priests, panting but satisfied and talkative; the saint, so handsome and sporty, smiling on his litter, with one leg up in the air as
if to start a minuet, and the candid dove about to spread its wings:
everything was joyful and earthy, nothing inspired the melancholy
anxiety that usually dominates religious ceremonies. Julián felt as
young and happy as the blessed saint himself. As he walked out
with Don Eugenio to enjoy the air, among the circle of dancers he
caught sight of Sabel in her best Sunday clothes, revolving with the
other girls to the rhythm of the bagpipe. This vision cast a shadow
on his bright day.

At that hour the parsonage of Naya was a culinary hell, if such
a place exists. In it were gathered Don Eugenio's aunt and two
cousins who, being young and fresh, were not allowed to live in
the parsonage; the housekeeper, a whining, hopeless, good old
woman who ran around like a stunned dove; and, in contrast, the
housekeeper of the priest of Cebre, an assertive woman with a local
reputation for her skill at churning butter and roasting capons,
who in her youth had been in the service of a canon in Compostela. This robust cook, with a slight moustache, a lofty bosom,
and a resolute air, had turned the house upside down in a few
hours. Since the day before, she had swept it with large and furious strokes and moved the old junk up to the attic. Then she had
begun to mobilize a formidable gastronomic army, soaking the
pork and garbanzos, and reviewing with the sharp glance of a true
commander-in-chief the contents of the insatiable pantry, which
was bursting with donations from the parishioners: baby lambs,
chickens, eels, trout, pigeons, jars of wine, butter and honey, par-

tridges, hares and rabbits, red and black sausage. After inspecting the state of the provisions she gave orders for maneuvers. The old women would pluck the birds; the young ones would scrub kettles, pots, and skillets to a golden shine; and a couple of village louts—one of them stupid with a vengeance—would skin cattle and clean game.

Had a master of Flemish painting—one of those who lavish poetry on the prose of domestic life—been present, how he would have rejoiced at the sight of the spacious kitchen and the busy fire that caressed the glowing belly of the kettles; at the plump arms of the housekeeper that blended with the no less plump red meat of the stew she was seasoning; at the flushed girls who frolicked with the village idiot like nymphs with a captive satyr, stuffing between his shirt and skin handfuls of rice and peppers! A few moments later, when the bagpiper and other players came in for their light breakfast—a stew of goat liver and giblets known in the area as *mataburrillo*—how worthy of his brush the painter would have found this scene of gargantuan appetite, gastric expansion, puffed-out cheeks, and jets of wine caught in the air amid jokes and laughter!

But all this could scarcely compare with the Homeric feast laid out in the dining room of the parsonage. Half a dozen boards resting on as many baskets lengthened the ordinary table. Large jars overflowing with aged red wine stood on the two clean table-cloths; big-bellied barrels equally full awaited their turn in a corner. The china was mixed; among tin and earthenware the eye struck an occasional piece of authentic Talavera, enough to capti-vate one of the many collectors devoted these days to the arcane science of crockery. The reverend priests began to take their seats at the table with profuse compliments and ceremony, each deter-mined to defer to others. Finally the places of honor fell to the obese archpriest of Loiro—the most respected among the neighboring clergy in age and dignity—who, to avoid the suffocating crush at the mass, had not attended the religious ceremony; and to Julián, whom Don Eugenio honored as a representative of the illustrious house of Ulloa.

Julián sat down somewhat self-consciously and felt his embarrassment grow as the meal progressed. A newcomer who had always refused party invitations, he was the target of everybody's attention. About fifteen priests and eight laymen sat at the magnificent table, among them the doctor, the notary and judge of Cebre, the young gentleman of Limioso, the nephew of the priest of Boán, and the notorious chieftain known by the nickname Barbacana.[2] Supported by the moderate party then in power, Barbacana ruled over the district and practically canceled the influence of his rival, Trampeta,[3] who was backed by the Unionists and mistrusted by the clergy. In short, the cream of the county was gathered there, with the exception of the marquis of Ulloa, who doubtless would come for dessert. The monumental, greasy bread soup with red sausage, garbanzos, and sliced boiled eggs now circulated in gigantic tureens and was eaten in silence but for a steady chomping of jaws. Now and then a priest ventured a word of praise for the accomplishments of the cook; and the host, watching covertly which of the guests ate slowly, urged them to take advantage of the soup and stew, for, he added, there was hardly anything else. Julián, wishing to be gracious to his host, attacked the soup and stew without reserve. Much to his alarm, the interminable twenty-six-course parade traditional at the feast of the patron saint of Naya began to march before his eyes—and this was not even the most plentiful in the archpriesthood, for Loiro far surpassed it.

In order to reach the prescribed number, the cook had not re-

2. "Whitebeard."
3. "Little Trick."

sorted to the artifice with which French cuisine normally disguises its dishes, christening them with new names or decorating them with trappings and frills. No, sir. In this virgin territory—praise the Lord!—Frenchy pepper sauces were completely unknown, and everything was pure, virile, and as classic as the pot stew. Twenty-six courses? The bill of fare is easily made up: roast chicken, fried chicken, chicken in a pepper and tomato sauce, stewed chicken; chicken with peas, with onions, with potatoes, and with eggs. Apply the same principle to beef, pork, fish, and lamb. Thus, without racking his brains, anybody can present twenty-six varied dishes.

How the cook would laugh if a French chef appeared out of the blue insisting on a menu limited to four or five main courses, alternating heavy with light fare and capitalizing on vegetables! "Vegetables!" the housekeeper of the priest of Cebre would say, as she laughed with all her heart and her hips, too. "Vegetables on the patron's day! They're only good for pigs!"

Julián, worn out and dizzy, had strength only to push aside the dishes that passed incessantly from guest to guest. At least they no longer watched him, for the conversation was heating up. The doctor of Cebre—a lean, ill-humored, and opinionated man—and the bearded and flushed notary public dared to tell jokes and anec-dotes. The nephew of the priest of Boán, a very enamored law student, talked about women and sang the praises of the young Molende ladies and the freshness of a baker's wife of Cebre, highly reputed in the area. At first the priests did not take part, and some guests, observing that Julián cast his eyes down, exchanged know-ing glances and pretended not to hear. But the reserve did not last. As jars and dishes were emptied, nobody wished to remain quiet, and the jokes grew increasingly bolder.

Doctor Máximo Juncal, who had just graduated from the Uni-versity of Compostela, fired a volley of loaded political remarks and malicious hints at a current scandal that greatly worried the revolutionaries of the provinces: Sister Patrocinio,[4] her scheming, her influence at court. Two or three priests became upset, and Barbacana, gravely turning to Juncal his florid beard, told him a plain enough truth: that "many speak of things they don't understand." To which the doctor, shooting gall through his eyes and lips, retorted that "the day of the great purge was coming," and that "then the greatest uproar of the century would rise, and the neo-Catholics would go tell it at the house of their father, Judas Iscariot."

Fortunately he made these terrible predictions while most of the priests were tangled in a theological debate, the necessary complement to every patronal banquet. They were so engrossed in it that none of those who might have responded violently paid any attention to the doctor's remarks: neither the coarse abbot of Ulloa; nor the bellicose abbot of Boán; nor the archpriest, who, as deaf as a post, yelled at the top of his lungs in political discussions, shaking the forefinger of his right hand as if to summon the wrath of heaven. At that point, while dishes of rice with milk, cinnamon, and sugar passed around and glasses of wine were drained, the dispute reached its climax. Arguments, proposals, objections, and syllogisms filled the air.

"*Nego majorem* . . ."

"*Probo minorem* . . ."

"Watch out, Boán! You're attacking grace underhandedly."

"Be careful, my friend. If you go any farther we'll lose the notion of free will."

"Cebre, you're on the wrong track; you're getting close to Pelagius."[5]

"Not me. I stick to Augustine."

4. A nun (1811–91) who played a role in politics as adviser to Queen Isabella II.

5. English monk and theologian (A.D. 360–420?) who denied the transmission of original sin.

"This proposition is acceptable *simpliciter,* but in any other sense it won't do."

"I'll quote as many authorities as you like. I bet you can't come up with half a dozen. Let's hear them!"

"It's common knowledge in the church since the early councils."

"It's a matter of opinion, *quoniam*! Don't give me councils!"

"Do you pretend to know better than Thomas himself?"

"How about you? Are you challenging the Doctor of Grace?"[6]

"No one can refute my point! Grace, gentlemen . . ."

"Let's not lose our wits! This is blatant heresy, pure and simple Pelagianism."

"How would you know? I'm ready to defend what you censure."

"Let the archpriest speak. I'm willing to bet that he won't dismiss my argument so lightly."

The archpriest was respected for his age rather than his theological knowledge; so the terrific uproar decreased to some extent when he straightened himself up with difficulty, his hands behind his ears and his face flushed with blood, to settle the controversy, if possible. But an incident diverted the general attention: the Ulloa heir walked in, followed by two hounds whose bells tinkled merrily to announce his entrance. As he had promised, he stopped for dessert and a glass of wine that he drank standing, for a flock of partridge was waiting for him in the mountains.

He was received with all sorts of courtesies. Those who could not honor him in person entertained Chula and Turco, who rested their heads on every knee, licking plates here and there and gobbling down an occasional cake. The gentleman of Limioso rose, determined to accompany the marquis in his cynegetic excursion: he had already made the necessary preparations, for he never left home without a gun on his shoulder and a bag at his waist.

6. Saint Augustine.

When the two gentlemen departed, the effervescence of the debate on grace had calmed down. In a low voice the doctor recited to the notary certain satirical political sonnets, which at the time circulated under the name of *belenes*. The notary delighted in them, particularly when the doctor emphasized the verses colored with salacious and piquant allusions. The untidy table, spotted with sauce and red wine, and the floor littered with bones thrown by the less orderly guests marked the end of the feast. Julián would have given anything to retire; he was tired and overwhelmed by his aversion to purely material things, but did not dare to interrupt the after-dinner conversation, particularly now that the guests were enjoying their cigarettes and gossiping about the most distinguished local folks. The subject was the gentleman of Ulloa and his ability to shoot partridges, and—Julián did not know how— the discussion immediately turned to Sabel, whom everyone had seen in the morning at the dance. They praised her figure, with signals and winks at Julián as if the conversation concerned him. The chaplain lowered his eyes as usual, while he pretended to fold his napkin; but unexpectedly feeling one of those momentary fits of anger that he could not restrain, he coughed, looked around, and dropped a few remarks that left the assembly speechless. Don Eugenio, when he saw the party spoiled, decided to stand up and suggest to Julián a walk in the cool garden. A few priests rose too and announced that they were going to say compline; others slipped away with the doctor, the notary, the judge, and Barbacana to play cards till nightfall.

The priest of Naya and Julián went out to the garden through the kitchen, where the servants, the priest's cousins, and the cooks and players were celebrating noisily. Jars of wine vanished steadily and the feast threatened to last until sunset. The garden, on the other hand, kept its quiet and poetic spring calm. A fresh breeze rocked the late blossoms of the pear and cherry trees and stroked the thick fig leaves by whose shade, on a soft, grassy slope, the two priests sat down. Don Eugenio protected his head from a siege of early flies with a checked cotton handkerchief. Julián was still flushed and burning with indignation; but he had also begun to regret his impatience, and he resolved to be more tolerant in the future. Although, considering the matter carefully . . .

"Would you like to steal a wink?" the priest of Naya asked, seeing him so gloomy and crestfallen.

"No. What I wish, Don Eugenio, is to apologize for my bad temper back in there. I admit that sometimes I'm . . . a little too rash . . . but then, talk of a certain kind drives me out of my senses, there's nothing I can do about it. Put yourself in my place."

"I do. But they tease me too every minute, about my cousins, and one must put up with it. They mean no harm: they just want to laugh a little."

"There are jokes and jokes, and I think that those concerning modesty and purity are too delicate for a priest. If out of human considerations one puts up with such talk, they may assume that one has lost one's scruples and is likely to go from words to actions. And who knows if some of the laymen—I won't say the priests, I don't wish to offend them—will believe that, in fact . . . ?"

The priest of Naya nodded comprehendingly, like somebody who admits the strength of a certain remark; at the same time, the smile that exposed his uneven teeth was a gentle and ironic protest against so much rigidity.

"One must take the world as it is," he murmured philosophically. "To be good is what matters, because who can silence other people? Every man talks about whatever he pleases and plays whatever jokes he wants. If your conscience is at peace . . ."

"No, sir, no; look here," Julián replied heatedly. "We must endeavor not only to be good, but to look it too; and if I may press my point, bad example and scandal in a priest are even worse than sin itself. You know that, Eugenio, you know it better than myself, because you're responsible for the healing of souls."

"You're making a mountain out of a molehill, as if everybody were already pointing their fingers at you. One needs a great deal of patience to live among these folks. At this rate, you won't have a moment's peace."

Julián, brooding and frowning, had picked up a little stick of wood from the ground and began to poke the grass with it. Suddenly he raised his head. "Eugenio, are you my friend?"

"Of course, always," the priest of Naya answered warmly and sincerely.

"Then be honest with me. Talk to me as in confession. Are people around here talking about . . . that?"

"About what?"

"About me having something to do with that girl, eh? You can believe me, I'd even swear it if it were permitted: the Lord knows that I detest that woman! I haven't looked at her face half a dozen times since I arrived at the house of Ulloa."

"There's nothing wrong in looking at her face, which is like a rose. Enough, calm down! It doesn't seem to me that anybody has funny ideas about you and Sabel. Obviously the marquis didn't invent the wheel and the wench has as much fun with her own kind as she pleases, as everyone could see today at the bagpipe dance; but she wouldn't have the nerve to make a fool of the marquis to his face with his own chaplain. For heavens' sake, let's not make him out to be so stupid!"

Julián turned around, kneeling rather than sitting on the grass, with his eyes wide open. "But the master . . . what's the master got to do with . . . ?"

The priest of Naya jumped up, although he had not been bitten by a fly, and broke into youthful mirth. Putting two and two together, Julián asked once more: "Then the boy . . . , Perucho . . . ?"

Don Eugenio's roaring laughter forced him to wipe his eyes with the checked handkerchief. "Please don't take offense," he mumbled, between laughter and tears. "Don't take offense at my laughing like this. It's just that, seriously, I can't control myself when laughter strikes; once I even got sick. This is like tick . . . tickling . . . unintentional . . ."

Don Eugenio smothered his fit of laughter and added: "I always thought you were a candid soul, just like our patron Saint Julián, but this is too much. To live in the house of Ulloa and not know what's going on in it! Or are you playing the fool?"

"Honestly, I suspected nothing, absolutely nothing. Do you think I would have stayed there a single day longer if I knew? Do you think I would condone concubinage in my presence? But . . . are you sure?"

"My friend, do I have to tell you the whole story? Are you blind? Haven't you noticed? Just look around you!"

"I don't know, when one is not in the habit of thinking evil . . . And the boy? Unhappy child! I feel so much pity for the boy. He's growing up like a Moor. Can you believe that parents can be so heartless?"

"Pooh! Children like this, born out of the church . . . If you listen to different people here and there . . . Everybody says whatever they please. The girl is as happy as a fish in water. Everyone who goes on pilgrimage to the shrines owes her a bit of money. This one treats her to cakes, that one to *resolio;* [7] somebody asks her to dance, somebody else pushes her . . . They tell so many stories. Did you notice the bagpiper playing today at mass?"

---

7. Liquor made with anise and coffee.

"A handsome lad with long whiskers?"

"That one. They call him "the Rooster." Well, they talk about whether he does or does not meet her by the roads. Who knows?"

Merry voices and peals of laughter came from behind the garden.

"It's my cousins." Don Eugenio said. "They are going to listen to the bagpipe, which is now playing by the cross. Would you like to come just for a while? Let's see if we can cheer you up. Back there at home some pray and others play. I never pray after a meal."

"Let's go," Julián answered, lost in thought.

"We'll sit at the foot of the cross."

Chapter 7

Julián felt very worried as he returned home, angry at himself for being a simpleton, blind to what everyone knew. He was as innocent as a dove, only in this wicked world one also has to be as cautious as a serpent. He could not possibly stay at the house of Ulloa; on the other hand, how could he live again at his mother's expense, with no other means than his fees for saying mass? And how could he suddenly leave his master, Don Pedro, who treated him so kindly? And the house of Ulloa, which needed a zealous and loyal restorer? All that was true enough, but what about his duty as a Catholic priest?

These thoughts nagged him as he crossed a cornfield bordered with pungent camomile. The night was balmy, and for the first time Julian appreciated the peace of the countryside, the calm that mother nature pours over our weary spirit. He looked up at the dark, high sky.

"God above all!" he whispered and sighed, thinking that he would have to live in a town of narrow streets and bump into people at every step.

He walked on, guided by the distant barks of the dogs. The massive structure of the house of Ulloa now appeared close. The wicket must be open. Julián was only a few steps away when he heard two or three screams that chilled his blood, like inarticulate shrieks of a wounded animal mingled with the cries of a child.

The chaplain was soon engulfed by the deep darkness of the corridor and the cellar, and he reached the kitchen quickly. He stood at the doorstep, paralyzed by what he saw by the dim candlelight. Sabel lay on the floor screaming desperately, while Don Pedro, mad with fury, struck her repeatedly with the butt of his gun. Perucho sobbed in a corner, his fists clenched over his eyes. Julián, without stopping to think, broke into the group and called the marquis at the top of his lungs: "Master, Master Don Pedro!"

The lord of Ulloa turned around and remained motionless and livid with rage, holding the gun by the barrel and panting, his hands and lips shaking frantically. He made no apology, nor any move to assist the victim, but instead stammered hoarsely: "Bitch, damned bitch! Make supper right away or I'll beat the living daylights out of you! Get up, or I'll get you up with the gun!"

Sabel, moaning in pain, sat up with the help of the chaplain. She still wore her fancy costume, in which a few hours earlier Julián had seen her dance by the cross and in the atrium; but the rich skirt was stained, the shawl hung limp from her shoulders, and one of its long silver pendants, smashed by a blow of the gun, stuck into the back of her neck and caused a little stream of blood. Five red bruises on Sabel's cheek showed plainly how the bold dancer had been struck down.

"Supper, I said!" Don Pedro repeated brutally.

The girl, wailing without a word, walked toward the corner where the child still sobbed and pressed him to her breast. The rustic angel continued to cry loudly. Then Don Pedro approached and said in a different tone: "What is this? Is there something wrong with Perucho?"

He touched the boy's forehead and felt something damp; then he looked at the palm of his hand and saw that there was blood on it. He clenched his fists and uttered a curse that would have horrified Julián, had he not known since that afternoon that here was a father who had just wounded his son. And the father reemerged, cursing himself, pushing the child's curls away from the contusion, dipping a handkerchief in water, and tying it with the greatest care around his head.

"See that you take good care of him," he shouted to Sabel. "And make supper right now! I'll teach you to waste time showing off at the festival, bitch!"

Sabel stood and stared at the floor. She was no longer moaning, but with her right hand she carefully felt her left shoulder, which must have been painfully bruised. In a low, mournful voice but with great determination, she stated, without a glance at her master: "Get someone else to make your supper . . . someone else to live here. I'm leaving, leaving, leaving . . ." And she repeated it obsessively, flatly, as if it were the most natural and inevitable thing in the world.

"What did you say, you scoundrel?"

"I'm leaving, I'm going to my poor little home. Who brought me here? Oh, my God!"

The girl began to cry bitterly. The marquis, on the verge of another outburst of violence, held his gun and ground his teeth in anger, when a new character entered the scene. It was Primitivo, who came out of a dark corner; one would think that he had been hidden there all the time. His presence had an immediate effect on Sabel's attitude. She trembled, fell silent, and restrained her sobs.

"Didn't you hear the master?" her father asked calmly.

"I he-eard, si-r, I-I heard . . ." the girl stammered, swallowing her tears.

"Then move and get supper ready. I'll see if the other girls have come back to help you. The Sage is out there; she can light the fire for you."

Sabel made no reply. She rolled up her sleeves and took a frying pan down from the rack. As if she had been called by one of her fellow sorcerers, the white-haired hag known as "The Sage" stepped sideways into the kitchen, with her large apron filled with logs. The marquis still held his gun; Primitivo took it respectfully and put it back in its usual place. Julián, resisting the temptation to comfort the child, decided that it was time to strike a diplomatic blow. "Would you like to take some fresh air, sir? The evening is very pleasant; we can take a walk in the garden."

And he thought to himself: "In the garden I'm going to tell him that I'm leaving, too. This house and this kind of life are not for me."

They went out to the garden. The frogs croaked in the pond, but not a single leaf on the trees stirred, so still was the night. The chaplain made bold to begin, for darkness encourages one to say difficult things. "Sir, I regret to inform you . . ."

"Hush! I know, no need to waste words. You caught me in one of those moments when a man is out of control. They say one should never beat a woman. Frankly, Don Julián, that depends on the kind of woman she is. There are women and women, by God! and certain things would be too much for the patience of Job himself if he rose from the dead. What I feel bad about is the blow the boy got."

"That's not what I meant," Julián murmured, "but if I may tell you the truth as is my duty, I don't think it's right to treat anybody like that; just because supper wasn't ready, it doesn't mean . . ."

"Supper not ready!" the master interrupted. "Supper not ready! Nobody likes to come back after a day in the mountains eating cold food and find nothing to eat, but if that accursed woman had done nothing more than that! This wench is playing tricks on me! Didn't you see her? Didn't you see her dancing wildly, shamelessly, all day in Naya? Didn't you see her, coming back with her escort? Or do you think that girls of her sort walk around all by themselves? Ha, ha, ha! I saw her with my very own eyes, and I tell you, if there's something I regret it's that I haven't broken one of her legs, so that she couldn't dance for a few months."

The priest remained silent, at a loss for an answer to such a revelation of furious jealousy. At last, he made up his mind to let go something that was stuck in his throat.

"Sir," he mumbled, "excuse me for taking this liberty. A person of your class should not concern himself with the comings and goings of the maid. People are malicious and will think that you have something to do with this girl . . . actually, everybody thinks so already. The thing is that I . . . well, I can't stay in a house where, according to public opinion, a Christian is living in concubinage. We are strictly forbidden to condone such a scandal with our presence and thus become accomplices in it. It grieves me deeply, Marquis. Believe me, it's been a long time since I've felt so sorry about anything."

The marquis, with his hand buried in his pocket, stopped walking. "Just a minute," he whispered. "You must try to understand what it means to be young and strong. Don't preach me a sermon, don't ask for the impossible. What the devil! I'm just a man like any other."

"I'm a sinner," Julián replied, "but I can see clearly into this matter, and because of the favors I owe you and the bread I've eaten at your table I'm forced to tell you the truth. Tell me honestly, sir, aren't you tired of this sordid life so beneath your birth and station? An ordinary kitchen maid!"

They were approaching the edge of the woods, where the garden ended.

"A shameless hussy, which is worse!" the marquis burst out after a pause. "Listen," he added, as they moved up to a chestnut, "that woman, Primitivo, that damned witch the Sage with her daughters and granddaughters, all that crew that turns my house into a hellhole, the whole village if necessary, should be crushed like this," and he pulled a twig of the chestnut and broke it into bits. "They're plundering me, they're eating me alive. When I think that slut hates me and prefers any barefoot peasant of those I hire to pound rye, I have a mind to bash her brains out, as if she was a poisonous snake."

Julián listened to all that misery of a sinful life in amazement, realizing how cleverly the devil casts his nets.

"But, sir," he began, "if you are aware of it yourself and you admit it . . ."

"Of course I'm aware of it! Am I so stupid as not to see that slut is slipping away from me, and that I have to chase her like a hare? Only among peasants is she happy, or with that witch who brings her gossip and takes her messages to the young bucks! She detests me. One of these days she's going to poison me."

"I'm shocked, sir," responded the chaplain energetically. "Why be so upset about something that's so easy to remedy? All you have to do is get rid of that woman!"

As both men had become used to the darkness, Julián now saw that the marquis not only shook his head but frowned.

"That's easy to say," the latter whispered listlessly, "but it's not so easy to do . . . There are practical difficulties. If I kick out this enemy I won't find anyone to serve me or cook for me. You won't believe it, but her father has threatened all the girls that he will put a bullet into anyone who comes here if his daughter leaves. And they know he's the kind of man who'd do it. One day I grabbed Sabel by the arm and took her to the door. That same evening all the other maids announced that they were leaving, Primitivo pretended to be ill, and I had to eat my meals at the parsonage and make my own bed for a week. Then I had to beg Sabel to come back. You'd better face it: they're more powerful than we. This clan that hang around them are their servants and obey them blindly.

Do you think I can save a single penny in this desert? Forget it! The whole village lives on me. They drink my wine and feed their hens with my grain; my mountains and woods supply them with logs, my granaries with bread. I collect the rent late and badly, and they owe me plenty of back payments; I breed seven or eight cows and I drink no more milk than would fit in the palm of my hand. In my barns there is a herd of oxen and calves that are never yoked to plow my land; they were bought with my money, oh yes! but they're put to collective use and never bring in any income."

"Why don't you get another steward?"

"Another steward? Do you think that's so easy? One of these two things would happen: either Primitivo would pick him from among his men, in which case nothing would be solved, or else Primitivo would put a bullet in his belly. The truth is that Primitivo is no steward, and it's worse than if he was, because he dominates everybody, including me; but I've never appointed him my steward. Here the steward used to be the chaplain. Primitivo may be illiterate, but he's as smart as the devil himself, and even when Uncle Gabriel was alive he was needed to do everything. Look, like it or not, the day he refuses to take charge I find myself stuck. Not to mention hunting, for in that he has no equal. If I lacked Primitivo it would be like having no hands or feet. In other matters it's just the same. Your predecessor, the abbot of Ulloa, was helpless without him; and yourself, who are here also as an administrator, be honest: can you manage on your own?"

"The truth is that I can't," Julián declared humbly, "but with time and practice . . ."

"Bah! No peasant will ever take orders from you, for you're a poor devil; you're too good-natured. They need people who know their weaknesses and outsmart them in their crooked ways."

As humiliating as this remark was to the priest's pride, he had to admit that it was accurate. Because he felt a little piqued, however, he was determined to make use of all his talents to achieve victory in such an unequal battle. And out of his noddle came the following platitude: "But, sir, why don't you leave the village for some time? Wouldn't this be the best way to put an end to it all? I wonder how a gentleman like you can live in these wild mountains all year around. Don't you ever get bored?"

The marquis looked at the ground, even though there was nothing worth looking at. The priest's idea did not catch him by surprise. "Leave this place!" he exclaimed. "And where the devil do I go? At least here, good or bad, I'm the king of the county. Uncle Gabriel told me a thousand times: in town you can't tell decent people from shoemakers. A shoemaker makes a fortune with his awl and looks down upon any of us, who are gentlemen from fathers to sons. I'm used to treading on my land and walking among trees that I can chop down if I want to."

"But, sir, Primitivo is the boss here!"

"So what! I can beat Primitivo black and blue whenever I'm fed up with him and the judge won't touch me. I don't do it, but I sleep with the certainty that I could if I wanted to. Do you think Sabel will turn me in for the blows she got from my gun today?"

This barbarian logic puzzled Julián.

"Sir, I'm not saying that you ought to leave for good, just for a while, to see how it goes. If you went away for some time, it wouldn't be so difficult for Sabel to marry someone of her own kind; you also might find a convenient arrangement yourself, a legitimate wife. Anyone can slip once; the flesh is weak. That's why it isn't good for a man to live alone, because he degrades himself; as a wise man once said: better to marry than burn in concupiscence, Don Pedro. Why don't you get married, sir?" he exclaimed, clasping his hands together. "There are so many honest, good young ladies!"

If it had not been so dark Julián would have seen the marquis's eyes flash.

"And do you think, you simple soul, that I've never thought of that? Do you think that I don't dream of a child that looks like me, that is not the son of a whore, that perpetuates the family name, and is called Pedro Moscoso after me?"

As he said this, the marquis beat his sturdy torso, his manly chest, as if he expected his long-awaited heir to spring out from it already grown and strong. Julián, full of hope, was about to encourage him in his good purpose; but suddenly he shivered, for he thought that he heard the rustling of an animal among the bushes behind him.

"Who's there?" he shouted as he turned around. "It seems that the fox is near."

The marquis took him by the arm. "Primitivo," he articulated in a whisper choked with anger. "Primitivo, who must have been observing us and overhearing our conversation for the last fifteen minutes. You're in trouble now. What a pair of fools we've been! May God and all the saints in heaven help me! I'm running out of patience, too. I'd rather go to prison than live like this!"

Chapter 8

Julián concocted a project while he shaved off the scanty blond hairs that grew on his cheeks. As soon as he finished washing and shaving, he would set out for Cebre on foot. There he would ask the priest for a cup of chocolate and wait in the parsonage for the stagecoach from Santiago to Orense, which arrives at noon. He would be very surprised if he could not find an empty seat. His valise was already packed. From Cebre he would send a servant for it. Making these plans, he gazed sadly at the gentle landscape, the garden with its sleepy pond, the darkness of the grove, the green meadows and the cornfields, the mountains and the clear sky; and his soul was enraptured by that sweet loneliness and silence, so much to his liking that he would gladly have spent the rest of his life there. It was not to be! God guides our steps according to his designs . . . No, it wasn't God, it was sin incarnated in Sabel that expelled him from paradise. This thought upset him and he cut his cheek twice with the razor. He almost cut himself yet a third time when someone slapped his shoulder.

He turned around. Don Pedro had undergone such a transformation that no one would have recognized him. He, too, had shaved carefully and rubbed his beard with scented lotion to make it softer and shinier. Reeking of soap and clean clothes, dressed in a gray suit, white vest, and blue bowler, and holding a coat on his arm, the lord of Ulloa looked like a different man, twenty times more civilized than the former one. Suddenly Julián understood and his heart leaped joyfully.

"Sir!"

"There! Hurry, we've got to rush. You must come to Santiago with me. We should be in Cebre before noon."

"Do you mean it, sir? It's like a miracle! I've just been packing. Heaven be praised! But if you think that I ought to stay here until . . ."

"Of course not! Traveling alone would spoil the whole thing for me. I'm going to surprise Uncle Manolo and get better acquainted with my cousins; the last time I saw them they were just little girls. If I lose my nerve now, I won't get it back in ten years. I've already sent Primitivo to saddle the mare and the donkey."

At that point a face that seemed sinister to Julián peeped through the door. The marquis must have had the same impression, for he asked impatiently: "What now?"

"The mare," Primitivo answered in an even voice, "is no good for the road."

"And why, may I ask?"

"She hasn't been shod," the hunter stated calmly.

"Damn you!" the marquis shouted, with his eyes ablaze. "And you tell me now! Isn't it your job to see that she's ready? Or do I have to take her to the smith myself?"

"I didn't know the master was going out today."

"Sir," Julián interrupted, "I'll walk. I was going to walk anyway. You can take the donkey."

"There's no donkey either," the hunter objected, without blinking or moving a single muscle of his bronze face.

"What? There is no what?" Don Pedro repeated, clenching his fists. "There—is—no—don—key? Let's see if you dare say that again to my face!"

The man of bronze did not flinch and restated coldly: "No donkey."

"By God, there will be one, and three more, for if there isn't you'll get down on all fours and carry me to Cebre!"

Primitivo, stuck to the doorstep, made no reply.

"Speak clearly: how is it there's no donkey?"

"The shepherd found it stabbed yesterday when he came back from the pasture. The master can see for himself."

Don Pedro uttered a curse and rushed down the stairs two steps at a time. Primitivo and Julián followed him. In the stable the shepherd, a boy with a stupid and scrofulous face, confirmed the hunter's story. At the back of the stable they saw the unfortunate animal shaking, with droopy ears and dim eyes. The black stream that flowed from its wounds had coagulated from the flanks to the hooves. In that murky stable full of cobwebs Julián felt as if he were at the scene of a crime. As for the marquis, he stood motionless for a moment and then suddenly grabbed the boy by his hair and pulled it furiously as he shouted: "This will teach you not to let your animals be killed! Take that, and that!"

The lad began to cry sheepishly, casting anxious glances at the impassible Primitivo. Don Pedro turned to the latter. "Get my bag and Don Julián's valise immediately. Move! We are going to Cebre on foot. If we walk briskly, we'll get there on time to catch the stagecoach."

The hunter obeyed with the same icy calm. He brought down the valise and the bag, but instead of loading them on his own shoulders he gave them to a couple of laborers and said curtly: "You're going with the master."

The marquis was surprised and looked at the steward with suspicion. Knowing that Primitivo never missed an opportunity to accompany him, he wondered at the hunter's inhibition this time. A shadow of mistrust quickly crossed Don Pedro's mind. And Primitivo, as if he could read his fears, tried to dispel them: "I must supervise the logging at Rendas Grove. The chestnuts are so thick that you can't see through them. The woodcutters are already there, but they can't manage without me."

The marquis shrugged. Perhaps, he reasoned, Primitivo wished to conceal in the woods the embarrassment of his defeat. However, knowing him as well as he did, he found it hard to believe that he would give up the game without having his revenge. He was about to say, "Come with me," but predicting resistance, he thought to himself: "What the devil! It's better to leave him. No matter what he's scheming, he won't stand in my way. And if he thinks he's a match for me . . ."

Nonetheless, he scrutinized the hunter's hard features, in which he seemed to detect a repressed and sly diabolical contraction.

"What is this fox plotting?" the master wondered. "We won't get away with this without one of his tricks. He'd better watch out; I feel up to anything today!"

Don Pedro went up to his room and came back with his gun on his shoulder. Julián looked at him, surprised that he should take the weapon to travel. Then he remembered something, too, and walked to the kitchen.

"Sabel," he called. "Sabel! Where's the child? I'd like to kiss him goodbye."

Sabel went out and came back with the boy clinging to her skirt. She had found him hidden in the barn among the cows, his favorite spot, and bits of grass and wild flowers still adhered to his curls. He looked lovely; the bandage around the bruise completed his resemblance to Cupid. Julián lifted him up and kissed him on both cheeks.

"Sabel, please wash him at least now and then, in the mornings."

"Let's go," the marquis urged from the door, as if he were afraid to approach the woman and the child. "It takes a while to get there; we're going to miss the stagecoach."

If Sabel wished to retain that fleeing Aeneas she showed no sign of it, for with the greatest calm she went back to her pots and pans. Don Pedro, though he had rushed Julián, lingered at the door for a couple of minutes, perhaps hoping secretly to get the young woman's attention; but finally he shrugged and started to lead the way on the trail that ran through the vines and ended at the stone cross. It was open although uneven country, and so the master was able to observe anything that moved on his right and left; not a single hare escaped his sharp hunter's eye. Even as he chatted with Julián about how surprised the de la Lages would soon be, and about the dark, threatening sky, the marquis's attention remained fixed on something that seemed to interest him greatly. He stopped briefly, thinking that he had descried a man's head in the distance, behind the wall that bordered the vineyard; but he was too far away to be sure. He redoubled his vigilance.

They were approaching Rendas Grove. From this point on the woods became thicker and one had to be more cautious. After skirting the grove, they reached the foot of the holy symbol and entered a rough and narrower path. They did not see anything suspicious. In the thick of the woods they heard repeated ax strokes and the "ham!" of the woodcutters felling chestnuts. Then, complete silence. The sky was covered with heavy clouds; the veiled sunlight, heralding a storm, could barely shine through. Julián remembered a melancholy detail—the cross they were about to reach, which marked the scene of a crime—and asked: "Sir?"

"Eh?" the marquis mumbled between his teeth.

"Isn't it true that somebody killed a man around here? Where the wooden cross stands. Why did they do it? Revenge?"

"A drunken brawl between two men coming back from the fair," answered Don Pedro curtly, all his attention on the thickets.

The dark cross was now upon them and Julián began, as usual, to whisper the Lord's Prayer very softly. He walked at the front and the master followed in his footsteps. The boys who carried the luggage were far ahead, eager to arrive at Cebre as soon as possible and have a drink in the tavern. Only a hunter's ear could have perceived the rustle of the leaves and the bushes as a human body made its way through them. The master did perceive it, soft but clear, and saw the barrel of a gun aimed so straight that the bullet could not miss its target: it was pointing not to his own chest but to Julián's back. The shock nearly paralyzed Don Pedro. It took him less than a second to recover, raise his rifle up to his face, and aim in turn at the hidden enemy. If the latter shot, his bullet was likely to meet another, avenging bullet. This situation did not last long; two opponents worthy of each other were face to face. The most intelligent one, knowing himself discovered, gave up. The marquis heard the gun that threatened Julián brush against the leaves as it was lowered. Primitivo came out of the grove, brandishing his old but reliable shotgun held together with twine. Julián rushed through the Gloria Patri and said politely: "Hello! Are you finally coming to Cebre with us?"

"Yes, sir," Primitivo replied, his face more than ever like that of a metal statue. "I'm no longer needed at Rendas, and perhaps I'll have a chance to shoot something down between here and Cebre."

"Give me that gun, Primitivo," Don Pedro ordered. "I hear the quail singing over there as if it was mocking me, and I forgot to load my weapon."

And as he said this he took the gun, aimed at random, and fired. A few leaves and twigs flew off a nearby oak, but no quail dropped.

"Damn it!" the marquis shouted in feigned annoyance as he thought to himself: "It wasn't a bullet; it was lead shot. He wanted to put some lead into his body. Of course! A bullet would have been too big a scandal, it would have alerted the law. He's a cunning fox."

And he said aloud: "Don't load again; no hunting today. The rain will catch us if we don't hurry up. March in front of us to show us the shortcut to Cebre."

"The master doesn't know it?"

"Of course I do, but sometimes I forget."

 # Chapter 9

As the bell had already rung twice and the servants did not seem to have heard it, the de la Lage girls, who did not expect important visitors so early in the day, came downstairs in person. In their dressing gowns and slippers, and with their hair still undone, they looked a sight. Therefore, they were taken aback to find themselves face to face with a handsome young man, who asked plainly: "Well, does anybody here remember me?"

They were tempted to run away; but the third one, who must have been about twenty and was less pretty than the others, murmured: "No doubt it's cousin Perucho Moscoso."

"Bravo!" Don Pedro cheered. "She's the smartest in the family."

And stepping forward with his arms open, he tried to hug her; but she slipped away and put out a fresh little hand, just washed with water and cologne. Immediately she went back into the house and called: "Papa, Papa! Here's cousin Perucho!"

The floor shook under elephantine steps. Señor de la Lage appeared, filling the house with his volume. Don Pedro hugged his uncle and was all but carried to the drawing room in his arms. Julián, who had sneaked behind the door not to spoil the effect of the cousin's arrival, came out of his hiding place smiling. After the girls had teased him and told him that he had grown very fat, he fled down the corridor in search of his mother.

When they were seen side by side, the resemblance between Señor de la Lage and his nephew was striking: the same majestic height, the same ample proportions, the same large bones and muscles, the same rich and vigorous beard; but while the nephew's titanic constitution, strengthened by outdoor exercise, was well proportioned, the uncle's was exuberant and plethoric. Constricted to a sedentary life, he clearly had flesh and blood in excess and did not know what to do with them. Without being exactly obesity, his corpulence spread in all directions: each foot was like a boat, each hand like a carpenter's hammer. He suffocated in formal dress, did not fit in small rooms, panted loudly in a theater seat, and at mass elbowed his neighbors to conquer more space. A magnificent specimen suited for mountain life and the warfare of feudal days, he wasted away pathetically in the vile idleness of the city, where he who produces nothing, teaches nothing, and learns nothing is good for nothing and does nothing. Oh, what a shame! Had he been born in the fifteenth century, this pure-bred Pardo de la Lage would have provided a subject for the archaeologists and historians of the nineteenth.

He praised his nephew's good looks and talked to him without ceremony, to make him comfortable. "But, my boy, how big you've grown! I think you're bigger than I. You always took after Gabriel and me rather than your mother, may she rest in peace. No, no trace at all from your father either. You are not a Moscoso or a Cabreira, my boy, but a Pardo altogether. You've seen your cousins, haven't you? Well, girls, what do you say to your cousin?"

"What do they say? They greeted me in the most formal way. I tried to hug that one over there and she put out her hand very politely."

"How silly! They're a bunch of prudes! Come at once and hug your cousin, everybody!"

The first to obey was the eldest. As he held her, Don Pedro could not but notice the generous proportions of the beautiful human frame that he was embracing. Quite a woman, his eldest cousin!

"You're Rita, if I'm not mistaken?" he asked, smiling. "I've got a terrible memory for names and I might get you all mixed up."

"Rita, at your service," the cousin answered in the same affable manner. "And this is Manolita, and that is Carmen, and that one is Nucha."

"Wait a minute! You'll have to repeat the names as I hug each one of you."

Two more cousins came to pay their tribute, saying merrily: "I'm Manolita, at your service." "I'm Carmen, at your service."

The third had hidden behind the folds of a damask curtain, as if she wished to avoid the affectionate ceremony; but her inhibition, far from doing her any good, spurred her cousin to exclaim: "Señorita Hucha, or whatever your name is, don't you think you'll get away; you owe me a hug."

"My name is Marcelina, but my sisters always call me Marcelinucha or Nucha."

She could not make up her mind to come out, and remained sheltered behind the red curtain. Her hands were folded over a white cotton shawl, on which her loose braids descended like two lines drawn with ink. Her father pushed her roughly, and the girl, blushing, crashed into her cousin, who hugged her tightly and brushed his beard against her cheek, so that she was forced to hide her face in his shirt front.

After these friendly preliminaries, Señor de la Lage and his nephew engaged in the inevitable conversation on the journey, its purpose, incidents, and adventures. The nephew was very reticent about the reason for his unexpected visit: well . . . he felt like getting away for a while, one gets tired of being always alone, a little variation is appreciated . . . The uncle did not insist, thinking to himself: "Julián will tell me all about it."

And he rubbed his enormous hands as he smiled at a thought

that he had entertained for a long time in his heart, but had never seemed as clear and promising as now. What better husband could any of his daughters want than the Ulloa cousin! Among the numerous examples of fathers anxious to marry off their daughters, none was more determined than Don Manuel Pardo, but none was more reserved about the method and procedure to follow. For that gentleman of old lineage felt a strong desire to see his girls wed; and yet under his deceivingly plain manner, his family pride was so fierce that he not only despised the ruses to which parents usually resort in these cases but was also very strict in his daughters' upbringing and the choice of their friends. He kept them locked up and isolated as in a castle and seldom took them out to public amusements. "The de la Lage ladies," he thought to himself, "must marry, and it would be contrary to Divine Providence if I did not find a tree onto which to graft the offspring of such a noble race properly; but I'd rather have them be wallflowers than marry a nobody, like some lieutenant stationed in town, or a shopkeeper who makes his living measuring cloth, or a doctor who takes the pulse of his patients. That, confound it, would be a vile profanation! The de la Lage ladies may give their hand only to their equals." Thus Don Manuel, who would never cast his nets for a rich plebeian, resolved at once to do everything in his power to transform his nephew into his son-in-law.

Did the little cousins conform to their father's views? The truth is that as soon as their cousin sat down to chat with Don Manuel, each one of them slipped away quietly to do her coiffure or to prepare a room for the newcomer and choice dishes for the table. It was agreed that the cousin would stay at home as a guest. A servant went to the inn for his luggage.

The meal was extremely cheerful. The kind of familiarity peculiar to second-degree relatives of opposite sexes soon established itself between Don Pedro and the young ladies: the relationship between cousins, unlike that between brothers and sisters, is spiced with a zesty hostility that generates humorous and gallant games. At the table there was a crossfire of the jokes, equivocations, and compliments that usually prelude more serious combats between man and woman.

"Cousin, I'm surprised that sitting as you are next to me you haven't poured me a glass of water."

"We country people are not very politic; you must teach me manners, for with a teacher like you . . ."

"You little piggy! Who said you can have seconds?"

"This dish is so delicious, it must have been your work."

"Don't get your hopes high! It was the cook's. I don't cook for you. So there!"

"Cousin, this little bite for me . . ."

"Don't steal from my plate, you greedy thing! I said I'm not giving it to you! There's the platter, help yourself!"

"Watch me steal it from you! If I catch you unawares . . ."

"No, you won't!"

And the girl would get up and dash off with the plate in her hands to prevent the theft of her meringue pie or half an apple, and the cousin would chase her around the table, and the game would be celebrated with peals of laughter as if it were the funniest in the world. The participants in this tournament were Rita and Manolita, the two eldest; as for Nucha and Carmen, they remained within the limits of a moderate cordiality, laughing at the jokes but not playing an active role in them. The only difference between them was that the face of the youngest, Carmen, reflected a permanent melancholy and overwhelming preoccupation, whereas Nucha's expressed only natural seriousness, not without placidity.

Don Pedro was in heaven. When he had decided to make the

trip, he had feared that his cousins might be formal and stuffy, something that would have made him very uncomfortable, for he was not accustomed to the company of fine ladies—a breed of "white larks" that he had never hunted. This warm welcome, however, instantly restored his self-confidence. His vigorous blood awakened, and feeling encouraged, he considered his little cousins one by one, trying to decide to which of them he should throw his handkerchief. The youngest was undoubtedly very pretty, pale, tall, slim, with black hair; but her ill-concealed hypochondria and the purple circles under her eyes diminished her appeal to Don Pedro, who was not inclined to romanticism. As for the third, Nucha, she looked very much like her younger sister, only in a plain version; her huge eyes, also black as mulberries, converged slightly, which gave her glance a peculiar vagueness and modesty. She was not tall, and her features could not be called correct, except for the mouth, which was a miniature. In sum, few physical charms, at least for those who hold in high regard the size and texture of our earthly covering. Manolita was quite a different type. Her youthful flesh and grace were admirable, but she had a flaw that some find very attractive in a woman and others, like Don Pedro, find repulsive: her feminine charms had a masculine touch, a fuzz on her upper lip that was gradually becoming a moustache, and a prolongation of the hairline above the ears and along the jaws that boldly imitated a beard. The eldest, Rita, had no defects. What Don Pedro found fascinating in Rita was not so much the beauty of her face as the generous proportions of her body and limbs, the roundness and broadness of her hips, her fully developed bosom, everything in the aggressive and harmonious curves of her vigorous figure that promised a fertile mother and an inexhaustible nurse. A superb vase, indeed, to contain a legitimate Moscoso, a splendid tree onto which to graft the heir of the Ulloas! What the marquis foresaw in such a glorious female was not sensual pleasure, but the numerous male offspring that she would bring into the world, in the same way as the farmer who contemplates a rich plot of land does not delight in its colorful flowers, but calculates the harvest that it may yield at the end of the summer.

After the meal they moved to the drawing room. The girls, who had dressed up for dinner, showed Don Pedro a number of knick-knacks: stereoscopes and picture albums, which at the time were considered elegant and uncommon. Rita and Manolita called their cousin's attention to their portraits, in which they appeared lean-ing against a chair or a pillar, the classical pose dictated by the photographers of the day. Nucha opened a tiny album before Don Pedro's eyes and asked eagerly: "Do you know him?"

It was a boy about seventeen years old, with a short haircut and in a uniform of the Academy of Artillery, who looked remarkably like Nucha and Carmen except for his bald head and their thick braids.

"He's my boy," Nucha said gravely.

"Your boy?"

The other sisters laughed noisily, and Don Pedro finally under-stood: "Oh, I know! He's your brother, my gentleman cousin Gabrieliño, the de la Lage heir."

"Of course, who else? But this sister of ours loves him so much that she calls him her boy."

Nucha, nodding in agreement, leaned forward and kissed the portrait with such passionate tenderness that the poor pupil at Segovia, victimized perhaps by cruel pranksters, must have felt something sweet and warm on his cheek and in his heart.

When the sorrowful Carmen saw her sisters entertained, she slipped away from the room not to return. Having exhausted all the curiosities of the drawing room, the girls marched their cousin through the house, from the attic to the woodshed. It was a roomy, decrepit old mansion like many others still left in monumental Compostela, a worthy urban counterpart to the rural house of Ulloa. The sober facade displayed a modern balcony that looked out of place and had been designed by Don Manuel Pardo de la Lage, who had the costly habit of remodeling. This architectural anachronism was a great consolation to the Pardo ladies, who were always there like birds perched on their favorite branch. It was there that they stitched and had their little garden in pots and boxes; there that they hung cages with canaries and linnets; but perhaps the blessed balcony was also put to other uses. The truth is that they found Carmen on it, leaning out and looking down at the street, so lost in thought that she did not hear her sisters come. Nucha pulled at her dress. The girl turned around and showed a touch of pink on her usually pale cheeks. Nucha whispered eagerly in her ear and Carmen left her position by the windows, silent and preoccupied as always.

Rita talked endlessly to her cousin about a thousand details: "From here you can see the best streets. That one is Preguntorio; it's very busy. That tower belongs to the cathedral. Haven't you been in the cathedral yet? You really haven't said a credo to the Holy Apostle, you heathen?" the girl exclaimed, flashing her eyes flirtatiously. "Shame on you! I must take you there so that you can meet the saint and hug him very, very tight. And haven't you seen the club? And Alameda? The university? Good Lord, you haven't seen anything at all, have you?"

"No, madam. You know that I'm a country boy who only got here last night. All I did was go straight to bed."

"Why didn't you come here right away, you ungrateful thing?"

"And upset you all in the middle of the night? I may be a farmer, but I'm not that rude."

"Anyway, today you must see some of the sights and then take a walk. There are lots of pretty girls around here."

"That I've already noticed, without going to Alameda," the cousin replied, throwing Rita a glance that she resisted with remarkable courage and repaid without the slightest coyness.

Chapter 10

Indeed, the marquis was shown a number of things that did not particularly interest him. Nothing pleased him and he was always disappointed, as often happens to country people who entertain exaggerated ideas of the city. He found, with good reason, the streets narrow, crooked, and ill paved, the ground muddy, the walls damp, the buildings old and darkened, the urban area small, commercial life stagnant, and the public places almost always deserted. As for all those things in an ancient town that may captivate a refined spirit—the great memories, the timeless artistic life preserved in monuments and ruins—Don Pedro knew of them as much as he knew of Greek or Latin. Moldy stones! He had enough of those at the house of Ulloa. A country gentleman of very rancid views, he found himself on a level with the most radical and vandalic democrats. Even though he had been in Orense and Santiago as a boy, he had his own fantastic notion of the ideal modern city: broad streets, regular buildings, everything brand new, a heavy police force. That was the least civilization could offer to its slaves. Granted, Santiago possessed two or three spacious buildings: the cathedral, the town hall, St. Martin's . . . But their merit, in the marquis's opinion, was overrated. A case in point was La Gloria, the portico of the cathedral. Some sculpture! Deformed saints and skinny, shapeless women. And the carvings on the pillars, how coarse! It would be interesting to see one of those scholars who study the meaning of a religious monument trying to demonstrate to Don Pedro that La Gloria contains high poetry and profound symbolism. Symbolism! Nonsense! The portico was very badly sculptured, and the figures on it looked as if they all had been squeezed through a sieve. Craftsmanship must have been terribly rudimentary in those days. To put it briefly, of all the monuments in Santiago the marquis concentrated on one of very recent manufacture: his cousin Rita.

The approaching festival of Corpus Christi somewhat invigorated the sleepy university town, and every afternoon there were elegant promenades under the trees of Alameda. Carmen and Nucha usually walked ahead; Rita and Manolita followed, with their cousin as escort. Their father covered the rear guard, in conversation with any of the elderly gentlemen who populate this town, where, by the law of affinity, there seem to live more old people than in other places.

Manolita often walked close to a very stiff young man with ridiculous airs and pretensions of elegance: his name was Don Víctor de la Formoseda, and he studied law at the university. Don Manuel Pardo was glad to see him approach his daughters, for Señor de la Formoseda was the heir of an irreproachable mountain estate and a by no means negligible fortune. But he was not the only mosquito buzzing around the de la Lage ladies. From the beginning, Don Pedro noticed that through the narrow and gloomy arches of Villar Street and the greenery of Alameda and Herradura they were followed by a young man with long hair, wrapped in a gray coat of an unusual, old-fashioned style. This man was like the girls' shadow; it was impossible to turn around without seeing him. Don Pedro also observed that whenever the constant pursuer appeared from behind a pillar or among the trees, Carmen's face brightened and her lifeless eyes shone. Don Manuel and Nucha, on the other hand, seemed anxious and upset.

Don Pedro, once alerted, kept his eyes open like the experienced hunter that he was. Nucha must not have had any admirer amid the crowd of students and idlers who flocked to the promenade, or if she did, she did not pay him any attention and remained serious and indifferent. In public, Nucha conducted herself with a gravity beyond her years. Manolita, on her part, never missed an opportunity to flirt with Señor de la Formoseda. Rita was almost as lively and provocative with her cousin as with the other men, and Don Pedro noticed that she responded to their looks and compliments with piercing glances. This worried the marquis of Ulloa. Perhaps because he was among those men easily attracted to vivacious women, he had an abysmal opinion of them, which he formulated to himself in very crude terms.

Julián and the marquis slept in contiguous rooms, for since his ordination Julián had gained status in the house. Though his mother continued to serve as housekeeper, the son sat at the family table, occupied one of the main bedrooms, and was treated, if not as an equal—a few class distinctions remained—at least with great kindness and respect.

The marquis, before he retired for the evening, went into Julián's room to chat and smoke a cigarette. The conversation was uneventful, for it always evolved around the same subject: Don Pedro's amazement at his resolution to leave the house of Ulloa and take a wife, an idea that in the past had always seemed utopian. Like all egoists, he considered his own actions and mutations very important and worthy of discussion, and constantly needed a subordinate or inferior at hand to concur on their extraordinary value and lend him a sympathetic ear.

The colloquy pleased Julián. Projects of marriage between cousins seemed to him as natural as the twining of the vine around the elm tree. Their families could not be better or closer, their classes more equal, or their ages more compatible; so the outcome was bound to be happy, because the marquis would thereby rescue his soul from the clutches of the devil, incarnated in impudent concubines. The only thing he did not like was that Don Pedro seemed to have chosen Señorita Rita; but he did not dare even to mention the problem, for fear that the marquis's Christian decision might be nipped in the bud.

"Rita is quite a woman," the latter said, explaining himself. "She looks as healthy as an apple, and her children will no doubt inherit her fine constitution. They'll grow even stronger than Perucho, Sabel's son."

Inopportune reminiscence! Julián, without exploring such physiological questions, hastened to reply: "The Pardo family has always been a healthy one, thank goodness."

One evening these confidential exchanges took a different turn, one extremely embarrassing to Julián, who felt responsible for the marquis and was afraid that a slip of his tongue might thwart his master's project.

"Do you know," Don Pedro ventured, "my cousin Rita strikes me as a little flighty. On our walks she's always wondering who does or does not look at her, who speaks to her or not. I'd swear she's fair game."

"Fair game?" the priest repeated, unable to make head or tail of the crass phrase.

"I mean . . . that she's agreeable to . . . you know . . . And when one takes a wife, it's no joke if she misbehaves with the first fellow that comes along."

"Of course, sir! The most precious treasure in a woman is her honesty and virtue. You mustn't let appearances deceive you. Señorita Rita simply has that kind of temperament, frank, lively . . ."

Julián thought that his elusiveness had saved the situation until, a few nights later, Don Pedro pressed him to speak out: "Don Julián, don't try to be mysterious with me. If I am to marry, at least I want to know how and whom. Everybody would have a good laugh if just because I come from the country these folks could pull the wool over my eyes. Then they could rightly say that I jumped out of the frying pan into the fire. It's no good to tell me that you don't know anything. You grew up in this house and have known my cousins since you were born. Rita . . . Rita is older than you, isn't she?"

"Yes, sir," Julián answered, seeing no reason to conceal her age. "Señorita Rita will soon be twenty-seven or twenty-eight. Then come Señorita Manolita and Señorita Marcelina, twenty-three and twenty-two—two little boys died in between—and then Señorita Carmen, who's twenty. When Master Gabriel was born—he must now be about seventeen, give or take a year—no one expected the lady of the house to have any more children, because her health was already failing. In fact, the last delivery was so difficult that she died a few months later."

"You must know Rita very well, then. Come on, let's have it!"

"Sir, I'm telling you the truth. I grew up in this house, yes, but I didn't mix with my masters, for I come from an entirely different class. And my mother, who is very pious, never allowed me to join the young ladies in their games, for the sake of modesty. You understand. With Señor Gabriel I did spend some time, but with the ladies it was "good morning" and "good evening" when I met them in the halls. Then I went to the seminary . . ."

"Bah! Are you trying to pull my leg? You have to know all about the girls. Your mother must have kept you informed. Am I right? You're blushing, that means I'm on the right track! Do you expect me to believe that your mother never told you a thing or two?"

Julián turned crimson. A thing or two! Of course she had told him! Since his arrival, the venerable matron who managed the de la Lage household had not spent a minute alone with her son without referring to a certain business that could only be disclosed to grave and religious men. Doña Rosario was not about to discuss it with envious gossips, oh no! She did not forget that she ate Don

Manuel Pardo's bread; but with serious and ponderous people like, for example, her confessor, the canon Don Vicente, or Julián, that fruit of her womb elevated to the highest position on this earth, who could deny her the thrill of making her own judgments on the master's and the ladies' behavior; of boasting about her discretion while she criticized, mildly and benevolently, certain actions that "if she were a lady" she'd never commit; and of hearing "respectable persons" praise her good sense and agree with her views? Had Julián heard a thing or two, good Lord, had he ever! But hearing them was one thing, repeating them was something else. How could he reveal Señorita Carmen's decision to marry, against her father's will, an insignificant medical student, a nobody, the son of a smith—what an insult to the eminent lineage of the Pardos!—a raving madman, who followed her everywhere like a lapdog, and besides was said to be a materialist and a member of various secret societies? How could he say that Señorita Manolita prayed to Saint Anthony that Don Víctor de la Formoseda would make up his mind to ask for her hand? And that, furthermore, she had written anonymous letters to Don Víctor to ill-dispose him toward the other young ladies whom he visited? And worst of all, how even to hint at *that business* about Señorita Rita that, if interpreted maliciously, might so damage her honor? He would rather have his tongue cut out.

"Sir," he stammered, "I think that the young ladies are very good and incapable of doing anything wrong, but if I knew the opposite to be true I should be very careful not to mention it, for my gratitude to this family would, so to speak, put a gag in my mouth."

He paused, realizing that he was only getting into more trouble. "Don't read anything into my words, sir. For goodness' sake, don't draw further conclusions from my inability to explain myself."

"Then you don't think," the marquis inquired, looking at the priest out of the corner of his eye, "that there is anything to

worry about? Fine. You find them all impeccable and irreproachable ladies; any one of them would make me a good wife, isn't
that so?"

Julián pondered over his answer. "If you insist on knowing
everything that's in my heart, frankly, although they are all very
charming, if I had to choose, I don't deny it, I'd choose Señorita
Marcelina."

"Wait a minute! She's a little cockeyed . . . and skinny. All she has
is good hair and a nice manner."

"She's a gem, sir."

"She must be like the others."

"She's like no one but herself. When Señor Gabriel lost his
mother as a baby, she took care of him so diligently that it was
something to see, because she wasn't much older herself. A real
mother could not have done more. Night and day, she always
carried the child in her arms. She called him her son: they say it
was quite a sight. It seems that carrying the child so much finally
exhausted her, and that's why she's not as healthy as her sisters.
When her brother left to go to school she fell ill. That's why you
see her so pale now. She's an angel, sir. Her only endeavor is to give
her sisters good advice."

"That means that they need it," Don Pedro argued maliciously.

"Good heavens! I have to be careful! You know that what's good
may always be better, and Señorita Marcelina borders on perfection. Perfection is granted only to a few. Señorita Marcelina, sir, is
so religious, and confesses and takes communion so often that she
is an inspiration to others."

Don Pedro meditated for a while, and then stated that he liked
women to be religious and that he considered piety indispensable
for their virtue. "So she's pious, eh?" he added. "Now I know what
makes her tick."

That was, in fact, the outcome of this conference in which

Julián, with more goodwill than diplomacy, tried to present
Nucha's candidacy. After that day her cousin teased her often,
with greater or lesser tact. When he made Nucha blush, he felt
the pleasure of a child determined to open a rosebud with his fingers, scratching the skin of her soul with impudent jokes and crass
familiarities that she rejected energetically. Such games irritated
the priest as much as the girl. After-dinner conversations were an
endless torture to him. Don Manuel's stories and anecdotes, which
always dealt with ill-smelling subjects—one of Señor de la Lage's
inveterate habits—merged with Don Pedro's improprieties to his
cousin. Poor Julián, with a slight frown and his eyes fixed on his
plate, went through sheer agony. He believed that to smear even in
jest the flower of virginal modesty was an appalling sacrilege. What
his mother had told him of Nucha and what he saw in her filled
him with religious awe, as if he were before a shrine that enclosed
a revered image. He never dared to call her by her diminutive,
"Nucha," which struck him as a name more suitable for a dog than
a person. When Don Pedro began to tell sordid jokes, the priest
would sit by her and talk to her of holy and peaceful things, like a
prayer or a church service that she attended frequently, and thus he
hoped to comfort her.

The marquis could not overcome his irritating attraction to
Rita. As his eldest cousin's sway over his senses grew stronger, the
instinctive suspicion that city females awaken in the country man,
who often mistakes their flirting for depravity, also increased. The
marquis could not help it: in his phrase, Rita was "awfully fishy."
She could be so uninhibited sometimes! She led him on and cast
her nets so openly, she relished men's adulation so much!

The villager who goes into town has heard a thousand stories of
pranks played on innocent greenhorns. Full of suspicion, he looks
in every direction, is afraid of being robbed in the stores, does not
trust anyone, and does not dare to go to sleep for fear that some-

body may steal his purse. Setting aside the distance that separates a farmer from the master of the house of Ulloa, this was the marquis's situation in Santiago. Primitivo's tyranny and Sabel's shameless betrayals in his own home did not humiliate him nearly as much as his little cousin's teasing here in town. Besides, it was one thing to have fun with a girl and another to take a wife. The woman destined to perpetuate the eminent name of Moscoso should be as clean as a mirror. And Don Pedro figured among those who do not consider clean any woman who has had a love affair—even of the most chaste and innocuous nature—with anybody but her husband. Mere glances in the street were serious sins. Don Pedro understood conjugal honor in a Calderonian, truly Spanish way: extremely indulgent in the case of the husband and implacable in that of the wife. And he refused to believe that Rita was not involved in some kind of liaison. As for Carmen and Manolita, he did not have to strain his imagination; it was plain to see what was going on. But Rita . . .

Don Pedro had no close friends in Santiago, just a few acquaintances made during his walks, at his uncle's house, or at the club, where, as every idle Spaniard did, he spent each morning and evening. There he was constantly chaffed on the subject of his cousin, and listened to the comments on Carmen's passion for the student and her permanent watch from the balcony, with her beau standing across the street. The marquis, always alert, observed the tone in which Rita's name was mentioned. On a couple of occasions he thought he detected traces of irony, and perhaps he was not mistaken; for in small towns, where no event is erased or forgotten, where conversation evolves endlessly around the same topics, where petty things are blown up and serious ones take epic proportions, a girl often loses her reputation before her virtue, and the most insignificant frivolities, recounted and criticized year after year, accompany the maiden to the grave. Moreover, the de la

Lage ladies, because of their name and beauty, their father's aristocratic airs, and the halo with which he liked to protect them, were
the target of considerable envy and gossip: when they were not
accused of pride they were pronounced to be flirts.

Notable among the club's battered furniture was a guttaper-
cha sofa that was the showpiece of the reading room and might
well be called the tribune of the slanderers, for three of the most
evil-tongued men in the world—a triumvirate worthy of further
attention—sat on it. Its most distinguished member was a master
in the science of evil knowledge. Just as scholars pride themselves
in knowing the most insignificant events of remote historical eras,
so this fellow boasted that he could say without the slightest error
what was the income of the twenty or thirty foremost families of
Santiago, what they ate, what they talked about, and even what
they thought. He would declare with great calm and solemnity:
"Yesterday the de la Lages had two main courses: beef stew and
croquettes; cauliflower salad; and for dessert preserves made by
the nuns."

When this type of information was checked, it always turned
out to be accurate.

This knowledgeable individual planted further suspicions in the
mind of the marquis of Ulloa, by merely dropping a few words
that, interpreted literally, seemed quite innocent, but when examined closely might mean anything. After celebrating Rita's cheer-
fulness, Rita's beauty, and the remarkable anatomy of Rita's body,
he added casually: "She's a splendid girl, but she has very few
chances to find a husband here. Girls of Rita's type always find their
better halves in outsiders."

Chapter 11

For a whole month Don Manuel Pardo had been asking himself: "When will the young fellow make up his mind to ask for Rita's hand?"

That he would ask for it Don Manuel never doubted. Tacitly, the marquis's position in that home was that of an accepted fiancé. The friends of the family allowed themselves open allusions to the approaching marriage, and in the kitchen the servants were already calculating how big a tip they might collect on the wedding day. When the girls retired for the evening they teased Rita; all day long they laughed fraternally with their cousin; and a gust of youthful merriment turned the old house into a noisy birdcage.

One afternoon, when the marquis was taking a nap, someone knocked loudly on the door. He opened: it was Rita in her dressing gown, with a handkerchief tied around her head, and her beautiful throat bare. In her right hand she brandished a huge feather duster. She looked like a very pretty maid, which far from discouraging the marquis only made his blood run faster.

"Perucho? Perucho?"

"Ritiña, Ritoña?" Don Pedro replied, as he devoured her with his eyes.

"The girls want you. We're busy cleaning the attic, which is filled with things from grandpa's times. It seems that you can find marvels there."

"And what good can I do? You don't expect me to sweep?"

"You'll sweep if we want you to. Come along, lazybones, sleepy-head!"

A steep stairway led to the attic, which thanks to three skylights was not too dark; but it was so low that the marquis could not stand upright in it, and the three girls constantly knocked their heads against the ceilings. Stored in that attic were discarded knick-knacks that in the past had contributed to the pomp and splendor of the Pardos de la Lage, and now lay in the company of dust and termites. Their only hope was to catch the girls' attention as they merrily searched for some old jewel that they could remodel according to the current fashion. With those withered relics one could write the history of the life and mores of the Galician nobility of the last two centuries. Remains of painted and gilded chairs; little lanterns with which the pages lighted the way for their ladies when they came back from their coteries, in the days when pub-lic lighting was unknown in Santiago; a military uniform from Ronda; bead-embroidered headdresses and handbags; jackets with striking flower patterns; faded silk stockings; skirts with flounces; rusty steel swords; theater programs printed on silk, announcing that the leading lady would sing an amusing ditty and the come-dian would perform a droll *petite pièce;* all lying in confusion with other similar trifles. Among the most eloquent and symbolic ob-jects were a set of Masonic emblems: a medal, a triangle, a mallet, a square, and an apron, spoils of a Francophile grandfather who was a Mason of the highest rank; and a fine purple jacket with colonel's badges embroidered in silver on the cuffs and the collar. This gar-ment had belonged to Don Manuel Pardo's grandmother, who, following a contemporary custom initiated by Queen María Luisa, wore her husband's uniform to sit comfortably astride her horse.

"Nice place you've brought me to!" Don Pedro said, choking in the dust and terribly upset because he could not move.

"This is what we want," Rita and Manolita retorted, with triumphant applause, "for no matter how hard you try, you can't run after us or play your tricks. This is our great chance! We're going to dress you up in this jacket and sword. Wait and see."

"I'm not in the mood for masquerades."

"Just for one minute, to see how it looks."

"I'm telling you, you're not going to dress me like a clown."

"What do you mean we won't? We've made up our minds."

"You'll regret it, I warn you. The first one to get near me will pay for it."

"And what will you do to us, you rascal?"

"I'm not telling you. You'll see."

The mysterious threat seemed to frighten the cousins, who for the moment limited themselves to harmless mischief and a few strokes with the duster. They made progress with the cleaning work. Manolita moved things around with her sinewy arms; Rita sorted them out; Nucha shook and folded them neatly. Carmen participated hardly at all in the hustle-bustle, and even less in the merriment; two or three times she vanished, doubtless to look out over the balcony. The others dropped her a few hints.

"How's the weather, Carmucha? Is it sunny or raining?"

"Are there lots of people in the street? Come on, tell us!"

"She's always daydreaming."

As the girls dusted the garments, they tried them on. Manolita, with her manly figure, looked very nice in the colonel's uniform. Rita was a delight in her grandmother's silk dressing gown. Carmen agreed to wear only an extravagant ornament, a triple tuft of feathers that in its day was called "the three potencies." The lace mantillas were reserved for Nucha. Meanwhile the sun was setting, and it was difficult to see anything through the cobwebs of the attic. The shadows favored the girls' designs; taking advantage of them, the two elder ones stole behind Don Pedro, and while

Rita planted a three-cornered hat on his head, Manolita threw a dove-colored jacket with a trim of blue and yellow flowers on his shoulders.

The result of this silly prank was instant confusion. Don Pedro, determined to take a memorable revenge, chased his cousins on all fours, because otherwise he could not move in the low attic; the girls squealed like mice and bumped into furniture and scattered knickknacks as they ran to the narrow exit to escape punishment. While Rita barricaded herself behind the remains of a gilded chair and a decrepit chest of drawers, the two least courageous girls fled; and when Manolita cleverly blinded her cousin for a second by flinging a shawl on his head, Rita, the natural leader of this mutiny, was also able to escape. In the twinkling of an eye, Don Pedro freed himself of the shawl by tearing it to shreds and rushed through the door and downstairs in pursuit of the fugitive.

He leaped down the steps impetuously and followed the hasty trot of his beautiful prey like a hunter used to tracking down elusive animals. He caught it around a bend of the corridor. The resistance was weak and interrupted by laughter. Don Pedro, who had promised to avenge himself and was determined to do it, applied his long and loud punishment close to an ear. Then he thought that the victim ceased to resist; but this malicious assumption proved to be wrong, for Rita took advantage of a brief truce to run away again, screaming: "Catch me again if you can, you coward!"

The marquis, spurred by his little taste of victory, forgot the dangers of the game and dashed after his cousin. By now she was engulfed in the darkness of the irregular and winding corridor that meandered through the house, breaking into unexpected angles and narrowing in some places like an ill-stuffed sausage. Rita had the advantage of being familiar with these nooks and crannies. The marquis heard a door squeak, a sign that the girl had sought refuge in the sanctuary of a bedroom. Don Pedro was not about to respect holy ground and pushed on the door behind which he thought Rita had retreated. The door resisted as if something stood against it; but Don Pedro's fists easily wrecked the frail barricade built with two chairs, which tumbled down with a great deal of noise. He entered the totally dark room and by instinct stretched out his hands so that he would not stumble upon the furniture. He heard something move in the darkness, felt the air around him, and touched a woman's body, which he gathered into his arms without a word, so that he could repeat the punishment. What a surprise! He met with the most stubborn and vigorous resistance, the most desperate protest, two little hands of steel that he could not dominate, a nervous body trying to break free, and at the same time deep and sorrowful moans, two or three suppressed screams for help. Confound it! This was quite different! Blind and carried away as he might be, the marquis could not but notice it. He felt more confused than ever before and released the girl.

"Don't cry, Nuchiña . . . hush, I'll let you go . . . I won't do you any harm. Wait a minute."

He hurriedly searched his pockets, struck a match, looked around, and lit a candle. Nucha, once she found herself free, was quiet but still on the defensive. The marquis once more apologized and comforted her. "Nucha, don't be such a child. I'm sorry, I really . . . I didn't think it was you."

Nucha, holding back her sobs, replied: "Even if it had been somebody else . . . It isn't right to be brutal with young ladies."

"But, my dear, your sister was after me, and when a woman is after me it's no wonder if she finds me. Be quiet, now; don't cry anymore. What's my uncle going to think of me? But, girl, are you still crying? You're very sensitive, aren't you? Let's see that face."

He raised the candlelight to Nucha's face. She was flushed and altered, and a tear trickled down each cheek; but when the light shone into her eyes, she could not help smiling slightly, and dried her tears with a handkerchief.

"My God! Who would ever dare! You're a little wildcat! There was even strength in your fists in those moments!"

"Go, now," Nucha ordered, recovering her seriousness. "This is my room, and I don't think it's proper for you to be in it."

The marquis took two steps to the door; then he turned around suddenly and asked: "Are we still friends? Peace?"

"Yes, as long as you don't do anything like that again," Nucha replied firmly.

"And what will you do if I come back?" the country gentleman asked, grinning. "You're capable of knocking me out with a single blow."

"Surely I'm not that strong. I'll do something else."

"What?"

"Tell papa, loud and clear, to call his attention to something that has not crossed his mind: that it isn't natural for you to live here, for you're not our brother and we are all unmarried girls. I know it takes nerve to tell papa what he should do; but he's not aware of this and doesn't think you capable of such tricks as you've played today. As soon as he knows he'll do something about it, and I won't have to whisper anything into his ears, for I have no right to give advice to my father."

"Why, you're saying it as if . . . it were a matter of life or death."

"Exactly."

With this unceremonious farewell the marquis left; through the whole dinner he remained sulky and self-absorbed and paid no attention to Rita's flattery. Although Nucha's face was still a little altered, she was as kind and composed as usual, tending to the service of the meal and order at table.

That night the marquis did not let Julián sleep, entertaining him until late with endless talk. For the next days there was a truce. Don Pedro went out and was often seen at the club, next to the slanderers' tribune. He wasted no time there but gathered information about matters that concerned him, such as, for example, his uncle's real financial position. People in Santiago said what he already suspected: that Don Manuel Pardo would leave the best part of his capital to his son Gabriel, who, with his monetary inheritance plus the estate, would sweep away practically the whole de la Lage fortune for himself. The girls' only hope was an unmarried aunt in Orense, Señorita Marcelina, who was also Nucha's godmother and lived like a rat in a hole, hoarding up her riches. This piece of news worried Don Pedro, who kept Julián awake a few more nights. At last he made a final decision.

One morning Don Manuel Pardo shivered with delight when he saw his nephew walk into his office with the indescribable expression of somebody who comes to deal with an important matter. Don Manuel had heard that when there are several sisters the difficulty lies in getting rid of the eldest, and then the rest drop on their own, like the beads of a necklace. Once Rita was married, the rest would be child's play. Sooner or later, the presumptuous Señor de la Formoseda would take care of Manolita; Carmen would forget about certain follies, and being so pretty, she would not lack a good match; and Nucha . . . Nucha certainly was no burden to him around the house, because she managed it admirably. Besides, as her godmother's presumptive heiress, she did not need the security of marriage. If she did not find a husband, she would live with Gabriel when the latter finished his studies and took possession of the de la Lage estate. With these reassuring thoughts, Don Manuel opened his ears to the dew of his nephew's impending words. What he heard was more like a shot.

"Why are you so shocked, Uncle?" Don Pedro said, inwardly enjoying the old gentleman's dismay and bewilderment. "Is there any problem? Does Nucha have another suitor?"

Don Manuel began to raise a thousand objections, omitting some that he was not about to mention. He emphasized the girl's youth and poor health, even her lack of beauty, and spiced this remark with unsubtle allusions to Rita's good looks and Don Pedro's poor taste in not preferring her. He patted his nephew on the shoulders and the knees; he cracked jokes; he tried to advise him as one advises a child who has to choose a toy; and finally, after telling in dialect several anecdotes suited to the occasion, he declared that he would give a dowry to the other girls when they married, but Nucha, as she expected to inherit her aunt's money . . . Alas, these were bad times! Then he faced the marquis and asked: "Let's see, what does that little mouse Nucha say?"

"You'd better ask her yourself, Uncle. I haven't told her much. We're too old to fool around."

Oh, what a storm swept the house of de la Lage for the next two weeks! Conferences with the father, whispering among the sisters, late vigils and early risings, slamming of doors, secret tears betrayed by eyes as swollen as balloons, irregularities at mealtimes, consultations with grave friends, the curiosity of idle maids who walked on tiptoes to listen behind the curtains, and all the dramatic trifles that accompany a serious domestic event. And as in a provincial town walls are made of glass, all Santiago gossiped frantically, enumerating the scandals that had taken place among the de la Lage ladies on account of their cousin. Rita was accused of insulting her sister because Nucha had stolen her fiancé, and Carmen of helping Rita because of Nucha's objections to her habit of gazing out the window. Nucha was also dubbed false and hypocritical. They threw mud at the father too, and someone repeated in a circle of close friends what Don Manuel had told him confidentially: "I wasn't about to let my nephew leave without taking one of the girls; he fancied Nucha, so I had to give her to him." It was taken for granted that the sisters never spoke to each other at table, and as proof people cited the fact that in the street Rita walked in front with Carmen, while their cousin followed behind with Don Manuel and Nucha, who lowered her head modestly. Gossip grew when Rita went to Orense to stay with her aunt Marcelina for a while—so she said—and Don Pedro moved to an inn, for it was not proper for the couple to live under the same roof so shortly before the wedding.

It took place in late August, once the papal dispensation arrived, with all the necessary requisites: exchange of courtesies, gifts from friends and relatives, lavishly decorated bonbon boxes, and a good trousseau of linen. The bride's outfit came from Madrid in a huge box. Two or three days before the ceremony a small package arrived from Segovia. It was a case that contained a simple gold ring and a card that read: "To my unforgettable sister Marcelina from her loving brother, Gabriel." The present from "her boy" made the bride cry profusely; she put it on the little finger of her left hand, where it would soon be joined by the other ring that she would receive in church.

They were married at dusk in a lonely parish church. The bride wore a rich black silk gown, a lace mantilla, and an ornament of diamonds. Afterward, the traditional Spanish refreshments were served only to the family and intimate friends: preserves, sherbets, chocolate, sweet wine, cake, a large assortment of pastries, everything arranged on solid trays and silver plates with much etiquette and art. No flowers decorated the table, except for the cloth roses on the cakes and on the pine nut tarts. Two candlesticks, tall enough to stand beside a funeral coach, added solemnity to the dining room; and the guests, still filled with the awe that the sacrament of marriage inspires, spoke as softly as they would at a wake, avoiding even the clicking of their spoons against the plates. It was like the last supper of a condemned criminal. It is true that the worldly and amiable Father Nemesio Angulo, Don Manuel's old friend, who had just sealed the couple's happiness with his blessing, attempted to enliven the party with two or three decently jocular remarks; but his efforts crashed against the seriousness of the guests. They were all—as the accepted phrase goes—deeply moved, including Señor de la Formoseda, who perhaps thought, "Will I be next?" and Julián, who although he saw his greatest wish fulfilled and his candidacy triumphant, felt a strange burden in his heart, as if a sinister foreboding loomed over it.

The bride, grave and solicitous, tended to all the guests. A couple of times her shaky hand spilled the wine that she was pouring to good old Don Nemesio, who occupied the seat of honor on her right. The groom, meanwhile, conversed with the men, and after leaving the table passed around his cigar case filled with excellent cigars. No one referred to the main event of the day or dared to crack the slightest joke that might offend the bride; but some of the gentlemen, as they took their leave, maliciously emphasized their "good night," while matrons and maidens kissed Nucha loudly and whispered in her ear: "Goodbye, Señora Moscoso. You're a *married lady* now; we can't call you 'señorita' anymore." And they accompanied this trivial remark with an affected giggle, looking up and down at Nucha as if they were trying to engrave her image in their memory. When they were all gone, Don Manuel Pardo walked toward his daughter, pressed her against his ample chest, and stamped affectionate kisses on her forehead. Señor de la Lage was really touched. It was the first marriage of one of his daughters, and he felt his heart overflow with fatherly feelings. As he took Nucha by the hand to her chamber, while Doña Rosario lighted their way with a five-branched candelabrum from the dining room, he could not utter a word. His eyes became moist and a smile of pride and happiness played on his lips. Finally, at the doorstep he managed to say: "If only your mother, may she rest in peace, could raise her head today!"

On the dresser two candlesticks were burning, as tall and majestic as those that had stood on the table. As there was no other light and no one had yet dreamed of the classic porcelain globe found in the voluptuous suite of every novel, the bedroom was filled with religious rather than nuptial mystery. The shape of the bed completed its similarity to a chapel; the red damask curtains, with their gold fringes, resembled the draperies of a church; and the starched snow-white sheets with lace trimmings had the chaste smoothness of an altar cloth. As the father withdrew, whispering, "Good-bye, Nuchita, my dear daughter," the bride clung to his right hand and kissed it with her dry, feverish lips. Then she was alone. She shivered like a leaf on a tree. A death-cold shudder ran through her nerves at every minute, caused by an indefinable and sacred terror rather than by conscious fear. This room, with its imposing silence and the tall, solemn candles, seemed to her the same temple where barely two hours earlier she had been on her knees. Now she knelt down once more. In the shadows between the head of the bed and its austere canopy she caught a glimpse of the old ebony and ivory crucifix. Her lips murmured the customary evening prayer: a Pater Noster for mamma's soul. In the corridor she heard the creaking of brand-new boots, and the door opened.

Chapter 12

The crumbs of the wedding feast were not yet stale when Don Pedro held a conference with Julián; they decided that it was imperative for the chaplain to return to the house of Ulloa right away, in order to make the necessary preparations and condition the burrow a little before the arrival of its owners. No sooner had Julián accepted the assignment than the master began to have second thoughts.

"Remember," he warned him, "that there you'll need a lot of pluck. Primitivo is a crooked man who could fool you a thousand times."

"God will help me. And he's not going to kill me, anyway."

"Don't say that twice," the marquis insisted, prompted by his conscience, which at this moment spoke loudly and clearly. "I have cautioned you before about Primitivo. He's capable of anything. However, I don't think he'd do something crazy just for the sake of it, even on the spur of the moment, when the desire for revenge blinds him. But still . . ."

This was not the first time that Don Pedro had shown a good knowledge of human character; but it was useless without the tact and moral sensibility that society expects nowadays from those who by birth, wealth, or power occupy a high place in it. The marquis proceeded: "Primitivo is not brutal, but he's the most cunning scoundrel in the world and will stop at nothing to get what he wants. Devil take it, I know this all too well! The day we came he tried to end our trip with a bullet; I wouldn't give a cent for your life or mine."

Julián shuddered and the color faded from his cheeks. He was not made of the stuff of heroes, as his face now proved. Don Pedro was infinitely amused by the priest's fear, for there was a streak of cruelty in him fostered by his gross existence.

"I'll bet," he said with a laugh, "that you say a prayer by the cross."

"Maybe I shall," Julián replied, pulling himself together, "but I'll go anyway. It's my duty and there's nothing extraordinary in my doing it. God will guide me. Maybe Primitivo's bark is worse than his bite."

"This is not the time for Primitivo to stop to think about proverbs."

Julián remained silent. At last he exclaimed: "Sir, if you only made up your mind to . . . throw that man out, just throw him out, sir!"

"Wait a minute. We'll make him toe the line, but throw him out . . . And what about the dogs and the hunts? And those folks and all that crew that nobody but he can handle? You'd better face it: I can't manage there without Primitivo. Try, just for the sake of it, to do any of the jobs that Primitivo can do in his sleep. Besides, what I tell you is the gospel truth: if you kick Primitivo out of the door, he'll come back through the window. I know him well, damn it, I do!"

Julián stuttered: "And . . . that other thing?"

"About the other things you can do as you please. I give you a free hand."

He had a free hand! If only he had also an effective recipe to make good use of it! Invested with this omnipotent authority, Julián felt pity for the shameless concubine and particularly for her spurious son. Was the poor innocent boy to blame for his mother's rogueries? It seemed cruel to cast him out of the house, which after all belonged to his father. Julián would never have accepted such an unpleasant task had Don Pedro's salvation and Señorita Marcelina's temporal happiness—despite the comments of the wedding guests, he continued to call her "señorita"—not been at stake. Not without apprehension, he crossed once again the gloomy wolf country adjacent to the valley where the house of Ulloa stood. Primitivo was waiting for him at Cebre, so they completed the journey together. The steward behaved so humbly and respectfully that Julián, who in contrast to Don Pedro was a poor judge of character but a good speculative and abstract thinker, gradually lost his mistrust and became convinced that the dog had no intention of biting. Primitivo's inexpressive face revealed neither resentment nor anger. With his usual laconism he commented on the rainy, unstable weather that had barely permitted them to cut the corn, gather the grapes, or accomplish any of the major farming tasks normally. The trail was, indeed, swampy and full of puddles, and as it had rained in the morning water dripped from the shiny pine needles and splashed on the riders' hats. Julián's fears had subsided and a pure joy had filled his spirit by the time he greeted the cross with true religious fervor. "Blessed be your name, my Lord," he thought to himself, "for you have allowed me to accomplish a good deed, pleasing to your eyes. A year ago I found vice, scandal, vileness, and evil passions at the house of Ulloa; now I bring to it a Christian marriage and the family virtues that you have consecrated. I, I have been the agent of your holy work. Thank you, my God."

The soliloquy was interrupted by excited barks; it was the marquis's dogs, which came out to greet the hunt master with joy, wagging their stumped tails and opening their mouths wide. Primitivo, who was extremely affectionate toward the dogs, patted them with his bony hand, and then pulled his grandson's nose playfully. Julián tried to kiss the child, but the latter ran away before he could catch him. Once again the priest felt pity and remorse when he saw the repudiated child. He found Sabel in her usual place, amid her pots and pans, but without the retinue of old and young village women, the Sage and her numerous descendants. In the kitchen reigned absolute order: everything was clean, calm, and solitary; the most exacting judge could not have found anything to criticize. The priest felt confused when he saw that things ran so smoothly in his absence, and feared that his arrival might upset them—an anxiety produced by his natural shyness. At dinner he was even more surprised. Primitivo, as gentle as a dove, reported to him in a soft voice everything that had happened through the last six months: how many calves had been born, what work had been undertaken, and how much rent had been collected. And while the father thus bowed to his higher authority, the daughter served him humbly and diligently, like a spoiled domestic animal begging for affection. Julián did not know how to take such a cordial reception. He thought that their attitude would change the next day, when, making use of the omnipotent power granted him by the marquis, he ordered the Hagar and Ishmael of that patriarchate to emigrate to the desert; but, unbelievable though it seemed, Primitivo's meekness remained unaltered even then.

"The masters will bring a cook from Santiago," Julián explained to justify the expulsion.

"Of course," Primitivo responded in the most natural tone. "In town they cook differently, and the master must now be used to it. It suits us well, because I was just going to ask you to write to the marquis and ask him to bring a new cook."

"You?" Julián said in amazement.

"Yes, sir. This daughter of mine wants to get married."

"Sabel?"

"Yes, sir, Sabel; with the bagpiper of Naya, the Rooster. Needless to say, she plans to move to her own home as soon as the ceremony is over."

Julián was overwhelmed with joy. He could not but think that God's providence was plainly visible in that affair. Sabel married and away from the house, danger exorcised; everything in order, salvation secured. Once again he thanked the good Lord, who removes difficulties when the wretched human mind cannot even cope with them. So great was the happiness that overflowed his heart that he felt embarrassed, and in order to conceal it from Primitivo he hastened to congratulate him and predict a bright future for Sabel in her new state. That same night he wrote the good news to the marquis.

The days went by, always peaceful. Sabel remained submissive, Primitivo complacent, Perucho invisible, the kitchen deserted. The only passive resistance that Julián detected concerned the management of the marquis's finances and estate. In this respect, he found it impossible to make the slightest progress. Primitivo firmly maintained his position as the real administrator, treasurer, and autocrat behind the scenes. Julián realized that Primitivo did not give a farthing for his "free hand," and even saw clear evidence that the hunter's influence in the domain of Ulloa was extending to the whole county. People from Cebre, Castrodorna, Boán, and places still farther away came often to consult with the steward in attitudes of servile humility. A straw could not move within ten miles unless Primitivo consented. Julián knew that he did not have the strength to fight him; moreover, he reckoned that the damage that Primitivo's bad management might do to the house of Ulloa was a lesser evil than the harm that Sabel had been about to cause. To cast the daughter away was the important thing; as for her father . . .

The truth is that the daughter had not yet left either; but she would leave, no question about it! Who could doubt that she was going to leave? Julián felt reassured by what he considered to be an unmistakable sign: on a certain evening, he surprised Sabel and the piper by the stacks of straw engaged in a colloquy more tender than edifying. The encounter made him blush; but he looked the other way and reflected that this was, so to speak, the waiting room to the altar. Confident of his victory over this wily female, he compromised with the steward, particularly because the latter never contradicted Julián or rejected his suggestions. If the chaplain conceived a plan, criticized a certain abuse, or insisted upon an urgent reform, Primitivo acquiesced, paved the way, and devised the means; that is, verbally. When it came to execution, that was another story; then the difficulties and hesitation began: today it was this, tomorrow that . . . No force can compare to inertia. To comfort Julián, Primitivo would say: "It is one thing to talk and another to act."

One had either to kill Primitivo or to deliver oneself into his hands: the priest realized that there was no way out. One day he went to unburden his heart to Don Eugenio, the abbot of Naya, whose wise reasoning always encouraged him greatly. He found him very excited about the political news that the few newspapers available in this remote part of the world had just confirmed. The navy had risen and deposed the queen, who had fled to France; a provisional government had been formed, and there were reports of a bloody battle on the bridge of Alcolea; the army had joined the coup, and the devil knew what . . .[1] Don Eugenio rushed about like a madman, ready to leave for Santiago without delay to get reliable information. What would the archpriest and the abbot of Boán say? And Barbacana? Barbacana was now in trouble: his sworn enemy Trampeta, a friend of the Unionists, would get the upper hand forever and ever, amen!

Amid the bustle of these events, the abbot of Naya paid hardly any attention to Julián's tribulations.

1. This was the liberal revolution of 1868, led by General Juan Prim.

Chapter 13

After a period of family life with his father- and sisters-in-law, Don Pedro began to miss his den. He could not get used to the archiepiscopal town. He suffocated within its high mossy walls, its narrow porticoes, its buildings with gloomy halls and dark staircases, which seemed to him dungeons and cells. It annoyed him to live in a place where a couple of raindrops kept everybody at home and instantly brought forth a sad vegetation of silk mushrooms, of enormous umbrellas. It irritated him to hear the perpetual symphony of the rain trailing down the gutters or clicking on the puddles formed on the paving stones. There were only two ways to relieve his boredom: to quarrel with his uncle or to play at the club. Although the marquis did not find these activities tedious—real tedium is a malaise reserved to refined people and sybaritic intellects—he felt an annoyance and suppressed anger born from the secret conviction of his inferiority. Don Manuel surpassed his nephew in the cultural varnish acquired through many years of urban life and the resulting contact with people, as well as in that legitimate pride in his name and birth that, according to his favorite expression, saved him from vulgarity. Aside from his fondness for after-dinner anecdotes that threatened, if not the modesty, the stomachs of his guests, Don Manuel was a man of courtesy and good manners. He was the sort of person to lead at a funeral, attend a meeting of the Economic Society of Friends of the Province, carry the banner at a procession, or be called into the governor's office for consultation. If he longed to retire to the country, it was not only to satisfy a wild desire to walk about without a tie and pay none of the ordinary tributes to society, but also to cultivate more modern and delicate hobbies: to grow a garden and fruit trees and to build, an activity that fascinated him and that was cheaper in the country than in the city.

His wife's gentle disposition, moreover, and the constant company of his daughters, had softened whatever uncouth tendencies Don Manuel may have inherited from the de la Lages; five cherished females will tame the most rustic man. That is why the father-in-law, although chronologically a generation behind the son-in-law, was morally several years ahead of him.

Don Manuel's attempts to polish his nephew were not only useless but counterproductive, for they rekindled his arrogance and fierce independence. Señor de la Lage hoped that his nephew would finally settle down in Santiago and close the house of Ulloa, visiting it only in the summer to enjoy his leisure and supervise his estate. While he thus advised his son-in-law, he dropped hints and allusions to indicate that he was not oblivious at all to what went on in the old burrow of Ulloa. This kind of pressure and imposition, as excusable as it was, irritated Don Pedro, who, in his own words, would not put up with intrusions nor let anyone manipulate him.

"For this reason," he declared one day in front of his wife, "we're going to leave soon. Since I grew up nobody has told me where to go. If sometimes I hold my tongue, it's because I'm not in my own house."

To be at someone else's home irked him. Everything he saw he found objectionable and unpleasant. Señor de la Lage's moderate and decorous pomp; his silver platters and candlesticks; his fine old furniture; his respectable acquaintances, selected from the cream of the crop in town; his harmless evening gatherings with canons and formal people who came to play cards; his obliging servants, sometimes negligent but never insolent or nosy—all this struck

Don Pedro as a living parody of his chaotic and crude existence at the house of Ulloa, of the meals without tablecloths, the windows without glass panes, and the familiarity with wenches and peasants. Instead of a healthy desire to emulate, it aroused in him nothing but mean envy and its companion, sour contempt. Only Carmen's mad love affair brought him some consolation; rubbing his hands, he celebrated the funny remarks that circulated at the club about the audacity of the student and the impudence of the girl. How furious his father-in-law would be! Damask chairs and rugs had no power to stop scandal.

The disputes between Don Pedro and his uncle grew more bitter and were eventually poisoned by political controversy, which is particularly heated among those who base their arguments on impressions rather than well-founded ideas. It must be admitted that the marquis belonged to this category. Don Manuel was not exactly an expert, but he had long been platonically affiliated with the moderate party, he read the newspapers regularly, and he knew the political routine. He had taken so seriously the fall of González Bravo and the departure of Queen Isabella that he lost his temper and nearly choked with anger every time his nephew, just to taunt him, made apologies for the revolutionaries and repeated the atrocities that the press and the people related about the fallen monarchy, pretending to believe them as an article of faith. His uncle refuted him energetically, raising his gigantic hands to heaven. "You people out there in the country," he said, "swallow everything, even the greatest nonsense. You don't have educated opinions, son, you simply don't. That's your problem! You look at things from a self-created point of view." Don Manuel must have learned this queer notion from some editorial. "You must base your judgments on experience and good sense."

"Do you think that out there we're all stupid? Well, maybe we even have more brains than you, and we see what you can't see." He alluded to his cousin Carmen, fastened on the balcony at this very moment. "Believe me, Uncle: there are fools sucking their thumbs everywhere. Yes, sir, there are!"

The debate then took a personal and aggressive turn. This usually happened at table, after a meal. The coffee cups clinked threateningly against the saucers. Don Manuel, shaking with rage, spilled the anisette as he lifted it to his lips. Uncle and nephew raised their voices, and after an intemperate remark or a harsh phrase came a moment of silence loaded with hostility, in which the girls looked at each other. Nucha would lower her head and roll little bread crumbs or fold all the napkins slowly and slide them into their rings. Don Pedro would stand up suddenly, push his chair aside, and, making the floor shake under his firm steps, go out to the club, where the card games went on day and night.

He did not feel at home there either. A certain intellectual atmosphere, which is characteristic of university towns, oppressed him. In Santiago nobody wants to pass for an ignoramus, and the marquis realized that its dwellers would amuse themselves at his expense if they knew that he was not strong in orthography and in other "ies" that were often mentioned there. His self-esteem as undisputed monarch of the house of Ulloa rebelled when he saw himself scorned by a few sickly professors or, worse yet, by students with old boots and brains heated from reading some modern author in the university library or in the reading room of the club. This kind of life was much too active for his mind, much too constricting and sedentary for his body; his blood itched for exercise and open space; his skin desperately longed for air, sunshine, and rain, for the caress of thorns and brambles. Oh, a full immersion in the wilderness!

He could not stand the social leveling that urban life imposes. He could not get used to being counted as a number in the city, after having been all his life the one and only lord of his feudal residence. Who was he in Santiago? Simply Don Pedro Moscoso; no, he was less than that: Señor de la Lage's son-in-law, Nucha Pardo's husband. Here his title had vanished like salt in the water thanks to one member of the slanderous triumvirate: a malicious old man who because of his advanced age and prodigious memory was in charge of investigating past events, just as the youngest member, whom we have already met, specialized in current ones. They were, so to speak, the chronicler and the analyst of the metropolis.

The chronicler, therefore, did his job. He traced the true and complete genealogy of the Cabreira and Moscoso families and proved step by step that the title of Ulloa could only belong to Duke So-and-So, grandee of Spain, et cetera; the *Peerage* corroborated these facts. Incidentally, while this business was being conducted, Don Pedro and Señor de la Lage became the target of many jokes. The latter was accused of having had a marchioness's crown embroidered on a set of sheets for his daughter's trousseau. The analyst confirmed this innocent weakness, specifying when and how the above-mentioned sheets had been embroidered, and how much the trinkets on the little crown had cost.

The impatient Don Pedro decided to depart before the worst of the winter was over, at the end of a very unreliable and chilly March. The coach left for Cebre before dawn. It was bitter cold. Nucha, huddled up in a corner of the uncomfortable vehicle, often raised a handkerchief to her eyes. Her husband addressed her none too gently: "One would think that you're not happy to come with me."

"What a thing to say!" the girl answered, uncovering her face and smiling. "It's natural that I feel sad to leave poor papa and the girls."

"I doubt if they will beg you to come back," the marquis mumbled.

Nucha fell silent. The coach jolted on the bumpy street that led out of town, and the driver shouted hoarsely at the horses. They came out on the road and the cumbersome vehicle now rolled on a smoother surface. Nucha resumed the dialogue and asked her husband about details concerning the house of Ulloa, a subject that always interested him. He depicted the beauty and healthiness of the country hyperbolically, extolling the antiquity of the mansion and the independent and comfortable life they would lead in it.

"You mustn't believe," he told his wife, raising his voice above the sound of the horsebells and the clattering of the windowpanes, "you mustn't believe that there are no refined people there. Some very good families live near the house: the young Molende ladies, who are very nice; Ramón Limioso, quite a gentleman. We'll also enjoy the company of the abbot of Naya, not to mention our own, the abbot of Ulloa, whom I brought myself. I own that one as much as I own my dogs, and if I don't order him to bark and fetch and carry, it's just because I don't feel like it. You'll see! Out there one is somebody, and is treated like somebody."

As they approached Cebre and entered Don Pedro's domain, his loquacity redoubled. He pointed at the chestnuts and the mounds of furze, shouting joyfully: "We're home, we're home! Every single hare that roams these woods is mine!"

When they arrived at Cebre his spirits rose even higher. Outside the inn stood Primitivo and Julián, the former with his enigmatic face of metal, the latter with the most affectionate smile. Nucha greeted him no less cordially. They unloaded the luggage and Primitivo brought Don Pedro his bright and lively chestnut mare. He was about to mount when he noticed that the animal prepared for Nucha was a malicious and stubborn tall mule, with one of those round saddles with a little hump in the middle that seem designed to eject rather than carry the rider.

"How come you didn't bring the little donkey for your mistress?" asked Don Pedro before he mounted, one foot on the stirrup and his hand clasping the mare's mane, looking askance at the steward.

Primitivo mumbled something about an injured leg, a "cold tumor . . ."

"And aren't there other donkeys around? Don't give me excuses! You had time to find ten of them!"

He turned to his wife and, as if to appease his conscience, asked her: "Are you afraid, my girl? You probably aren't used to riding. Have you ever tried this sort of saddle before? Can you sit up straight on it?"

Nucha stood hesitantly and picked up her dress with her right hand while she held her travel bag in the left. At last, she murmured: "I can stay on it all right. Last year at the baths I rode on all sorts of unusual saddles. Only now . . ."

She suddenly let go her dress, ran to her husband, and threw an arm around his neck, hiding her face on his chest as she had done the first time, when she was forced to hug him. And there, in a sort of murmur or sweet whisper, she finished her broken sentence. The marquis's face expressed surprise and at the same time immense joy, jubilant pride, exultant victory. He pressed his wife to him with a tender and protective gesture and burst out at the top of his lungs: "If there is a single tame donkey within ten miles and God himself keeps it in heaven and doesn't want me to have it, I must bring it to you, upon the word of Pedro Moscoso. Wait, girl, just wait a minute . . . or rather, go into the inn and sit down. Let's see, a bench, a chair for the lady . . . You just wait, Nuchiña. I'll be back in a trice. Primitivo, come with me. Keep warm, Nucha."

If not in a trice, in half an hour he returned, breathless, leading by the bridle a plump, quiet, reliable donkey in full riding gear: the property of the judge of Cebre's wife herself. Don Pedro took his wife in his arms, lifted her onto the saddle, and arranged her clothes solicitously.

Chapter 14

As soon as master and chaplain were able to talk in private, Don Pedro, without looking Julián in the face, asked: "What about *her*? Is she still around? I didn't see her when we arrived."

And, as Julián frowned, he added: "So she *is* around. Before we came I'd have bet a hundred pesos that you hadn't found a way to get rid of her."

"Frankly, sir," Julián stammered, quite upset, "I don't know what to say. This thing has become more and more complicated. Primitivo swore up and down that the girl was going to marry the bagpiper of Naya."

"I know him," Don Pedro grumbled between his teeth, while his face darkened.

"Naturally, I believed it. Besides, I saw for myself that the bagpiper and Sabel are indeed . . . involved."

"Did you find out all that?" the marquis inquired ironically.

"Sir, I . . . although I'm not very good at such things, I tried to gather information so that they couldn't fool me. I asked around and everybody agrees that they are planning to marry; even Don Eugenio, the abbot of Naya, told me that the lad had asked for his papers. And in truth, if the wedding hasn't taken place yet, it's because there is some problem or mistake with the blessed papers."

Don Pedro stood silent until, at last, he burst forth: "You're a happy soul. They could never have fooled me with such stories."

"To tell you the truth, sir, if they intended to deceive me, they're nothing but big rascals. And as for Sabel, if she's not crazy for the player, she pretends it really well. Two weeks ago she went to Don Eugenio and fell on her knees, crying and begging him in God's name to hurry up the marriage, because that day would be the happiest in her life. Don Eugenio told me, and Don Eugenio wouldn't make it up."

"The slut, the shameless slut!" Don Pedro blurted out furiously as he paced the room. He soon calmed down, however, and added: "I'm not in the least surprised, and I'm not saying that Don Eugenio is lying; but you . . . you're a simpleton and a poor devil, for the problem is not Sabel, do you understand? but her father, her father! And her father has duped you like a child. That woman, I'm sure, is dying to split off; but Primitivo is capable of killing her rather than letting her go."

"In truth, I was beginning to suspect that. I can assure you that I was sniffing something . . ."

The master shrugged contemptuously and said: "High time! Leave this business to me. And how's everything else?"

"They've been as meek as lambs. They haven't opposed me in anything."

"And behind your back they've done whatever they pleased. Really, Don Julián, sometimes I have a good mind to feed you some pap as if you were a pigeon."

Julián replied, with a contrite air: "You're absolutely right, sir. We won't get anywhere if Primitivo opposes us. You were right when you warned me about that last year. And lately, I think he's even more respected, not to say feared. Since this revolution broke out and we've been hearing alarming news every day, I've thought that Primitivo is mixed up in these plots and recruits partisans around the province. Don Eugenio has no doubt about it, and he also says that for a long time he's got a lot of people under his thumb by lending them money at interest."

Don Pedro was silent. At last, he raised his head and asked:

"Do you remember that in Cebre I had to look for a donkey for my wife?"

"How could I forget!"

"Well, the judge's wife—you may laugh—the judge's wife agreed to lend it to me because Primitivo was with me. Otherwise . . ."

Julián had not given any thought to this incident that had so vexed the marquis. When their conference was over, Don Pedro slapped the chaplain's shoulder. "And why haven't you congratulated me yet, Señor Inconsiderate?"

Julián did not understand. The master, beaming with joy, explained himself. Yes, sir, by October, the season of chestnuts, the world could expect a real and legitimate Moscoso heir, as beautiful as the sun, to boot.

"And why shouldn't it be a little Señorita Moscoso?" Julián asked, after many warm congratulations.

"Impossible!" shouted the marquis, putting his soul in his words. And as the chaplain broke into laughter, he added: "You mustn't say that even in jest, Don Julián. One doesn't joke about such things. It has to be a boy, or else I'll wring its neck, whatever it is. I already instructed Nucha to make sure that she gives me a male. I could break one of her ribs if she dares disobey me. God won't play this trick on me. In my family there has always been male succession: Moscosos breed Moscosos, this is proverbial. Didn't you notice it when you were eating dust in the archives? But you're capable of not having even noticed my wife's condition."

And so he was. Not only had Julián not noticed it, but such a natural possibility had never crossed his mind. His veneration for Nucha, greater every day, led him to think that she was invulnerable to the physiological accidents that befall the rest of the females of this world. Nucha's appearance justified this bit of nonsense. The absolute candor of her vague eyes, which seemed lost in contemplation of her inner world, had not diminished since her marriage; her cheeks had become a little fuller, but still blushed bashfully at the slightest provocation. If there was any visible variation, any sign that proclaimed the transition from virgin to wife, it was perhaps that her modesty had grown stronger and more conscious: instinct raised to the level of virtue. Julián never ceased to wonder at Nucha's seriousness when a bold joke or an offensive word wounded her ears; at her natural dignity, which like a second skin or an invisible shield protected her even from sinful thoughts; at the kindness with which she repaid even the slightest consideration, expressing her gratitude in quiet but sincere words; at the serenity of her whole being, like that of a peaceful sunset. To Julián, Nucha appeared as the ideal biblical wife, the poetic model of the strong woman who, still with the halo of innocence around her brow, promises future strength and majesty. With time, this grace must become severity, and the dark braids turn silver, and even then this pure brow will be clean of sin and free of guilt. Oh, this gentle spring was the harbinger of a rich maturity! When Julián thought about it, he congratulated himself again on the role he had played in his master's wise choice.

With unselfish satisfaction, he told himself that he had contributed to the creation of a situation that was pleasing to God and necessary for the orderly progress of society: Christian marriage, the blessed bond whereby with admirable inspiration the church serves both spiritual and material needs, sanctifying the latter by means of the former. By its nature, Julián reflected, this holy institution shuns impudent extremes and paroxysms, romantic and foolish transports, ardent and raucous turtle-dove courtships. For this reason, on those occasions when the husband permitted himself certain liberties more despotic than tender, the priest surmised that the wife must suffer immensely, maintaining her composure while her candid modesty was injured. He inferred that her lowered eyelids, intense blushing, and silence were a mute protest against familiarities that were inappropriate within a chaste conjugal relationship. If such things happened at table, for example, Julián averted his eyes and pretended to be distracted, or raised his glass to his mouth, or turned his attention to the dogs that were sniffing around. Then he would feel such subtle scruples that they were almost ungraspable. As perfect a wife as Nucha made, her virtues and condition summoned her to a yet higher state, closer to that of the angels, in which a woman preserves her virginal purity as her greatest treasure. Through his mother Julián knew that Nucha had shown an inclination to monastic life, and he began to deplore obsessively that she had not entered a convent. If Nucha was a good woman for a man, she would be even better as the bride of Christ; and that chaste marriage would have left the flower of her corporal innocence intact, and sheltered her forever from the tribulations and struggles that afflict the world.

The thought of these struggles reminded him of Sabel. Who could doubt that at this point her presence in the house was already a threat to the legitimate wife? Julián did not anticipate imminent risks, but foresaw problems to come. This appalling illegal family, clinging to the old house like the ivy on the crumbling walls! Sometimes the priest had an impulse to take a broom and sweep away all this accursed breed. But just when he was most determined to do it, he stumbled on the selfish indifference of the master and the passive, invincible resistance of the steward. Something happened that made matters even worse: the cook brought from Santiago began to sulk and complain that she did not understand this stove, that the logs did not burn well. Sabel, very solicitous, helped her, and a few days later the cook, tired of country life, took her leave rather abruptly. Sabel replaced her with no further ceremony than grabbing the handle of the pan when the other woman relinquished it. Julián had no chance to protest against this change of ministry and the return to the old regime. In truth, the spurious family conducted itself with the greatest humility: Primitivo was never to be found unless he was called; Sabel vanished as soon as she left the meals on the fire under the care of the kitchen maids; the boy seemed to have evaporated.

The priest, nevertheless, lived in constant fear. What if Nucha found out? And, no doubt, she would find out at any moment! Unfortunately, the new wife had a tendency to walk around the house, inquire about everything, and inspect the remotest places, like attics, wine cellars and wine presses, dovecotes, granaries, dog-houses, pigsties, chicken coops, stables, and barns. Julián was terri-fied that by some fatal accident on one of these visits Nucha might have a sudden and appalling revelation. At the same time, how could he object to the diligent wanderings of a housewife around her dominion? The young lady seemed to bring happiness, cleanli-ness, and order into every corner of the mansion; she was greeted by the dust swirling around the brooms and the sunbeams shining into nooks and crannies that thick cobwebs had kept in darkness for years.

Julián accompanied Nucha in her explorations in order to pre-vent, if possible, any unfortunate event. Indeed, his intervention was useful one day when Nucha found a certain featherless chick in the chicken coop. This incident deserves some careful attention.

Nucha had noticed that the hens never laid any eggs, or if they did, they were nowhere to be seen. Don Pedro maintained that the accursed hens consumed several bushels of rye and millet every year and still did not produce anything. They cackled, however, at the top of their lungs, a sure sign that they were about to lay the eggs. The triumphal hymn of the productive hens played against the subdued clucking of the brooders; the nests felt gently warm, and the hay had been pressed down and had taken the shape of the egg. But that was all: there was not enough even for a wretched omelet. Nucha kept her eyes open. One day, as she heard the cackle of announcement, she ran fast to the chicken coop and glimpsed a small child huddled at the background, hiding like a mouse. Only his bare feet could be seen through the straw of the nests. Nucha pulled at them and the rest of the body came out; finally his hands appeared, holding the dish that the lady of the house craved, the eggs that the boy had just smuggled and broken: so the omelet was half made or, at least, beaten.

"You little rascal!" Nucha exclaimed as she dragged him out into the light of the yard. "I'm going to give you the works, you rogue! Now we know who's the fox that eats the eggs! Today I'm going to beat your behind black and blue!"

The miniature thief battled and kicked. Nucha felt sorry for him and assumed that he was crying disconsolately. For a moment she could hardly see his face, but when she pulled his hands away from it she realized that the little brat was actually laughing. She also caught a glimpse of the ragged urchin's extraordinary beauty. Julián, who had been an uneasy witness to the scene, stepped forward and tried to take the child away from Nucha's arms.

"Let me have him, Don Julián!" she begged. "How handsome he is! Look at his hair and his eyes! Whose child is this?"

The prudish priest had never been so tempted to lie, but he did not know what to say. "I think . . ." he stammered and choked, "I think he's Sabel's, the girl who's doing the cooking these days."

"The maid? Is that girl married?"

Julián's confusion grew. This time, he felt a lump in his throat suffocating him. "No, madam, not exactly . . . You know . . . unfortunately, country women around here . . . aren't always chaste . . . Human weakness . . ."

Nucha sat on a stone bench outside the chicken coop without letting go of the child, while she tried to get a better view of his face. He struggled to cover it with his arms and hands, and squirmed like a trapped rabbit. Only his hair was visible—his rebellious chestnut curls, tangled with bits of straw and specks of dry mud—and his sunburned neck.

"Julián, do you have some pennies there?"

"Yes, madam."

"Here, my boy. Let's see if you stop being afraid of me."

The incantation had the desired effect. The boy stretched out his hand and quickly buried the coins in his bosom. Then Nucha saw the plump face with its dimples, graceful and classic at the same time, like that of the bronze cupids that hold burners and lamps. A smile between mischievous and angelic crowned this masterpiece of nature. Nucha smacked both of his cheeks loudly. "How lovely! God bless him! What's your name, son?"

"Perucho," the little boy answered unashamedly.

"My husband's name!" the young lady replied with vivacity. "I'll bet he's his godson, don't you think?"

"It's his godson, his godson," Julián hastened to confirm, wishing he could put a cork in this smiling mouth of fleshy cupid lips; as he could not do it, he tried to steer the conversation away from such dangerous ground. "What were you going to do with the eggs? If you tell me, I'll give you two more pennies."

"I sell them," Perucho declared concisely.

"So you sell them, eh? We have a businessman here. And whom do you sell them to?"

"To the women from around here who go to town."

"And, let's see, how much do they pay you?"

"Two pennies a dozen."

"I'll tell you what," Nucha said affectionately. "From now on, you'll sell them to me at this very same price. You're so pretty that I don't want to get upset and scold you, no, sir! We're going to be best friends, you and I. My first gift to you will be a pair of trousers. You're not exactly tidy."

In fact, the child's fresh and luxuriant flesh showed through the torn, coarse drawers; its whiteness was not totally concealed by the dirt and mud that covered it, for lack of a more decorous garment.

"The little angel!" Nucha muttered. "I can't believe that they neglect their children like this! It's a miracle they don't die of cold. Julián, we've got to dress this baby Jesus."

"Some baby Jesus!" Julián rumbled. "The devil himself, God forgive me! Don't pity him, señorita. He's a little rascal, naughtier than a monkey. You can't imagine the pains I took to teach him to read and write, to make him wash this little nose and these paws! But it's useless! And he's as sound as a bell, for all his rough life. This year he's fallen into the pond twice already, and the last time he nearly drowned."

"Come on now, Julián. What do you expect him to do at his age? He can't behave like a grown-up. Come with me, dear; I'm going to find you something to keep these little legs warm. Don't you have any shoes? We must order a pair of strong wooden shoes. And I shall give his mother a piece of my mind and tell her to scrub him every day. You'll teach him his daily lessons all over again, or we'll send him to school. That will be the best!"

No one could have dissuaded Nucha from her generous resolution. Julián was terribly afraid that some catastrophe might ensue from such closeness. His good nature, however, rekindled his interest in this pious work that he had already undertaken once without success. In it he saw the greatest proof of Nucha's moral beauty; he saw the hand of God in Nucha's wish to look after this wild limb from so vile a tree. Nucha, meanwhile, amused herself with her protégé. She enjoyed his very shamelessness, his rascally instincts, his greediness to collect eggs, fruit, and coins, his fondness for wine and tasty morsels. She intended to straighten up this tender young tree, to polish his skin and his spirit at the same time. "Another Herculean task," the priest said.

Chapter 15

At that time Señor and Señora Moscoso began to pay visits to the neighboring aristocracy. Nucha rode the donkey and her husband the chestnut mare, and Julián accompanied them on the mule. Some of the marquis's favorite dogs always joined the march. Two servants in their Sunday clothes—embroidered waistbands and brand new felt hats—served as footmen, swinging their green staffs as they walked and tending to the beasts when the riders dismounted.

The first visit was to the judge's wife in Cebre. The door was opened by a bare-legged maid. As soon as she saw Nucha get off her donkey and arrange the flounces of her dress with the handle of her parasol, she ran like mad into the house, screaming as if it were on fire or thieves were breaking in: "My lady! Oh, my lady! There's a lady and a gentleman!"

Nobody answered her distressed cries. After a few minutes, the judge himself appeared in the hall, with profuse apologies for the girl's clumsiness: they could not possibly imagine how hard it was to train her; one had to repeat the same thing to her a thousand times, but it was to no avail, she still hadn't learned to announce visitors properly . . . As he murmured these words, he hooked his elbow and offered his arm to Nucha to go upstairs. The stairway was too narrow for two people to climb it side by side; so Señora Moscoso had the greatest difficulty in clinging with her fingertips to the arm of the good gentleman, who was two steps ahead of her with his body all twisted.

As they reached the door of the drawing room, the judge began to fumble anxiously in his pockets while he muttered unintelligible and confused syllables to himself. Suddenly he let go a sort of frightful roar: "Pepa . . . Pepaaaaa!"

They heard the pattering of bare feet, and the judge faced the maid: "Where's the key? Where in the name of Judas have you put the key?"

Pepa left hurriedly again. The judge, shifting from the most furious hoarseness to the most mellifluous sweetness, pushed the door open and said to Nucha: "This way, my dear lady, this way, if you'd be so kind."

The room was in complete darkness. Nucha stumbled upon a table, while the judge repeated: "Will you be so kind as to sit down, my good lady? Excuse me."

The light that bathed the room once the shutters were opened allowed Nucha to see the sofa and two matching chairs covered in blue rep, the mahogany table, and, in front of the sofa, a cinnamon-colored rug in the shape of a ferocious Bengal tiger. The judge strained himself to make his visitors comfortable, inquiring persistently whether the marquis preferred to sit facing the light or with his back against the window. At the same time, he cast anxious glances about, for he began to worry about his wife's delay. He tried to maintain a conversation, but his smile was more like a contracted grin, and he often looked sternly at the door.

At last they heard the rustle of starched petticoats in the corridor. The judge's wife came in, flushed and hurriedly groomed for the occasion, as the details of her dress made plain. She had crammed her respectable dimensions into a girdle, but had not managed to button her silk bodice all the way up; her chignon of false hair, placed on her head in a rush, was tilted toward her left ear; one of her earrings was unfastened; and as she had had no time to put on her shoes, she struggled to hide her cloth slippers under the pompous flounces of her silk dress.

Although Nucha was not inclined to mock people, she could not help being amused by the attire of this lady, who passed as the paragon of high fashion in Cebre. She smiled to Julián up her sleeve, and winked imperceptibly at the necklaces, trinkets, and brooches displayed on the lady's throat. The judge's wife, on her part, devoured the bride from Santiago with her eyes to size up her simple outfit. The visit was brief, for the marquis wished to pay his respects to the archpriest that same day, and the parish of Loiro was at least a league away from the village of Cebre. The departure was as ceremonious as the arrival. Nucha was escorted downstairs and the host and hostess renewed their offers of hospitality and services.

To go to Loiro it was necessary to ride far into the mountains and follow a trail bordered by cliffs and precipices; it became viable as it approached the archpriest's dominions, extensive and prosperous in the past, but now considerably maimed by the confiscation of church property. The parsonage retained signs of its former splendor and had a monastic air. As they walked into the hall, the marquis of Ulloa and his wife had the impression that they were in a chilly underground crypt with a vaulted ceiling, where the human voice echoed in a strange and solemn way. Two human beings descended the broad steps, bordered by a monumental balustrade, slowly and totteringly, like a couple of bears on their hind legs. They were a monstrous couple, whose deformities were all the more visible when they appeared together: the archpriest and his sister. Both of them were panting; their painful breathing sounded as if it came from a wounded victim. Their faces—purple with blood under the skin—were surrounded by a halo of flesh, formed by their triple chins and the rolls of fat on the back of their necks. As they turned around it could be seen that, on the same spot where the archpriest's tonsure shone, his sister exhibited a little gray chignon, identical to those worn by bullfighters. Nucha, who was still amused at the thought of the judge's reception and his wife's dress, smiled to herself again, especially as she followed the *quid pro quos* of the conversation caused by the deafness of the respectable brother and sister. The hosts, honoring the country tradition of hospitality, ushered the reluctant visitors into the dining room. The sight of the dining table would have made even a stone laugh: a crescent had been cut at each end of it, no doubt to accommodate those two gigantic bellies comfortably.

The return to the house of Ulloa was enlivened with comments and jokes about the visits. Even Julián cast aside his usual formality and reserve to make fun of the cut-away table and the showcase of cheap jewelry displayed on the neck and bosom of the judge's wife. They looked forward to similar visits to the young Molende sisters and to Señor Limioso and his relatives, which certainly would be no less amusing, on the following day.

They left the house of Ulloa early, for they needed the whole long summer afternoon to complete their program. It might still not have been possible if they had found the Molende ladies at home. A country girl who walked by with a bunch of hay explained with difficulty that the misses "was gone" to the fair of Vilamorta, and only heaven knew when they would come back. Nucha was sorry to hear it, for she liked the young ladies, who had already visited her at the house of Ulloa; theirs were the only youthful faces, the only voices reminiscent of the lively chatter of her sisters, whom she could not forget. They charged the girl to deliver their compliments, and headed up the mountain toward the house of Limioso.

The rough road zigzagged around the mountain. The thick leaves of the vineyards on both sides met above it, as if to erase it. At the top, shining in the sunset, stood a building with a tower on the left and a roofless, decrepit dovecote on the right. It was the mansion of the Limiosos, once a rock castle, a hawk's nest hung on the dark and steep slope of the lonely hill, behind which the majestic heights of the inaccessible Pico Leiro rose against the horizon. In the whole neighboring territory, perhaps in the whole province, there was no older or prouder noble mansion, nor any other that the peasants called "palace" with greater respect.

Seen from a short distance, the house of Limioso seemed deserted, which intensified the melancholy impression made by the dilapidated dovecote. There were signs of neglect and decline everywhere: the courtyard was overgrown with nettles; not only the glass panes, but the frames themselves, were missing from the windows; a few broken shutters, pulled out from their hinges, swung like shreds from a torn dress. Parasitic plants crept up to the rusty iron grates of the first floor; threads of wretched, dry ivy ran along the crevices between the crumbling stones. The gate was wide open, as if the house dwellers had no fear of thieves; but to the muffled thud of horsehooves on the grassy courtyard some asthmatic barks responded. A mastiff and two retrievers charged against the visitors, wasting through their gullets the little energy they had, for these beasts were nothing but bristly coats on skeletons, whose bones threatened to poke out at any moment. The mastiff was literally unable to make the effort to bark; his legs shook and his tongue hung far out between his decaying, yellowish teeth. The retrievers were calmed by a word from the marquis of Ulloa, with whom they had hunted many times. The mastiff, on the other hand, seemed determined to die in fulfillment of his duty, and quieted down only when his master, the lord of Limioso, came out.

Who in these mountains does not know the direct descendant of Galician knights and paladins, the tireless hunter, the staunch traditionalist? At this time, *Ramonciño* Limioso was just over twenty-six years old; but his moustache, eyebrows, hair, and all his features had already a melancholy gravity and dignity that at first sight was somewhat bemusing. The sad arch of his eyebrows gave him some

similarity to the portraits of Quevedo; his thin neck called desperately for the classic ruffled collar; and instead of the crop he
was holding, it was easier to picture an old-fashioned sword in
his hand. Whenever this lanky body, this worn-out jacket, these
trousers with kneepads and a couple of patches appeared, it was
beyond doubt that Ramón Limioso, for all his poverty, was "a true
gentleman from old stock"—as the villagers said—and not one of
those who have kicked and punched their way up.

His gentlemanliness was evident in the way he helped Nucha off
the donkey, in his natural gallantry when he offered her not his arm
but, according to the ancient custom, two fingers of his left hand,
on which the lady of Ulloa could rest her right. With a decorum
worthy of a minuet step, the couple entered the house of Limioso
and climbed up the outside stairway that led to the cloister, whose
venerable, worm-eaten steps threatened imminent collapse. The
cloister's ceiling was like a sample of lace: patches of velvety blue
sky peeped through the tiles and beams. Sheltered behind the coat
of arms of the Limiosos—three fish swimming in a lake, a lion
supporting a cross—roughly carved on the capital of each pillar,
the young swallows chirped sweetly in their nests. Things became
even worse when they reached the antechamber. For many years,
moths and age had played havoc with the boards of the floor.
The Limiosos, who doubtless could not afford to lay new floors,
had limited themselves to throwing a few loose planks across the
exposed beams. The host walked through this dangerous room
always holding out his two fingers to Nucha, who did not dare to
ask for firmer support. Each board on which she stepped rose and
quivered, revealing underneath the dark depths of the wine cellar,
with its barrels wrapped in cobwebs. They stepped over the abyss
unflinchingly and entered the drawing room, which at least had a
solid floor, although broken in many places and almost reduced to
dust by the insects.

Nucha stood in amazement. In a corner of the room she caught a glimpse of a superb piece of furniture inlaid with tortoiseshell and ivory, almost hidden by a large heap of corn. On the walls hung some smoky, grime-covered oil paintings, in which now and then stood out the writhing leg of a martyr, or the haunch of a horse, or the round head of a cherub. Opposite the pile of corn there was a platform covered with Córdoba leather, which still retained its rich colors and intense gold decorations; in front of the platform, a set of magnificent carved chairs, also covered with leather, formed a semicircle; and between the corn and the platform, seated on unpolished oak stumps like those used by the poorest peasants, two wiry, pale, upright old women in Carmelite habits were . . . spinning!

Señora Moscoso had never expected to see anyone spin, except for peasant women and characters in novels; so she was strangely impressed by these two Byzantine statues—for that is what they resembled, with their perfect immobility and the stiff folds of their garb—handling the spindle and the distaff, and putting them down at the very moment of her entrance. The heir of Limioso had visited Nucha once in the name of these two statues, who were his aunts on his father's side. His father, who was paralyzed and bedridden, also lived in the house, but no one had ever laid eyes on him. His existence was like a myth, a mountain legend. The two old ladies rose and stretched out their arms to Nucha so simultaneously that she did not know to which she should go first. She felt an icy kiss, the lipless kiss of an inert skin, on both cheeks at the same time. She also felt that her hands were held by other fleshless, dry, mummified hands, and understood that they were leading her to the platform and offering her one of the tall chairs. No sooner had she sat on it than she realized with terror that the seat was giving in, sinking under her, that the chair was coming apart noiselessly and without resistance. With the instinct of the pregnant woman she got to her feet and left the last symbol of the Limiosos' splendor to crumble down definitively.

They left the ruinous estate at nightfall. Without revealing their common thoughts, maybe because they were not even conscious of them, they remained silent on the ride home, oppressed by the ineffable sorrow of things gone.

Chapter 16

The heir of the Moscosos must have been ready to come into this world, for Nucha incessantly sewed miniature garments, which looked like doll's clothes. Despite her industriousness, her looks did not deteriorate; on the contrary, it was as if every little step that the baby took toward the light of day had a beneficial effect on the mother.

One could not say that she had grown fat, but her form was filling out; what used to be flat and angular was now slightly rounded. Her cheeks had turned rosy, although her forehead and temples were veiled by a light cloud. Her black hair seemed richer and shinier, her eyes less vague and more moist, her mouth fresher and redder. Her voice had acquired deeper undertones. The natural enlargement of her frame was not excessive or unbecoming; it simply lent her body that sweet gravity we see in Mary's figure in the paintings of the Visitation. The posture of her hands, spread on her belly as if to protect it, completed the analogy with the iconography of such a tender scene.

Don Pedro, it must be admitted, behaved very well to his wife through this period of expectation. Putting aside his usual excursions to the mountains and cliffs, he took her out punctually every evening for healthy and gradually longer walks. Nucha leaned on his arm while they wandered through the valley in which the house of Ulloa lies hidden. When she felt tired, they sat on a stone fence or on a slope. Don Pedro tried to satisfy her most insignificant whims. On occasion, he even displayed some gallantry, bringing her wild flowers that had caught her eye, or handfuls of strawberries and blackberries. As gunshots always upset Nucha's nerves, he never took his gun along, and expressly forbade Primitivo to hunt in the valley. It seemed that he had slowly begun to shed his rugged bark, and that his wild and selfish heart was changing and bringing forth the gentle feelings of husband and father, like the little flowers that bloom in the cracks of a wall. If this was not the Christian marriage that the good priest dreamed of, it certainly looked like it.

Julián blessed the Lord every day. His devotion had been, if not reborn, for it had never died, rekindled. As Nucha's critical hour approached, the chaplain remained longer on his knees after mass to thank God; he prolonged the litanies and the rosary; he put all his heart and soul into his daily prayers, as well as into two devout novenas, one to the Virgin of August and one to the Virgin of September. He considered the cult of Mary especially suited to the occasion, given his increasingly firm conviction that Nucha was the living image of Our Lady, as far as any woman conceived in sin can be.

One October evening at dusk, Julián was sitting on his window bench, engrossed in the reading of Father Nieremberg, when he heard hurried steps on the stairs and recognized Don Pedro's boots. The master's face beamed with joy.

"Any news?" Julián asked as he dropped the book.

"Do I have news! We were taking a walk and we had to rush back."

"Have you sent to Cebre for the doctor?"

"Primitivo is on his way."

Julián made a face of displeasure.

"You don't have to be afraid. I sent two more men after him. I wanted to go myself, but Nucha doesn't want me to leave her now."

"The best thing is for me to go too, just in case," Julián said. "Even on foot and in the dark . . ."

Don Pedro burst into one of his loud and scornful peals of laughter. "You!" he yelled, always laughing. "What an idea, Don Julián!"

The priest lowered his eyes and frowned. He felt somewhat ashamed of his cassock, which rendered him useless for the smallest kind of service in such a critical situation. Apart from being a priest he was a man, and as such he must not penetrate the chamber where the mystery was taking place. Only two males had that right: the husband and the one Primitivo had been sent for, the representative of human science. Julián shrank at the thought that Nucha's modesty was about to be profaned and her pure body handled as a corpse on the anatomy table, as a piece of lifeless matter that no longer houses a soul. He realized that he was frightened and in pain.

"Call me if you need me, sir," he murmured in a faint voice.

"A thousand thanks, my friend. I just came to break the news to you."

Don Pedro rushed down the steps whistling a folk song. The priest stood motionless for a moment. Then he ran his hand across his forehead, moistened by light perspiration, and looked at the wall. Among several pictures in gilt frames, he chose two: one of Saint Ramón Nonato and another of Our Lady of the Sorrows with her dead son in her arms. He would have preferred an image of Our Lady of Milk and Good Birth, but he did not have one, and had not given much thought to the subject until then. He removed the objects lying on the dresser and propped up the pictures on it. Then he opened the drawer where he kept a few wax candles for the chapel, took out a couple, inserted them into brass candlesticks, and set up a little altar. As soon as the frames projected their yellow light on the glass that covered the pictures, Julián felt ineffable consolation. Filled with hope, the priest reproached himself for having considered his presence useless in these circumstances.

Useless! In fact, he had the most important responsibility of all, namely, to pray for protection from heaven. He knelt down and began to say his prayers with great faith.

Time passed by without interruptions. No news came from below. About ten o'clock Julián felt that his knees had become restless, his limbs sore, and his head giddy. He managed to stand up, staggering. Someone came in. It was Sabel, at whom the priest stared in surprise, for it had been a long time since she last entered his room.

"The master says, will you come down for dinner?"

"Has your father come back? Has the doctor arrived?" Julián inquired anxiously, not daring to ask more specific questions.

"No, sir. It's a *little morsel* from here to Cebre."

In the dining room Julián found the marquis eating with a hearty appetite, like a man whose pittance is served two hours late. Julián tried to imitate his calm, so he sat down and spread his napkin. "How's the mistress?" he asked eagerly.

"Oh, rather uncomfortable, as you can imagine!"

"Do you think she may need something while you're here?"

"No. Filomena, her maid, is up there. Sabel will help her too, if necessary."

Julián did not reply. Indeed, his thoughts were not to be revealed. It was revolting that Sabel should attend the legitimate wife, but if this did not occur to the husband, who would dare to point it out to him? On the other hand, Sabel really had domestic experience and would, no doubt, be useful. Julián noticed that the marquis's mood had changed and that he had grown impatient. The priest hesitated to question him, but at last he made up his mind. "Will . . . will the doctor get here in time?"

"In time?" the master replied, chewing and gulping down angrily. "Don't worry, he'll be in time all right! These refined ladies are very delicate and difficult about everything. And when they don't have a strong constitution . . . If only she were like her sister Rita!"

He banged the glass on the table and added sententiously: "City women are miserable things. They're made of glass. I tell you, she's so weak and prone to convulsions and fainting! What the devil, spoiled is what they are! Spoiled from childhood!"

He slammed his fist on the table again, stood up, and left the chaplain alone in the dining room. Julián, who did not know what to do with himself, decided that it was better to resume his conference with the saints. He went up to his room. The candles were still burning, and the priest knelt down once more. Hours and hours went by with no other sound than the wail of the wind around the chestnut trees, and the deep moan of the water in the dam of the mill. Julián felt prickling and soreness in his legs, cold in his body, and heaviness in his head. Once or twice he glanced at the bed, and each time the thought of the poor woman suffering downstairs held him back. He was ashamed of yielding to temptation, but his eyelids closed and his head, drunken with sleep, sank on his chest. He lay down in his clothes and promised himself to resume his task right away. When he awoke, the sun was already up.

When he saw that he was still dressed, he remembered everything, and chided himself for being so weak; then he wondered if the new Moscoso heir had already arrived into this world. He rushed downstairs rubbing his eyes, still half asleep.

In the antechamber of the kitchen, he bumped into Máximo Juncal, the doctor of Cebre, who wore a gray comforter around his neck, a brown felt coat, boots, and spurs.

"Have you just arrived?" the priest asked in surprise.

"Yes, sir. Primitivo says that he and two other fellows knocked on my door last night and nobody answered. It's true that my maid is a little deaf, but still, if they had knocked hard enough . . . Anyway, I didn't get the message till dawn. It looks like there's still plenty of time, though. It's her first delivery, after all, and these battles usually go on and on. I'll go in and see how she is."

He followed Don Pedro, holding his riding whip and clinking

his spurs, so that the military image that he had just used seemed quite fitting; anyone would think that he was the general who comes to secure victory with his presence and command. His resolute air inspired confidence. Shortly afterward he came out again and asked for a cup of hot coffee, for he had left his house in a hurry without breakfast. They served the master some chocolate. The physician pronounced his professional verdict: they would need a great deal of patience, because this business was going to be long. Don Pedro, disgruntled and with his face puffy from sleeplessness, insisted on knowing if there was any danger.

"No, sir, no," Máximo replied, as he melted the sugar and poured rum in his coffee. "If any problems arise, here we are. Hey, Sabel, a small glass!"

He poured some more rum in the liqueur glass and tasted it as the coffee cooled. The marquis offered him a full cigar case.

"Many thanks," said the doctor, lighting a Cuban cigar. "For the time being, we must wait and see. The lady is a beginner, and not very strong. In the city women receive the most antihygienic education: girdles to make narrow what must be broad; confinement indoors to produce chlorosis and anemia; sedentary life to fabricate lymph at the expense of blood. Country women are infinitely better prepared for the great battle of pregnancy and childbirth, which is, after all, woman's real function."

He continued to expound his theory, striving to prove that he was not unacquainted with the latest and boldest scientific hypotheses, bragging of his hygienic materialism, and extolling at length the beneficial effects of Mother Nature. It was obvious that he was a smart fellow, well read, and ready to contend with other people's illnesses; but his own bilious, sallow complexion and his pale dry lips did not indicate a robust health. This fanatic of hygiene did not match words with deeds. Rumor had it that rum and a baker girl of Cebre, who was certainly healthy enough for any hygienic doctor, were to blame.

Don Pedro chewed his cigar furiously and ruminated on the doctor's views. Strangely enough, they concurred in every way with his own, despite the gap that separates a modern scientist from a virgin mind quite unbiased by reading. This gentleman of old also believed that woman must be above all well equipped to perpetuate the human race. The opposite would be a crime. He often recalled, with nearly incestuous pangs of conscience, the solid bust of his sister-in-law Rita. He also recalled Perucho's birth, one day when Sabel was kneading dough; before the bread was cooked, the child was already screaming and saying in his own way that he was a creature of God and needed nourishment. These memories brought to his mind a very important matter.

"Tell me, Máximo, do you think my wife will be able to nurse the child herself?"

Máximo began to laugh, savoring the rum. "Let's not ask for the moon, Don Pedro. Nurse! This august function requires a vigorous nature and a sanguine temperament. The lady can't nurse."

"She's the one who wants to do it," the marquis said contemptuously. "I thought from the beginning it was madness, even though I didn't realize that my wife is so weak. Anyway, now we have to make sure that once the baby is born he doesn't starve. Is there time for me to go to Castrodorna? The daughter of Felipe, the caretaker, the big girl, do you know her?"

"Of course I know her! A great cow! You have a doctor's eye. And she gave birth just two months ago. The only thing is, I don't know if her parents will let her come. I believe they're honorable people within their class, and don't want anybody to know about their daughter."

"Fiddlesticks! If she resists, I'll drag her here by the braids. I won't put up with any nonsense from my renters. Is there time to go or not?"

"There's time, yes. I wish we could finish soon, but it doesn't look like we will."

When the master left, Máximo poured himself another glass of rum and said confidentially to the chaplain: "If I were in Felipe's shoes, I'd give Don Pedro a piece of my mind. When will these landlords understand that a renter is not a slave? This is how things are in Spain; plenty of talk about revolution, freedom, human rights . . . And in the end, only tyranny, privileges, and feudalism, for what is this but a return to the days of bondage and the injustice of slavery? I need your daughter, so I snatch her against your will. I need milk, a human cow, so if you don't feed my baby willingly you'll feed him by force. But I'm shocking you. No doubt, you don't share my social views."

"No, sir, I'm not shocked," Julián answered calmly. "On the contrary, it amuses me to see you so heated. Because, what could Felipe's daughter like better than to serve as a wet nurse in this house? She'll be supported and pampered, she won't have to work. Think about that."

"And her freedom? Do you want to abolish freedom and individual rights? Suppose that the girl prefers her honest poverty to all these benefits and advantages you mention. Isn't it outrageous to drag her here by her braids just because she's a subordinate's daughter? Naturally, you don't think so; a man who dresses from the head down could not think otherwise. You must be all for feudalism and theocracy, am I right? Don't deny it!"

"I don't have any political views," Julián stated peacefully. Suddenly he remembered something and added: "Wouldn't it be a good idea to see how the mistress is doing?"

"Oh, at the moment I'm not really needed there, but I'll go and see. Don't let them take away the rum bottles, will you? I'll be back in a jiffy."

He returned promptly, made himself comfortable in front of his glass, and tried to resume the political conversation, of which he was inordinately fond. Deep inside he preferred to be contradicted, for then he grew hot and excited and came up with unexpected arguments. Those violent disputes that ended in screams and insults expanded his stagnant bile and activated his digestive and respiratory process, making him feel infinitely better. He argued for hygienic reasons: these gymnastics of the larynx and the brain unblocked the channels of his liver.

"So you don't have any political ideas? Don't give me that, Father Julián. All black-feather birds fly backward, let's face it. If you say the opposite, you'll have to prove it: what do you think of the revolution? Let's see what you say to this: do you support freedom of worship? Do you agree with Suñer?"[1]

"The things you come up with, Don Máximo! How can I agree with Suñer? Isn't he the one who said those horrible blasphemies in the Congress? The Lord have mercy on him!"

"Speak clearly. Do you see eye to eye with the abbot of San Clemente de Boán? He says that Suñer and the revolutionaries will be persuaded not with arguments, but with shots and blows. What do you think?"

"People say things like that in the heat of the moment. A priest is a man like any other, and in a dispute he can get upset and say the most terrible things."

"Indeed! And by the same token, he may have illegitimate 'interests,' he may want to be well off at the expense of his neighbors' stupidity, he may feast on the capons and goats of his parishioners . . . This you can't deny."

"We're all sinners, Don Máximo."

"And he can do even worse things than that . . . that we all know about, don't we? There's no need to get upset."

"Yes, sir. A priest can do all the wrongs in the world. If we were immune to sin, things would be very easy for us: saved from the

1. Atheist deputy who advocated a Spanish federal republic.

very moment of ordination, no joke! In truth, ordination imposes on us stricter duties than those of all other Christians, and therefore it is twice as difficult for us to be good. In order to strive for perfection as we are required at ordination, we need, aside from our own efforts, the grace of God. No easy task."

He said all this so simply and sincerely, that the doctor calmed down for a while. "If they were all like you, Don Julián . . ."

"I'm the last, the worst. Don't rely on appearances."

"Come on, now! The others are a nice lot. And not even the revolution has undermined their power. You won't believe what they've been plotting these past few days to butter up that bandit Barbacana."

Julián, who was not informed on the matter, remained quiet.

"Just imagine," the doctor explained. "Barbacana has under his orders another butcher, a fellow from Castrodorna known as 'One-eye,' who constantly flees back and forth from Portugal, because one night he stabbed his wife and her lover to death. It seems that recently the police got hold of him; but Barbacana wanted him free, so he and the Holy Joes sweated so much over the matter that he was released on bail and now is walking around. So despite all the fuss, here we are, under the rule of the infamous Barbacana."

"But," Julián objected, "I've heard that when Barbacana is not in power there's a worse chieftain named Trampeta, who bleeds the poor peasants dry with his plots and machinations. So, one way or the other . . ."

"Well, there's some truth in that; but look here, at least Trampeta is not arming guerrillas. Barbacana, on the other hand, must be destroyed, for he is in touch with the Carlist juntas of the province and intends to rouse the county to a bloody rebellion. Do you support Don Carlos's candidacy to the throne?"[2]

2. Don Carlos was the brother of Ferdinand VII, who reigned from 1814 to 1833.

"I told you that I don't have any opinions on these matters."

"What you don't have is any desire to argue."

"Frankly, Don Máximo, you're right. I'm worried about that poor lady and what might happen to her. Besides, I don't know anything about politics. You may laugh at me, I really don't. I only know how to say mass. Incidentally, I haven't said it yet, and until I say it I can't have breakfast, and my stomach is . . . I'll offer this mass for our present need. I can't," he added with a certain sadness, "give the mistress any other help."

He walked out of the room, leaving the physician surprised to find a priest who shunned political discussions, which in those days replaced theological ones at each patron's saint's meal. Julián said mass with utmost attention to the details of the ceremony. The acolyte's bell tinkled clear and crystalline in the empty old chapel. From outside came the chirps of birds in the trees of the garden, the distant creak of cart wheels rolling to work, and all sorts of pleasant, calming, and reassuring country sounds. It was the mass of Saint Ramón Nonato, which he had chosen for this particular circumstance. When the priest pronounced, "ejus nobis intercessione concede, ut a peccatorum vinculis absoluti . . . ,"[3] he felt as if the painful chains fastened around the poor little virgin—for so she was to the chaplain, even in these moments—broke loose and left her free, joyful, and radiant, the happiest of mothers.

When he returned to the house, however, there were no signs that this had happened. Instead of the rushed comings and goings of the servants that always indicate a transcendental event in the house, he noticed an ill-omened calm. The master had not come

---

The Carlists were the conservative party that supported Don Carlos's claims to the throne. They outlived their candidate and waged several wars against the liberals throughout the nineteenth century.

3. "Grant us that by his intercession, free of all the bonds of sin . . ."

back; granted, Castrodorna was a long way from the house of Ulloa. They had to sit at table without him. The doctor made no more attempts to start an argument because he, too, was a little worried about the delay of the heir. To the credit of the opinionated hygienist, it must be admitted that he took his profession seriously and respected it as much as Julián respected his. Proofs of this were his very obsession with hygiene and his cult of health, inspired by modern writings that have replaced the God of Sinai with the goddess Hygieia. To Máximo Juncal, immorality was synonymous with scrofula, and duty was very much like a perfect oxidation of assimilating elements. He forgave himself certain follies because his hepatic channels were obstructed.

At this moment, the danger looming over Señora Moscoso aroused his desire to fight the real evils of the earth: pain, illness, death. He ate distractedly and drank only two glasses of rum. Julián, who barely touched his food, asked now and then: "What do you suppose is going on up there, Don Máximo?"

He ceased to ask when the doctor, in a low voice, gave him some details in technical terms. Night was falling. Máximo rarely left the patient's room. Julián felt so sad and lonely that he began to think he would go up and light his altar to enjoy, at least, the company of the candles and the little pictures. Then Don Pedro burst in like a gust of wild wind, pulling by the hand a girl of earthy complexion, a castle of flesh: the classic type of the human cow.

Chapter 17

Let Máximo Juncal examine carefully the source of the milky flow of this powerful animal; after all, this is his business. To everybody's amazement, the marquis had brought her seated in front of him on the saddle of his own mare, for there was no other transportation available in Castrodorna, and Don Pedro was too impatient to let her walk. To this day, the mare shivers at the thought of that memorable journey, when she had to carry at once the present representative of the Moscosos and the future Moscoso's wet nurse.

Don Pedro's spirits fell when he learned that his heir had not yet arrived. At this moment, he thought that the impending event would never take place. He rushed Sabel with dinner, for he had a ferocious appetite. Sabel served it personally because that day Filomena, the maid who usually waited at table, was very busy. Sabel was fresher and more desirable than ever. The luscious flesh of her bare arms, the copper brilliancy of her hair, the mellow tenderness and sensuality of her blue eyes, contrasted sharply with the situation of the woman who was enduring cruel torments and almost dying not far away.

It was long since the marquis had seen Sabel at such close range. One could say that he scrutinized rather than looked at her for several minutes. He noticed that she did not wear earrings, and that one of her ears was torn; then he recalled that it was he himself who had split it in two, when he smashed her eardrop with the butt of his gun in a fit of brutal jealousy. The wound had healed, but the ear had now two lobes instead of one.

"Doesn't the mistress sleep at all?" Julián asked the doctor.

"Now and then, between labor pains. But it is precisely this drowsiness that I don't like at all. There isn't any progress or regularity, and worse yet, she's losing strength and getting weaker every time. She hasn't had a bite for practically two days; she confessed to me that long before she told her husband, she felt sick and couldn't eat anything. These little naps are very fishy. It seems to me that rather than sleeping, she actually faints."

Don Pedro rested his head listlessly on his closed fists. "I'm convinced," he said emphatically, "that these things only happen to young women brought up in the city with a lot of nonsense and scruples. Girls around here don't give a damn about fainting spells. They put down half a gallon of wine and get the job over with in a jiffy."

"No, sir, there's all sorts of them. The lymphatic nervous types collapse. I've had cases . . ."

He explained in detail some of these cases, although not too many, because his medical experience was still short. He favored patience: the best midwife is the one who can wait. There comes a moment, nonetheless, when to lose one second is to lose everything. As he spoke thus, he savored sips of rum.

"Sabel!" he called suddenly.

"What do you want, Don Máximo?" the girl answered solicitously.

"Where did you put the case I brought with me?"

"In your room, on the bed."

"Very well."

Don Pedro glanced at the doctor and understood. Julián, on the other hand, alarmed by the silence that followed the dialogue be-

tween Máximo and Sabel, interrogated him indirectly to find out
what the mysterious case contained.

"Instruments," the physician answered dryly.

"Instruments? What for?" the priest asked, feeling drops of sweat
ooze from the roots of his hair.

"To operate on her, what the devil! If we could hold a medical
consultation here, perhaps I'd let things follow their course; but
as it is, everything that may happen is my own responsibility. I
can't sit here twiddling my thumbs and get caught by surprise like
a fool. If at dawn she's even more exhausted and I see no signs of
progress, we'll have to make a decision. You may start praying to
the blessed Saint Ramón, chaplain."

"If it were a matter of praying!" Julián said candidly. "I've hardly
done anything but pray since yesterday!"

This humble confession provided the doctor with a pretext for
telling numerous funny stories, in which devotion and obstetrics
mingled gracefully and Saint Ramón played a prominent role. One
of them referred to his professor at the hospital of Santiago, who
whenever he entered the delivery room and saw the picture of the
saint with its candles would shout furiously: "Gentlemen, you'll
have to make up your minds between the saint and me, for if I
fail I shall be blamed, and if we succeed he will be credited with a
miracle." He also told a rather grotesque story about roses of Jeri-
cho, ribbons of the Virgin of Tortosa, and other pious talismans
used on critical occasions. At last he stopped chatting, overcome
by sleep, with the help of the rum. In order not to pass out entirely
in the comfort of the bed, he lay down on the bench in the dining
room, with a basket for a pillow. The master had folded his arms
on the table and dropped his head on them; a slight whistle, a prelude to a snore, announced that sleep had attacked him, too. The
tall grandfather's clock, with a tiresome sound, struck midnight.

Julián was the only one awake. He felt chilled to the bone, while his cheeks burned with fever. He went up to his room, soaked a towel in fresh water, and applied it to his temples. The candles on the altar had extinguished themselves. He replaced them and put a pillow on the floor to kneel on, for that pesky prickling in his legs was very troublesome. And, in high spirits, he started the difficult path to prayer. Sometimes his strength failed him, and his young body, wrapped in the gray mist of slumber, craved the clean sheets. Then he folded his hands and dug his fingernails into his flesh to stay awake. He wanted to pray with devotion, to be fully aware of what he was asking of God, not to pray by heart. But he was fading away. He recalled Christ's prayer in Gethsemane and the difference, so wisely established, between the willingness of the spirit and the weakness of the flesh. He also evoked a biblical passage: Moses praying with uplifted arms because, should he lower them, Israel would be defeated. Then he decided to put into practice something that had floated in his imagination for a while. He removed the pillow to let his knees rest on the blessed floor; he raised his eyes, searching for God beyond the religious pictures and the beams on the ceiling; and opening his arms like a cross, he began to pray fervently in this position.

The atmosphere became icy cold. A feeble brightness, paler and dimmer than moonlight, shone from behind the mountain. Two or three birds twittered in the garden. The rumor of the water mill became softer and less mournful. Dawn, which had merely touched this corner of the world with one of her rosy fingertips, dared to stretch out her whole little hand. A joyful and pure radiance bathed the slate rocks, which glittered like polished steel, and entered the priest's room, devouring the yellowish light of the candles. But Julián did not see the dawn, he did not see anything. Actually, he did. He saw those lights that our perturbed blood ignites in our brain, those purple, greenish, sulfur-colored tiny stars that flutter without illuminating, which we see as we feel a buzz in our ears and the frantic pulse in our arteries, about to burst. He felt that he was fainting, dying. His lips no longer uttered sentences, only a murmur that still retained the tone of prayer. In the midst of his painful vertigo he heard a voice that seemed to resound like a bugle. The voice said something. Julián understood only two words: "A girl."

Breathing a deep sigh, he managed to get up with the help of the person who had just come in, who was no other than Primitivo; but he was hardly on his feet when a terrible pain in his joints and the sensation of a hard blow on his skull brought him down to the floor again. He fainted.

Downstairs Máximo Juncal washed his hands in a pewter basin held by Sabel. His face showed the joy of triumph mixed with the perspiration of the struggle, which was quickly cooling in the morning chill. The marquis, tense and sullen, frowned and paced the room. He had that expression, grim and stupid at the same time, that vigorous people dominated by the laws of matter acquire after a sleepless night.

"Now let's be happy, Don Pedro," the doctor said. "The worst is over. We have achieved what you wished most. Didn't you want the baby to come alive and unharmed? Well, there she is, safe and sound. It's been a bit hard, but finally . . ."

The marquis shrugged his shoulders contemptuously, as if to belittle the physician's accomplishment, and rumbled something between his teeth. Meanwhile, he resumed his pacing up and down the room, with his hands in his pockets and his trousers as tense as his mood.

"It's a little angel, as the old wives say," Juncal added, seeming to relish the gentleman's annoyance, "only it's a female little angel. Such things must be accepted; no system has yet been invented to send a request to heaven that explains clearly which is the sex desired."

Another onslaught of rage and abuse came out of Don Pedro's lips. Juncal burst into laughter as he dried his hands with a towel.

"At least half of the blame, sir, must be put on you," he exclaimed. "Would you be so kind as to give me a cigarette?"

Don Pedro, as he offered him his open cigarette case, asked a question. Máximo grew serious before he answered. "I didn't say that . . . and I don't think so. It's true that when the battle is so long and hard, the fighter may come out of it handicapped; but nature is wise, and while it puts women through such severe trials, it also brings them the most unexpected compensations. This is not the time to think about that, but to let the mother recuperate and bring up the little girl. I fear some immediate misfortune . . . We'll see. The lady has come out of it so exhausted . . ."

Primitivo entered the room and, with no sign of alarm or fear, asked Don Máximo to go upstairs, for there was something wrong with the chaplain, who looked as if he were dead.

"Let's go, my good man, let's go. This was not in the program," Juncal murmured. "This priest is as much a woman as a man! How poor his build is! This one certainly won't grab a gun if there is an uprising, as that oaf the abbot of Boán dreams of!"

Chapter 18

For many days Nucha had one foot on the gloomy threshold of death, as if she wondered: "Shall I enter? Shall I not?" The horrible physical torture that played havoc with her nerves; the fever that consumed her brain when the wave of useless milk invaded her breasts; her distress at not being able to offer her baby this liquor that was drowning her; the exhaustion of her whole being, from which life slipped away drop by drop, irreversibly—all this pushed her toward death. On the other hand, summoning her back were her youth, the will to survive that stimulates every organism, the science of the great hygienist, Juncal, and particularly a small pink soft hand, a tight fist that peeped out between the lace of a little dress and the folds of a shawl.

The first day that Julián was permitted to see the patient, she had been up only a few times to lie, wrapped in coats and blankets, on an old broad sofa. She was not yet allowed to sit up, and her head rested on folded pillows. Her lean and emaciated face, framed in shiny black hair, seemed as yellow as that of an ivory statue. Her eyes strayed even more, because in the past few days the optic nerve had weakened considerably. She smiled sweetly to the priest and pointed toward a chair. Julián pierced her with a glance full of compassion, the revealing glance that we try in vain to conceal when we approach a seriously ill person. "I think you're looking very well, señorita," the chaplain said, lying like a rogue.

"You, on the other hand," she retorted languidly, "look a little worn out."

He confessed that, indeed, he had not been feeling too well since . . . since he had caught a cold. He was too ashamed to give an account of his sleepless night, his fainting spell, and the strong moral and physical impression made on him by these events. Nucha began to talk about unimportant things, and then asked suddenly: "Have you seen the little one?"

"Yes, señorita, the day she was baptized. The little angel! She cried when she tasted the salt and felt the cold water."

"Ah! Now she's at least a fourth bigger than she was then, and she has become so lovely!" Raising her voice and straining herself, she called: "Nurse! Nurse! Bring the baby."

They heard steps as of a colossal statue, and in came the earth-colored lass, all puffed up in her new dress of blue merino trimmed with a black velvet strip. She resembled the old female giant of the Cathedral of Santiago called "La Coca." Like a bird perched on a large trunk, the infant lay on the generous bosom that nourished her. She was asleep with the calm, sweet, and insensible breathing that makes the sleep of children sacred. Julián could not take his eyes from her.

"Blessed child of God!" he whispered, gently pressing his lips on her bonnet because he did not dare to touch her forehead.

"Hold her, Julián. You'll see what an armful she is. Nurse, give him the baby."

She did not weigh more than a bouquet of flowers, but the chaplain swore over and over that she seemed made of lead. The nurse stood by and waited while Julián sat with the girl in his arms.

"Let me hold her for a while," he begged, "as long as she sleeps. Surely she won't wake up soon."

"I'll call you when I need you. Leave us, nurse."

The conversation evolved around a commonplace that was very dear to Nucha: the charms of the little one. She had a great many of them, yes, sir, and anyone who doubted it was a fool. For example, she opened her eyes in the naughtiest way and sneezed with incomparable mischief; with her little hand she squeezed your finger so hard that it took the strength of a Hercules to release it. She performed still other tricks that should rather be kept quiet than recorded in the chronicle. As she enumerated them, Nucha's emaciated face grew animated, her eyes sparkled, and once or twice laughter parted her lips. But suddenly her face darkened, and her eyes brimmed with ill-repressed tears.

"They won't let me nurse her, Julián. A whim of Señor Juncal, who does nothing but talk about hygiene here and hygiene there. I don't think it would kill me to try for a couple of months, just two months. Maybe I'd feel better if I didn't have to lie forever on this sofa, with my body imprisoned and my imagination running wild. I have no peace as it is. I'm always afraid that the nurse will drop my baby or let her drown. Now that she's close to me I'm happy."

She smiled to the sleeping child and added: "Don't you see the resemblance?"

"To you?"

"To her father! She's his spit and image, particularly in the lines of her forehead."

The priest did not express his opinion and changed the subject. Through the days that followed he continued to fulfill the charitable duty of visiting the sick. Nucha, during the long period of her convalescence and complete loneliness, needed somebody willing to perform this pious task. Máximo Juncal came every other day but was nearly always in a hurry, because the number of his patients was on the rise—they called him from as far away as Vilamorta. The doctor talked about politics, breathing out an odor of rum and trying to tease and irritate Julián; indeed, if Julián had been capable of anger, he would have found good reasons for it in the news that Máximo Juncal brought: demolished churches, antireligious scandals, Protestant chapels erected here and there, freedom of education and worship, freedom of this and that . . . Julián limited himself to deploring these excesses and hoping that things would improve. This attitude did not give Máximo ammunition for one of his favorite disputes, so beneficial for the expansion of his bile and so animated when he stumbled upon stubborn Carlist clergy, like the archpriest or the abbot of Boán.

Except for the visits of the feisty doctor, peace and quiet reigned over the sick woman's room. Only the baby's cries, promptly hushed, interrupted it. The chaplain read aloud from *The Christian Year*, and the atmosphere became pregnant with stories of novelistic and poetic flavor: "Cecilia, an exceedingly fair and illustrious Roman lady, dedicated her body to Jesus Christ. Her parents gave her in marriage to a gentleman named Valeriano, and the wedding was celebrated with festivities, merriment, and dance. Only Cecilia's heart was sad." The narration proceeded with the mystic wedding night, Valeriano's conversion, the angel that protected Cecilia's chastity, and the glorious epic finale of her martyrdom. Sometimes the hero was a soldier, like Saint Menna, or a bishop, like Saint Severo. The narrative, detailed and dramatic, described the interrogations by the judges, the quick bold responses of the martyrs, the flagellation with ox sinews,[1] the rack, the thumbscrews, the red-hot ax blades applied to their sides . . . "And the knight of Christ held his heart valiant and still, his face serene, and a smile on his lips—as if it were not himself but another who suffered—mocking his torments and asking that they be increased." These readings had a fantastic effect, particularly in the cruel winter evenings, when the dry leaves from the trees whirled and danced and the thick cotton clouds drifted slowly past the panes of the deep-set window. Far in the distance the dam moaned endlessly, and the carts, loaded with corn and pine

1. Euphemism for ox penises.

branches, squeaked. Nucha listened attentively, her chin rested on her hand. From time to time her bosom heaved with a sigh.

It was not the first time since the birth of the child that Julián had noticed a great sadness in the lady. The priest had received a letter from his mother that perhaps contained the clue to Nucha's misery. Apparently Señorita Rita had been so persuasive with her old aunt from Orense that the latter had disinherited her god-daughter and appointed Rita her sole heiress. Furthermore, Señorita Carmen was crazier than ever for her student, and in town rumor had it that if Don Manuel Pardo refused his consent, the girl would elope. Terrible things were happening with Señorita Mano-lita, too. Don Víctor de la Formoseda had left her for a working girl, the niece of a canon. In sum, Doña Rosario prayed the Lord to grant her patience in so many tribulations, for those of the Pardo home were also her own. If all this had reached Nucha through her husband or her father, it was not surprising that she sighed so. On the other hand, her physical deterioration was all too apparent. Now the only Virgin Nucha resembled was the emaciated image of the Virgin of Solitude. Juncal felt her pulse religiously, prescribed nutritious food, and observed her with alarming persistence.

As she tended to her child, Nucha revived. She took care of her with feverish dedication, insisting on doing everything herself, and delegating to the nurse only her nourishment. The nurse, she said, was a barrel full of milk that was there so she could turn on the tap and let the stream flow when necessary: no more and no less than that. The analogy was quite exact: the wet nurse had the shape, color, and intelligence of a barrel. As such, she also had a capable belly. It was a pleasure to see her eat, or rather devour, in the kitchen. Sabel entertained herself filling her plate and cup to the brim, putting half a loaf of bread in front of her, and fattening her like a turkey. In the presence of such a dull creature, Sabel acted like a princess, like a paragon of good taste and refinement. As in this world everything is relative, those who lived in the lower levels of the mansion looked upon the nurse as a funny and grotesque savage and laughed at her blunders, although they were capable of even greater ones. In truth, the nurse was an object of curiosity not only to the peasants but, for different reasons, to the ethnographer. Máximo Juncal gave Julián some interesting details on the subject.

In the valley where the nurse's village lies—located in the farthest boundaries of Galicia, bordering Portugal—women possess a distinct physical condition and mode of life: they are a type of Amazons, remnants of the Galician wars chronicled by Latin geographers. As these days they can battle with no one but their husbands, they farm as vigorously as they used to fight, and run around half naked, displaying their firm, strong flesh. They plow, dig, harvest, and load carts with branches and produce; like caryatids, they bear on their shoulders the heaviest burdens; and they live without the assistance of men—if not without their intervention—for the men of the valley usually emigrate to Lisbon at age fourteen in search of jobs, return to their country for a couple of months to marry and propagate the race, and flee as soon as they have fulfilled their mission as drones in the hive. In Portugal sometimes they hear news of conjugal infidelity, and by night they cross the border and stab the sleeping lovers to death: this was the crime committed by One-eye, Barbacana's protégé, whose story Juncal had also related. Generally, however, the females of Castrodorna are as chaste as they are wild.

The nurse, with her incredibly broad hips and stout, coarse limbs, was a worthy specimen of her race. Nucha had to struggle to make her dress sensibly and exchange the short green woolen skirt, which hardly covered her bare calves, for a longer and more decorous one. The only thing she tolerated willingly was a bodice, the classic garment of the wet nurse that allows the replete

udders to overflow, and the characteristic large round earrings, the
Roman *torquis*, used by the women of the valley since the dawn
of time. It was an ordeal to force her to put on her shoes daily,
because all her acquaintances reserve them for special holidays. It
was like a penitence for her to learn the name and use of even the
most simple objects. To convince her that the baby whom she fed
was a delicate frail being that should not be wrapped in rags of
red wool, carried in a basket lined with fir leaves, and left in the
shade of an oak tree at the mercy of wind, sun, and rain, like a newborn of Castrodorna, was to ask for the impossible. Máximo Juncal, who advocated hygienic techniques along with the miraculous
virtues of nature, had some difficulty reconciling both extremes;
so he solved the dilemma with an appeal to his latest reading, Dar-
win's *Origin of Species*, and the application of certain laws of environment, heredity, et cetera, which made him conclude that the
nurse's method would either blow up the baby like a firecracker or
strengthen her admirably.

Nucha, just in case, decided not to make the test and to look
after her treasure herself, leading the busy and fussy existence of
a mother, in which hot soup is an event and lukewarm water a
disaster. She washed, dressed, and swaddled her little daughter,
watched over her when she was asleep, and entertained her when
she was awake. Life moved on, monotonous and busy at the same
time. The good chaplain witnessed these tasks and learned little by
little what he considered to be the arcane mysteries of the coiffure
of a baby. He even became familiar with the multiple objects that
constitute the trousseau of the newborn: caps, binders, diapers,
minute crocheted shoes, and bibs. These snow-white garments,
adorned with lace and embroidery, scented with lavender, warmed
up over a brazier—the most healthy and domestic heat of all—
often lay in the priest's lap. Meanwhile, the mother put the baby
face down on her waterproof apron and ran the sponge time and

again over her silky flesh, raw and irritated because of the extreme delicacy of the skin; she sprinkled it with refreshing starch powder, and pressing the buttocks with her fingers to create dimples, she showed them to Julián, exclaiming joyfully: "Look, how lovely! She's getting so plump!"

Julián, who had seen only chubby cherubs on altarpieces, had limited knowledge of child nudes. But he said to himself that, although original sin had corrupted all flesh, what was in front of him must be the purest and holiest thing in the world: a lily of innocence. The little head still had tender scabs covered with blond fluff, and released that peculiar odor of a dove nest inhabited by unfledged chicks. The hands, whose fingers resembled those of a child Christ in the act of blessing, were already rounded with tender fat. The pink, waxen face; the moist, toothless mouth, like a pale coral taken from the sea; the tiny feet, whose heels were red from continuous and graceful kicking—all these trifles generated those mixed emotions that small children awaken even in the most barren soul, a complex and humorous feeling that combines compassion, dedication, some respect, and a great deal of gentle mockery without the bitterness of satire.

In Nucha, exalted by her nervous temperament and sickly sensitivity, the sight of her daughter made a deep impression typical of the maternal honeymoon. To this soft bun that still seemed to retain the gelatinous texture of the protoplasm, that lacked self-consciousness and lived only for physical sensations, the mother attributed sense and knowledge. She poured out her soul in frantic kisses, and claimed that the child understood everything and performed a thousand clever tricks; why, she even laughed quietly, in her own way, at the sayings and deeds of the nurse. "Notions that nature instills with a very wise purpose," Juncal explained. Happy was the day when the first smile dispelled the comic seriousness of the minute face, and opened with a heavenly expression the narrow line of its lips! It was inevitable to recall the commonplace simile of the morning light dispelling darkness. The mother was beside herself with joy.

"Once more, once again!" she cried. "Sweetheart, darling, laugh, my precious, laugh!"

For the time being, the smile refused to return. The doltish nurse even refused to acknowledge the feat, something that infuriated the mother. The next day, the honor of rekindling the brief spark of the baby's intelligence fell to Julián, as he dangled God knows what glittery trinkets before her eyes. The chaplain had gradually lost his fear of the child, who he thought at first would melt like butter in his fingers. While the mother rolled the binder and warmed up the diaper, he was in the habit of holding the baby on his lap.

"I trust you more than the nurse," Nucha said confidentially, disclosing her secret jealousy. "The nurse is incapable of doing anything right. Just imagine, to part her hair she puts the comb on her chin and runs it across her mouth and nose slowly, until she stumbles upon the middle of her forehead; this is the only way she can do it! I was determined not to let her eat with her fingers, but I couldn't get anywhere. Now she eats meat with a spoon. It's grotesque, Julián. Any day she's going to hurt my baby."

The priest perfected his technique of holding the baby in his arms so that she didn't cry or scream. An incident about which we should perhaps remain silent strengthened his friendship with the little one: a certain warmth that he felt once through his trousers . . . What an event! He and Nucha celebrated it with merriment and laughter, as if it were the funniest thing in the world. Julián jumped with delight and held his sides, which ached with laughter. The mother offered him her waterproof apron, but he refused; he already had an old pair of trousers destined to perish in these circumstances, and on no account would he renounce feeling this warm wave. Its contact melted that snow of austerity frozen on his virgin, feminine heart since the days of the seminary, since he had given up family and home to enter the priesthood. At the same time, it lighted in him a mysterious fire, sweet and expansive, of human tenderness. The priest began to love the child blindly, to imagine that if he saw her die he would die too, and to have other extravagant notions of the kind that he rationalized by telling himself that, after all, the little thing was an angel. He never tired of admiring her, of devouring her with his eyes, of contemplating her liquid and mysterious pupils, which seemed to float in milk, and at whose bottom serenity itself seemed to lie.

A painful thought haunted him from time to time. He remembered his dream of instituting in this home a Christian marriage modeled after the Holy Family. Alas! The holy group was incomplete: Saint Joseph either was missing or, worse yet, had been replaced by a priest. The marquis was hardly seen. Since the birth of his daughter, instead of becoming more domestic and sociable, he had returned to his old ways, his hunts, his visits to abbots and gentlemen who owned good dogs and liked the mountains, his excursions to distant hunting grounds. Sometimes he would spend a whole week away from the house of Ulloa. His speech had become rougher, his temper more selfish and impatient, and his way of expressing his wishes and commands harsher.

Julián detected even more alarming signs. He watched uneasily how once again Sabel resumed her role of favorite sultaness amid her former court. The Sage and her progeny, with all the talkative old wives and ragged beggars of the village, populated the house and fled quickly when the chaplain approached them, with suspicious bundles in their bosoms or under their aprons. Perucho did not hide any longer; on the contrary, he was always sitting on the floor in everybody's way. In sum, things were returning to their former state.

The good chaplain tried to deceive himself and pretended to believe that all this meant nothing; but an accursed coincidence forced him to open his eyes when he did not want to. One morning he rose earlier than usual to say mass, and decided to ask Sabel to have his chocolate ready in half an hour. In vain he knocked on the door of her room, which was close to the tower where Julián slept. He went downstairs, hoping to find her in the kitchen; but as he walked past the door of the large office next to the archives, to which Don Pedro had moved since his daughter's birth, he saw the wench come out of it, bleary eyed and with her clothes in disarray. The psychological laws that apply to guilty consciences required that Sabel be confused; but it was Julián who was upset. Not only was he upset, but he went back to his room with the strange sensation that someone had struck a terrible blow to his legs and broken them. As he entered his bedroom, he thought something like: "Let's see who has the nerve to say mass today!"

Chapter 19

No, he did not have the nerve. Some mass he would say, with his mind in this chaotic state! Until he could subdue his mutinous thoughts and make a firm and valid decision, Julián did not even dare to think of the holy sacrifice.

It was clear enough. The situation was the same as that of two years earlier. Ugly vice and infamous sin were driving him away from this house. It was not legitimate for him to remain here a minute longer. With all due respect, this Christian marriage—in a way, his own work—had gone to the dogs. There was no trace of home left, except a cesspool of vice and sin. Therefore, he had to move on.

However, some things in this world are easier said than done. Difficulties rose in his way like a mountain: to find an excuse, to take his leave, to pack his belongings . . . The first time he had tried to leave the place it was hard enough; now, the mere thought of going away had the same effect as a bucket of cold water on his soul. Why did it bother him so to leave the house of Ulloa? After all, he was a stranger in it.

Actually, not a complete stranger . . . He lived spiritually linked to the family by bonds of respect, affection, and habit. And above all, the child. The memory of the child cast a kind of spell on him. He could not explain the great anguish that he felt at the thought that he would never hold her again in his arms. Indeed, he had grown fond of the little doll! His eyes filled with tears.

"They were right in the seminary," he mumbled with discour-

agement. "I'm very shy and very much like women, who get upset
so easily. Some priest I am, ordained to say mass! If I'm so crazy
about children I shouldn't have chosen this career. No, no. What
I'm saying is a greater piece of nonsense yet. If I like children and
I have the vocation of tutor or nursemaid, what prevents me from
looking after those who walk the roads barefoot, begging for alms?
They are children of God, as much as this poor little one here. I
did wrong, terribly wrong, to take such a fancy to her. The thing
is that only a dog—not even a dog!—could kiss such an angel and
not love her!"

Later he resumed his meditations and added to himself: "I'm
a fool, a simpleton. Why did I have to come back a second time?
I shouldn't have done it. I should have foreseen that the master
would end up like this. My lack of energy is to blame. At the risk
of my life I should have driven out this scum, if not by words
by blows. But I don't have the stomach, as the master well says,
and they are stronger and slyer than I, even if they are also more
brutish. They have deceived me, they have fooled me. I haven't
kicked that shameless girl out in the street, and they have laughed
at me. Hell has triumphed!"

Throughout this soliloquy he had begun to take linen out of a
drawer of the dresser in order to pack. Like every irresolute person, he was in the habit of acting impulsively and taking steps that
helped him to deceive himself. As he filled the valise, he reasoned
to himself: "My God, my God, why should there be so much evil
and stupidity on this earth? Why does man let the devil catch him
with so coarse a hook and so vile a bait?" As he said this, he lined
up his stockings in the trunk. "Possessing a pearl among women,
a wife with the true essence of female strength, the most chaste of
all"—this superlative came to his mind as he folded his new cassock
carefully—"how can he fall for a worthless wench, a maid, of all
people, a shameless scouring maid, who has fun with the first peas-

ant that turns up!" As the monologue reached this point, he was trying unsuccessfully to accommodate his tall hat in such a way that the lid of the valise would not crush it. The noise of the valise as he closed it and the harmonious squeak of leather sounded like an ironic voice that answered him: "That's why, that's exactly why."

"Is this possible?" the good priest whispered. "Is it possible that the very abjection, indignity, and foulness of sin should attract, stimulate, and like a fiery pepper, whet the appetite of the jaded palates of the slaves of vice? And those who fall are not people of little means, but high-born noble gentlemen, gentlemen who . . ."

He stopped to count a pile of handkerchiefs that lay on the dresser: "Four, six, seven . . . Why, I had a dozen, all marked with my initials. Clothes disappear easily around here." He counted once more: "Six, seven . . . One in my pocket, eight . . . Perhaps there's one at the wash . . ."

Suddenly he dropped them. He had just remembered that he had tied one of these handkerchiefs under the baby's chin, to protect her neck from her drooling. He sighed deeply and, opening the valise again, realized that the silk of his hat had been damaged by the lid.

"It doesn't fit," he thought, and his failure to accommodate his hat seemed an insurmountable difficulty to the trip. He looked at the clock: it struck ten. About this time the baby had her soup every day, and it was the funniest thing to watch her, with her nose smudged with pap, struggling uselessly to grab the spoon. She would be so charming! He decided to go downstairs. The next day he would find a way to pack his hat and make up his mind to take off. Twenty-four hours more or less would not make any difference.

For most people, the balm of procrastination is tantamount to an infallible drug. One should not decry its use, considering the great comfort it brings. In truth, life is a series of postponements, and there is but one final decision, the last. So Julián had the bright idea of waiting a little. He felt calm, even happy. His temperament was not especially jovial; he had rather a tendency to a kind of morbid and dreamy deliberation, like an anemic maiden. But at this point he breathed such a great sigh of relief for having found a solution that his hands shook while he briskly unpacked stockings and linen and generously released the hat and the cloak. Then he ran downstairs toward Nucha's room.

Nothing happened to make that day different from any other, for the only variation was the greater or lesser number of times that the baby was fed, or the number of diapers hung to dry. In this peaceful retreat, however, the chaplain saw a terrible tragedy unfolding quietly. Now he understood Nucha's repressed sighs and melancholy. As he watched the emaciated face, the pale complexion, the eyes, larger and vaguer than ever, and the beautiful mouth, always contracted except when she smiled at her daughter, he inferred that the lady must know everything, and a deep sorrow invaded his soul. He reproached himself for having even thought of going away. If the lady needed a friend, an advocate, where should she find one but in him? And, no doubt, she would need one.

That same evening, before he went to bed, the priest witnessed a strange scene that plunged him in greater confusion. As the oil in his lamp had burned out and he could not pray or read, he went to the kitchen for more fuel. Sabel's soirée was very well attended. The benches by the fire were occupied by girls who spun or peeled potatoes while they listened to the jokes of Uncle Pepe of Naya, an old fellow who was all mischief. Whenever Uncle Pepe came to the Ulloa mill to grind a sack of wheat, he spent the night there, after enjoying a bowl of greasy soup and pork slabs that the hospitable Sabel offered him. He paid his fee by telling spicy stories. On the kitchen table, which the family had not used since Don Pedro's wedding, not far from the dim candlelight, the remains of a more succulent feast lay scattered: leftover meat on greasy plates, an uncorked bottle of wine, half a cheese—all of it piled in a corner, as if surfeit had pushed it aside contemptuously. Spread in a row on the free space left on the table were half a dozen cards that, if they had not become oval in shape from much use like those of Rinconente and Cortadillo,[1] competed with them in filth and stickiness. María, the Sage, stood in front of them and consulted them meditatively, pointing with a finger as black and knotty as a twig. The horrendous sibyl bent over in the glow of the lively fire on the hearth and the light of the lamp. She was a frightful sight, with the expression of a witch at a black mass, a coarse mane, and a monstrous profile with a huge goiter that disfigured her neck and outlined a second infernal face, without eyes or lips, smooth and shiny like a baked apple.

Julián stopped at the top of the stairs to contemplate the superstitious practices that would surely be interrupted if the sound of his slippers betrayed his presence. Had he known in depth the obscure and not wholly discredited art of fortune-telling, how much more interesting he would have found the scene! Down there he would have seen gathered, as in the cast of a drama, all the characters that played a role in his life and occupied his imagination. That king of clubs, in his blue train trimmed with red, with his feet in a symmetrical position and the heavy green club on his shoulder, would have seemed quite formidable, had Julián realized that he represented a dark married man (Don Pedro). The queen would have appeared less ugly if he had understood that it symbolized a young lady, also dark-haired (Nucha). He would have kicked the queen of hearts for her insolence and drunkenness had he considered that it personified Sabel, a blond unmarried woman. The greatest shock would have been to recognize himself—a fair young man—in the jack of hearts, which was blue, to be precise, although all the colors were covered with filth.

1. Two rogues in Cervantes's exemplary novel of the same name.

What would have happened later, if as the old hag shuffled the cards, divided them into four piles, and proceeded to interpret their fatal meaning, had he heard distinctly every word that came out of the appalling dungeon of her mouth? There were parallels between the queen of clubs and the eight of hearts that foretold nothing less than enduring sacred loves; appearances of the eight of clubs that announced rows between husband and wife; meetings of the queen of spades and the queen of hearts—the latter with her legs up in the air—that carried gloomy omens of widowerhood by death of a wife; although, on the other hand, the five of hearts prophesied a happy later union. Only Sabel, the beautiful maid, listened to all these pronouncements that the sibyl made in a low voice. With her arms folded behind her back and her face flushed, Sabel bent over the oracle, which seemed to arouse in her curiosity rather than joy. The rumpus that followed Uncle Pepe's jokes smothered the old woman's whispers. From his location upstairs, Julián's glance took in the table, pillar, and altar of the frightful ritual, and without being seen, he was able to see and overhear some of it. As he listened and tried to understand the voices that reached him confusedly, he leaned on the railing and made it creak, a sound that caused the witch to raise her horrid mask. She gathered up the cards in a jiffy. The chaplain descended, a little embarrassed by his accidental spying, but so alarmed at what he had encountered that he did not even think of censuring the practice of sorcery. The witch rushed to explain in her usual servile tone that this was a mere pastime "to amuse themselves a little."

Julián went back to his room in a state of great agitation. He did not know what was going on in his own mind. He had always suspected that Nucha and her daughter ran serious risks in the house of Ulloa, but now they seemed so obvious and imminent! Terrible situation! The chaplain tortured his overexcited brain; they would kidnap the child and starve her to death, perhaps they would poison Nucha. He tried to pull himself together. Bah! Murder is not all that common in this world, thank heaven. There are judges, magistrates, executioners. This bunch of rascals would be content to exploit the master, feed on his property, and take command, trampling on the dignity and domestic rights of the mistress. But . . . what if they were not content with that?

He turned up the oil lamp, rested his elbows on the table, and tried to read the works of Balmes, which he had borrowed from the priest of Naya. In Balmes he found a pleasant spiritual solace, and he preferred the company of his charming and persuasive intellect to the scholastic depths of Prisco and Saint Severino. At this time, however, he could not make out a single line of his philosophy, distracted by the sad sounds from outside, the constant moan of the dam, the wiles of the wind. His overheated imagination distinguished amid these lamentations another still more pitiful, because it was personal: a human cry. What nonsense! He ignored it and continued reading. But then he thought he heard again the sorrowful "ah!" Could it be the dogs? He leaned out of the window: the moon was sailing in a cloudy sky, and from the distance came the howl of a dog, that gloomy howl that the peasants call "the scenting of death" and interpret as a sure sign that somebody is about to expire. Julián, shivering, closed the window. He did not excel in courage, and his instinctive fears increased in this mansion, which sometimes still intimidated him as much as in the early days. His lymphatic temperament did not possess the secret of certain mechanisms that help to dispel the terrors and ghosts of the imagination. He had proved capable of taking any serious risk if he thought that his duty required it; but he could not do it calmly, with the lofty contempt for danger and with the heroic countenance that are the privilege of muscular, red-blooded people. Julián's courage was a shaky kind of courage, so to speak; it was the brief nervous impulse characteristic of women.

He had just resumed his conference with Balmes when . . . God help us! There was no doubt now! A piercing shriek of terror flew up the spiral staircase and entered through the half-open door. What a scream! The lamp danced in Julián's hands. He rushed down the steps, however, unconscious of his own movements, as happens in the terrifying falls of our dreams. He ran past the rooms along the endless corridor toward the archives, from where the horrible scream had come. The candle, swinging wildly in his right hand, projected bizarre shadows on the lime walls. He was about to cross the passage that divided the archives from Don Pedro's room when he saw . . . Good heavens! Yes, here was the scene, just as he had imagined it: Nucha standing against the wall, her face contorted with panic, her eyes not only vague but unbelievably astray. In front of her, her husband brandished a huge weapon. Julián threw himself between them. Nucha cried out again: "What are you doing! It's running away, it's running away!"

Then the deluded priest understood what had happened, to his great embarrassment and confusion. A spider of incomparable size and monstrous belly, swinging on eight hairy legs, crawled rapidly up the wall, trying to escape from the light. It raced so speedily that the marquis could not reach it with his boot. Suddenly Nucha came forward, and in a voice that was at once solemn and frightened, repeated naively what she had said a thousand times in her childhood. "Saint George, stop the spider!"

The ugly insect stopped when it entered the area of shadow. The boot fell on it. Julián, by a natural reaction of irrational glee after his recent fear, was about to burst out laughing when he realized that Nucha had closed her eyes, leaned on the wall, and covered her face with a handkerchief.

"I'm fine, just fine," she whispered. "It's only my nerves . . . It'll go away . . . I'm still a little weak . . ."

"Such a fuss for a trifle!" the husband replied with a shrug of his shoulders. "You city women are so spoiled! I've never seen the likes of it. Don Julián, you must have thought the house was tumbling down! Everybody to bed! Good night."

It took the priest a while to fall asleep. He pondered over his terrors and acknowledged how ridiculous they were. He promised to overcome this faintheartedness of his, but the anxiety remained buried in the deepest recesses of his mind. No sooner had sleep descended upon him than he was attacked by a legion of anguishing, dark nightmares. He started to dream of the big old mansion of Ulloa. As dreams are always based on real impressions mingled, unhinged, and scrambled by the chaotic power of the imagination, Julián did not see the den as he had always seen it, with its vast, square mass, its spacious rooms, its broad, harmless gate, and its stout, conventual likeness to an eighteenth-century building. It was still the same, and yet its shape had changed: the garden, with its boxwood and pond, was now a large and deep moat; the solid walls were riddled with loopholes and crowned with battlements; the gate was transformed into a drawbridge with rattling chains. In sum, it was a true feudal castle, which did not lack even the romantic touch of the Moscoso banner waving on top of the tower. Undoubtedly, Julián had seen a painting or read a frightening description of these bogeys from the past that our century restores so lovingly. The only thing in the castle reminiscent of the house of Ulloa was the majestic coat of arms, but even there an important difference existed. Julián saw clearly that the emblematic stones had become animated, the pine tree was green and moaned with the wind, and the two rampant wolves moved their heads and howled gloomily. Julián, fascinated, looked up at the top of the tower and saw an alarming figure in it: a knight in iron armor and a lowered visor. Although not a single inch of his body was exposed, Julián, with the power of divination that dreams confer, recognized Don Pedro's face behind the visor. Don Pedro, furious and threatening, flourished a strange weapon, a steel boot, that he was about to drop on the priest's head. Julián made no attempt to avoid it; neither did the boot complete its fall. It was an unbearable anxiety, an endless agony. Suddenly he felt a hideous owl with white hair perched on his shoulder. He tried to scream, but in dreams the scream always freezes in the throat. The owl laughed quietly. In order to escape from it, he leaped into the moat, only it was not a moat anymore but the dam of the mill. The shape of the feudal castle also suffered inexplicable mutations. Now it looked like the classic tower that the images of Saint Barbara always hold in their hands: a structure of painted cardboard made with perfectly square pieces. Behind the window he saw the pale, contorted face of a woman. This woman stepped out of the window—first one foot, then the other—and began to climb down. Astonishing! It was the queen of clubs, the same dirty, greasy queen of clubs! Under the wall the jack of spades awaited, a rare blue creature with a black-striped tail. But gradually Julián realized his mistake. The jack of spades! It was no other than Saint George himself, the brave knight-errant of the celestial army, fighting a dragon that looked like a spider, in whose powerful mouth he thrust his spear again and again. Sharp and glittering, the spear came down and sank in deeper. Surprisingly, Julián felt the thrusts in his own side. He sobbed quietly, striving to speak and beg for mercy. Nobody came to his rescue, and the spear had already pierced through his body. Suddenly he woke up to a painful twitch in his right hand, which lay crushed under the weight of his body. He had been sleeping on his left side, a position most conducive to nightmares.

Chapter 20

Terrifying nightmares usually seem risible at the crack of dawn; but Julián, as he jumped out of his bed, could not overcome the impression of his dream. His overexcited imagination continued to boil. He looked out of the window and found the landscape gloomy and sinister. In fact, the celestial vault was overcast with heavy, dark clouds that sent pale reflections; sudden gusts of wind, some silent and others whistling, bent down the trees. The chaplain descended the spiral staircase to say mass, which, because of the poor condition of the feudal chapel, he almost always performed in the parish. On his return, as he approached the house of Ulloa, dry leaves whirled around his feet, a chill ran down his spine, and the huge stone den faced him, imposing, ominous, and terrible like a prison and the castle of his dreams. The building, attacked by the fearsome north wind under a canopy of black clouds, appeared threatening and sinister. When Julián entered it, his heart lost a beat. He quickly crossed the icy-cold vestibule, the cavernous kitchen, and the empty halls, and ran for shelter to Nucha's bedroom, where he was customarily served chocolate at her orders.

He found her more out of sorts than usual. The fatigue that permanently marked her sharpened features was now aggravated by a contraction and a look of anxiety that denoted great nervous tension.

She held her daughter in her arms and, when Julián arrived, hastily signaled him not to speak or budge, for the little angel had become lethargic in the warmth of her bosom. Leaning over the baby, Nucha breathed upon her the better to induce sleep, and with feverish movements arranged the knitted scarf, which wrapped this budding life as the cocoon envelops a silkworm. The child blinked a few times and then shut her eyes, while her mother rocked her to a lullaby that she had learned from the nurse, whose theme was a sad repetition of *lai . . . lai*! the long, slow wail of all popular Galician songs. The singing became fainter and fainter until it extinguished itself in the melancholy, sweet sound of a single letter, a prolonged *ehhhh*. Walking on her tiptoes, Nucha placed her daughter in the cradle very delicately, for the little girl was so clever—according to her mother—that she immediately noticed the difference between the cradle and human arms, and was capable of waking from the deepest slumber if she detected the substitution.

For this reason, Julián and Nucha talked in a low voice, while the latter crocheted a pair of shoes that looked like little bags. Julián began by asking if she had recuperated from the fright of the previous day.

"Yes, but I still feel queer."

"I'm not fond of those disgusting bugs either. I had never seen such big ones until I came to the country. In the city there are hardly any."

"I," replied Nucha, "used to be very brave, but since . . . since the little one was born, I don't know what's the matter with me. It looks like I've become a little silly; I'm afraid of everything."

She interrupted her knitting and raised her face. Her large eyes seemed even larger, her lips shivered slightly. "It's an illness, an obsession; I admit it, but I can't help it. I only think of scary things, of horrors. You heard how I screamed yesterday because of that blessed spider. Well, at night when I'm alone with the baby—for the nurse sleeps as if she were dead; one could fire a cannon in her ear and she would not wake up—I would constantly dream up similar scenes if I didn't restrain myself. I'm too ashamed to tell Juncal, but I see very strange things. The clothes I pin up always take the shape of a hanged man or a shrouded corpse risen from its coffin. It doesn't matter how I arrange the night candle before going to bed, while the oil lamp is still burning; in the end, as soon as I turn off the lamp and light the candle, it will cast extravagant shadows. Sometimes I see people without heads; or on the contrary, I see only their faces with each particular feature, the mouth wide open, grimacing . . . These puppets painted on the screen move, and when the windows rattle with the wind, as they did last night, I begin to wonder if they are souls from the other world, moaning."

"Señorita!" Julián broke in painfully. "That's against our faith! We must not believe in ghosts and witchcraft."

"Oh, I don't!" the lady replied with a nervous giggle. "Do you think that I'm like the nurse, who says she's seen the *companya*— the procession of ghosts with their candles—in the middle of the night? I've never believed such nonsense; that's why I'm telling you that if I'm haunted by visions and monsters I must be ill. Señor Juncal's favorite topic is 'get stronger, produce more blood.' It's a pity one can't buy blood at the chemist's, don't you think?"

"Or that those of us who are healthy can't give it to the ones who . . . need it."

The priest said this hesitantly and blushed to the roots of his hair, for his first impulse had been to exclaim: "Señorita Marcelina, here's my blood at your disposal."

The silence produced by this impulsive reaction lasted a few seconds, through which both stared at the landscape beyond the deep, broad window. At first they did not really see it, but little by little its somber appearance penetrated through their eyes, despite themselves, into their very souls. The mountains appeared black, hard, and solid under the extremely dark dome of the stormy sky;

the valley was illuminated by the pale clarity of an anguished sun; the chestnuts were sometimes motionless and sometimes shaken by gusts of furious wild wind. Chaplain and mistress exclaimed at the same time: "What a sad day!"

Julián pondered over the curious coincidence of Nucha's terrors with his own, and thinking aloud, he burst out: "Señorita, one must admit that this house . . . I don't want to speak ill of it, but . . . it's a little frightening, don't you think?"

Nucha's eyes lighted up, as if the priest had guessed a feeling in her that she did not dare disclose. "Since the beginning of winter," she whispered, talking to herself, "I don't know what's wrong with it, it just doesn't look the same. The walls themselves have grown thicker, and the stones darker. It's silly, I know, but I don't dare leave my room; I, who used to search every corner and walk around the whole place! The only remedy is to get out of here. I have to go to the basement and see if I can find the linen trunks. Please come with me, Julián, now that the girl is asleep. I want to put an end to these apprehensions and this nonsense."

The chaplain tried to dissuade her. He feared that she would tire, that she might catch cold passing through the halls and the cloister. The lady's only answer was to put down her knitting, wrap herself in a shawl, and start to walk. Their muffled steps resounded as they marched briskly through the row of large, almost empty rooms. From time to time, Nucha showed her alteration and anxiety by turning her head to see if her escort still followed her. A bunch of keys swung in her right hand. They came out onto the upper cloister and climbed down a very steep stairway to the lower one with stone arches.

Having reached the small patio enclosed by the austere cloister, Nucha pointed at a pillar with an inlaid iron ring from which still hung a rusty link. "Do you know what this is?" she whispered faintly.

"I don't," Julián responded.

"Pedro says," the lady explained, "that his ancestors kept a black slave chained here. Can you believe that such cruelty existed? Those were bad times, Julián!"

"Señorita, Don Máximo Juncal, who thinks only of politics, talks about this all the time. But look: every age has its horrors. There's plenty of brutality today, and religion is perishing amid all this uproar."

"But since here we see only the atrocities of the lords of old," Nucha remarked, stating in simple terms an observation with ample historical and philosophical implications, "we don't think much of the present ones. Why are people such bad Christians?" she added, with her lips parted in candid astonishment.

As Nucha spoke, the sky darkened. Lightning suddenly illuminated the depths of the cloister. The lady's face, tinged with greenish light, acquired the tragic expression of a religious image.

"Blessed Saint Barbara!" the chaplain implored piously, while he shivered. "Let's go back upstairs, señorita. It's thundering! This year we haven't had our autumn storms, and now we shan't go through the equinox without them. Shall we go up?"

"No," Nucha protested, determined to fight her own terrors. "This is the basement door. I wonder which key it is."

She searched for it at length among the bunch. When she introduced it in the lock and pushed the door open, another blast of lightning bathed in ghostly light the space she was about to enter. Thunder rolled, first quietly and then hoarse and formidable, like a human voice swollen with wrath. Nucha stepped back in fright.

"What's the matter, my dear señorita? What's wrong?" the priest cried.

"Nothing, nothing!" the lady of Ulloa stammered. "When I opened the door I thought that I saw a huge dog sitting in there that got up and tried to bite me. Do you think that I'm going crazy? I could swear it was here."

"For goodness' sake, señorita! It's just that it's cold here and it's thundering, and it's madness to search the basement at a time like this. Withdraw to your room, I'll look for whatever you need."

"No," Nucha replied energetically. "I'm fed up with my own silliness. I want to go in first, just to prove to you that I don't care for this nonsense. Do you have a match?" she called, already from inside.

The chaplain struck a match, and by its dim light they saw the basement, or rather they glimpsed the walls oozing moisture. A jumble of useless objects rotted away in the corner—a collection of formless things, whose very amorphousness made them all the more vague and frightening. In the shadows of this almost underground place, among the clutter of old junk left to the rats, the leg of a table sketched a mummified arm, the sphere of a clock became the white face of a corpse, and a pair of riding boots that stuck out among rags and papers and was eaten away by insects evoked the fantasy of a man assassinated and hidden there. Nucha, nevertheless, marched resolutely toward the damp and intimidating chaos, and with the muffled, altered voice of those who have just won a great triumph over themselves, she cried: "Here's the trunk. Somebody will carry it up later."

She came out very lively and satisfied with her prowess, the winner of a hand-to-hand struggle with the old house that terrified her. As they climbed up the narrow steps, she was startled once again by the roaring thunder, which sounded louder and nearer than before. It was necessary to light the altar candle and pray the Trisagio.[1]

1. Special prayer to ask for protection from a storm.

And they did so promptly. The candle was placed on Nucha's dresser: an orange-colored wax candle, with many drips and a sputtering wick that did not burn well at all. Before they knelt down, they closed all the window shutters so that the glaring eye of the lightning would not blind them at every second. The wind blew with renewed fury. Thunder resounded just above the mansion of Ulloa, as if a squadron of cavalry were galloping over the roof, or a giant were pushing and rolling a huge boulder over the tiles. How fervently the priest began to say the mysterious Trisagio! Befuddled in the face of divine wrath, which shook the house violently, as if it were a shack, he murmured:

> From sudden death
> by lightning and fire,
> spare this Trisagio and protect
> those who pray, and remember . . .

Suddenly Nucha rose to her feet screaming, ran to the sofa, and threw herself down on it, seized by hysterical laughter that sounded like crying. Her hands twitched, tugged at the hooks of her dress, or pressed her temples, or dug into the cushions of the sofa and scratched them furiously. Julián, despite his inexperience, realized what was happening: the inevitable spasm, the outburst of ill-repressed terror, the price that poor Nucha had to pay for her boast of courage.

"Filomena, Filomena! Here, here . . . Water, vinegar, that little bottle . . . Where's the bottle from the pharmacy of Cebre? Loosen her dress. Of course I'm turning around, my good woman, you don't need to tell me. Cool pads on her temples . . . Who cares about thunder—forget about it! Help your mistress. If nothing else, fan her with this sheet of paper. Are her clothes loosened? Is she under the covers? I'll give it to her drop by drop . . . Let her breathe the vinegar deeply . . ."

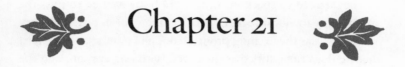

Chapter 21

A few days later, Señora Moscoso's health had somewhat improved, whereupon the priest revived and his withered face brightened, too. The marquis seemed very busy organizing a hunting expedition to the distant mountains of Castrodorna, on the other side of the river. The weather was favorable, the nights icy cold and clear; soon there would be a full moon, and everything promised success. On the eve of their departure several men came to spend the night: the notary of Cebre, the gentleman of Limioso, the priests of Boán and Naya, and a furtive hunter, an infallible professional hunter, known in the area as "Rat-nose"—a most appropriate nickname, given his dark complexion and quick, sparkling eyes. The house was filled with noise: tinkling bells, the scratching of dog claws on the wooden floors, sonorous voices, and orders to have all the hunting gear ready by dawn. Dinner was cheerful and noisy. The guests joked, estimated how many partridges would fall, savored in advance the victuals they were going to take to the mountains, and refreshed their throats with glorious aged red wine. Nucha retired before coffee and dessert were served to go back to her child. Then Primitivo and the Rat came up from the kitchen, and the comrades in future glory and tribulation began to socialize and compete in smoking and drinking. For a thoroughbred hunter it was the sweetest moment, the instant of true happiness: it was the time for cynegetic anecdotes, and most of all for lies.

They agreed to speak in turn, for nobody wanted to miss the opportunity to fabricate his own fib, and the stories reached astonishing levels as the evening progressed. The hunters sat in a circle, and the dogs slept curled at their feet, with one eye shut and the other open, the eyelid twitching. Sometimes, when the chuckles and jokes subsided, the dogs "played the guitar," that is, scratched themselves in unison like a true orchestra, barked in their dreams, cocked their ears, and sighed with resignation. Nobody paid them any attention.

Rat-nose had the first word: "Perhaps you won't believe me, but it's as true as we all have to die and the earth will swallow us. To be precise, it was Saint Silvester's day . . ."

"Then the witches were probably loose," the priest of Boán broke in.

"If it was the witches or the devil, I don't know; but as sure as we are accountable to the Lord for our deeds, what I'm about to tell you happened to me. I was lying low, real low, following a partridge," and the Rat squatted, according to his timeless habit of demonstrating everything that he said, "because I had no dog or anything like it with me; and I was about, if you forgive my saying so, to straddle a fence, when I hear the pitapat of a hare. It was running faster than lightning! So, I turn my head just like this, if you forgive my saying so, hold my gun tight, and suddenly bam! something from the other world goes over my head, and I fall down from the fence."

Explosion of questions, laughter, and protests.

"Something from the other world?"

"A soul from purgatory?"

"But what was it? A person, an animal? What the devil was it?"

"Open the door! This lie doesn't fit in this room!"

"May God save me and grant me glory as it is true!" Rat-nose shouted, with the most contrite face in the world. "It was, if you forgive my saying so, the shameless hare itself, which leapt over me and knocked me off the fence!"

The clarification aroused sheer delirium. Don Eugenio, the abbot of Naya, literally ached with laughter, holding his sides with both hands and shedding tears. The marquis of Ulloa burst out in loud guffaws; even Primitivo modulated a hoarse, opaque laughter. Good old Rat could not open his mouth without unleashing hilarity.

In every reunion of hunters—men partial to practical jokes—there is a designated buffoon, a minstrel, a clown; this role fell by right upon the professional, who was only too glad to perform it. He was used to spending nights and days in the open while he awaited the hare, rabbit, or partridge and to tightening a rope around his waist like a savage on those many occasions when he lacked even a crumb of bread to eat. The wretched little Rat was therefore elated when he stumbled upon fine gentlemen who carry to the hunting ground full wineskins and cooked pork and cigars, and swelled with pride when they laughed at his tall tales. He had learned to tell them in a naive tone, with great seriousness and conviction, and to respond to mockery by invoking God and all the saints in heaven to support his wild accounts.

On his feet, with his hands in the pockets of his trousers, which were patched up like a world map, his nose and mouth the color of rancid fat twitching in a funny, quick manner, he awaited requests for new episodes as unlikely as that of the hare. But now it was Don Eugenio's turn.

"Have you heard," asked the latter, still crying and shaking with laughter, "what happened between Canon Castrelo and a very witty gentleman, Ramírez of Orense?"

"Canon Castrelo!" the priest of Boán and the marquis exclaimed. "He's a good one! His lies are as big as the bell tower of the cathedral!"

"Well, you're going to hear how he met his match where he least expected it. One night there was a card game at the club. Castrelo, as usual, began to rattle off his hunting tales—a pack of lies! Once he had his fill, he tried to drop the big one, and, very, very serious, he said: 'You know, one morning I went to the mountains and I heard a suspicious sound coming from the bushes. I got close very slowly, and the noise continued without pause. I get closer, and at this point I don't have any doubt: there's big game hiding in there. I load, aim, and shoot. Bam, bam! What would you think I killed, gentlemen?' Everybody named a different animal: was it a wolf? a fox? a wild boar? Somebody even ventured a bear. Castrelo just shook his head until, at last, he declared: 'It wasn't a wolf, or a fox, or a wild boar. It was . . . a Bengal tiger!' "

"Come on, Don Eugenio, none of that!" the hunters shouted unanimously. "How would Castrelo dare? They'd have punched him in the nose right there!"

Don Eugenio, unable to raise his voice over the general racket, signaled with his hand to indicate that the best was yet to come. "Patience!" he cried at last. "Be patient, I'm not done yet. Well, as you can imagine, there was a lot of fuss at the club. They started to insult Castrelo and call him a liar in his face. Only Señor Ramírez remained collected, and tried to calm down the rioters. 'Don't be surprised. I'll tell you something that happened to me when I was hunting, which is even more extraordinary than Father Castrelo's adventure.' The canon begins to feel suspicious, and the audience listens: 'One morning I went to the mountains, and from the brush came a noise, a suspicious noise. So I get close, and the noise goes on and on, and I get closer. By now I don't have any doubt: there's big game hiding in there. I load, aim, fire. Bam, bam! And what do you think I killed, your reverence?' 'How on earth am I supposed to know? Was it a lion?' 'No!' 'Then it must have been . . . an elephant!' 'Nooo!' 'Then . . . whatever you want, by Jupiter!' 'A queen of clubs, Father Castrelo, it was a queen of clubs!' "

A few moments of bewilderment followed. The Rat laughed with a kind of loud hiccup, Señor Limioso hoarsely and gravely; the priest of Boán, unable to restrain his hilarity, stamped the floor and slammed the table.

"Hey, Rat-nose!" Don Eugenio called, "have you ever stumbled on a tiger? Fill your glass, and tell us if you've run into one around here, come on."

The Rat put down half a pint. His tiny eyes shone. He wiped his lips with the sleeve of his greasy jacket and proceeded to say in a sincere, candid tone: "When it comes to *trigers* . . . up in these mountains there aren't no trigers, and if there was, I'd have killed them already. But I'll tell you what happened to me once in August, on Saint Mary's Day."

"At ten minutes past three in the afternoon?" Don Eugenio asked.

"No. It must have been eleven in the morning, maybe earlier. I swear it by the light shining upon us. I was coming back from shooting doves in a field, and I ran into Uncle Pepe's little girl, from Naya, who was pulling a cow just like this," and he rolled an imaginary rope around his wrist. 'Good day.' 'Nice and good.' 'Will you give me those birds?' 'And what do I get for them, lass?' 'I don't have a penny.' 'Then let me suck from the cow, I'm dying of thirst.' 'Go ahead, but don't suck her dry.' I kneel like this"—the Rat went halfway down on his knees before the abbot of Naya— "I milk the cow in the palm of my hand, and forgive my saying so, I gulp the milk. How fresh it was! 'Lass, may Saint Anthony keep your cow.' I walk, and walk, and walk, and after a while I get so sleepy. I feel numb all over. 'Let's take a nap!' I go straight up into the mountain, and when I find a place where the bushes are taller than me, I lie down like this, if I may say so, I take off my hat, and I drop it like this—mind you!—on the grass. And I sleep and don't wake up till an hour and a half later. I grab my hat to leave and, as true as we all have to die and rise again on Judgment Day, underneath I find a snake fatter than my right arm, forgive me for saying so!"

"But no fatter than your left arm?" Don Eugenio interrupted slyly.

"Much fatter!" the Rat proceeded, "and all coiled up and up, so that it could fit in there, sleeping like the blessed."

"What about snoring, did it snore?"

"The damned thing had sniffed the milk and then had the notion to hide under my hat. I knew what it was up to. It was fixing to sneak into my mouth, if you forgive me for saying so!"

There was a great uproar, which the priest of Boán moderated somewhat by reminding the audience of many similar cases: people claiming that they had found snakes in stables, or that they had climbed into babies' cribs to drink the milk from their stomachs.

Julián found the evening cheerful and entertaining, for the merriment and humor of the hunters dispelled his anxieties of the past few days: his fear of the Sage, Primitivo, and the house of Ulloa; and his gloomy forebodings, intensified by Nucha's nervous terror. Don Eugenio, seeing him in such a good disposition, urged him to join them for the next hunt. Julián declined, under the pretext that he had to say mass and pray at the canonical hours. In truth, he did not want to leave Señorita Marcelina alone; but Don Eugenio insisted so much that at last he agreed to join them for the first day.

"I'll have none of that," the jocular priest replied. "We'll take you with us tomorrow morning, and we'll come back early the day after tomorrow."

All resistance would have been in vain, particularly at such a time, when the rumpus increased and the wine in the jugs decreased. Julián knew that these rough-and-ready men were quite capable of dragging him by force if he refused to go of his own accord.

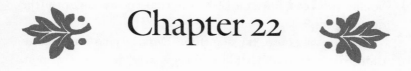

Chapter 22

And so he had to leave at daybreak, his teeth clattering with cold as he rode the tame little mule and endured the jokes of the hunters about his clothes, which were rather unsuitable for the occasion: he had no sheepskin jacket, no leather boots, no wide-brimmed hat, and no offensive or defensive weapons of any kind.

The day began clear and splendid. Frost crystals sparkled on the grass, and the cold earth trembled and steamed slightly at the first caress of the sun. The hunters marched at a brisk and athletic military step on the ground hardened by the winter freeze.

They reached the hunting site about nine o'clock and then scattered over the mountain. Julián, who did not know what to do with himself, stayed near Don Eugenio and watched him perform two cynegetic feats and stuff into his game bag two partridge chicks still warm with life. It must be clarified that Don Eugenio had no reputation as a great shot; for this reason, when the hunters assembled at midday to eat at an oak wood, the priest of Naya appealed to Julián as a witness to testify that he had seen him shoot them down on the wing.

"What do you mean by 'on the wing,' Don Julián?" everybody asked him.

As the chaplain was unable to answer such an insidious question, it occurred to the hunters that it would be amusing to give him a gun and a dog and send him to shoot something. Willy-nilly, he had to consent. They chose Chonito, an infallible purebred hound with a cleft nose, the keenest and most dependable of all the dogs present.

"As soon as you see the dog stop," Don Eugenio explained to the novice hunter, who hardly knew how to hold a deadly weapon, "you must get ready and encourage him to go; when the partridges come out, take aim, and when they spread their wings, shoot. It's the easiest thing in the world."

Chonito walked with his nose on the ground. His flanks twitched impatiently; now and then he turned around to see if the hunter still followed behind. Suddenly he broke into a trot toward a bush, and then stood tense and motionless, like a bronze statue waiting to be placed on a pedestal.

"Now!" the priest of Naya shouted. "Julián, make him go in!"

"Go in, Chonito, go in," the chaplain whispered languidly.

The dog, surprised at the soft tone of the order, hesitated. Finally he charged into the bushes. Immediately there was a flapping of wings and the flock came out flying in all directions.

"Now, you fool, now! Shoot!" Don Eugenio shouted.

Julián pulled the trigger. The birds flew speedily and disappeared out of sight in a second. Chonito, confused, looked at the shooter, at the gun, at the ground. The noble animal seemed to be inquiring with his eyes where the wounded partridge had fallen, so that he could retrieve it.

Half an hour later the same scene—including Chonito's disappointment—took place again. Nor was this the last time. Later on in a field the dog roused another flock, so numerous and so well placed within range that it was impossible not to hit two or three birds, even shooting at random. Julián fired once more. The hound barked with enthusiasm and excitement . . . but not a single partridge dropped. Chonito then fixed on the chaplain an almost human look full of contempt, turned around, and ran away like mad, ignoring the imperative voices that called him.

It is difficult to put into words how this spark of intelligence was celebrated at dinner. Julián was mercilessly teased, and as penance for his clumsiness he was condemned to sit out, tired though he was, and wait for hares.

The December moon looked like a polished silver disk hanging from a dark glass dome. The sky appeared higher and wider through this transparent, calm, and almost boreal atmosphere. Frost was forming, and the air seemed riddled with myriads of tiny, sharp needles, which pricked the flesh and concentrated all vital warmth in the heart. But for the hare, wrapped in its rich mantle of soft and luscious fur, it was a night to munch the tender buds of the pines, the fresh grass heavy with dew, the aromatic plants of the forest; it was also a night of love, a night to pursue the shy maiden of slim ears and brief tail, to surprise her, move her, and drag her to the dark depths of the pine wood . . .

On these nights, the hunters wait in ambush behind the pine trees and the underbrush. Lying on their stomachs, the barrels of their guns covered with paper so that the smell of powder may not reach the keen-scented nose of the hare, they apply their ears to the ground, sometimes for endless hours. The light, irregular hop of the game reverberates clearly on the frozen ground; then the hunter shivers, straightens up, plants his knee firmly on the earth, rests his gun on his right shoulder, tilts his head, and fingers the trigger nervously before he pulls it. Finally, by the moonlight, he makes out a fantastic monster that, leaping prodigiously, appears and disappears like a vision. The darkness of the trees alternating with spectral and oblique moonbeams makes the helpless hare seem enormous; the contrast enlarges its ears, renders its leaps fantastic and terrifying, its movements dazzlingly quick. But the hunter, with his finger already on the trigger, refrains from shooting. He knows that the phantom dashing across his firing range is the female, the Dulcinea chased and courted by innumerable suitors in heat. Her modesty keeps her in the warren during the day until at night, hungry and tired, she comes out to eat the tips of the pine shoots. At least three or four anxious males run after her, seeking romantic adventures. If the lady is allowed to pass by, none of her nocturnal beaus will stop his mad race, even when he hears the shot that reaps his rival's life, even when he stumbles on his bloody corpse, even when the stench of powder warns him: "At the end of your romance is death!"

No, they will not stop. Perhaps the cowardly instinct inherent in their species will prompt them to hide briefly behind a bush or a rock. But at the first imperceptible erotic whiff carried by the constant breeze, at the first breath of the female that drowns out the scent of the pine resin, the ardent pursuers will race again with renewed zest, blind with love and seized by desire, and the watch-ful hunter will drop them one by one at his feet, on the very grass where they dreamed of making their nuptial bed.

Chapter 23

For some time the chaplain had had a happy, victorious rival in the heart of the little Ulloa heiress: Perucho. All he had to do to conquer her was introduce himself. One day he tiptoed into the room and stole unheard up to the crib. Once in a while Nucha offered him candy and small coins, and the boy, as usually happens with tamed wild animals, developed such familiarity and attachment that it was difficult to get rid of him. He was to be found in the most unexpected places, like a spoiled kitten.

The baby instantly bewildered him. Neither the new chicks coming out of the eggs, nor Linda's puppies, nor the cow's calves monopolized Perucho's attention like this. He did not understand how and whence this new creature had arrived, and lost himself in thought on this subject. He hung around the crib constantly, risking a smack or two from the nurse; unless they ordered him out, he stood still, self-absorbed and enraptured, while he sucked his finger and looked more than ever like those garden cherubs who with their attitude seem to say: "Silence." Never before had he been quiet for so long. As soon as the baby became conscious of the world around her, she made it clear that if Perucho was interested in her, she was no less interested in Perucho. Both characters immediately acknowledged their mutual importance, and this recognition was followed by obvious signs of harmony and happiness. The moment the little girl spotted Perucho her eyes shone, and from her half-open mouth came, together with the warm and crystalline saliva of her teething, a most sweet gurgle. She stretched out her hands anxiously and Perucho, who understood her orders, bent his head before her and closed his eyes. Then the baby satisfied her whim by pulling his curly hair at will, and sticking her finger- tips into his mouth, ears, and nose, accompanying these motions with the same gurgle and a shriek of joy when, for example, she found his earholes.

After a couple of months of nursing, a child's temper grows sour, and as the teething process begins, crying spells and tantrums become more frequent. When this happened to her girl, Nucha used Perucho's presence as a talisman. One day the baby would not stop crying, and it was necessary to resort to more drastic mea- sures: Perucho had to sit in a low chair and hold the little one in his arms. He sat quiet and still, hardly daring to breathe, with his eyes fixed and wide open. He looked so handsome that one could have devoured him with kisses. Without transition the baby passed from rage to peace, and opened her large, toothless mouth to laugh: she laughed with her lips, her eyes, her dancing feet, which gently kicked Perucho's thigh. The boy was so charmed that he did not dare even to turn his head.

As the child's awareness grew, Perucho racked his brains to bring her toys that amused her immensely. Who knows how the little rascal managed to find new things everywhere—flowers, live birds, crossbows of cane, and all sorts of rubbish, which was what she preferred! One day he would show up with a frog tied by a leg, contorting itself grotesquely; or, beaming with pride, he would bring her a newly born mouse, so tiny and scared that it was pitiful to see. The little devil specialized in animate toys. Inside his torn cap, riddled with holes, he stored lizards, butterflies, and "little creatures of God"; in his pockets and inside his shirt, nests, fruit, and worms. The lady of the house gently pulled his ears. "If you bring any more disgusting things in here . . . you'll see. I'll hang you from the chimney and smoke you like sausage." Julián tolerated this intimacy until he discovered another of a less innocent kind. Since that morning when he saw Sabel leave Don Pedro's room, he had felt a chill down his spine every time he stumbled on the little boy and realized the affection that Nucha bestowed on him.

One day the priest walked into the lady's room and beheld an unexpected sight. A colossal earthenware bowl filled with steaming hot water stood in the middle of the chamber. Perucho and the heiress of Ulloa were bathing naked, the boy holding the baby tightly in his arms. Nucha had squatted down to keep watch over them.

"There was no other way to make her take her bath," she explained when she noticed Julián's astonishment, "and Don Máximo says that baths are good for her."

"It isn't she that surprises me," the chaplain replied, "but he, who's more afraid of water than of fire. I can't believe that he's taking a bath!"

"To be with the baby," Nucha answered, "he would let me bathe him in boiling tar. Here you have them, in their glory. Don't they look like brother and sister?"

As she asked this question in all simplicity, Nucha glanced up at Julián. His immediate discomfiture was so revealing, so eloquent and profound, that Señora Moscoso, leaning on one hand, rose suddenly and stood up to face him. In these features consumed by long illness; in this fine skin, through which a net of veins was visible; in these large, moist, vague eyes surrounded by blue circles, Julián saw a horrible light of certainty, shock, and terror flash behind the eyelashes. He remained silent. He had no courage to articulate a single sentence or to pull himself together.

The baby smiled in the pleasant warmth of the bath. Perucho, holding her by the armpits and calling her all sorts of affectionate nicknames, swung her in the pellucid liquid and opened her thighs so that she could feel the touch of the water everywhere, imitating faithfully what he had seen Nucha do. The scene took place in one of the smallest rooms of the house, which was divided into two by an oversized and mistreated eighteenth-century screen decorated with fantastic landscapes: rows of pointed trees that looked like so many lettuce heads, mountains similar to cheeses of Saint Simón, clouds in the shape of bread rolls, houses with a red roof, two windows, and a door, always facing the viewer. The screen hid Nucha's bed, with its gilded canopy and baroque pillars, and the baby's crib. The lady, after she had remained still for a few seconds, suddenly seemed to recover her mobility. She bent over the bowl and tore her daughter from Perucho's arms.

The infant, surprised and frightened by the violent interruption of her amusement, broke into disconsolate crying. But her mother did not pay her any attention; she ran behind the screen, dropped the baby into the crib, tucked her in hurriedly, and came out at once. Perucho sat in the water, rather shocked; the lady seized him by the shoulders, by the hair, and pushed him cruelly, stark naked as he was, across the room and out the door.

"Get out!" she said, paler than ever, her eyes flaring. "I don't want to see you in here again. If you ever come back I'll whip you, do you hear? I'll whip you!"

She disappeared behind the screen again, and Julián followed her, confused, unable to understand what was happening. Her head was lowered and her lips trembled. With shaky hands she arranged the covers over her daughter, whose crying already had the inflections of an adult's sorrow.

"Call the nurse," Nucha ordered dryly.

Julián rushed to obey her. At the doorstep something lay across the floor. He lifted his foot: it was Perucho, naked and curled up, crying silently; one could see only the large, glistening tears and the anguished spasms of his chest. The chaplain felt sorry for the boy and lifted him up. His flesh, still wet, was blue and stiff. "Here are your clothes," he told him. "Take them to your mother so that she can dress you. Hush."

Perucho, insensitive as a Spartan to physical pain, thought only of the injustice committed against him. "I wasn't doing anything wrong . . .," he stammered, short of breath. "Nothing wrong, no . . . thing . . ."

Julián returned with the nurse. It took the baby a long time to find consolation in her breast. She applied her mouth to the nipple, and then suddenly grimaced, sobbed, and began to cry painfully. Nucha abandoned her retreat behind the screen and walked mechanically to the window, signaling Julián to follow her. Both distraught, they contemplated each other for a few minutes, she questioning him with imperative eyes, he determined to deceive, to lie. Certain things present problems only when considered in cold blood; in critical moments instinct solves them with wonderful confidence. Julián was prepared to violate the truth without scruples.

At last Nucha said hoarsely: "You mustn't think this is the first time it has occurred to me that . . . the boy is . . . my husband's son. I've already thought of it; but it was always as brief as lightning, the sort of idea one casts away as soon as one conceives it. Now . . . this is altogether different. The minute I saw your face . . ."

"For heaven's sake, Señorita Marcelina! What has my face got to do with it? I beg you, don't get upset. This has to be the devil's work. My God!"

"I'm not upset," she answered, breathing hard and running the palm of her hand across her forehead.

"God help us! You're in a state, señorita. Your color is changing. I can see an attack coming on. Do you want your medicine?"

"No, a thousand times no! I'm perfectly all right, it's just a little tightness in my throat. It happens often, it's like a lump in here;

and at the same time I feel as if something were drilling into my temples. Now, to the point: tell me what you know; don't spare me anything."

"Señorita . . ." Julián then decided inwardly to resort to the so-called Jesuitic subterfuge, which is simply the normal recourse of those who detest lies but do not dare tell the truth. "Señorita . . . I curse my face. What a notion you had! I never thought of such a thing. No, madam, no."

The wife looked even harder into the chaplain's eyes and asked him two or three specific, decisive questions. It was time for Jesuitic resourcefulness again or, in other words, for the white lie.

"You may believe me, why should I tell you something that isn't true? I don't know who the boy's father is. No one knows for sure. Most likely, it is the girl's lover."

"How do you know that she has a . . . lover?"

"That's as plain as daylight."

"And are you sure that the lover is a village lad?"

"Yes, madam, a young man, and handsome, too. He's the one who plays the bagpipe at the festivals of Naya and everywhere else. I saw him come here a hundred times last year and . . . they went together. Furthermore, I know from the horse's mouth that they are getting their papers in order to marry, yes, madam, straight from the horse's mouth. So, you see . . ."

Nucha breathed again and raised her right hand to her throat, which was undoubtedly oppressed by the familiar suffocation. Her features became somewhat calmer, although they did not regain their usual composure and charming serenity; the frown and erratic look persisted.

"My girl!" she whispered. "My girl in his arms! No matter what you say and swear, Julián, we must remedy this situation. How am I going to live like this? You should have warned me before! If that woman and the boy don't leave I shall go mad. I'm sick. These things hurt me . . . They hurt me."

She smiled bitterly and added: "This is my luck. I've never harmed anyone. I married to my father's taste, and . . . look how things are turning out."

"Señorita . . ."

"Don't deceive me, not you." She emphasized the last two words. "You grew up in my house, Julián. For me you're part of the family. I have no other friend here. I need your advice."

"Señorita," Julián exclaimed vehemently, "I would gladly give the blood in my veins to spare you all the troubles of this world."

"Either that woman gets married and leaves," Nucha declared, "or . . ." Here she interrupted her sentence. In certain critical moments the mind contemplates two or three truculent, extreme solutions that the tongue, more cowardly, does not dare formulate.

"But, Señorita Marcelina, don't kill yourself like this," Julián insisted. "It's all in your imagination, señorita, just in your imagination."

She held his hands between hers, which were burning. "Tell my husband to send her away, Julián. For the love of God and his blessed Mother!"

The touch of these feverish hands and the supplication stirred the chaplain beyond words. Without stopping to think, he exclaimed: "I've told him so many times!"

"You have!" she said, shaking her head and folding her hands.

They spoke no more. From the fields came the hoarse croaking of the crows. Behind the screen the baby cried inconsolably. Nucha shivered and finally said, as she tapped her knuckles on the windowpanes: "Then, I shall tell him."

The chaplain whispered as if he were praying. "For goodness' sake, señorita, don't let your head spin. Forget about it."

Señora Moscoso closed her eyes and leaned her face on the window glass. She struggled to compose herself: the vitality and serenity of her character were trying to survive the violent storm, but her shoulders shook convulsively and betrayed the tyranny of her nerves over her weakened organism. The trembling gradually decreased and then ceased altogether. Nucha turned around, with dry eyes and her nerves already tamed.

Chapter 24

Shortly after these events the stagnant and sleepy life of the house of Ulloa underwent a change. A certain witch, more powerful than María, the Sage, entered the scene: it was politics, if a tangle of village intrigues and miseries merits this name. Everywhere the cloak of politics covers ignoble, selfish interests, apostasy, and vileness; but at least in the city the appearance—and sometimes the goals—of the struggle assumes grandiose dimensions. The magnitude of the arena lends nobility to the fight, greed rises to the level of ambition, and on occasion, material gain is sacrificed to victory for victory's sake. In the country, on the other hand, not even hypocrisy or pretensions achieve the semblance of a lofty general purpose. Ideas play no part in the game, but only people, and at their worst: resentment, hatred, vindictiveness, wretched profit making, microscopic vanity. A sea battle in a puddle.

One must admit, however, that in revolutionary days political passion and fanatic faith in theories infiltrated everything, and like a hurricane blew through the noxious atmosphere of ordinary village plots. At the time the fate of Spain hung on parliamentary debates and a cry uttered here or there, in an armory or in the thick of a mountain. Every two or three weeks vital questions were examined and discussed, in the hope that definitive solutions might be found. Problems that the legislator, the statesman, and the sociologist must study for years before they can come to grips with them, a revolutionary crowd will solve in a few hours by means of a heated session in parliament or a clamorous demonstration in the street. Between breakfast and lunch a whole society was reformed; over a cigar new principles were formulated. The two great solutions for our race lay at the bottom of the whirlpool, both strong because they rested on a secular basis slowly baked in the oven of history: absolutism and constitutional monarchy, which at the time was disguised as democratic monarchy.

The commotion of the clash echoed in all directions, including the wild mountains that surround the house of Ulloa. Here, too, everyone played politics. In the taverns of Cebre on the day of the fair there was talk of religious freedom, individual rights, the abolition of conscription, federation, and plebiscite—pronounced according to everybody's fancy, of course. After services, funerals, and solemn masses, the clergy lingered in the atrium and argued passionately about symptomatic and eloquent recent events, like the first appearance of the notorious *four sextons,* and other trifles of the sort. The young gentleman of Limioso, a hard-boiled traditionalist like his father and grandfather, had made two or three mysterious incursions into the Miño territory, on the other side of the Portuguese border, and rumor had it that he held conferences with certain sly fellows in Tuy. It was also said that the ladies of Molende were busy those days making cartridge belts and other military implements, and that they had received secret warnings that their house would be searched.

The experts in the matter, however, realized that any armed uprising in Galician territory would founder; and that, regardless of the rumors about mobilization in Portugal, the coming of troops, appointment of officers, et cetera, the real battle would not take place in the field but in the ballot box, although it would be equally bloody. At that time the area was governed by two formidable chieftains, a lawyer and the secretary of the town council of Cebre: this little village and its surrounding countryside trembled under their power. Because they were tireless opponents, their struggle,

like those between Roman dictators, could end only with the defeat and death of one of them. To write the chronicle of their
exploits, revenges, and manipulations would be an endless task.
Lest someone think that their feats were laughable, it is necessary to clarify that some of the crosses erected by the roads, some
charred roofs, some men imprisoned for life, could testify to this
unrelenting antagonism.

It is important to know that neither of the two rivals had any
political ideas or cared a fig about what was at stake in Spain;
but for strategic reasons, each of them embodied a tendency and
a party: Barbacana, a moderate before the revolution, now declared himself a Carlist; Trampeta, a Unionist under O'Donnell,
had moved to the fringe of victorious liberalism.

Barbacana was more serious and authoritarian, more stubborn
and implacable in his personal vengeance, more certain when he
struck a blow, more hypocritical and greedy, more skillful in covering his treacherous methods of fleecing the poor peasant. In addition, he was a man who preferred to use legal means and abide
by the law: he argued that there is no better way to finish off an
enemy than to wrap him up in paper. If Barbacana was not responsible for as many crosses by the roads as his rival, his pervasive
influence was evident, formerly in the stinking district prisons and
currently in the walls of Ceuta and Melilla.[1] Trampeta, on the other
hand, although he did justice to his nickname by also participating
in shady lawsuits, usually acted more recklessly and violently than
Barbacana, and therefore was less able to secure his retreat. Thus on
several occasions his opponent caught him red-handed and nearly
destroyed him. Trampeta, to even the score, possessed great ingenuity and audacity, unexpected expedients with which to avoid
being seriously compromised. Barbacana's forte was to prepare an

1. Spanish colonies in northern Africa.

ambush from his room and retrieve the corpse later; Trampeta performed the deed in person and successfully. The county abhorred
both of them, but Barbacana's gloomy countenance inspired more
terror. On this occasion Trampeta, who represented the prevalent
official ideology, felt confident enough of his impunity to burn half
of Cebre if necessary, and beat, sue, and confiscate the other half.
Barbacana, with his superior intelligence and education, understood two things: first, that he was leaning on a more solid wall,
on the kind of people who would not desert their friends; second,
that whenever he wished to move with all his weapons and bag-
gage to the other side, he could always sink Trampeta's ship. He
already had a scheme for the coming election of deputies.

With tireless energy Trampeta pulled the rug from under the
feet of the government's candidate. He traveled frequently to the
city to hold conferences with the governor. On these trips the secretary, reckoning that one can never be too cautious, took along
his pistols and his pluckiest partisans, for he knew that Barbacana
depended on a few tough men, especially the fearsome One-eye of
Castrodorna. Each of these visits proved to be very fruitful for the
secretary and his followers. Barbacana's bastions fell one by one.
State monopolies, bailiwicks, prison guards, road workers—the
whole official staff of Cebre was shaped to suit Trampeta's taste.
Only the judge, protected from above by a prominent relative of
his wife, resisted. Trampeta also succeeded in convincing people
to look the other way on many issues, to stick their heads into the
sand on others, and in some cases, to become entirely blind; afterward, by virtue of the authority with which he had been invested,
he declared with his hand on his heart that he guaranteed victory
at the coming elections in Cebre.

Throughout this period Barbacana lay low. He limited himself
to giving his lukewarm, matter-of-fact support to the candidate
proposed by the Carlist junta of Orense, who was recommended

by the archpriest of Loiro and other active priests, like those of Boán, Naya, and Ulloa. It was clear that Barbacana entertained no hopes of success. The candidate was a respected person from Orense, a cultivated and loyal traditionalist; but he had no roots in the county and, apparently, no political cunning. His colleagues themselves did not get along with him, because they regarded him as a bureaucrat rather than a man of action and intrigue.

In this state of affairs it was observed that Primitivo, the hunt master of the house of Ulloa, went to Cebre very often. As in this village nothing passed unnoticed, it was also observed that, besides his usual visits to the taverns, Primitivo spent long hours at Barbacana's house. The latter lived practically confined at home because Trampeta, drunk with power, threatened that Barbacana would "pay his debt" in a *corredoira*—that is, a deep gorge. The lawyer, however, took the risk of appearing in public accompanied by Primitivo. Influential priests and subordinate leaders walked in and out of his house; many of them also went to the house of Ulloa, some for lunch and others in the evening. And as there is no well-kept secret among many people, the region and the government soon heard the great news: the junta's candidate had graciously withdrawn, and in his place Barbacana supported Don Pedro Moscoso, known as the marquis of Ulloa, as the independent candidate.

As soon as he got wind of the plot, Trampeta seemed seized by Saint Vitus's dance. Every other day he traveled to the city and explained himself profusely in the governor's office.

"The one to blame," he said, "is that pig, the archpriest. He and the rebellious priest of Boán are spurring that miser, the steward of the house of Ulloa, who in turn has involved that ill-bred master of his who sleeps with his daughter. Some candidate," he shouted at the top of his lungs, "they have chosen! At least the other one was an honest man!" (He yelled even louder when he reached this point about honesty.)

When the governor saw that the liberal leader had lost his temper, he realized that things were not going well, and he asked sternly: "Didn't you guarantee our victory, regardless of the candidate they present?"

"Yes, sir, I did," Trampeta hastened to reply. "But who would have expected a trick like this?"

Full of rage and contempt, he stumbled on his own words and insisted that no one could have thought that the marquis of Ulloa, a gentleman who cared only for hunting, would go into politics; that despite the power and prestige of the house of Ulloa among the peasants, the mountain aristocracy, and the clergy, the attempt would be doomed if it had not been taken up by Barbacana and a powerful subordinate leader, who up to now had oscillated between Barbacana's and Trampeta's parties, but this time had made his choice. He was no other than the steward of the house of Ulloa himself. A resolute man as clever as a fox, who had plundered the house of Ulloa and quietly enriched himself at its expense, he counted on many secure votes from numerous people who owed him money. This rascal, protected by the great litigator Barbacana, would carry with him the whole district unless they took drastic action.

Anyone who is in the least acquainted with electoral mechanisms will not doubt that the governor lost no time in telegraphing the following order: in spite of any obstacle, the judge of Cebre and the few stalwarts that Barbacana still had in the district should be removed. The governor had hoped to win Cebre without resorting to extraordinary measures or gross arbitrariness, for he knew that although uprisings were unlikely in this territory, human blood was often spilled over electoral ballots. This new coalition, however, forced him to cast aside his scruples and endow the illustrious Trampeta with unlimited powers.

While the secretary took preventive steps, the lawyer did not let the grass grow under his feet. The marquis accepted his nomination instantly and with glee. Don Pedro had no political ideas, although he leaned toward absolutism, believing naively that it would reestablish the privileges that flattered his aristocratic pride, such as entails and primogeniture. Aside from this, he partook of the peasants' indifferent skepticism and, unlike the gentleman of Limioso, was incapable of dreaming of a quixotic charge across the Miño border at the head of two hundred men. But though he lacked political passion, his vanity prompted him to accept. He was the first personality in the province, and his family the most distinguished; since time immemorial, his lineage had towered above the county nobility. It was on the strength of this argument that the archpriest of Loiro insisted that he must represent the district. He simply said, using an expressive plural and closing his fist: "We've got the county in here."

As soon as the news spread, the gentleman became the object of flattery from various people who came to pay him homage: all the neighboring gentry, practically the entire clergy, and Barbacana's numerous followers, under his personal leadership. Don Pedro beamed with satisfaction. He fully realized that Primitivo was behind the scenes, but after all, he was the anointed one. During these days he was extremely cordial and in an excellent mood. He patted his daughter and gave orders to put a new embroidered dress on her to impress the ladies of Molende, who had promised to the representative of the mountain aristocracy no less than one hundred votes. All new candidates go through a period of time in which they court their candidacy as one courts a girl, shaving with great care and displaying their physical charms. He, too, polished his looks, deplorably neglected since his return to the house of Ulloa; and as he was then at the height of his masculine beauty, the milkers of the electoral cow boasted about their handsome candidate for the Congress. At that time political passion took advantage of stature, hair color, and age.

As soon as the pot began to boil, the house of Ulloa opened

its doors to everybody. Filomena and Sabel marched through the rooms carrying trays with sweet wine, sherry, and cakes. One could hear the tinkling of spoons inside coffee cups and the clinking of glasses against each other. Down in the kitchen Primitivo presented his friends with wine from Borde, cod stew, and large plates of pork and vegetables. Often the guests upstairs joined the ones downstairs to argue, laugh, and tell salacious stories; they also excoriated—any softer word would be inadequate—Trampeta and his crew, and amid laughter, cigars, and exclamations they stirred up the vast detritus of major and minor frauds on which the secretary's fortune rested.

The priest of Boán, a stubborn old man with fire in his eyes and a reputation as the best shot in the district after Primitivo, said: "This time we've got them, *quoniam!*"

Nucha did not attend the meetings of the committee. She put in an appearance only when the visitors required it or when she had to supply necessary items for the perpetual banquet; afterward she fled. Julián also came seldom to these reunions, and when he did he spoke hardly at all, thus confirming the abbot of Ulloa in his opinion that stylish chaplains are good for nothing. However, as soon as the committee found out that Julián wrote with a beautiful hand and an impeccable orthography, his services were required for all important letters. In addition, another task fell upon him.

The archpriest of Loiro, who had been a close friend of Don Pedro's mother, Doña Micaela, wished to go through the entire house again and visit the chapel, in which he had said mass several times while the lady ("God rest her soul") was alive. Don Pedro showed him around indifferently. The archpriest received a shock when he entered. The chapel was practically roofless; the rain streamed down the altarpiece; the garments on the images looked like rags; everything lay in the cold neglect and peculiar sadness of abandoned churches. Julián had grown tired of dropping useless hints to the marquis about the pitiful condition the chapel was in; but the archpriest's astonishment and lamentations hurt the vanity of the Ulloa heir, who deemed it appropriate at a time like this to do some cosmetic repairs. A new roof was quickly built, and a painter from Orense painted and gilded the side and central altarpieces, with the result that the chapel was transformed. Don Pedro showed it with pride to priests, gentlemen, and Barbacana's landlords. The only thing that remained to be done was to dress the saints decently and sew ornaments and altar cloths. Nucha undertook this job under Julián's supervision. To do their work, they sought refuge in the solitary chapel, away from the hubbub of the electoral club. Between the two of them they undressed Saint Peter, combed the Immaculate Virgin's curls, trimmed Saint Anthony's sackcloth, and scrubbed the nimbus of the Christ child. Even the charity box of the souls in Purgatory was carefully washed and polished, and the naked, languid, tortured souls surrounded by red flames came to light in all their edifying ugliness. This occupation was delightful to Julián. The hours went by insensibly in the quiet precinct, which smelled of fresh paint and cattails, brought by Nucha to decorate the altars. He felt no need to talk while he set a leaf of silver paper on a wire stalk or rubbed the glass of an urn with a damp cloth. A peaceful inner happiness filled his soul. Sometimes Nucha simply gave him directions from a low chair, with her child in her arms, for she would not leave her for a minute.

Julián worked for the two of them, climbing on a ladder to the top of the altarpiece. He dared not ask about her private affairs, or inquire if she had reached a definitive agreement with her husband regarding Sabel; but he noticed the lady's discouragement, the black circles under her eyes, her frequent sighs, and drew logical conclusions from these signs. He also perceived other symptoms that agitated his imagination and preoccupied him. Nucha had showed lately a vehement, exalted motherly love. No sooner had she left her daughter than, restless and alarmed, she rushed to see if anything was wrong with her. One day when she did not find her where she expected, she began to shriek desperately: "They've taken her away from me, they've stolen my daughter!" Fortunately the wet nurse appeared just then with the baby in her arms. Sometimes Nucha kissed her so frantically that the child broke into tears; or she contemplated her enraptured, with a sweet, ineffable smile, and then Julián would think of the pictures of the Virgin Mother in wonderment at her own miraculous maternity. But while the moments of quiet affection were brief, fear and anguished tenderness were constant. She did not allow Perucho to approach them. Her expression changed when she spotted the boy; and he, forgetting his devilish adventures, his thievery, and his fondness for the stables, crawled to the entrance of the chapel and waited in ambush. When the little one came out, he greeted her with all sorts of blandishments that she repaid with cherubic giggles and unrestrained joy, launching her little body forward, impatient to exchange the nurse's arms for Perucho's.

One day Julián noticed in Nucha something still more serious. It was not only a melancholy air, but an overwhelming physical and moral depression. Her eyes were swollen and burning, as if she had cried for a long time, her voice faint and tired, her lips dry and cracked from fever and insomnia. It was no longer the thorn of pain slowly piercing her heart, but a dagger suddenly thrust in to the hilt. This sight overrode the priest's caution. "You're ill, señorita. You're not well today."

Nucha shook her head, trying to smile. "I'm fine. It's nothing."

"For heaven's sake, señorita, don't deny it! I see it as clear as daylight. Señorita Marcelina, my patron Saint Julián help me! Can't I be useful to you, give you some help and comfort? I'm a humble, useless person, but my good will, señorita, is as big as a mountain. I tell you from the bottom of my heart, I wish you'd order me to do something—something!"

As he made these protestations, he brandished a chalk-covered rag and rubbed it hard over the metal frames of the prayer cards, without looking at them.

Nucha lifted her eyes, and in them flashed a brief impulse to cry, to protest, to ask for help. But the flame quickly extinguished itself and the lady, with a slight shrug, repeated: "I'm fine. It's nothing, Julián."

On the floor stood a basket full of hydrangeas and green branches cut to fill the flower vases; Nucha began to arrange them with the graceful skill and delicacy that she displayed in all domestic chores. Julián, half fascinated and half afflicted, followed with his eyes the arrangement of blue flowers in crockery vases, the movements of the frail hands through the green leaves. He saw a clear, heavy drop fall on them that did not come from the dew still clinging to the hydrangeas. Almost simultaneously his attention was drawn to something that chilled his blood: there was a round purple ring on Señora Moscoso's wrist. With sudden clarity the chaplain looked back two years: The screams of a woman beaten with the butt of a gun rang again in his ears; he remembered the kitchen, the raging man . . . Forgetting himself completely, he dropped the prayer cards and seized Nucha's hands to make sure that the sinister mark really existed.

A number of people began to walk in through the door—the ladies of Molende, the judge of Cebre, and the priest of Ulloa—led by Don Pedro, who brought them here to admire the work of restoration. Nucha turned around hurriedly. Julián, confused, stammered an answer to the ladies' greetings. Primitivo, from the background, riveted on him his direct, scrutinizing eyes.

Chapter 25

If an election lasted very long, it would be the death of its leaders from sheer exhaustion and physical and mental overexertion. Bitter hatred, constant fear of treason, ardent promises, threats, rumors, numerous journeys and letters back and forth, messages, plots, sleeplessness, and irregular meals make for a delirious and intolerable existence. With regard to the practical disadvantages of the parliamentary system, there was full agreement between the mare and the donkey that, together with the strong young stallion recently purchased by the steward for his personal use, constituted the stables of the Ulloa estate. Fine things they thought of the election in their equine and mulish minds, as they panted broken-winded after a rough trot, with their wretched bodies bathed in sweat!

And what can we say of the little mule that Trampeta rode to the city! It had become so skinny that its ribs stuck through the skin. Day and night the notorious chieftain traveled the highway, and at every trip the election seemed more difficult and uncertain. In the governor's office Trampeta shouted desperately that it was necessary to show strength, to dismiss some people and appoint others, to scare, to promise. Above all, the government's candidate had to loosen his purse strings; otherwise the district was lost, lost!

"Didn't you tell me," the governor vociferated one day, tempted to send the secretary to hell, "that this election would not be costly, that our opponents couldn't afford any expenses, that the Carlist junta of Orense wouldn't contribute a single cent, that the house of Ulloa didn't have a cent either, because despite its large income it is always in debt?"

"Well, sir, you see," Trampeta answered, "all this is true enough, but there are times when a man . . . has to change his plans, as you well know." (This was Trampeta's favorite expression.) "The marquis of Ulloa . . ."

"The marquis, my foot!" the governor interrupted impatiently.

"Well, folks are in the habit of calling him so. Let me tell you, for the last month I've been spreading to the winds that there is no such marquis, that the government has *expopiated* his title to give it to a liberal, and that it is Charles VII who offered him the title of marquis, in preparation for the return of the Inquisition and additional taxes, as you well know . . ."

"Go on!" exclaimed the governor, who seemed very nervous that day. "You were saying that the marquis, or whatever he is, given the state of affairs . . ."

"A couple thousand *duros*[1] more or less won't matter to him, sir."

"If he didn't have them, might he have borrowed them?"

"But of course! He must have asked his father-in-law in Santiago, and since his father-in-law in Santiago doesn't have a cent to spare, as you well know . . . then he must have got it from his father-in-law in the house of Ulloa."

"Do you mean that this Carlist candidate's got two fathers-in-law?" inquired the governor, who could not help being amused by the secretary's gossip.

"He wouldn't be the first, as you well know!" Trampeta said, laughing at the drollery. "You understand what I'm talking about, don't you?"

"Oh, yes! That girl who lived in the house before Moscoso got married and who has a son by him. You see, I remember."

1. The Spanish currency is based on the *peseta*. There are five *pesetas* in a *duro*.

"The son . . . Only heaven knows whose child he is, sir . . . for the mother herself is not quite sure."

"Fine, but this has nothing to do with the election. To the point: Moscoso's resources . . ."

". . . have been provided by his steward, Primitivo, the unofficial father-in-law. Now you ask me: how can a mere steward have so much money? And I say: from making loans at eight percent a month—even more in hard times—and scaring everybody so that they'll pay their debts to the last wretched cent. And you say: where does that thief Primitivo get the money he loans? And I answer: from his master's pockets, robbing him from the sales of produce, charging one price and paying him another, mismanaging the property and rents; in a word, cheating him, as you well know, by hook or by crook. And you say . . ."

This mode of dialogue was a Trampetian oratorical device that he used when he wanted to persuade an audience. The governor interrupted him: "If you allow me, I'll say it myself. Why should that rascal lend his master the fortune that he has so painstakingly stolen from him?"

"I'll be damned!" the secretary swore. "Nobody lends this kind of money, as you well know, without some kind of mortgage or guarantee. Primitivo wasn't born yesterday. This way he secures both his capital and his control over the master."

"I understand," the governor replied keenly; and trying to show his perceptiveness, he added: "His master's candidacy will benefit him, by strengthening his influence in the territory and increasing his freedom of action."

Trampeta looked at the governor with the mixture of wonder and cunning that people of humble status show when they hear their superiors make a stupid remark.

"As you well know, sir," he began, "it's nothing of the sort. Don Pedro, as candidate of the opposition, or as an independent, or as whatever they want to call him, isn't worth a fig to them. If Primitivo joined forces with your humble servant or with Barbacana, pardon my *expession,* he would accomplish whatever he wished, d'you know what I mean? He doesn't need his master to run for the Congress at all. Besides, Primitivo was always one of us, until he got this idea into his head. There's no fox like him in the whole province. He'll end up destroying both Barbacana and me."

"But, then, why has Barbacana taken Don Pedro's side?"

"Because Barbacana follows the priests wherever they go. You know his style. You or me may be here today and gone tomorrow; but the priests are always here, and so are the gentry: the Limiosos, the Méndezes . . ." The chieftain, giving free rein to his resentment, clenched his fists and added: "I'll be damned! As long as we don't sink Barbacana's ship there's nothing for us to do in Cebre."

"Fine; then find a way to sink it. I'm certainly willing."

Trampeta brooded for a while, scratching his goatee with his square, cigar-blackened thumbnail. "What I can't figure out is what that snake Primitivo will gain if his master wins. Now he profits by two things: what he gets from the mortgage, and what he claims as campaign expenses, for, as you well know, he fixes the bills as he pleases. But if they win, and Don Pedro is sworn in as a deputy and goes to Madrí[2] and there borrows money from other people— which he's sure to do—and gets his eyes opened to his steward's foul play, and forgets the wench and the boy, then . . ."

Once again he scratched his goatee meditatively, as if searching for the solution to a very intricate problem. His sharp intellectual faculties were on full alert, but he could not unravel the mystery.

"To the point," the governor insisted. "The main thing is to avoid a humiliating defeat. Our candidate is a cousin of the minister's. We have guaranteed our victory."

2. Madrid, in Trampeta's dialectical speech.

"Against the candidate of the junta of Orense."

"Do you expect that they will split hairs like that? We must win against no matter whom. Let's not beat around the bush: do you think that we'll have to turn tail and run, yes or no?"

Trampeta could not make up his mind. At last he lifted his face, proud as a great strategist who is always capable of inventing a ruse to deceive his enemy. "Look," he said, "so far Barbacana has not been able to finish me off, although he has played a few on me. When it comes to playing games nobody can beat me, but I don't come up with my best tricks until I'm in the thick of it; then the devil himself could not devise the things that occur to me. There's something stirring in here," and he struck his dark forehead with his fist. "I just can't get it out yet. But it will come out, as you well know, when the *critrical* moment arrives." And, flourishing his right arm up and down several times like a sword, he added pompously: "Fear not, we shall win!"

While the secretary parleyed with the highest civil authority of the province, Barbacana received the archpriest of Loiro, who had come to find out personally how things were going in Cebre. He sprawled in the lawyer's office, sniffing Macuba snuff from a silver box; probably nobody else in Galicia used this brand, smuggled into the country with great mystery and at a high cost.

The archpriest, known in Santiago as "Enveloping Envelopes" [3] because of an unfortunate and candid question that he had asked in a store, had been the most valuable electoral instrument in the province when he was merely the abbot of Anles. On one occasion, when they told him that the election he was running was lost, he shouted furiously: "The priest of Anles a loser?" and kicked the ballot box with such might that he shattered it into a thousand pieces

3. The humorous nickname is based on the archpriest's redundant use of identical words in French and Spanish, which betrays his ignorance of French.

THE HOUSE OF ULLOA 211

and scattered the ballots to the winds. By this simple method, he succeeded in taking his candidate to victory. The feat earned him the Great Cross of the Catholic queen Isabella. Obesity, age, and deafness prevented him from taking part in this election; but he maintained his addiction to the electoral process, and there were few things he enjoyed more.

Every time the archpriest came to Cebre he stayed a while in the post office, where people discussed politics to exhaustion, read newspapers from Madrid, and criticized every governor and statesman in the country. One could often overhear statements like: "If I were the president of the Council of Ministers, I'd settle the matter in a jiffy," or: "If I were in Prim's shoes, I wouldn't stop at such a trifle." From time to time, a cleric would raise his voice above the others and exclaim: "Put me in the pope's place, and you'll see how quickly I solve the problem."

When he left Barbacana's house the archpriest went to the post office, where he met the judge, the court clerk, and Don Eugenio, who stood by the door loosening his mare and getting ready to mount. "Wait a minute, Naya," he called to him familiarly, using the name of his parish according to priestly custom. "I'm going to read the newspaper reports and then we can ride together."

"I'm headed for the Ulloa estate."

"So am I. Tell the folks in the inn to bring my mule."

Don Eugenio obeyed diligently. Shortly afterward both clerics, wrapped in ample cloaks, with their hats tied under their chins so that the gusty wind would not blow them away, descended the steep road at the quiet pace of their beasts. Naturally, they talked about the impending battle, the candidate, and other particulars regarding the election. The archpriest saw everything in a rose-colored light, and was so certain of victory that he even thought of taking the band of Cebre to the house of Ulloa to serenade the elected deputy.

Don Eugenio seemed cheerful, but did not share these high expectations. The government is very strong—the devil take it!—and when it sees trouble coming it resorts to coercion and settles elections with the help of the civil guard. All this parliamentary stuff is, as the abbot of Boán says, a shameless farce.

"Well, this time," the archpriest replied as he struggled to free himself from his pelerine, which the wind wrapped around his face, "this time we'll make them choke on it. At any rate, the district of Cebre will send to the Congress a decent individual, a native of this county, the head of a respected old home, who understands us better than those scoundrels from outside."

"That's very true," answered Don Eugenio, who seldom disputed other people's views openly. "I'm as pleased as anybody that the house of Ulloa should represent Cebre. If it weren't for certain things that we all know . . ."

The archpriest pulled a serious face and took a pinch of snuff. He loved Don Pedro dearly; one could say that he had known him since he was born, and besides, he respected the aristocracy as a matter of principle.

"All right, all right," he grumbled, "let's forget all that gossip. Everybody has flaws and must account to God for his sins. We have no business meddling with other people's lives."

Don Eugenio, as if he had not heard these remarks, repeated all he had learned at the post office, where the news delivered by Trampeta to the governor was laced with scandalous commentaries. He spoke in a rather loud voice, so that the archpriest, despite his poor hearing, now further impaired by the wind, could follow the gist of his speech. The mischievous and malicious priest of Naya enjoyed enormously seeing the archpriest flushed and bloated, with his hand around his ear like a funnel and his nose stuck keenly into his snuffbox. According to Don Eugenio, Cebre waxed indignant against Don Pedro Moscoso. The peasants loved him well, but in town, where Trampeta's protégées ruled, horrors were circulated about the house of Ulloa. Since the marquis's nomination Cebre had seethed with a holy hatred of sin, a rebuke of concubinage and illegitimacy, an astonishingly exquisite sense of moral rectitude. It is worth noting that this fit of virtue struck only the secretary's satellites, most of whom were rough people of less than exemplary behavior. The archpriest went on a rampage when he heard these things.

"Pharisees, scribes!" he hissed. "And then they call us hypocrites! Look how modest, honorable, and bashful these uncircumcised natives of Cebre have become!" On the archpriest's lips, *uncircumcised* was a terrible insult. "As if a single one of that bunch of rascals hadn't earned time in prison! Hit them hard, I say, hard!"

Don Eugenio could not restrain his laughter.

"Seven years, it's been no less than seven years," the archpriest stammered, somewhat calmer but panting because of the wind, "since this business that now so shocks them started in the house of Ulloa. And damn it if they ever gave it a thought! But now, with elections coming . . . This accursed wind! We're going to be blown off, my boy."

"They even say worse things," the priest of Naya shouted.

"What? I can't hear a word in this hurricane!"

"That there are more serious rumors still," Don Eugenio shouted as he drew his restless little mare close to the reverend mule of the archpriest. "They say they're going to shoot us all. I, for one, have already been threatened by the secretary with indictment and prison."

"What indictment? Bend your head a little. That's right. Although we are alone, I don't want to speak too loudly."

Don Eugenio, clinging to his friend's cloak, told him something that the wings of the northeast wind took away at high speed, with a sharp and mocking whistle.

"Damnation!" the archpriest roared, unable to think of another word.

It took him a couple of minutes to recover his power of speech and spit into the increasingly wild and furious wind an anthology of insults against the infamous scandalmongers of Trampeta's party. The sly Don Eugenio let him ventilate his rage and then added: "There's still more!"

"What else can there be? Are they also saying that Don Pedro attacks travelers in the highways? Uncircumcised rabble, with no God and no law other than filling their bellies!"

"They claim that the news comes from somebody within the house."

"What? The devil take the wind!"

"That the source of information is within the house of Ulloa itself, do you understand?" and Don Eugenio winked.

"I understand. Heartless curs, scorpion tongues! A lady from such a good family, who's honesty itself—no offense to anyone—to slander her like this, and with an ordained minister of God! The worthless petty liberals we have around here sell their souls so cheap! The world is in disarray, Naya, in disarray!"

"They also say . . ."

"Heavens, aren't you done yet? What a storm is coming, Holy Mary! What wind!"

"Listen to me. What I'm going to tell you doesn't come from them but from Barbacana. He says that this person in the house—Primitivo, as you may have guessed—is going to pull a big one on us in this election."

"What? Are you kidding? Ho, mule! Let's see if I can hear you. You were saying that Primitivo . . ."

"It's not certain yet, it's not certain," the abbot of Naya shouted, finding the whole scene as funny as a comedy.

"Good gracious, this is too much! Are you trying to drive me crazy? I've got enough with the confounded wind! I don't want to hear it! I don't want to hear any more!" As he said this, a sudden gust of wind lifted his cloak upward, so that the archpriest looked like the familiar painting of Venus on her shell. As soon as he had managed to rearrange his attire, he put his mule into a trot. Now the only voice he heard along the road was that of the northeast wind, which, shaking chestnut and oak trees, intoned a majestic symphony in the distance.

Chapter 26

After the initial impression had subsided, Julián did not dare to cross-examine Nucha about what he had seen. He even hesitated, and not without reason, to go to her room. Despite his trusting nature, he suspected that somebody was spying on him. Who? Everyone: Primitivo, Sabel, the old witch, the servants. Just as at night one feels, without seeing it, the damp mist that penetrates the skin, Julián felt mistrust, malevolence, suspicion, and hatred closing around him. It was indefinable but evident. He attended two or three services in which he thought that the priests addressed him with hostility, the archpriest frowned at him, and only Don Eugenio treated him cordially. But maybe these were only vain delusions, and he might just have imagined that at table Don Pedro followed the direction of his eyes and watched his every move. This anxiety was aggravated by his irresistible compulsion to glance at Nucha often, to see out of the corner of his eye if she was thinner, if she ate with a good appetite, or if there were any new marks on her wrists. The dark circle of the first day had taken on a greenish hue and then disappeared.

Finally the urge to see the baby overrode Julián's reservations. After the restoration of the chapel was complete, he could see her only in her mother's room; and that was where he went, for the kiss he had stolen in the hall as the nurse carried her in her arms was not enough for him. The baby was coming out of that stage when infants look like a bundle of rags, and though she had not lost the appeal of all weak, helpless creatures, she had a charming personality, having grown more at ease in her movements and aware of her actions. By turns, she would pose as a Murillo angel; or pick up an object and take it to her warm mouth, impatient at her delayed teething; or, performing with wonderful grace a captivating movement of all small children, she would stretch out with absolute abandon not only her arms, but her whole body, to whoever earned her favor: what wet nurses call "getting on with people." Lately the child laughed louder, and her melodious, brief, sudden outbursts of joy were comparable only to the twitter of a bird. No articulate sound had yet come out of her mouth; but by onomatopoeia, which according to some philologists is the basis of primitive language, she was able to express clearly all her attachments and whims. Her skull began to solidify, although in the middle the crown still pulsated. Her hair, as soft as fur, grew darker and thicker every day. Her tiny feet straightened out, and her toes—formerly curled, with the big toe up and the other little pink buttons down—became used to the horizontal position of the walking human being.

Each major step in her life was a surprise and an immense pleasure to Julián, confirming his fatherly devotion to the creature who did him the honor of pulling his watch chain, fingering the buttons of his vest, and spilling saliva and milk on him. There was nothing he would not do for his idolized little girl! Sometimes his love stirred terrible impulses in him, like the wish to seize a stick and crack Primitivo's ribs, or to take a whip and do the same with Sabel. But, alas! no one can take the place of the master of the house; and the master of the house . . . This Christian marriage weighed heavily upon the chaplain's conscience. His intentions had been noble, but the fruit was bitter. He would give his heart's blood to see Nucha in the convent!

What course should he follow at this point? Julián foresaw the enormous disadvantages of a direct intervention. Convinced of his principles, capable of enduring to death, he lacked the mainspring of human action: initiative. Beyond question things were confused, twisted, and out of joint in the house of Ulloa. The chaplain witnessed the drama in fear of a tragic end, particularly after he saw the notorious wrist marks, which had remained in his heated mind. He appeared melancholy; his rosy complexion turned as yellow as wax; he prayed even more than usual, fasted, and said mass with an ardor worthy of the time of the Christian martyrs; he wished to offer his whole life for the well being of Señorita Marcelina; but except for those moments of sheer nervous energy, he was unable to take any step or measure, even the simplest one, like writing a note to Señor Manuel Pardo de la Lage to inform him of what was happening to his daughter. He always found pretexts to postpone every action, as trifling as, for example, "Let's wait until the election is over."

He hoped that if the master was elected, left his den, and got away from the wicked people who spun their net around him, God might touch his heart and induce him to change his behavior.

One thing worried the good chaplain a great deal: would the marquis travel to Madrid alone, or would he take his wife and child with him? Julián swore to God that he wished the latter, although the thought of it filled him with sorrow. The possibility of not seeing the child for months or years, of not bouncing her on his knees, of his remaining there face to face with Sabel, as in a dark well inhabited by a viper, seemed intolerable. It would be hard enough to see the mistress leave, but the girl . . .

"If they left her with me," he thought, "I'd take care of her beautifully."

The decisive battle was approaching. The house of Ulloa bustled with activity. Partisans and gossips came and went with messages, orders, and counterorders, as in a military headquarters. In the stables there were always guest horses and mules munching mountains of feed; in the spacious rooms one could hear the incessant creak of tall boots, the stamp of heavy shoes, even the click-clock of wooden clogs. Julián stumbled on frantic, bellicose priests who talked about the burning issue and wondered why he did not take part in it. On such a solemn and critical occasion, the chaplain of Ulloa had no right to eat or sleep!

He continued to notice that some abbots seemed aloof or resentful, especially the archpriest, who was the most attached to the family. Whereas the priest of Boán and even Don Eugenio of Naya concentrated mainly on political success, the archpriest cared more for the prestige of the estate and the good name of the Moscosos.

Everything indicated that, despite the government's enormous display of strength, the master of the house of Ulloa would be the winner. From the count of votes and the census, it was clear that Trampeta's most crooked tricks would be useless against the numerical superiority of his opponents. In the district the government counted only on what was pompously called the official element. Admittedly this sector, owing to the submissiveness of the peasants, is very powerful in Galicia, but in Cebre it could not counteract the influence of the priests and gentlemen who supported the formidable Barbacana. The archpriest exuded happiness. Strangely enough, Barbacana himself was the only one who had reservations. Preoccupied and in a worse mood every day, he frowned whenever a priest walked into his office and, rubbing his hands with glee, reported new converts and more votes.

How difficult these elections were, good heavens! How close the fight to conquer inch by inch, by means of all sorts of wiles and schemes! Trampeta seemed to have multiplied himself into half a dozen men who played his tricks in half a dozen places simultaneously. Substitutions of ballots, delays and advances in the schedule, forgeries, threats, and beatings were not peculiar to this election; but new touches of unprecedented subtlety added to the usual stratagems. In one polling place the cloaks of the marquis's voters were splashed with turpentine and surreptitiously set on fire, so that their unfortunate wearers rushed out screaming, never to return. In another, the electoral table was placed on the landing at the top of the stairs. The voters had to climb up in single file, because twelve men who worked for Trampeta stood in line on the steps the whole morning, vigorously punching and kicking anyone who tried to elbow his way. In Cebre itself, craftier methods were put into practice.

There went the priests, cheering on the flock of voters so that they would not panic at the moment to cast their ballots. In order to avoid risks, Don Eugenio, making use of his right to intervene, placed one of his most loyal peasants at the table, with strict instructions not to lose sight of the ballot box for a moment. "Do you understand, Roque? Don't look away from it even if the end of the world should come." The churl took his position, with his elbows on the table and his cheeks on his hands, staring intensely at the mysterious pot out of the corner of his eye, as if attempting a hypnotic experience. He sat motionless, hardly breathing, as though carved in stone. Trampeta himself, as he made his rounds, grew impatient at the sight of the petrified witness, for another container stuffed with ballots more to the taste of the mayor and the secretary of the committee was concealed in wait for an opportunity to replace the legitimate one. He ordered one of his henchmen to bribe the watchman by inviting him to a bite or a drink, resorting to all kinds of flattery. It was a waste of time. The guard did not even glance at the man who addressed him. His round hairy head, protruding jaw, and unblinking eyes composed the portrait of obstinacy itself. It was necessary to remove him, because the critical hour—four o'clock—was approaching, and the exchange of ballot boxes had to be effected. Trampeta grew restless, questioned his partisans about the watchman's biography, and found out that he was involved in a lawsuit whereby his oxen and fruits had been confiscated. Trampeta sneaked up to the table, put his hand on the man's shoulder, and shouted: "You won the lawsuit!"

The peasant jumped, electrified. "What are you talking about?"

"It was decided yesterday at the High Court."

"You're mad."

"I'm telling you, you won."

In the meantime the secretary of the committee performed the exchange of ballot boxes unheard and unseen. The mayor rose solemnly. "Gentlemen, we are going to proceed with the counting of votes!" People rush into the room; the reading of ballots begins; the priests look at each other in terror when the name of their candidate does not appear.

"Did you leave your seat?" the abbot of Naya asks the guard.

"No, sir," he answers with so much conviction that no suspicion is possible.

"Somebody has sold us out," the abbot of Ulloa mumbles hoarsely, casting a glance of distrust upon Don Eugenio. Trampeta, with his hands in his pockets, laughs up his sleeve.

Such procedures decimated considerably the votes for the marquis of Ulloa, reducing the fight at last to a scramble for a small number of votes that would decide victory. When the time came, the Ulloists took their triumph for granted; but totally unexpected desertions, bordering on abominable treason, of supporters who were thought to be absolutely reliable, for whom the steward of the house of Ulloa himself had vouched, tipped the scales to the government's side. No one had been able to foresee or prevent this vile, sudden blow. Primitivo, belying his usual impassibility, raged and hurled absurd threats against the turncoats.

Barbacana, on the other hand, behaved stoically. The lawyer learned about the definitive defeat in the afternoon as he sat in his office, surrounded by three or four people. The archpriest came in, crimson with contempt and fury, bellowing like a whale stranded on a beach. He collapsed on a leather chair and, taking his hands to his throat, pulled away his stock and tore open his shirt and vest. Tremulously, with his spectacles tilted on his nose and the snuff-box clutched in his left fist, he wiped away his sweat with a scented handkerchief. The chieftain's calm drove him mad.

"I can't believe it, confound it! I can't believe that you're sitting there so cool and collected! Do you know what's going on?"

"I don't fret about things that are only to be expected. When it comes to elections, nothing can surprise me."

"Did you expect this?"

"Of course. Here's the abbot of Naya, to ratify that I prophesied it. I don't summon dead witnesses."

"It's true," Don Eugenio corroborated contritely.

"Then, for goodness' sake, why play the fool like this?"

"We couldn't give up the district without putting up a fight. Would you have liked that? Legally, we are the winners."

"Legally . . . damn! Legally, perhaps, but who cares about legalities? Those damned traitors deserted us when everything depended on them. The blacksmith of Gondas, the two Ponlles, the veterinarian!"

"Those are not traitors; don't be so innocent, archpriest. They are simply subordinates. The Judas here is somebody else."

"What? Oh, I understand! Well, if that's true—and I'm reluctant to believe it—the punishment of Judas would not be enough for this traitor. But, my good man, why didn't you intercept him? Why didn't you warn us? Why didn't you unmask that scoundrel? If the marquis of Ulloa knew that he had a traitor at home, he would tie him to a bedpost and whip him. His own steward! I don't understand how you can take this so calmly!"

"We'll reveal the truth later; but look, when elections hinge on one person and there's no way to prove his good or bad faith, it's pointless to make one's suspicions public. It's better to sit still and wait for the blow, put these suspicions to the test, and if nothing happens, keep one's mouth shut and file them in one's memory."

As he said "file them," the chieftain beat his chest, which resounded deeply, just as Saint Jerome's must have resounded when he hit it with the notorious stone. Indeed, Barbacana bore some resemblance to the Saint Jeromes of the Spanish school, withered and bony, with long tangled beards and a dark fire in their black pupils.[1]

"They won't get away with this one," he added sternly, "and we shall waste no time. No one ever owed anything to Barbacana who didn't pay. As for the Judas, how did you expect us to unmask him if now, as in the time of Christ's crucifixion, he has the bag in his hand? Tell me, archpriest, who has given us the ammunition for this battle?"

"Who? Actually, the house of Ulloa."

"Did they have it at their disposal? Yes or no? That's the catch. These stately homes stand on sheer vanity. The marquis, rather than confess that he doesn't have the money and borrow it from an honest person—like myself, for instance—borrows it from a rogue, a snake who's soaking him dry."

"The things those nincompoops of the junta of Orense are going to say of us! They'll say that we are a bunch of good-for-nothing simpletons. It's the first time in my life that I have lost an election."

"In a nutshell, what the junta will say is that we chose a very weak candidate."

"Wait a minute!" the archpriest exclaimed, ready to make a stand for his beloved marquis. "We don't agree . . ."

Here ended the discussion. The audience, consisting of the

---

1. Pardo Bazán refers to a painting of Saint Jerome by José Ribera (1588–1652) at the Museo del Prado in Madrid.

abbots of Naya and Boán and the gentleman of Limioso, bore the humiliation of defeat silently. Suddenly a terrible uproar, made by the loudest and most discordant sounds that can attack the human eardrum, invaded the room. Frying pans scraped with iron spoons and forks; cooking pots played as cymbals; chocolate beaters spinning frantically inside casserole dishes; heavy pestles tolling like horse bells inside copper cauldrons; cans tied to a cord and pulled over the floor; plates tapped with iron rods; and above all, the hoarse, gloomy sound of the horn, the horrendous outcry of numerous human throats, with that hollowness that comes from excess of wine. Actually, the blessed musicians had just finished off a fat wineskin generously provided by the secretary of the town council. In those days, country voters were not yet aware of certain social refinements; they did not know how to ask for "the wine that boils and froths," as they would some years later, and settled for the hearty red wine of Borde. Wine vapors and the sour smell of the mob, drunk with something besides victory, together with the sound of the coarse instruments and the wild uproar, penetrated through Barbacana's windows. The archpriest straightened his spectacles. His congested face betrayed anxiety. The priest of Boán frowned. Don Eugenio was inclined to take the whole matter as a joke. The gentleman of Limioso, resolute and calm, walked up to the window, lifted the curtain, and looked out.

The serenade continued, relentless and frantic, scratching the air the way a bunch of cats in heat scratch the roof. Suddenly, amid the grotesque riot, rose a clamor that in Spain always has a good deal of tragic effect: a cry of death.

"Death to Don Carlos!"

A number of "deaths" and "long lives" followed.

"Death to the priests!"

"Death to tyranny!"

"Long live Cebre and our deputy!"

"Long live national sovereignty!"

"Death to the marquis of Ulloa!"

More provocative and distinct than the others came this cry: "Death to the rabid thief Barbacana!"

And all the voices repeated unanimously: "Death to him!"

Immediately a man of sinister countenance who had remained hidden in a corner appeared by the lawyer's table. He was not dressed like a peasant, but like a lower-class city dweller: black cloth jacket, red waistband, gray bowler hat. His short whiskers emphasized the hardness of his face, which was marked by prominent cheekbones and a broad forehead. One of his deep-set green eyes flashed with a feline expression; the other, motionless and veiled with a thick white cloud, seemed made of opaque glass.

Barbacana opened a drawer of his desk, produced two huge horse pistols—no doubt prehistoric—and examined them to make sure that they were loaded. Staring at the apparition, he seemed to offer him the weapons with a slight lift of his eyebrows. In reply, One-eye of Castrodorna pulled from his waistband the tip of a knife with a yellow handle and quickly hid it again.

The archpriest, whose nerves had weakened with obesity and age, suffered a shock. "Stop this nonsense, my friend! Just in case, I think it would be a good idea to slip out by the back door. I'm not about to wait here for these uncircumcised savages to bring us grief."

But by that time the priest of Boán and the gentleman of Limioso, together with One-eye, formed a group ready for action. The gentleman of Limioso, faithful to his old aristocratic blood, waited quietly, without arrogance but with a fearless heart. The abbot of Boán, born to fight in a guerrilla war rather than to say mass, fondled the pistol with glee in anticipation of danger; had he been a horse, he would have neighed with happiness. One-eye crouched like a tiger behind the door, ready to spring and tear to pieces the first who came in.

"Have no fear, archpriest," Barbacana whispered gravely. "Their bark is worse than their bite. These loudmouths won't even dare break one of my windows, but we'd better be prepared to bare our fangs, just in case."

Death cries resounded, but in fact, not a stone was thrown at the windowpanes. The gentleman of Limioso drew near again, lifted the curtain, and called Don Eugenio.

"Look, Naya, look out there. It doesn't seem that they are about to get close and throw stones. They're dancing."

Don Eugenio walked up to the window and burst into laughter. Amid the drunken crowd, a jailer and a bailiff at the service of Trampeta were trying to spur the loudest rioters to assault the lawyer's house. They pointed at the door, indicating by eloquent gestures how easy it would be to knock it down and get in. But the mob, which despite its drunkenness had not lost its caution or the wise apprehension felt by the peasant in the presence of the landlord, pretended not to understand, and limited itself to howling and battering pots and pans with renewed fury. In the middle of the circle the most inebriated, the true human wineskins, leaped like madmen to the beat of pestles and casserole dishes.

"Gentlemen," Ramón Limioso said in a grave, hoarse voice, "it's a shame that these rogues should lay siege on us here. I have a mind to go out and make them run till they reach the town hall."

"My good man," the abbot of Boán grumbled, "you speak little, but well. Let's frighten them, *quoniam*! A sneeze of mine would suffice to scare away half a dozen of these sponges."

One-eye did not utter a word; only his green eye shone with a phosphorescent light as he glanced at Barbacana, as if asking him permission to take part in the enterprise. Barbacana nodded his approval, but at the same time signaled him to put away the knife.

"You're quite right," the gentleman of Limioso exclaimed, as he craned his neck and swelled his nostrils with an arrogance that rarely disturbed his languid, sad face. "These people require the stick and the whip. It would be a shame to sully the weapon you use for partridges and hares, which are worth far more than they— except for their souls, of course."

As he said the last words, he crossed himself.

"Let's be careful, men," the archpriest murmured with difficulty, his hands stretched out to calm down the overheated spirits. How far away were the bellicose days when he had secured an electoral victory by a kick!

Barbacana did not oppose the plan; on the contrary, he went to another room and came back with a bundle of sticks and canes. The priest of Boán refused to carry any weapon other than his walking stick, which was formidable. Ramón Limioso, true to his contempt for the rabble, seized the thinnest whip, his riding crop. One-eye brandished a kind of lash, which in his vigorous right hand would snap out with terrific effect.

They descended the stairs cautiously, trying to smother their footsteps—a precaution that the diabolical racket outside rendered quite superfluous. The lawyer's cook had barred and locked the door as soon as she heard the uproar of the mutiny. The abbot of Boán unbolted it impetuously, and One-eye lifted up the crossbar and turned the key in the lock; clergy and laymen fell on the mob without warning, with clenched teeth and blazing eyes, brandishing whips and clubs.

Five minutes later Barbacana, who was surveying the battlefield from behind his window, smiled quietly, or rather spread his lips to expose his yellow teeth, and grabbed the window bars with nervous violence. The drunkards screamed and ran in every direction, as if a cavalry regiment had charged against them. Some stumbled and fell on their faces, and One-eye's lash coiled around their bodies, drawing squeals of pain from their throats. The Limioso heir struck them with less cruelty but more contempt, as if they were a herd of swine. The priest of Boán hit with tireless energy and regularity. Don Eugenio of Naya, incapable of playing in earnest his role of avenger, insulted, laughed at, and flogged the drunks at the same time. "Move, you drunken sot, you soaker, you wino! Take this, and that, and come for more, you wineskin! Go sleep it off, you pig! Take yourself back to the tavern, barfly, barrel of wine! Go to jail and vomit up all the alcohol you've put in your bellies!"

The street was now clean, sparkling like silver. A deep silence had followed the uproar, the death cries, and the raucous serenade. The spoils of battle—pots, pestles, horns—lay on the ground. From the stairs came the clamor of the victors, who climbed up celebrating their triumph. Don Eugenio led them into the room and then sprawled in an armchair, clapping and chuckling heartily. The priest of Boán followed him, wiping his sweat. Ramón Limioso, serious and still melancholy, simply handed his crop over to Barbacana without a word.

"Fled . . . they've all fled!" the abbot of Naya stammered, amid loud peals of laughter.

"I ground them as one grinds wheat!" the priest of Boán exclaimed, his chest puffed out with pleasure.

"For my part," the young aristocrat explained, "if I had known that they are such cowards and would run away without putting up a fight, I certainly wouldn't have taken all this trouble."

"Don't trust them," the archpriest remarked. "By now Trampeta may well be sneering at them in the town hall, and he's capable of marching those uncircumcised barbarians in here personally to give the doctor"—this is what his close friends called Barbacana— "a fright. Just in case, it is wiser for these gentlemen to spend the night here. I have to say mass in Loiro tomorrow, and by now my sister must be scared to death; otherwise . . ."

"None of that," Barbacana answered peremptorily. "These gentlemen are going back home. There's nothing to fear. All I need is this fellow," he added, pointing at One-eye, who was crouched in his corner again.

It was impossible to persuade the chieftain to accept the guard of honor offered to him. On the other hand, there was no sign at all of new disorders. No distant voices of electoral winners sounded. The sleepy silence peculiar to small, lifeless villages fell heavily upon Cebre. Three heroes of the great raid, accompanied by the archpriest, rode off toward the mountain. They were not crestfallen, as befits defeated voters, but joyful, chatting, joking, and celebrating profusely the beating administered to the drunken serenaders. Don Eugenio was inspired, timely, cheerful, witty, particularly when he imitated the howls of those wretches and their falls on the muddy street, and enacted the "grinding."

Barbacana remained alone with One-eye. Had one of the pummeled musicians dared to show his head and peek through the chieftain's window, he would have seen that the shutters, out of negligence or contempt, had not been closed; through the curtains he would also have glimpsed the heads of the lawyer and his ferocious defender outlined against the back of the room by the light of the oil lamp. No doubt they were discussing an important matter, to judge by the length of their conference. An hour or more went by from the time when they lighted the lamp until they closed the shutters, leaving the house quiet, bleak, and gloomy, as if it hid a dark secret.

Chapter 27

Nucha was the one who felt the electoral defeat most deeply. After the election both her physical and her mental condition grew weaker. She hardly came out of her room, where she lived tied to her daughter night and day. At table she ate little and said nothing. Julián, who did not take his eyes away from the lady, sometimes noticed that she moved her lips, like a person obsessed with a single idea who speaks silently to herself. Don Pedro, more intractable than ever, did not bother to start a conversation. He chewed vigorously and ate heartily, with his eyes riveted on the plate if not on the ceiling beams, but never on his table companions.

To the chaplain Señora Moscoso seemed so worn out and exhausted that one day he overcame his inexplicable reservations and called Don Pedro aside to ask him in a shaky voice if it would be necessary to call Señor Juncal.

"Are you crazy?" Don Pedro replied, striking him with a contemptuous look. "Call Juncal after what he did to me at the election? Máximo Juncal will never cross this doorway again."

The priest did not answer. A few days later, on the way back from Naya, he accidentally met the doctor. The latter stopped his horse, and without dismounting answered Julián's questions.

"It may be serious. She was very weak after delivery and needed conscientious care. Nervous women require spiritual peace to heal physically. Look, Julián, we would have to talk for hours if I were to tell you what I think about that unhappy lady and that house. I won't say any more. A fine deputy you were going to send to the Congress! His parents should have sent him to school first."

"It may be serious . . ." This in particular remained on Julián's mind. It might be serious, indeed, and what means were at his disposal to exorcise illness and death? None. He envied doctors. His power could heal only the spirit, and in this case it was useless, for Nucha did not confess to him. In truth, he was confused and troubled by the very thought of hearing her in confession and seeing her beautiful soul bare.

Often, however, he had considered the possibility that any day Nucha, in search of comfort and relief, might throw herself at his feet at the court of penitence and beg for advice, strength, and resignation. "And who am I," Julián wondered, "to guide a person like Señorita Marcelina? I don't have the age, the experience, or the wisdom for it; and worst of all I also lack virtue, for I ought to accept all her sufferings for her greater glory in the afterlife. But I'm so evil, so carnal, so blind, so inept, that I constantly question divine goodness, just because I see this poor lady in the throes of adversity and temporary tribulations. This has to stop," the chaplain decided, not without effort. "I must open my eyes, for I have the light of faith that's denied to unbelievers, to heathens, to mortal sinners. If Señorita Marcelina asks me to share with her the burden of the cross, I'll teach her to embrace it with love. Both she and I must understand the meaning of this cross, which is the way to the only true happiness. As satisfied as the mistress might be here in this world, how long could her joy last, and how perfect could it be? Even if her husband . . . appreciated her as she deserves, even if she were the apple of his eye, would she by virtue of this affection be free of problems, sickness, old age, and death? And when the hour of death comes, what does it matter if this insignificant, perishable life has been more or less merry and peaceful?"

Julián always kept at hand a copy of *The Imitation of Christ*. It was a quaint but excellent translation by Father Nieremberg in the modest edition of the Religious Library. The cover featured an engraving of little artistic value, which gave the priest great consolation whenever he looked at it. It represented a hill: Calvary. Jesus slowly climbed the narrow path leading to his ordeal, with the cross on his shoulders and his head turned toward a monk, who in the distance carried another cross. Although the picture was bad and its execution worse, the engraving breathed a kind of melancholy resignation suited to the chaplain's moral situation. After he had contemplated it for a while, he thought he felt an overwhelming yet sweet heaviness on his shoulders, a perfect calm, as if he lay—he told himself—at the bottom of the sea, surrounded by water but not drowning. Then he would read paragraphs from the magic book, which penetrated his soul as a red-hot iron penetrates flesh:

"Why do you fear, then, to take up the cross that leads to the kingdom? The cross is health, the cross is life, the cross is protection against the enemy, the cross is infused with divine mercy, the cross is strength of mind, the cross is joy of the spirit, the cross is the ultimate virtue, the cross is perfect sanctity . . . Take, therefore, your cross, and follow Jesus . . . Remember, everything is in the cross, and in order to attain it we must die. There is no other way to life and true peace than that of the holy cross and constant mortification . . . Dispose and order all things according to your wish, and you will see that willingly or by force you must suffer; and thus you shall find always the cross, either in the pain of the body or in the tribulations of the spirit . . . When you reach a state in which your affliction is sweet and pleasant to you for the love of Christ, then think yourself fortunate, because you shall have found Paradise on earth."

"When shall I reach this blessed state, my Lord?" Julián whispered, putting a mark in the book.

Sometimes he had heard that God grants what the mind has prayed for in the act of consecrating the host. Julián asked with fervor to attain that state in which his cross—no, his poor mistress's—became sweet and pleasant to her, as Kempis said.

In the rejuvenated chapel Nucha always knelt down to listen to mass, and withdrew when Julián said the thanksgiving. Without turning around or taking his attention away from prayer, Julián knew exactly when the lady rose, and heard her imperceptible steps on the new wooden floor. One morning he did not hear them. This simple fact disturbed his peace while he prayed. When he rose he saw Nucha standing with her forefinger on her lips. Perucho, who readily helped with mass, was snuffing the candles with a long cane. The lady's eyes said plainly: "Get this child out of here."

The chaplain ordered the acolyte to finish up. The latter lingered a bit to fold the maundy towel. At last he left, reluctantly. The smell of flowers and fresh varnish filled the chapel. Through the red taffeta curtains at the windows came a warm light that shed life on the flesh of the saints on the altar. Nucha's paleness assumed a shade of pink.

"Julián?" she asked in an imperious tone, unusual in her.

"Señorita," he answered in a low voice, out of respect for the holy place. His lips trembled and his hands grew cold, because he thought that the terrible moment of confession had come.

"We must talk, and it has to be here. Anywhere else there's always somebody watching."

"It's true."

"Will you do what I'm going to ask you?"

"You know that . . ."

"No matter what it may be?"

"I . . ."

His confusion increased. His heart pounded furiously. He leaned against the altar.

"You must," Nucha stated, fixing her eyes—now vacant rather than vague—on him. "You must help me flee this place."

"Fl . . . flee," Julián stammered, astounded.

"I want to leave with my daughter. Return to my father. To be successful, we must keep it a secret. If they find out, they'll lock me up, they will take away my baby, they will kill her. I know that they will kill her."

Her tone, expression, and attitude were those of a woman who has lost her mind, a woman compelled by nervous excitement bordering on delirium.

"Señorita," the chaplain began, no less alarmed, "do not stand; sit down on this pew. Let's talk sensibly. I know what you're going through, señorita. We must be patient, prudent. Please, calm down!"

Nucha collapsed on the pew. She breathed with difficulty, as if her lungs could not fulfill their function. The light shone through her pale ears, which seemed detached from her skull. When she had gathered her strength, she spoke quietly. "Patience and prudence! I have as much as any woman can have. Let's not pretend, you know how long I've had this thorn inside me: since the day when I decided to find out the truth. It wasn't too hard. I mean, yes, it cost me . . . a struggle, but that doesn't matter now. For my own sake I wouldn't think of going away, for I'm not well and I figure that I . . . won't last. But what about my daughter?"

"Your daughter . . ."

"They are going to kill her, Julián. These . . . people. Don't you see that she's in their way? Don't you see it?"

"For the love of God, I beg you to pull yourself together. Let's talk calmly, sensibly . . ."

"I'm sick of being sensible!" Nucha retorted angrily, as if she had heard a piece of nonsense. "I have begged, and begged. I have exhausted every means I can think of. I won't wait, I can't wait any longer. I waited until the election was over because I hoped that we would leave this place, and with it my fears. I'm afraid of this house, you know that, Julián, terribly afraid, particularly at night."

By the light filtered through the crimson curtains, Julián saw the lady's enlarged pupils, her parted lips, her raised eyebrows, the expression of mortal terror painted on her face.

"I'm very frightened," she repeated with a shiver.

Julián cursed his awkwardness. How he wished to be eloquent! But he could think of nothing to say, nothing! The mystic consolations he had prepared and treasured, the theory of embracing the cross . . . Everything shattered against this willful, throbbing, boundless pain.

"Ever since I came here," Nucha continued, "this big old house sent a chill down my spine; but now it isn't the whim of a spoiled girl, no. They want to kill my baby, you'll see for yourself! The moment I leave her with the nurse I'm on burning coals. Let's be done with it soon; we must take care of this right away. I came to you because I can't trust anyone else. You love my child."

"I love her, indeed . . . ," Julián stammered, almost speechless with emotion.

"I'm alone, alone," Nucha replied, running her hand over her cheeks; her voice was broken by restrained sobs. "I thought that I might confess to you, but it would be meaningless. I wouldn't obey if you ordered me to stay here. I know it's my duty: a wife must not leave her husband. My decision when I married was . . ."

Suddenly she stopped, faced Julián, and asked:

"Don't you agree that this marriage had to fail? My sister Rita was almost engaged to Pedro when he asked for my hand. Through no fault of mine, Rita and I haven't spoken to each other since then. I don't know how that happened; God knows that I did nothing to attract his attention. Papa advised me to marry my cousin anyway. I followed his advice. I made a resolution to be good, love him dearly, obey him, see after my children . . . Tell me, Julián, what did I do wrong?"

Julián folded his hands. His knees were so weak that he nearly fell to the ground. "You're an angel, Señorita Marcelina," he said enthusiastically.

"No," she replied, "not an angel, but I don't remember having hurt anyone. I took good care of my little brother Gabriel, who had poor health and had lost his mother . . ."

As she uttered these words, the cup overflowed; her tears ran, at last. Nucha breathed more easily, as if these childhood memories tempered her nerves, and crying relieved her.

"I loved him so much that I thought to myself: if I ever have children, I couldn't possibly love them more than my brother. Later I realized that was nonsense: a mother's love is infinitely greater."

Gradually the sky clouded over and the chapel darkened. The lady spoke with melancholy calm. "When my brother went to the artillery school, all my endeavor was to please papa and compensate as well as I could for mama's absence. My sisters preferred their walks, for they are pretty and fond of entertainment. They called me plain and cross-eyed, and said that I wouldn't find a husband."

"I wish you hadn't!" Julián exclaimed, unable to restrain himself.

"I laughed at them. Why should I want to marry? I had papa and Gabriel to live with forever. If they died, I could go into a convent; I liked the Carmelites, where Aunt Dolores is. In sum, I'm not to blame at all for Rita's grief. When papa informed me of my cousin's intentions, I told him I didn't want to steal my sister's fiancé from her, and then papa . . . kissed my cheeks over and over as he did when I was a little girl, and—I still can hear him now— he answered me: 'Rita is silly . . . hush.' But no matter what papa said . . . my cousin still liked Rita!"

After a few moments of silence, she continued: "You see, I don't have anything for my sister to envy. I've swallowed so much gall, Julián! When I think of it, I feel a knot in here."

At last the priest managed to express some of his feelings: "I'm not surprised. I feel the same way. Night and day I brood on your misfortune, señorita. Ever since I saw that mark on your wrist . . ."

For the first time during the conversation Nucha's pale face blushed, and her eyes clouded over under the lowered eyelids. Her reply was elusive. "You know," she whispered with a hint of a bitter smile, "I always have to pay for wrongs I haven't committed. Pedro insisted that I should claim my share of mother's inheritance from papa, because papa refused to give him a certain amount of money that he needed for the election. He was also very angry because Aunt Marcelina, who planned to make me her heiress, will probably leave her fortune to Rita. I don't have anything to do with that. Why are they killing me? I know I'm poor, there's no need to remind me every minute. Anyway, that's the least of my concerns. It hurt a great deal more when my husband told me that the house of Moscoso has no succession because of me. No succession! What about my daughter, child of my heart?"

The unfortunate lady wept quietly, without sobbing. Her eyelids already had the reddish tinge that painters give to the Virgin of Sorrows. She added: "I don't care for myself, I can endure to the very last moment. They may treat me one way or another . . . the maid may take my place . . . fine, patience; it's a matter of being patient, of suffering, of letting oneself die slowly. But my daughter is at stake. There's another child, a son, an illegitimate son. The girl is in the way. They'll kill her!"

She repeated solemnly and very slowly: "They will kill her. Don't look at me like that. I'm not crazy, only very agitated. I've made up my mind to go back to my father's house. I don't think that's a sin; neither is taking my daughter with me. And if it is, don't tell me, dear Julián. It's an irreversible decision. You'll come with me, because I'd never be able to carry out my plan by myself. Will you accompany me?"

Julián tried to raise an objection, but . . . which? He himself did not know. The lady's affectionate words and the feverish determination of her speech won him over. Could he refuse to help this unfortunate woman? Impossible. Did he consider how difficult and preposterous her project was? It did not occur to him for a moment. Being so naive, he found such an absurd escape easy. Would he oppose it? He, too, had always felt an intense fear, not only for the baby but for the mother. Had he not thought a thousand times that their lives might be in imminent jeopardy? Besides, he would attempt anything in the world to dry the tears from those pure eyes, to soothe that anxious bosom, to see his mistress safe, honored, respected, surrounded by loving care in the paternal home.

He pictured the scene of the flight. It would take place at dawn. Nucha would be wrapped in plenty of warm clothing. He would carry the sleeping baby, who would also be well wrapped. Just in case, he would put a bottle of hot milk in his pocket. If they walked briskly, they would reach Cebre in less than three hours. There they would have some soup. The child would not go hungry. They would take the stagecoach and sit in the most comfortable place, the front compartment. Every turn of the wheels would take them farther from the house of Ulloa.

Very quietly, as in confession, they began to discuss and decide these details. Another sunbeam split the clouds, and the saints in their niches seemed to smile benevolently upon the couple on the pew. Neither the Virgin Mary with loose curls and a white and blue robe on her body; nor Saint Anthony, cuddling a chubby Baby Jesus; nor Saint Peter, with his triple crown and keys; nor even the archangel Saint Michael, the knight with the flaming sword, always ready to cleave and strike Satan—none of them revealed on their freshly painted faces the slightest anger against this chaplain engrossed in the preliminaries of a regular abduction, whereby he would snatch a daughter away from her father and a wife away from her lawful husband.

Chapter 28

At this point, in order to complete the story, it is necessary to draw upon the recollections forever impressed in the mind of the handsome boy, Sabel's son, of the events that occurred on that unforgettable morning when for the last time he helped the good Don Julián with mass—after which, by the way, he usually received two pennies.

The first thing Perucho remembers is that when he left the chapel he lingered sadly by the door, because that day the chaplain had not given him anything. For a few moments he stood there meditating and sucking his thumb, until the very loss of the customary pennies threw some light on the matter: his grandfather had promised him two more if he let him know whenever the mistress stayed in the chapel after mass. He reckoned with remarkable mathematical accuracy that, as he had lost two pennies from one supplier, it was imperative to get them from another. No sooner had he conceived such a bright idea than his feet grew restless and he started to run as fast as he could in search of his grandfather.

He sneaked through the kitchen and into the room below, which served as Primitivo's office. Pushing open the door, he saw his grandfather sitting at a large old table, which was buried under a great sea of papers scribbled with clumsy figures and notes written by a rather unskilled hand. The desk and the room in general attracted Perucho in the way that topsy-turvy places and the accumulation of ill-assorted things always attract children, for they imagine that each heap of objects is an unknown world, a cache of inestimable treasures. Perucho rarely entered this room. His grandfather usually ordered him out, lest he might surprise certain financial operations that the steward wished to conduct without witnesses. When his grandson came in, Primitivo's metallic face was blended with the heap of bronze and copper coins that he was distributing in columns, aligned in perfect formation. Perucho stood dazzled at the sight of such fabulous wealth. Here were his two pennies! A tiny nugget from this gold mine! Filled with hope, he delivered his message as loudly as he could: the mistress was in the chapel with the chaplain, and they had sent him away.

He was going to add, "And you owe me two pennies for the information," or some similar remark, but his grandfather did not give him a chance. With the feline quickness that characterized all his movements, he rose from the armchair, causing a whirlpool in the sea of coins and the fall of several towers, which gave in to their own weight with a loud clash. Primitivo rushed to the inner rooms of the house. The boy remained there, facing the two strongest temptations he had suffered in his life. One was to eat the provocative red and white candy that beckoned him from a tin box. Although it would be more flattering for our hero to have overcome this gluttonous whim, we must confess, to honor the truth, that he stretched out a hand moistened with saliva and fished out one, two, three pieces of candy, until he had gobbled up the entire contents of the box. When he had satisfied this urge, he felt another, which was no less than to help himself to the two pennies from the heap that lay in front of him at his disposal. He was tempted not only to collect his rightful wages, but also to take some seductive rusty pennies, locally known as "lucky pennies"; with the logic of his childish mind, he preferred them to the coins of greater value. Generally, these pennies represented everything that Perucho could acquire and enjoy. For a penny, at the fair or the procession, the baker gave him candy or plenty of crullers; for a penny, he got enough thread for his spinning top, and the fireworks salesman gave him a great deal of powder to make little trails; for a penny he purchased a strip of cardboard matches, church music coarsely printed on yellow paper, or clay roosters with a whistle in a none-too-decorous part. And all this lay within his hand's reach, like the candy, and no one could see him and tell on him!

The wild angel rose on tiptoe, stretched out his hands, and buried them in the copper sea. For a long time he ran them over the surface, without daring to close them. Finally he seized a handful of lucky pennies and clenched his fist tight, with an intensity peculiar to children, who are always afraid that happiness may slip through their open fingers. He remained motionless, not daring to bring this sinful right hand with its load of booty to the haven of his bosom, where he stored all his plunders. It must be remembered that Perucho was a confirmed thief who appropriated eggs, fruit, or anything he craved without qualms; but with the superstitious respect that makes the peasant consider money the only sacred property, he had never touched a coin. One of those fierce battles between duty and passion sung by the muses of drama raged in Perucho's soul. The good and the bad angels pulled at each one of his ears, and he did not know which to follow. Terrible dilemma! But to the joy of heaven and mankind, the spirit of light prevailed. Was it the first awakening of that sense of honor that compels men to heroic sacrifices? Was it a drop of Moscoso blood that really ran in his veins, and by the mysterious power of heredity guided his will like a rein? Was it an early fruit of Julián's and Nucha's lessons? What is certain is that the boy opened his hand and spread his fingers apart, so that the lucky pennies fell from his fist and clattered among the others on the heap.

By no means had Perucho given up his two pennies, honestly earned by the swiftness of his legs. Giving them up was the last thing on his mind! The same embryo of conscience where the

Decalogue had been written since the dawn of time, and which had cried from the depths of his being, "Thou shall not steal," said with no less energy, "You have a right to claim what is yours." Obeying its command, the child ran off in pursuit of his grandfather.

By accident he stumbled on him in the kitchen, where he was asking Sabel something in a low voice. Perucho walked up to them, tugged at his coat, and exclaimed: "My two pennies!"

Primitivo ignored him and continued to talk with his daughter. As far as Perucho could understand, she was explaining that the master had gone out at dawn to shoot partridge chicks, and by now must be on the road to Cebre. The old man uttered a curse of which he was particularly fond and that Perucho used to repeat for the sake of boasting, and without further ado, he left.

Perucho claimed later that he was surprised to see his grandfather leave without his gun and wide-brimmed hat, two items that he always carried with him. This thought must have occurred to him afterward, in the light of the events that followed. At the time, his only idea was to catch up with Primitivo, whom he found at the top of the road. Even though the hunter was as fast as lightning, the lad ran just as quickly.

"Go to the devil! What do you want?" Primitivo rumbled when he saw his grandson.

"My two pennies!"

"I'll give you four if you help me look for the master on the mountain. When you see him, tell him what you told me, understand? That the chaplain has shut himself up in the chapel with the mistress, and that they threw you out to be alone."

The cherub opened his mouth and riveted his clear pupils on the fascinating snake eyes of his grandfather. Without waiting for further instructions, he darted off in the direction that he instinctively assumed the master had followed. He raced with clenched fists, scattering pebbles and clumps of dirt as he galloped off on his calloused feet. Unmindful of the thorns, he tore across the furze, trampled on the flowers of the pink briers, leaped over bushes as tall as himself, scared away the hare hidden in the strawberry bushes or the magpie perched on the lower branches of the pine. Suddenly he heard human steps and spotted the master as he came out of the oak wood. Mad with joy, he approached him to deliver his message, thinking that it would be appreciated; but it was received with the same infamous crude word that his grandfather had blurted out in the kitchen. The master fled toward the house of Ulloa, as if a tornado had carried him away.

Perucho stood confused and in suspense for a few moments. He says that soon, however, the promised cash, which by now amounted to the respectable sum of four pennies, spurred him on again. In order to obtain it, it was necessary to find his grandfather and inform him that he had met the master. This task should be an easy one, for he more or less remembered the spot where he had left Primitivo. Through shortcuts and trails viable only to rabbits and himself, he dashed in search of the steward. As he climbed a ruinous wall that supported a vine growing on the steep slope of the mountain, he perceived footsteps on the other side of the little fortress. His fine hearing detected that they did not belong to the hunter. With the instinct of the child of nature left to his own devices, he crouched behind the wall, so that only his forehead remained visible. Beyond question, these were human steps, quite different from a rabbit's hops on the leaves, or the quick, repeated, brief taps of dog or fox claws. Human steps they were, although fearful, muffled, and deliberate, an indication that somebody was trying to hide. And in fact, the boy soon spotted a man creeping among the bushes, a man whom he had heard mentioned perhaps a hundred times in autumn evenings, with great exclamations of terror. The gray bowler, the red waistband, the trimmed whiskers outlined on the tallow-colored face, and above all the blind white eye, cold as a piece of granite from the road—in sum, the unsettling countenance of One-eye of Castrodorna—startled the boy. One-eye clutched his short, wide blunderbuss against his chest. After turning in all directions the only star that shone on his ugly face, pricking his ear, and, so to speak, sniffing the air, he walked up to the wall and knelt down behind the brambles and briers that garnished it.

Perucho stood as if stuck to the wall, with his feet on the crevices of its surface. He did not dare to breathe, move, or climb down, because this evil-faced, watchful stranger filled him with the irrational terror that children experience in the presence of unknown dangers. As strong as his desire for the four pennies was, he dared not descend the wall for fear that, at the noise, this weapon, whose wide mouth no doubt vomited fire and death, would be pointed at him. Ten seconds of anguish passed. Before the boy could come to grips with his terror, a new incident took place. Once again he heard steps, not timorous as of somebody who is hiding, but the hasty steps of someone who rushes to his destination. On the road below the wall he glimpsed his grandfather walking toward the house of Ulloa. Undoubtedly, his sharp eye had spotted the master and he was trying to catch up with him. Primitivo, whose only thought was to find Don Pedro, marched distractedly, without looking in any particular direction. At last he reached the wall. Then the child saw something terrible, something that he would remember years later and even for the rest of his life. The man who lay in ambush rose, and with his fierce eye flashing, lifted the formidable black carbine to his face. A cloud of smoke drifted up and was instantly dissolved in the air; through its last veils, Perucho's grandfather spun on himself like a top and fell on his face, no doubt biting the grass and the mud of the road in his last convulsion.

Perucho declares that he has never known whether it was panic or his own will that prompted him to climb down the wall and roll rather than run down familiar shortcuts, so that he bruised his body and tore his clothes, paying no attention to one or the other. He bounced like a ball among the knotted vines and leaped over the stone wall that divided them; he flew like an arrow across the cornfields; he waded creeks up to his waist rather than lose time following the stepping-stones; he scrambled over fences three times taller than himself; he ran through hedges and jumped over lowlands and ditches; and not knowing how, he found himself back in the house of Ulloa, scratched, bloody, sweaty, out of breath. Automatically he returned to the starting point, the chapel, and entered it, totally oblivious to the four pennies, the initial motive of all his adventures.

This morning was fated to be rich in extraordinary surprises. Perucho knew that in the chapel people spoke quietly, walked slowly, even held their breath; the slightest slip in this matter usually cost him a stern rebuke from Don Julián. So instinct and habit overrode fear and confusion, and he stepped reverently into the sacred place. What he saw there shocked him even more than his grandfather's demise. Leaned against the altar, shivering from head to toe, Señora Moscoso looked pale as a corpse, her eyes closed and her face tense. Before her the master, with a threatening gesture, shouted rapid words that the child did not understand. The chaplain, whose hands were clasped and whose face wore an expression of terror and pain that Perucho had never beheld on a human face, beseeched the master, the mistress, the altar, the saints . . . Suddenly he stopped his supplications and with fiery eyes faced the marquis, as if to challenge him. Perucho half comprehended indignant phrases, phrases overflowing with wrath, furor, outrage, insults; and ignorant of the cause of such a row, he concluded that the master was violently angry, that he was going to strike the mistress, perhaps kill her, blow Don Julián to pieces, overturn the altars, maybe burn the chapel . . .

The boy then recalled similar scenes in the kitchen of the house of Ulloa, whose victims had been his mother and himself. On those occasions the master had the same expression on his face and the same tone of voice. And amid the confusion that dominated his tender mind, amid the terrors that gathered to overpower him, an idea rose triumphant above the others. That the master was going to knock down his wife and the chaplain was beyond question. Every sign indicated that this was the day of the general slaughter. Who knew if the master, once he had finished with his wife and Don Julián, planned to kill the baby? This thought revived in Perucho all the activity and energy that he usually mustered in his hazardous enterprises in corrals, chicken coops, and stables.

He slipped out of the chapel easily, determined to save the life of the Moscoso heiress at all costs. How was he going to do it? There was no time to mature his plan; it was necessary to act quickly, without stopping at anything. He sneaked through the kitchen unseen and ran upstairs. Once he reached the upper rooms, where the family lived, he smothered his steps so much that the sharpest ear would have mistaken them for the murmur of the air stirring a curtain. What he feared was that the door of Nucha's room might be locked. When he saw it ajar, his heart leaped with glee.

He pushed on it with the softness of the cat that conceals its claws. The accursed door was in the habit of squeaking, but his push was so gentle that now it hardly whined. Perucho hid himself inside the room, behind the screen. Through one of its many holes he peeped to the other side, where the crib was, and saw the baby asleep and the nurse lying on her face on Nucha's bed, snoring loudly. This human log was not likely to wake up. The boy would be able to carry out his plan safely. It was important, however, not to awaken the baby, lest she arouse the house with her screams. Perucho held her as if she were a fragile and precious glass doll. His rough palms, used to flinging stones and slapping oxen's foreheads, suddenly became exquisitely delicate. The baby, wrapped in a knitted shawl, did not even grumble when she passed from the crib to the arms of her precocious kidnapper. The latter held his breath and addressed his quick, furtive, cautious steps—like a cat carrying her kittens by the nape in her mouth—to the cloister, to avoid a possible surprise in the kitchen.

In the cloister he halted for about ten seconds to meditate. Where could he hide his treasure? In the haystack, in the straw loft, in the granary, in the stable? He opted for the granary, the darkest and least frequented spot of all. He would go down the steps, steal across the cloister into the stable, run through the threshing floor, and then nothing would be easier than hiding in their haven. No sooner said than done.

The ladder stood leaning on the granary.[1] Perucho began to climb, a rather difficult operation with the baby in his arms. It was necessary to use hands and feet to go up the narrow vertical steps, but Perucho could not count on his hands. He concentrated all the energy of his will on his big toes, which seemed almost prehensile in the way they adapted and adhered to the wooden rungs, polished with use. When he was halfway up he was about to roll down the ladder, so he clutched the baby tighter against his chest. The child awoke and began to cry. Let her cry! Not a living soul could hear her here; only a few hens ran on the threshing floor, competing with two piglets for a few cabbage leaves. Perucho entered triumphantly through the door of the granary.

The spikes of corn were not yet piled up to the ceiling, so there was sufficient space for two minuscule people like Perucho and his protégée to make themselves comfortable. The boy sat down with the baby in his arms, and tried to hush her with profuse flattery and sweet words, especially diminutives, which acquire a peculiar charm on the lips of the peasant. "My little queen, my beauty, my little lump of sugar, hush, hush, and I'll tell you *perty, perty* little

---

1. The typical Galician granary (*hórreo*) is built on stilts.

things. If you don't hush, the bogeyman will come and eat you up! Look, here he comes! Hush, little sun, white dove, little rosebud!"

Not by virtue of these exhortations, but because she had recognized her favorite friend, the infant's crying subsided. She looked at him and, with a blissful smile, ran her hands over his face, babbled, drooled, and looked around her curiously, realizing that she was in a strange place. In front, around, below, everywhere, she was surrounded by a sea of golden spikes, which at Perucho's slightest movement rolled down in gentle cascades. The sun filtered through the interstices of the granary and spread brighter, moving stripes of light. Perucho understood that the spikes were an endless source of amusement for the little one. Now he presented one to her in his hand; now he built a kind of pyramid with many of them, which the child knocked down—or imagined that she did, for it was actually a kick from Perucho that performed the miracle. She laughed with all her heart and gave clear and impatient signs that she wished the game to proceed.

Soon she tired of it. Thanks to Perucho's presence, however, she remained in a good mood. Her gentle, smiling eyes stared at Perucho and seemed to say: "What game could be better than being together? Let's enjoy this privilege, which has always been denied us." In light of her sweet disposition, Perucho surrendered to the pleasure of entertaining her however he wished. He would press a finger on her cheek to make her laugh; or run his hand up her body, darting like a lizard; or make ferocious grimaces, rolling his eyes, clenching his fists, puffing out his cheeks, and bellowing furiously; or lift her high in the air and pretend to drop her suddenly on the corn spikes. Finally, afraid of tiring her, he picked her up, sat down cross-legged, and began to rock her as gently and tenderly as her own mother.

A nagging whim, a powerful desire, came over him. Desire for what? On those occasions when he had been admitted to the privacy of Nucha's room to share the baby's life, he had never dared to do it. Fear of being scolded or sent away, a vague religious respect that restrained his roguish nature, embarrassment, inexperience of his lips, which had never kissed anyone—all this combined prevented him from satisfying an aspiration that he deemed ambitious and almost sacrilegious. But now the treasure was his, now the baby belonged to him. He had won her in fair combat, he owned her by right of conquest, a right that even savages understand! Bringing his face forward as if he were about to savor a delicacy, he touched the child's forehead and eyes. Then he unfolded the shawl and uncovered her legs, warm as little sausages, which began to kick with joy as soon as they were free. Perucho raised one foot to his lips, then the other, alternating them thus for a while. His kisses tickled the baby, who chuckled and then suddenly became serious; but soon she began to feel chilly, and with the vulnerability to temperature changes peculiar to small children, her little feet grew almost icy cold. When Perucho realized, he breathed on her repeatedly as he had seen the cow do to her calves, wrapped her again in her swaddling clothes and shawl, and rocked her in his arms. The most glorious conqueror could not have felt prouder or more satisfied than Perucho, convinced as he was that he had rescued the baby from certain decapitation and brought her into safety where no one could find her. Not for a moment did he think of the hard, sunburned grandfather lying out there by the wall. It is not unusual to see a child who has been crying desperately by his dead mother's body comfort himself with a toy and a few chocolates; perhaps the memory and the sorrow will return later, but the brutal first impression of pain is gone forever. This was the case with Perucho. The happiness of possessing his beloved baby, the glory of defending her life, effaced the recent tragic events. He did not remember his grandfather, nor the shot that had struck him down as he used to strike down partridges.

And yet fear and gloom seemed to hold sway over his imagination, to judge by the tale that he began to narrate solemnly to the baby, as if she could understand his words. From where did this tale, a variation of the ogre legend, come? Had Perucho heard it one evening by the fire, while the old women wove and the young ones peeled chestnuts? Was it a creation of his fantasy, agitated by the terrors of so exceptional a day?

"Once upon a time"—the tale began—"there was a very bad king, a big rascal, who ate people and living *presons*. This king had a *perty* baby, perty like a flower of May, and tiny, tiny like a grain of millet." Perucho meant a grain of corn. "And this devil of a king was going to eat her, for he was the bogeyman and had an ugly face, more uglier than the devil himself!" Perucho grimaced horribly to dramatize the king's incomparable ugliness. "And one night he says, says he: 'Tomorrow morning very early I shall eat the baby . . . like this, and like that.'" He opened and closed his mouth, flapping his jaws like the flycatchers in the cathedral. "And there was a little birdie up on the little tree, and he heard the king and said, he said: 'Eat her you won't, you ugly bogeyman.' And birdie goes, and what does he do? He flies in through the window. And the king was asleep." He laid his head on the spikes and snored loudly to mimic the king's sleep. "And birdie goes and pecks out one of his eyes, and now the king's got just one eye." He shut his left eye, demonstrating how the king had lost it. "And the king wakes up and cries, and cries" (parody of crying) "with just one eye, and birdie laughs, sitting perty on the little tree. And he goes, and hops, and says, says he: 'If you don't eat the baby and you give her to me, I'll give you your eye back.' And the king says: 'All right.' And birdie married the baby, and always sang perty songs, and played the bagpipe" (bagpipe solo). "And they lived happily ever after, and the king orders that I tell you the tale again!"

The baby did not hear the end of the story. The music of the words, which meant nothing to her, the warmth, the satisfaction of Perucho's company, imperceptibly lulled her back to sleep. Perucho, amid the usual hullabaloo with which horror tales end, saw her shut her eyes. He arranged the bed of corn spikes as best as he could, tucked her in the shawl as Nucha did, so that her little nose would not get cold, and resolutely took his position as sentry in a corner by the door, leaning on a heap of corn. But owing to immobility and exhaustion or to the effect of so many accumulated emotions, his head grew heavy too and his eyelids began to close. He rubbed them with his fingers, yawned, and for a few minutes struggled with his encroaching drowsiness . . . and lost. The two angels sheltered in the granary slept in peace.

Among the figures that populated Perucho's anguished nightmare, he saw an animal of immeasurably enormous proportions, a wild beast that approached him howling, roaring, ready to swallow him at once or squash him under one of its paws. His hair stood on end, his flesh shivered, and a chilly sweat bathed his brow. What a horrible monster! It is coming, it attacks Perucho, its claws tear his flesh, its huge body falls like an immense rock upon him . . . The boy opens his eyes . . .

Raging furiously, screaming, beating him black and blue, kicking him, and pulling at his curls was the nurse, larger and more brutal than ever. We must say that Perucho behaved like a hero. He lowered his head and barred the entrance to the granary, and for a few minutes he defended his prize with the wall of his body. But the nurse's bulk and weight crushed and paralyzed him, rendering him helpless. When the half-suffocated, wretched boy felt the leaden statue release him, after she had almost flattened him to the ground, he looked back. The baby had disappeared. Perucho will never forget how desperately and long he wept, while he writhed amid the corn spikes.

Chapter 29

Nor will Julián forget the day when these extraordinary events took place, the most tragic day of his life, when things that he could never have imagined actually happened: he was accused by a husband of unlawful conspiracy with his wife, a husband who claimed to have been offended, who threatened him, who shamefully banished him from his house forever; and he saw the unfortunate lady, the truly outraged wife, impotent to refute the ridiculous and despicable calumny.

What would have happened if they had carried out their escape plan the next day? Then they would have had to bow their heads and plead guilty! To think that only five minutes earlier it had not even occurred to them that Don Pedro and the world would interpret the situation in this way!

No, Julián will never forget it. He will not forget those unforeseen tribulations; the sudden courage, unknown to himself, that he summoned at the critical moment in order to throw in the husband's face everything that burned in his soul; the rebuke; the indignation that had been restrained by his usual timidity; the confrontation provoked by the vile insult; the terrible words, which for the first time came to his lips, versed only in words of peace; his challenge to the marquis, from man to man, as he walked out of the chapel. No, he will not forget the appalling scene, no matter how many years may bend his shoulders and how much white hair may frost his brow. Nor will he forget his hasty departure, without time to pack; and how he saddled the mare with his own inexperienced hands; how, with a skill improvised by urgency, he mounted, spurred, and rode off at full gallop, everything done mechanically, as in a dream, before the momentary rebellion of his blood died down. He had not seen the baby and kissed her good-bye, because he knew that if he did he would be capable of throwing himself at the master's feet and begging him humbly for permission to stay at the house of Ulloa, even as a shepherd or a farmer.

He will not forget either how he left the stately house and took the road that on the day of his arrival had seemed so sad and gloomy. The sky is cloudy. A thickening dark canopy threatens the clarity of the sun. The pine trees, twining their tops, whisper persistently, poignantly, sweetly. Every gust of wind carries the healthy scent of resin and the honeyed aroma of broom. At a short distance the cross raises its arms of stone, stained with golden lichen. Suddenly the mare balks, shivers, rears . . . Julián lets go of the rein and clings instinctively to the mane. A bundle, a man, a corpse, lies on the ground; the grass around him is drenched with blood, which is beginning to cake and blacken. Julián remains nailed on the spot, powerless, possessed by a mixture of amazement and gratitude to Providence that he cannot explain and that, nonetheless, subjugates him. The face of the corpse is pressed to the earth. It does not matter: Julián has recognized Primitivo, the traitor. He does not speculate, he does not wonder who murdered him. Whatever the instrument may have been, it has been guided by the hand of God! He pulls away his mare, crosses himself, and rides off forever; from time to time, he turns around to look at the black form outlined against the green grass and the dull whiteness of the wall.

Chapter 30

Ten years constitute a stage not only in the life of an individual, but also in the history of a nation. Ten years complete a process of renewal; ten years rarely pass in vain, and he who looks back is usually surprised by the distance covered in a decade. But certain places, like certain people, let a tenth of a century pass unnoticed. There stands the house of Ulloa to prove this truism. The massive lair, defying time, appears as heavy, gloomy, and forbidding as ever. No useful or ornamental renovations can be appreciated in the furniture, the garden, or the fields. The wolves on the coat of arms are not any tamer; the pine tree has no new sprouts; the same symmetrical ripples of petrified water bathe the pillars of the majestic bridge.

The village of Cebre, on the other hand, pays tribute to progress. In the phrase of an enlightened native son who reports to the newspapers of Orense and Pontevedra, it has introduced moral and material improvements. The tobacco store is no longer the only center of political discussion. A society of education and recreation, and of arts and sciences—as its regulations state—has been founded to this end, and a few little stores, which the aforementioned Cebrean calls "bazaars," have been opened. Admittedly, the two chieftains still fight for their petty empire, but by now it seems certain that Barbacana, who represents reaction and tradition, will yield to Trampeta, the living embodiment of progressive ideas and the new age.

The malicious say that the secret of the liberal candidate's success lies in the fact that his opponent, today a *canovist*, [1] has grown old and decrepit, having lost much of his nerve and of his indomitable and at the same time treacherous character. Be that as it may, the truth is that Barbacana's influence has weakened and decreased.

Someone else has aged rather prematurely: the former chaplain of the house of Ulloa. His hair is streaked with silver, his lips sunken, his eyes cloudy, his shoulders bent. He walks slowly on the narrow path that meanders through vineyards and thickets to the chapel of Ulloa.

What a humble church! It rather looks like a peasant's shack, the only mark of its sanctity being a cross above the portico. It is a sad and humid place. The grassy atrium is damp at all hours—even in full sun—as if wet with dew. The atrium is built higher than the peristyle of the church, which is sinking, entombed by the earth that slowly slides down the nearby hill. In a corner of the atrium stands a small isolated bell tower with a cracked bell in it. In the middle, a low cross at the top of three stone steps lends the picture a pensive, poetic touch. Here, in this corner of the universe, Jesus Christ lives. But how lonely! How forgotten!

Julián stopped in front of the cross. He looked much older, and also more manly. Some of the features on his delicate face were sharper, firmer; his lips, pursed and pale, revealed the severity of the man used to repress every outburst of passion, every earthly impulse. Manhood had taught him what the true worth and rightful crown of the pure priest ought to be. He had become as tolerant of others as he was stern with himself.

Treading the atrium of Ulloa made a curious impression on him. He felt that somebody very dear to him walked about alive, resuscitated, filling him with her presence, warming him with her breath.

---

1. Supporter of Cánovas del Castillo, leader of the conservative party in power between 1875 and 1881.

Who could it be? Heavens above! He was struck by the notion that Señora Moscoso was alive, even though he had read the announcement of her death! No doubt the strange hallucination was caused by his return to Ulloa after a ten-year parenthesis. Señora Moscoso's death! Nothing would be easier than to see for himself. There was the churchyard. All he had to do was go toward the wall overgrown with ivy, push open the wooden door, and enter.

It was a gloomy place, despite the absence of languid willows and cypresses, whose theatrical and majestic appearance contributes so much to the solemnity of burial grounds. The church walls bordered it on one side; on the other three it was bounded by thick walls covered with ivy and parasitic plants, and by the gate, which connected the entrance with the atrium. Through the wooden lattice of the gate the mountain looked sharp, remote, and purple, owing to the early hour. It was that time of the day when the sun, not yet very warm, begins to rise toward its zenith, and nature shivers with the morning coolness, as if emerging from a bath. An aged olive tree bent over the gate, its branches sometimes shaken by the quick fluttering of the innumerable noisy sparrows that nested in it. A huge hydrangea grew opposite it, withered and stooped after the heavy seasonal rain, gracefully infirm, with its clumps of languid blue and yellow flowers. This was the extent of the decoration in the cemetery. The vegetation, however, was so vicious and exuberant that it inspired repulsion and superstitious terror, and induced all sorts of fantasies. By mysterious transmigration, in these tall, thick nettles, in this rank grass, in these vigorous thistles, whose flowers had the fallow hue of wax, may have been incarnated the souls—in a sense also vegetative—of those who slept here forever: those who had never lived or loved, or pursued one of those lofty, generous, purely spiritual and abstract ideas that stir the conscience of the artist and the thinker. It seemed as if a human substance—the substance of a

crude, atavistic, inferior humanity steeped in ignorance and matter—nourished and gave its energy and abundant sap to this flora,
gloomy by virtue of its very luxuriance. On the uneven ground,
which contrasted with the smooth platform of the atrium, the foot
sometimes detected the hardness of an ill-covered coffin, and then
a softness that aroused as much horror and fright as stepping on
the flabby limbs of a corpse. An icy-cold breeze, a peculiar odor of
mold and putrefaction, a truly sepulchral atmosphere, rose from
the irregular ground, replete with the dead piled upon each other.
Amid the damp greenery, streaked by the slimy trails of snails and
slugs, stood the black wooden crosses outlined with white, which
bore curious inscriptions riddled with spelling mistakes and quaint
errors. Julián's feet tingled with restlessness and the sensation that
he trod on something soft and living, or at least something that
had once had sensibility and life. Suddenly he was startled: on one
of the crosses, taller than the rest, there was a name written in white
letters. He approached and deciphered the inscription, ignoring
its orthographic lapses: "Here lie the ashes of Primitibo Suárez,
his relatibes and friends prey to god for his soul." On this spot the
ground protruded to form a mound. Julián muttered a prayer and
walked away quickly, thinking that he felt the bronze body of his
formidable enemy under his feet. At that moment a white butterfly
flew from the cross—one of those late butterflies that fly slowly, as
if chilled by the cold air, and soon land on the first favorable place
they find. The new priest of Ulloa followed it and saw it rest on a
miserable mausoleum, tucked between the corner of the wall and
an angle on the side of the church.

   The insect stopped there, and so did Julián. His heart beat fast
and his sight clouded over. For the first time in many years, his
spirit was disturbed and he was wholly beside himself. The shock
was so deep and harrowing that he could not explain how it seized
his being and pulled him out of his natural state. It knocked down

walls, jumped over fences, dodged obstacles, and overthrew everything with the superhuman power of long-repressed emotions that
at last overflow and tyrannize the soul. He did not even notice
the incongruity of the mausoleum, built with stone and lime and
decorated with skulls, bones, and other funereal emblems by the
inexperienced hand of some village dauber; he did not need to
spell out the inscription, for he was certain that where the butterfly had landed there rested Nucha, Señorita Marcelina, the saint,
the victim, the little virgin, always candid and heavenly. There
she lay alone, abandoned, betrayed, abused, slandered, her wrists
wounded by a brutal hand and her face consumed with sickness,
terror, and pain . . . These thoughts froze the prayer on Julián's
lips. The flow of existence went back ten years; and in one of those
transports that in him were as rare as they were sudden and irresistible, he fell on his knees, opened his arms, and kissed the grave
ardently, crying like a child or a woman, rubbing his cheeks against
the cold surface, and digging his nails into the lime until it came off.

He heard laughter, whispering, and a merriment unsuited to
the place and the occasion. He turned around and stood up in confusion. There before him was a bewitching pair lighted by the sun,
which had reached almost to the center of the sky. The boy was the
most handsome adolescent that fantasy could have dreamed of. If
as a child he had looked like the Cupid of antiquity, the lengthen-
ing lines that distinguish puberty from childhood now gave him
the appearance of the archangels and heavenly heralds of biblical
pictures. Like them, he combined feminine beauty and curly locks
with a certain graceful and masculine severity. As for the girl, quite
tall for eleven, her astonishing resemblance to her poor mother
at the same age broke Julián's heart: identical long black braids,
identical pale face, although less transparent, darker, more perfectly oval, with brighter eyes and a firmer gaze. Of course Julián
recognized the couple! How often had he held them in his arms!

Only one detail made him doubt if these charming youths actually were the illegitimate child and the true heiress of the Moscosos. Whereas the clothes of Sabel's son were of fine materials and a style between that of the prosperous villager and the gentleman, Nucha's daughter wore an old calico dress and shoes so battered that she might as well have been barefoot.

Autobiographical Sketches
by Emilia Pardo Bazán

Reader and Friend: The worthy publishers of the new Library of Contemporary Novelists, which begins with my novel *The House of Ulloa*, have asked me to write a few autobiographical notes, more extensive than a preface but more succinct than a complete autobiography. I shall gladly honor the request of Cortezo & Company; firstly because I wish to support a press that popularizes Spanish literature by means of the exquisite collection Arts and Letters, and secondly because its proposal suits my taste.

I have always liked writings of an intimate nature in which the author reveals himself and serves to the public tidbits of his life, not as food for frivolous curiosity but as a substantial dish spiced with decorous frankness. I have noticed that in foreign countries refined intellectual gourmets regard this genre as a delicious aperitif and a delicacy. In it—they say—the writer appears less guarded and more spontaneous, exposing his moral makeup, preferences, habits, and obsessions; these clues take us to conclusions that the sharpest critic cannot gather from *external* writings alone. These works are almost the equivalent of making the author's acquaintance. What interesting data, unpublished details, eloquent documents, remain in them for future research! Unlike political news, literary news is comparable to a good wine: as it ages its value increases. While an author's life or a historical period slips away, its contemporaries, who have all the facts at hand, often ignore it; but let half a century pass, and as the acquisition of exact details becomes more difficult, these gain a special interest. I should add that it is not necessary that they pertain to universally known, first-rate writers.

Thus in France, for example, not only do memoirs, autobiographies, letters, and diaries proliferate, but erudition also pursues tirelessly the most obscure and debatable aspects of the lives of writers and poets: whether Molière's wife limped on the right or the left foot; whether Diderot's affair with Madame Puisieux was or was not detrimental to his career, and whether his affair with Miss Wolland, on the other hand, helped and encouraged him; whether André Chénier's[1] quarrel with his brother José María lasted only a few months or persisted for so long that it had an influence on the great poet's tragic end; whether Blaise Pascal favored or opposed his sister Jaqueline's decision to become a nun; and in sum, other particulars of this nature, which sometimes border on the trivial or exceed the subtle.

Around here, on the contrary, neither writers nor readers have shown any inclination toward the confidential genre. Be it out of modesty, as Philarète Chasles[2] believes, or pride, Spanish authors frown even on prefaces, except when they are written by somebody else's hand; and they are so reluctant to talk about themselves clearly and in detail that after they die the most conscientious biographer cannot revive their personalities, and the literary historian is at pains to discover the intimate link between *the man and his work*.

Who would not love to find today some autobiographical note by Cervantes that might shed light on obscure points of his life and deeds? But there is no need to refer to a peerless genius; any discovery regarding an inferior or mediocre figure would delight the historiographer.

It is not pure vanity to speak of oneself, providing it is done opportunely and moderately, with respect for modesty and with the intent of sincerity; but is sincerity possible—one may reply— when the writer analyzes himself, not alone with his conscience but before thousands of people? I respond that it is. Furthermore, a wish to confess, an irresistible urge to communicate to the public our deepest feelings and thoughts, runs like an electric current from the heart to the hand that moves the pen across the white page. After all, art is nothing but a communion between the individual soul and the collective soul, if I may call them so. And now, to the point.

I can trace my earliest literary memory to an important and already distant historic date: the end of the African war, to which I dedicated the first gifts of my muse. The merit of the poems can be easily inferred, considering that I was approaching the age when the Catholic church grants children the ability to think. Nevertheless, my remembrances of the period and of the patriotic enthusiasm stirred by the events of the time are indelible, whereas more recent memories are easily erased.

In those days the struggle with the Moroccan empire was the main topic of conversations, newspapers, and books.[3] No doubt, if the Spaniards had taken advantage of their victory as vigorously as they had fought and won, and if they had understood the grounds of their enterprise, we might have reaped great benefits from O'Donnell's sterile campaign, which produced only a cargo of Moorish money. Among the journals to which my father subscribed stood out *La Iberia*, whose editor was his friend and fellow believer Calvo Asensio. I devoured (I do not know when I began to read fluently, for I do not recall ever learning to spell) articles, clippings, news sections, poems, camp letters, and accounts of exploits by Prim, Ros de Olano, and other commanders whom I deemed far superior to Bernard and Roland.[4] When the peace was signed and we knew that part of the victorious army would disembark in La Coruña, I felt exultant and wished that my shoulders would sprout swallow wings, so that I could fly to the high seas and there welcome the ships transporting the troops.

I shall never forget the day of the triumphal march into the city. A splendid sun shone on the bayonets and naked swords; it rendered the colors of the national flag—pierced by bullets—gayer, shinier, and bolder; it drew enameled reflections from the leaves of the laurel crowns; and it descended like a bath of glory on the tanned, smiling faces of the boys and limber hunters, whose uniforms boasted with martial coquetry the dust, tears, and tatters of the fight. I stood on a balcony of Real Street, my forehead level with the railing. While the young ladies, objects of my envy, dominated the scene, waving embroidered handkerchiefs and throwing bouquets and crowns with rose petals and long ribbons, I rose on tiptoe or struggled to squeeze my head between the railing bars to take a better look at the parade and, lacking other gifts, to cast my glances and my soul to the winners. Whoever has not seen the return of the national troops carrying winged victory in the folds of the flag cannot say that he has lived!

When the ranks broke, the joy in the street was even greater than on the balconies and porches. Good old women who had once had children "in the service of the king" and kept a soft spot in their hearts for soldiers, kissed and hugged them profusely. The young ones smiled at them and the men offered them their cigar cases. Neighbors fought over the cumbersome task of housing them; no one wanted to give up his conqueror. A sergeant and two volunteers from the Basque infantry fell to us; theirs were the regiments that had participated the least in the Moroccan war, for they had been organized at the last minute to prevent criticism of the privileges of the Basque provinces, whose system of self-rule exempted them from joining in national warfare.[5] When our shy and respectful boarders walked through the door, I thought that they were supernatural beings descended from a world more perfect than ours. How becoming were the deep blue garments, the loose-fitting trousers, the black boots, and particularly the graceful berets! How virile their sunburned complexions, overgrown beards, and puffed-out chests! Later I realized that they were but three sturdy lads with the rugged, honest air typical of the Basques, but at the time they struck me as the epitome of masculine gallantry.

Everyone was disposed to treat them royally. We lavished presents upon them, debating which would be more to their taste. First we suggested sherry, Cuban cigars, and fancy meals; then we prepared their beds in the best room of the house. I shall mention a detail that I remember clearly as proof of our hospitality toward those men, who no doubt were brave, even though they had had no opportunity to demonstrate it. All housewives know that the most exquisitely embroidered bedding sets are saved in the closet for special occasions. The finest chambray of our wardrobe was spread on the beds of the Biscayan mountaineers, under old family quilts of rustling damask with embossed initials. Half an hour later another boarder arrived: Uzuriaga, commander of the regiment and also a friend and fellow deputy of my father in the government of 1854. Then we had to face a dilemma. Uzuriaga was going to sleep between sheets inferior to those of his soldiers! Should we interchange them? After careful deliberation, we decided to leave things as they were, lest the good Biscayans be offended.

Uzuriaga impressed me rather less than the volunteers. I believed—I do not know why—that in general the real heroes were not among officials but among rank-and-file soldiers. This is why I was surprised to find a great banquet prepared in honor of the commander. I ran around the dining room and the corridors, as children are wont to do when something unusual happens in the house, bothering everyone, inquiring into everything, admiring the decorated serving plates, clusters of pastries, candles, toothpick cases, and flower vases on the table, and the bottles lined up symmetrically on the sideboard. I surmised that the end of the war and the march of troops in La Coruña meant something very important and worth celebrating that related not to the government—which at home we often criticized—but to something greater, loftier, and more majestic, worshiped by all: the nation. Seeing that the grown-ups paid me no attention and that I had no one with whom to share my enthusiasm, I withdrew to my bedroom and scribbled my first poems, which, I gather, must have been *quintillas*.[6] Oh, how I dreamed of seeing them printed in the papers, which in those days published a great many poems with decorated borders!

It was long before another poetic spark struck my mind. I declare that the sublime thrill of patriotic love precedes the conscious idea of its cause, and that we feel it in our childhood as much as in our youth or maturity. In my case, this is one of the emotions that have not been altered by readings, studies, the ups and downs of life, or certain sophisms that nowadays pass for the last word in philosophical disillusionment, and in truth are only atrophy of the soul and a symptom of the decadence of nations. In this respect I find myself—I say it proudly—on the same level as a woman of the people.

Another incident, although not related to modern history, stands out amid my first memories. We used to spend our summers in Rías Bajas, in the province of Pontevedra. Surrounded by the Herculean arms of a sea worthy of the Neapolitan coast and blessed with a climate also reminiscent of Italy, it is one of the loveliest areas in the Galician countryside: a shore of fine beaches with minute, glittery grains of sand and mother-of-pearl shells, bordered by aloe trees; a place where the ash-colored Galician sky becomes clearer and brighter, and where the inhabitants have lighter blood, dark hair, and pale skin, approaching the meridional type. On this privileged spot we own a vast and picturesque estate and a very old mansion called Torre de Miraflores, which has nothing to do with the gloomy house of Ulloa. While they repaired the decrepit tower, we rented a residence in Sangenjo, a charming fishing village at the foot of our property. The owner left us the furniture, including a collection of books that I still can see in my mind's eye, sprawled in disorder on old bookcases painted blue and motheaten. What a discovery!

I was one of those children who read anything that falls into their hands, even wrappings of doughnuts and spices; the kind who sit all day quietly in a corner with a book, their eyes surrounded by black circles and squinting from the strain on their still tender optic nerves. Any story that I found and liked I would read five or six times, and later I would recite entire chapters, particularly from *Don Quixote*, without omitting a comma. Then I pronounced myself in permanent closed session in that little room. Sometimes, through the windows that overlooked the main square of Sangenjo, I heard a loud row of women selling sardines, or a melancholy song of fishermen pulling their boats. No one could drag me out of that room. Books, a great many books that I could handle, peruse, remove from and put back on the shelves!

From all of them I remember just one, but that one I remember so vividly that I would be certain to recognize it if I saw it now in the same edition. It was a multivolume Bible with notes and beautiful pictures. I plunged into it, forbidding myself to skip any part of such an incomparable whole. I particularly enjoyed Genesis, whose magnificence I felt vaguely, the dramatic Exodus, and the exquisite and novelistic stories of Esther and Ruth. On the other hand, I did not much care for the inspired voices of the Prophets or the cooing of the beloved in the Song of Songs. To complete the sketch of an eight- or nine-year-old girl engrossed in these readings, I must add that perfect innocence has the ability of the bee to extract honey from the most poisonous flower. I can guarantee that, although I felt the magnitude of biblical poetry with surprising intensity, the crude passages, so numerous in the Old Testament, did not arouse my curiosity or cloud over the clear sky of my childish fantasy; and before my eyes passed the Oriental sinners, Tamar, Lot's daughters, she "who lay with Uriah"—as the sacred text goes—without my understanding their naughtiness.

In Madrid, where we spent the winters, I attended a French school, the cream of the crop among elitist schools of the day, highly patronized by the royal family. I was only a day student. The principal, a spruced-up old woman with strands of gray hair that showed under the headdress typical of her country—a cap with lace and ribbons—treated us worse than galley slaves. At lunch she served an imaginary stew, and for dessert the oldest peanuts, the blandest hazelnuts, the most petrified chestnuts that could be purchased in town or country. I think that she deliberately kept them in a closet until they reached the point when the pupils could not sink their teeth into them. There has never been a stingier Frenchwoman, common as her type is. As for spiritual nourishment, *Telemachus* and La Fontaine's[7] fables day and night, plenty of mythology, small doses of geography, and now and then a solar eclipse through smoked glasses, an experiment that seemed to me the ultimate in astronomical science. There was also a positive aspect: as we were not allowed to speak Spanish, the not-so-dull pupils left the place chattering in French like parrots.

Finally we settled down in La Coruña. In the large, quiet, imposing old house in which I had no one to play with, I discovered a treasure similar to the one in Sangenjo. Next to the iron doors of the archives there were two more that looked equally forbidding. One day I found them half open and caught a glimpse of a nest of books. I courted it incessantly until it was put at my disposal, for my parents looked favorably upon my fondness for reading. How many evenings I devoted to the pleasure of unexpected discoveries! And yet there was nothing in the library particularly appealing to me: it was the collection of a cultivated man with a taste for politics, jurisprudence, and agriculture, more interested in social than literary issues. Amid these tedious books, however, I stumbled on others that captivated me. I could not say how many times I browsed through *La conquista de México*, by the elegant Solís, or reread Plutarch's *Lives*. The latter, incidentally, earned me a few philippics from a good gentleman of our coterie who was appalled to hear that a ten-year-old brat, loquacious to boot, admired and celebrated Cato, Brutus, and other flaming pagans of the same breed.

Whenever someone called me "doll," my comfort and haven was a corner of the couch reserved for another guest, who still lives and continues to call me "baby" as he did then. Known as "the naturalist" and self-styled "bug expert," he is a prestigious entomologist from Havana who sought retreat in a village close to La Coruña. In his luggage he carried things that fascinated me: collections of tropical butterflies, rare insects skillfully hunted and dissected. He told us about his hunts, excursions, travels, and adventures with so much color, vividness, and charm that I always drew near him, tugged at his coat, and begged: "Tell me about bugs."

Behind the iron doors I also found Cervantes's *Novelas ejemplares* yawning in the annoying company of *La Etelvira*, *El castillo misterioso* (The mysterious castle), *Los huérfanos de la aldea* (The orphans of the village), and some more dull novels of the scary, weepy genre, which I devoured with the appetite of tender age. The good Abbot Barthélemy and his *Viaje del joven Anacarsis* (Travels of young Anacarsis) appealed to me; but it was superseded by Cantú's *Historia de cien años* (History of one hundred years),[8] and by several studies of the French Revolution, which seemed to me the most interesting drama in the world. Strangely enough, in my childhood—an age that is usually exclusive in its affections—I liked the ferocious Jacobins as much as the gentle Girondists, and

I mourned both Madame Roland's decapitation and the torture of the poor little prince imprisoned in the Temple.[9]

By now I had scrutinized everything. The only remaining temptation was the top shelf, on which several volumes set aside by my father slumbered. These were the apple of Eden. When they had been rearranged I had been told, "Don't touch those," without too much insistence on the prohibition, for the shelf was high enough to keep me away from the forbidden fruit. But the devil himself is not as resourceful as a curious girl. Taking advantage of a moment of solitude, I piled up bound dictionaries and illustrated magazines—about a dozen in total—to make a platform for a chair; on top of the chair I put another one, precariously balanced in the air. Then I began to climb, in imminent danger of breaking my neck, clinging to the bookshelves and relying on my device as little as possible, until, to my ineffable delight, my hand seized the mysterious volumes. One after another I threw them on the floor, onto which I jumped and squatted to savor my prey. I opened one of the books, examined the cover, looked at the vignette . . . I cannot explain what I felt. I think that it was boredom, contempt, and rage rather than embarrassment. I remember that, without reading a single line from any of them, I tossed them up with such a steady hand that they landed in their former place, at the back of the shelf.

It was a purely instinctive reaction. A twelve-year-old girl brought up among serious people, with no friends other than her parents and a circumspect confessor, I was certainly incapable of much perversity; therefore, it is impossible for me to say why I rejected the book so angrily. I must add that since then I have read a few that make that one—Pigault-Lebrun's *El mozo de buen humor*[10]—appear a model of modesty, as far as freedom of language and scenes is concerned; and yet they have what the impudent French author lacks: real charm and literary beauty. Without Petronius's perfection and irony, without the wit and aphorisms of the archpriest of Hita, without Delicado's sharp eye for detail, without Brantôme's humorous naiveté,[11] dirty books disgust me or send me to sleep. From their authors I expect twice as much talent, and when they lack it I prefer any life of a saint, *Año cristiano* (Christian year), or an innocent book of miracles.

That treasure protected by the iron doors was more beneficial to me than the teachings of some of my tutors at home. I secretly rebelled against piano lessons and pronounced useless all that grinding up and down and over and over the scales, which finally boiled down to "a little practice" for my fingers. Away with Liszt! I begged for Latin instead of piano; I wanted to read the *Aeneid,* the *Georgics,* and Ovid's *Elegies,* which lay scattered in the iron closet. But nobody honored my preferences, which, I admit, were a little unusual for a young lady. I continued to pound the keys, and it was even said that I made progress. I believe that my grudge against pianos was born then.

Music such as I can appreciate and enjoy revealed itself to me in poetic lines: in Ercilla's not-so-harmonious octaves, in the beat of Racine's alexandrines, in Malo's none-too-good translation[12] of the *Iliad,* and above all in the magic of Zorrilla, the king of melody and the Verdi of our poets.[13] Despite the pleasant sound of Zorrilla's *Poema a Granada* and *Cantos del trovador,* spiritually Homer satisfied me more. As soon as I had pencil and paper I had to sketch Achilles' head in his proud, feathered helmet, Minerva, Apollo, and bearded old men who were supposed to be Priam rescuing Hector's body. Today I have the foolish vanity to remember that the three books I most enjoyed in my childhood, with no need of encouragement from adults, were the Bible, *Don Quixote,* and the *Iliad.*

I composed a few poems furtively, for a certain modesty always surrounds these poetic activities. Not all of them remained as unknown as they should have; some ended up printed in Soto Freire's

Almanaques or in *Soberanía nacional* in Madrid. Incidentally, to one of these *Almanaques* I submitted a short story or outline of a novel—perhaps my first prose lines—in which some people from our circle saw a dramatization of a contemporary tragedy. I never intended to write about real events, though reminiscences of the current topic of conversation may have unconsciously rushed to my pen.

Shortly afterward Señor Salustiano Olózaga, the greatest parliamentary orator of the second constitutional term and a good friend and political leader of my father, passed through La Coruña, which had been the stage for some of his adventures as a persecuted plotter. The afternoon he spent at our home was memorable for me. I could not take my eyes off the white curls on his head, his opaque paleness, his veiled eyes, expressive as myopic eyes usually are, his beautiful, patrician old age. As often happens to children, I was unable to assess him objectively, and so I raised him to a pinnacle as if he were one of Plutarch's illustrious men in the flesh. Embarrassment, confusion, and enthusiasm seized me when the progressive leader asked me to read a sonnet in which I said with some vehemence that the nation "in you beholds its saving anchor." As soon as I finished, something like heavenly music poured in my ears. Olózaga, in brief and carefully chosen sentences, emphasized by a still vibrant and powerful voice, paired me with the Argensolas[14] and the best sonnet makers in the universe. Now I see clearly that there was little else the good gentleman could say; but consider the impact that his praise had on me. Those days were quite different from ours, when every summer political figures and celebrities move from Madrid to provincial towns. In the period to which I refer, it took resolution to make a long trip in the stagecoach. The railroad was like a fantastic dream in the Galician imagination that did not come true until fifteen years later. The Olózagas of this world did not walk through one's door every day.

In my whole childhood I met hardly any famous writer, other than the pleasant fabulist and charming old man Don Pascual Fernández Baeza. He was a senator decorated with I do not know how many crosses, whom I used to call "Baeza fables" and on whose knees I climbed—just think how long ago it must have been—to hear him recite his poems and to repeat them immediately from memory. This harmless old man, who looked like the living image of classicism and whose bent shoulders and shaky head cried out to rest in an academic chair, was—who could imagine it!—my first teacher of rhetorical indiscipline. "My little one," his kind toothless mouth said, "don't ever read Hermosilla! [15] And if you do, send him to the devil, do you understand? To the devil! Write poems your way, no rules! Forget about rules! They are only good to ruin everything. Don't count the syllables, do you hear? Count by ear, it's enough. If you can't count by ear and you start using your fingers, do you know what will come out of it? A monster. Most of all, be careful with Hermosilla!" I became convinced that Hermosilla was worse than the devil himself, and his works inspired in me a mixture of curiosity and terror.

The numerous tempting anecdotes that come to my mind would exceed the limits of these sketches, so I shall close the chapter of childhood memories with an episode that illustrates my idea of the novel at the time. At fourteen I was allowed to read everything: history, poetry, science, Cervantes's novels, and Quevedo's songs.[16] The only authors still frowned upon were Dumas, Suë, George Sand, Victor Hugo, and other devotees of French romanticism. Whenever their books were mentioned in my presence, it was implied that none could be more pernicious for a young lady. The censorship that is normally applied to the novel in general was reserved for these works, as if no others existed in the world. Of *El judío errante* (The wandering Jew) [17] I heard such things that I came to regard it as the quintessence of human iniquity. As is usually the case, however, the very insistence upon the poisonous elements in those books aroused in me an irresistible curiosity; I concluded that they must be dangerous indeed, if in my home, where people read so much and discussed literature so freely, only they were condemned. Even my uncle, General of Artillery Don Santiago Piñeiro, a curious Voltairian gentleman so fond of numismatics that for a tarnished coin he would travel miles and turn the world upside down, damned "those novels" in a long diatribe and suggested that I be introduced to Fernán Caballero.[18] In fact, I was allowed to read Caballero in reward for a sample of needlework.

One day I was at the house of one of the few friends I had of my age. As soon as we were alone in her father's office, my eyes turned to the shelves filled with books. I let out a scream of joy when I read on the spine of a heavy volume: Victor Hugo: *Nôtre Dame de Paris*. There was no struggle between duty and passion; the latter won without a fight. If I asked for the book they would never give it to me; at best, they would consult my parents, and then I might as well say good-bye to Victor Hugo. So I stole it and took it home hidden under my coat, and then put it in a small desk where I kept ribbons and earrings. At night I tucked it under my pillow and read until the light went out, oblivious to the time. How I relished the story of Esmeralda and Captain Febo, the angelic sacrifice of Quasimodo, the wicked plots of Claude Frollo! Here is a real novel, I thought, savoring every bit of it; here nothing seems natural and common, as in Cervantes, nor are these events of the sort that occur every day, as in Fernán Caballero; here everything is extraordinary, immense, and fateful, and so the author should not be judged by normal standards, because he is a rare genius. This influenced my concept of the novel for many years; I thought that it required a prodigious imagination and that, therefore, it was beyond my reach. The possibility of eventually writing a novel myself seemed as remote as that of receiving a royal crown.

Three important events in my life succeeded each other rapidly: my formal introduction to society, my marriage, and the outbreak of the revolution of September 1868. When my father was elected deputy to the Congress in 1869, we began to spend the winters in the capital and the summers in Galicia. My natural love of literature went into a long hibernation. To a sixteen-year-old wife from an austere family, who had been confined to the company of ponderous relatives and friends, Madrid offered a bustling court and an elegant society that, although dispersed and maimed by the revolution, shone no less for those who had never frequented it before. In the morning, formal calls or riding lessons; in the afternoon, rides along La Castellana; in the evening, balls and the theater; in the spring, concerts and bullfights with the matador Tato; in summer evenings, sometimes a ride to Casa de Campo or La Ronda, and occasionally a tour of El Escorial or Aranjuez. Pleasant pastimes indeed, which curbed my tendency to isolation and a certain shyness resulting from my childhood life and hobbies; but as they repeated themselves winter after winter, I began to feel a void in my soul, a tremendous anxiety, like the man who goes to bed on the eve of a duel and in his dreams fears that he will not wake up in time to fulfill his duty.

During the summers I had no time to retire and concentrate, for they were filled with amusements, parties, and excursions through Galicia on horseback, by carriage, or on foot—delightful journeys that opened my eyes to the outside world, revealed to me the natural kingdom, and prepared me to become the tireless landscapist that I am today, in love with the gray clouds, the aromatic chestnut trees, the foamy rivers imprisoned in ravines, the dewy meadows and sunken trails of my homeland.

Undoubtedly the September revolution opened a new period in our literature. Major political upheavals always influence and modify art: it is such a well-known principle that it needs no demonstration. The later years of Isabella II's rule were marked by artistic stagnation; perhaps a roaring storm was necessary to awaken those who slumbered and to engage in the fight those already alert, so that from the earth covered with wreckage and irrigated with blood a new generation might spring. The hurricane strengthened the lungs; the ongoing argument soon matured intellects and drew sparks from word and pen. The very literary interim of the early revolutionary years—when the muses remained silent, except for brilliant parliamentary oratory and a caustic satirical press—was beneficial, as rest is for the soil before it is sown. Those who had survived the previous age recuperated; the new ones jumped into the arena with the irresistible impetus of hope.

Distant rumors of the resurgent literary movement came to me wrapped in the delicate aroma of tea parties or in the whirlwind of carriage wheels. I would turn my head to listen for a moment, and gradually pay more attention. The *Gritos* (Cries) that were building Núñez de Arce's reputation, the first dramas by Echegaray, the last by Tamayo, and *Carmañola*, by Nocedal,[19] at whose premieres members of the Catholic Youth applauded until they tore their gloves while members of the Cudgel party cracked ribs, worried me sometimes. But in those days the tendency was to leave aside literary merit and give preference to politics. That the revolution had brought about the most horrendous decadence in taste was an axiom supported by facts. The epidemic of can-can and comic operas was hitting hard; we heard *Ojo huero* (Bad Eye) or the rigadoons of *Barba Azul* (Bluebeard) play constantly. Offenbach reigned, and in elitist coteries Gabino Martorell read his five-line poems of protest, while an explosion of laughter discreetly smothered behind fans followed the notorious passage:

> When did the monks' teachings show
> what the can-can today shows?

The theater, thank goodness, remained free of this infection, only to meet with the public's indifference. I saw Matilde Díez in the sunset of her career perform with charming mischief *Mari-Hernández la gallega* (Mari-Hernández the Galician girl); I enjoyed the healthy humor of Mariano Fernández; Catalina had not yet crumbled down; and Rafael Calvo's vigorous youth held a good deal of promise, as did Elisa Boldún, also in blossom. I never missed a dramatic or comic performance, and my literary proclivities revived. Needless to say, in my spare time I hacked two or three dramas, which I wisely placed under lock and key as soon as I completed them. Though I lack the nerve to disinter them from their grave, I gather that they must have been imitations of old-fashioned plays. Unbeknownst to me, one of them came close to being performed, after a disloyal copyist gave it to a second-rate theater to study. Fortunately, I discovered the plot in time and put the manuscript in a safe place.

There was no point in devoting much energy to arts and letters, for the already chaotic political scene became further complicated by the thorny religious issue. Regardless of the opinions of superficial people, who cannot differentiate between passing historical detonators and transcendental factors, and naively assume that a civil war is fought over a few millions from England or France, the religious problem was the most serious of all. Brutal excesses of anticlerical demagoguery; the Congress turned into the headquarters of blasphemy; religious images shot to pieces; artistic monuments demolished with stupid viciousness; nuns harassed and treated like women of the street; greedy confiscations; and in sum, systematic attacks on Catholicism, which in our country grows deeper and stronger when it comes under fire, triggered off the inevitable reaction, either in the form of periodic acts of violence and public rituals of vengeance, or in that of Carlist gangs.[20] I do not remember in exactly which of the early revolutionary years

I witnessed one of those scenes that remain in the memory forever. A priest walked up Toledo Street with his elbows tied together, escorted by the civil guard. In front of him a swarm of urchins marched in formation raising their bare knees, while rascals and whores surrounded and reviled him. Amid their quick steps and the whirlwind of the mob, I caught barely a glimpse of a halo of snow-white hair around the clean-shaven tonsure. He was not even a political prisoner, as I later found out, only a suspect.

My numerous recollections of the revolutionary period do not belong here; therefore, I shall not dwell on the political atmosphere of the coteries, the crusades against King Amadeo of Savoy,[21] and the spirit of the Carlist insurrection, although to a degree they affected me. Clearly, amid that turmoil my beloved literature, of which I thought with increasing nostalgia, could not stay afloat. I cannot even count as a fruit of my ill-satisfied literary vocation a few poems of the moment, which circulated widely and ended up printed in gold letters on silk, through no fault of mine. Artistically, God knows they weigh heavily on my conscience: what is born of political feeling extinguishes itself with it.

After the king's departure the horizon appeared darker than ever. My father was determined to die for politics together with the honest progressive party, whose dream had been to reconcile religious interests with constitutional freedom. In this state of affairs we moved to France, hoping that from Paris we might calmly watch the muddy waters of the revolution run unrestrained. God knows how we managed to cross the border without incidents. All the travelers we knew feared that in Alsasua we might encounter Carlist forces, victorious in Oñate the day before.

Far from the Spanish helter-skelter and with fewer social connections than in Madrid, I led a kind of life more conducive to reawakening intellectual needs. In leisurely moments, after I had visited a museum or a historical monument, or at some hotel at night, I picked up my books and reviewed my English, for I had decided to read Byron and Shakespeare in their language. That same year on the banks of the Po and by the Canal of Venice, I savored the poetry of Alfieri and Ugo Foscolo, and the prose of Manzoni and Silvio Pellico;[22] in Verona I saw Juliet's balcony, in Trieste the Palace of Miramar, and in the great Exhibition of Vienna the progress of industry, which I contemplated with a touch of romantic contempt. It was a beautiful, profitable trip, during which my literary call summoned me with sweet urgency.

Indeed, I scribbled my first pages of prose on the tables of inns and on my knee in the train, with rusty quills and dull pencils: the indispensable travel diary, which does not deserve to be published. After that it became imperative for me to be always engaged in some project or study, a sign that the idle happiness and carelessness of my youth was giving way to meditation.

When I returned to Spain I noticed that, aside from regional unrest, civil war, and other ups and downs in the political tragedy, minds were captured by a new intellectual movement, which stirred not only thinkers and scholars but the press and even private circles, clubs, and coteries. This novelty was called German philosophy or Krausism.[23] Its adepts became the subject of a thousand extravagant and contradictory stories, capable of inflaming even the most incombustible curiosity. Some regarded them as Messianic redeemers of mankind, initiated in a sort of gnosticism or esoteric science, which with a single verb would regenerate our corrupt society and solve the burning issues of our century. Others decried them as sophists, cheats, and madmen, more harmful than the shirtless fanatics of Cartagena.[24] Some dismissed them as materialists, atheists, or pantheists, capable of worshiping onions and leeks like the Egyptians. Others, finally, professed that they were excessively charitable, pious, and given to prayer. What infuriated people most was the specialized language—gibberish, as many said—of the flamboyant sect, full of unknown and abstract terms that smacked strongly of Germanisms. I still chuckle when I remember one of my uncles on my mother's side, a sensible and wise country gentleman who had been a progressive deputy in the Congress in 1854. I can see him walk into my room in Compostela with a newspaper in his hand, covered with the dust of the trip from his estate, yelling before he even said good morning: "What does it say here, my girl, what does it say? Let's see if you can explain it to me. I've read it ten times already and I can't get the gist of it." And he pointed at a passage that, if I am not mistaken, began like this: "Attentive to our own conscience, we are in a state of mutation from our very selves with which we are, nonetheless, properly and truly intimate."

Being far more updated on the subject than my uncle, I tried to make sense of the texts that expounded the doctrine. Only a few were available in Spanish, most of them translated by Krause's disciples and commentators. Despite my papal license, those heterodox readings somewhat upset my Catholic conscience; therefore, in order to take the antidote together with the poison, I turned to another class of authors equally unknown to me, the mystics and ascetics. As soon as I put down *Mandamientos de la humanidad* (Commandments of humanity), I washed away the bitter taste in my mouth with the sugary *Filotea*, a subtle analysis of passion, a gentle breviary in which the roses of virtue have no thorns. When I finished *El ideal*—also of humanity—I embraced *Las moradas* (The abodes).[25] The result of this exercise was predictable, for in me the cult of beauty and form was quite natural. Krausist books seemed as heavy as lead, and their barbaric Spanish irritated me. On the other hand, I fell in love with the supreme perfection, platonic serenity, and luminous poetry that overflows the pages of Granada[26] and Saint Theresa of Avila.

My curiosity soon subsided. Krause struck me as a theosophist, a visionary with a passionate dreamy soul, the opposite of the type of pure thinker that, in my view, Kant embodied.[27] By then, serious people who prided themselves in philosophizing in the German way protested against the Krausist impetus and tried to counteract it with Kantian or Hegelian criticism.[28] My brief reading of Krause in translation revealed to me Kant's powerful intelligence, just as a traveler who stops to read an inscription learns of the existence and value of a magnificent monument. He was the first philosopher that I read with admiration, undaunted by the obscurity of his prose; in my unauthorized opinion, his style becomes transparent once we follow the thread of his clear, forceful reasoning and detect his muscular thought under the heavy clothing of the form.

When I first became acquainted with German philosophy I enjoyed the friendship of several members of this school, which boasted many brilliant disciples. Their trademark was a certain moral rigidity combined with innovative, unusual ideas. Unlike most philosophers, who store their principles away between pages of their books, they showed an excessive and sometimes petty determination to apply theirs to all things in life. In the words of a very talented writer, they were the devil's penitents, that is, the most ascetic heretics of all times. Theirs were the kinds of obsession that do not last, as the premature disintegration and demise of the school prove. Going back to my topic, when I realized that the adepts of Krausism deemed some knowledge of German necessary, I devoted myself to studying it. As soon as I acquired its rudiments, however, I preferred to put my heart and soul into Goethe, Schiller, Bürger, and Heine.[29] Although it would be more flattering to deny it, I declare unabashedly that, except for the expert, it is best to read metaphysical works in French translation. French reduces the complicated German word order to Latin structures, which reassure and illuminate the mind eager to grasp the depths of the text, when this is at all possible.

Now I understand how much I owe to the curiosity that prompted me to browse through Krausist documents. Thanks to that curiosity my reading became regular, methodical, and thoughtful, turning from mere pleasure into study. I developed my mind, set in motion my intellectual capabilities, and acquired the solidity every artist needs in order not to drift like a cork in the sea.

Admittedly, I ran the risk of growing fond of Krause, for his very shallowness and emphasis upon ethics and aesthetics render him insidious and alluring; but that was not the case. Krause's *harmonism* was useful to me as preparation for reviewing, not with total conviction but with the same pleasure we derive from a beautiful poem, Schelling's famous concept of identity, the *I that wills itself* of the eloquent Fichte,[30] Kant's pure reason, Hegel's debatable but brilliant aesthetic theories. And once I developed a taste for it, it helped me to travel back in time to Saint Thomas, Descartes, Plato, and Aristotle. I shall not pretend that I knew them well enough to select the best from each, or that I am well versed in their ideas. The fruits I reaped were more modest, but adequate to satisfy my intellectual needs. I became persuaded that my higher concerns required mystical philosophy, which ascends to God by way of love, and my earthly ones, criticism, a curious discipline that does not walk on stilts and so does not risk a fall.

Men can hardly imagine how difficult it is for a woman to teach herself and fill the gaps in her education. Males attend primary school as soon as they can walk and talk, then public or private school and the university, linking their studies in a continuous sequence. I am aware that much of what they learn is routine, perhaps bothersome and superfluous. Still, it is a strengthening exercise and a basis for later developments. They prepare themselves to pass from the known and elementary to the advanced; they become acquainted with words and ideas that generally remain as inaccessible to women as the fencing foil or the craftsman's tool. One day they attend the class of an eminent professor; the next, they prepare for an exam or compete for an administrative position, testing, like the boxer about to jump into the ring, the flexibility of their limbs. They enjoy every advantage; the disadvantages are reserved for women.

Conscious that my education was poorly grounded, my erudition superficial, and my readings random, I decided to upgrade and interrelate them and to fill the empty spaces in my knowledge, assigning myself homework as I did when I was a little girl with my needlework, and organizing my time. I found that the morning, when sleep has cleared and refreshed the mind, was very conducive to study. The hours I devoted to these occupations were so calm and peaceful that I longed for the whitewashed walls, the leather chair, the crucifix, the skull, and the blackened table of a convent cell. The method I adopted severely prohibited the reading of novels and other books of mere entertainment—this is how I categorized the novel at the time. What I am about to write seems difficult to believe, and yet it is true and deeply significant. Around 1874 and 1875 not only had I not read their work, but I was unaware that Pérez Galdós and Pereda existed, and had barely heard of Valera and Alarcón.[31] One day, as I was walking under the porticoes of Villar Street in Santiago, my eyes were drawn to a series of red and yellow volumes entitled *Episodios nacionales* displayed in a bookstore window.

"What do you think of those?" I asked a gentleman who was with me. "A historical work, isn't it? I'll have to buy it."

"Oh!" he answered. "It isn't a historical work, just a few novels. They aren't worth much."

I leave to him the responsibility for his judgment, but I take upon myself that of having forgotten the little volumes, except to joke about the "eggs and tomatoes"—the shrill note of color so unusual in a book cover—whenever we happened to walk by the window. Novels for a loyal reader of Kant and Spinoza! If I read them I would feel that I was losing time and credibility, like a white-haired professor asked to dance a waltz or play social games. The only distraction I allowed myself was writing a few poems and articles. Poetry, with its rhythmic and musical elements, still swayed my senses, still controlled my nerves, as it does today, and had the power to plunge me in a morbid melancholy that is only a step away from the relief of tears. At least in normal circumstances, however, I was beginning to enjoy the much healthier and more spiritual delights of prose. Translation exercises also induced me gradually to fall in love with the Castilian language, to discover its secrets and treasures, its character and rich harmony, and to become a tireless collector of words—words in which, aside from their contextual value, I find an inexplicable beauty, color, radiance, and aroma of their own, just as a lapidary stops to admire the size, glitter, and purity of a gem before he sets it.

About that time Núñez de Arce did me a favor for which I shall be grateful the rest of my life: he broke a word of honor that he had given spontaneously. I am going to tell the story, if only to put a brief, sad smile on the lips of the distinguished bard. I was still spending the rough season and even spring in Madrid. Once I mentioned to a friend of Núñez de Arce how much I enjoyed his *Gritos de combate*, and he promised to bring the author and introduce us. When he came, my first impression was of surprise that a man so small could create such massive, resonant, and manly poetry, worthy of being recited by a modern Simonides,[32] dominating as from the top of a rock the whisper of a restless crowd and the uproar of political-religious combat. Soon in the sour, saddened face of the Castilian poet I saw something that called for a seventeenth-century costume and the brush of Pantoja,[33] and that was perfectly in keeping with the character of his muse. We conversed amiably and I recited by heart some of his compositions;

he was very flattered, so he said, because ladies usually did not like his poems. My turn came and I did my repertory. There is no need to mention that Núñez de Arce raved about it, because between a courteous man and a poetess this is expected. The thing is that he also encouraged me to publish those beauties, and with generous energy offered to write a preface as my introduction and passport. Coming from him, such a gift had to be accepted. We agreed that I would do the necessary trimming to the manuscript and send it from Galicia. I cut, polished, and pruned my bush of poems; I divided them, had them rewritten in clear, elegant longhand, and sent them to their destination. But the heat of the moment had passed, and the poet's good intentions had gone where even the best of them go. Of that preface he never wrote a single line. How sincerely grateful I am for that!

I have noticed a curious phenomenon. Writers, whether they be mediocre or excellent, perceptive critics or not, grow inordinately fond of the fruits of their poetic genius, and entertain high hopes of winning the favor of the proverbial nine muses, whose palm leaves of virginity have not prevented them from flirting with the entire universe. Though writers have small regard for the rest of their production, they would give their little fingers for the poet's laurel crown. To know that in Spain there is a rhymer around every corner—a fact recorded by popular wisdom—will not cure them from their obsession; nor will the accepted axiom that the vague and divine essence of poetry is not captured within metric patterns, but may extend freely to the realm of prose, as we see in Cervantes, more poetic in *Don Quixote* than in *Viaje al Parnaso* (Travel to Parnassus). What else can I say? The coldness, indifference, and silence of the public and the contempt of critics will not dissuade them, because, ignoring the distracted and misled current generation, they appeal to a fair-minded posterity. The less attention they get from the reader, the more they treasure their beloved rhymes, as mothers do with unfortunate children. A few days ago I was talking to Luis Vilart. This diligent and remarkable man of letters confessed to me a particular weakness for his poems, and his intention of collecting and printing them neatly. Who is not aware of Menéndez y Pelayo's[34] preference for his rhymes above all the products of his intellect? Does this not apply to Valera? Has Cánovas del Castillo[35] laid down his lyre? Did Cervantes himself, the best Spanish prose writer, not glory in his poetry?

It is far from my intention to judge the poems of these authors, and even farther to compare them to my own, which I declare to be the worst in the world. I am free, however, of the common affliction of these brilliant minds: therefore my gratitude to Don Gaspar. Instead of defending my poetic property, I tend to conceal my verses as if they were so many sins—indeed, this is what I consider them to be. Poetry satisfies me only when it is almost perfect and original, in the sense that I understand originality; that is to say, when it dramatizes fully and sincerely the poet's personality. I know that nobody is born without a seed, as common people assume mushrooms are, and that in poetry and prose all of us have ancestors and teachers; but the poet is in greater danger of imitating clichés. I possessed a natural ability to rhyme. After reading the work of an author three or four times, I seemed to detect its basic traits. I remember that the humorous and discreet Campoamor[36] spent a whole morning trying to demonstrate how simple it would be for me to write short poems *like his*. He teased me thus on account of certain essays that I had shown him innocently. His little joke amused and at the same time cautioned me, for I am all too familiar with the poet's ways and his mischievous prose writings.

But then, giving lyric relief to a deep new feeling, I wrote a collection of brief poems entitled *Jaime*. Although to the extent that they were sincere they had a right to come to light, I had my doubts about the form. For this reason and for their intimate nature, they might have remained unknown if my dear friend Francisco Giner[37] had not read them and found them publishable. He kindly presented me with a lovely edition of three hundred copies, which was never submitted to critics or newspapers. Another friend in Paris, Leopoldo García Ramón, has put out a new edition, a typographical jewel worthy of the shelves of a bibliophile princess: just two copies in eighteenth-century Baskerville characters on Japanese paper, bound in Smyrna leather sprinkled with gold iris flowers—a luxury I never dreamed of for my rhymes, which would be even greater if the tears that the book has drawn from many other mothers crystallized into pearls and were set on the cover.

Jaime, my first child, was born in July 1876. As soon as the quarantine ended, I, despite my worries and chores as a nursing mother, put into practice the plan that I had conceived in Madrid: to enter a contest in Oviedo in memory of Father Feijóo.[38] In approximately twenty days I wrote my *Ensayo crítico* (Critical essay), which a clerk copied as soon as the messy pages left my hands. It was my timidity that prompted me to participate in the contest, I admit. I thought it wiser to submit my first attempt to the nine members of the committee rather than the public, a moral entity that fills me with awe. I was eager to engage in combat because I did not anticipate formidable rivals. On that I was wrong, for out into the arena came two women, one of them a writer of masculine intelligence and solid formation, the other a thinker who had collected numerous laurel crowns from the Academy of Moral and Political Sciences; and a male professor from the Central University who had instigated some recent student riots. The committee made a split decision, and then agreed on a tie between Señora Arenal[39] and me. The faculty of the University of Oviedo issued the final verdict, which was favorable to me.

I must say that I see the serious flaws of my work at least as clearly as my merciful judges did. When I wrote it I was not as familiar with the eighteenth century as the topic required, for often this period, the least known in Spanish literature, is pitilessly sacrificed to the previous two golden centuries. Because of this lack of authority on the subject, my book, overflowing with the restless blood of my literary youth, sprawled and lost itself in digressions. My inexperience was painfully evident, in that my mind was unable to follow a strict plan and my pen to penetrate and exhaust the subject or remain within its limits. Now I could not reprint *Ensayo crítico* without redoing it totally, preserving a minimal part of the original. With this explanation I hope to answer those people who ask me benevolently why I have not made a new edition of that insignificant piece.

At the same contest I won first prize in poetry, a golden rose, for an ode that sings the glories of Feijóo. Often the awards given at contests are of little merit or taste, but mine turned out to be quite nice—nicer, in fact, than the laureate ode itself. It is a truly artistic jewel made in Santiago, where the great Renaissance tradition of Spanish goldsmiths lives on: a life-size rose with a thorny, gracefully bent stem, the veins and shades of the leaves in fine green enamel, and the calyx half open; imitating nature, some petals are closed and others spread to reveal the stamens and the seed at the core. This solid gold flower, so heavy in the hand, when pinned on the breast or the head becomes as light as if it had just been cut from the bush.

After that contest I never thought of entering another. After the birth of my son we had moved to La Coruña. Through almost three years I did not interrupt my studies, except to draft sporadic articles. I still had a vague fear of facing the public with a book. As a child who hesitantly ventures its first steps, I tried my hand at various topics, attaching no importance to those loose pages. I could easily have sent them to Madrid, but I preferred the obscurity of regional journals. As an exception, my articles "Darwinismo" and "Poetas épicos cristianos" appeared in *La ciencia cristiana*, published in Madrid by the philosopher Juan Manuel Orti. Orti and Lara's magazine had a polemic rather than literary orientation, although it showed a commendable respect for the purity and clarity of the Castilian language, which the editors preserved as zealously as their orthodoxy. Among its contributors there were some serious, highly qualified men: Friar Ceferino González, at that time bishop of Córdoba, Father Mir, Father Mendive, Navarro Villoslada, and the editor himself (not to mention the pope, whose encyclicals sometimes took a third of an issue). Apart from these churchmen, I believe that I was the only one who did not wear trousers. Every submission was examined and revised in the light of theology before it went to the press; its content and expression were measured on a highly sensitive scale that detected the slightest deviation. It was forbidden to write about art for art's sake, without relating it to morality; even stylistic images and colorful descriptions were suspicious. It goes without saying that, despite my good intentions, a temperament as curious, uninhibited, and open as mine was bound to overstep the narrow boundaries of *Ciencia cristiana*.

I admit, however, that I profited greatly by my collaboration with *Ciencia cristiana*. I had to scrutinize every line and present a certificate of good conduct for every word; writing was a hard intellectual and verbal exercise, which no doubt trained me for my next work, *San Francisco de Asís*. Incidentally, in this book there is a chapter on Franciscan philosophers that brought about my definitive disagreement with Señor Orti. A translator of Jungman and a staunch Thomist, he disapproved of my adherence to the mystical criticism of Saint Bonaventura, Duns Scotus, Ockham, and Roger Bacon.[40] Everyone knows that the eternal issue of the Middle Ages continues to be the subject of heated debates, as we can see in the controversy between Friar Ceferino and the Franciscan Father Malo, between the Dominican Father Fonseca and Menéndez y Pelayo.[41]

Tired of my long pilgrimage up the road of Greek and German thought and Scholasticism, I found rest in the gentle bosom of mystic philosophy. The spiritual fatigue caused by my sustained reading of heavy works forced me to turn my attention to the life around me. Not only did I indulge in poetry, but I contemplated the novel as a pleasant recreation. It attracted me for the very reasons I had scorned it in my intolerant youth, and unconsciously I began to change my queer notion of it and to regard it as an open field where creativity and imagination could roam freely. As I read more in foreign languages than in my own, I started with Manzoni's *Los novios* (The betrothed) and *Cartas de Jacobo Ortis* (Letters of Jacob Ortis);[42] I proceeded with Walter Scott, Bulwer-Lytton,[43] and Dickens, and then George Sand and Victor Hugo, without ever suspecting the existence of the contemporary Spanish novel!

The only possible explanation of my ignorance lies in my life as a married woman in a provincial town, devoting to my studies whatever free time family and society left me. In those days I knew by heart who and how many were Draper's opponents;[44] I kept up with the progress of thermodynamics; I subscribed to *Revue philosophique* and *Revue scientifique*; I devoured books like *El sol* (The sun), by Father Secchi, or Haeckel's *Historia natural de la creación*;[45] my favorite newspapers were *La fe* (Faith) and *El siglo futuro* (The next century). My literary period went by, and I heard its voice as one of those distant rumors that have no echo in our distracted spirits. One day, discussing *Amaya o los vascos en el siglo VIII* (Amaya or the Basques in the eighth century)—a curious historical novel published then in *Ciencia cristiana*—a friend of mine who was versed in the subject recommended Valera and Alarcón and praised the *Episodios nacionales*, although on the whole he said he found it lengthy and "ponderous." I paid my first tribute to the Spanish novel by reading *Pepita Jiménez*, and then *El sombrero de tres picos* (The three-cornered hat).[46] After that I needed no more guidance.

Between Cervantes, Hurtado, or Espinel[47] and the present-day novelists I found the same resemblance as between the portrait of a family ancestor in old-fashioned garb and a descendant in modern clothes. To discover them gave me great pleasure and spurred me to take a stab at the novel myself. This thought had never entered my mind in the days when I assumed that the business of the novel was to hurl the hero, shrouded alive and with a cannonball chained to his feet, from the top of a tower into the sea; or to push him headlong into the queen's chamber as soon as he arrives in the capital, in order to learn of her loves and misfortunes and perform unprecedented exploits to save her honor. If the novel consists in descriptions of familiar places and mores and the characters of the people who surround us, in that case—I thought—I dare try. And I began to work.

I entitled my first piece *Pascual López, autobiografía de un estudiante de medicina*, and sent it to a friend in Madrid who was going to recommend it to *Revista de España*. This was a necessary precaution, for outside Galicia my name was known only among the not very numerous readers of *Ciencia cristiana*, some of whom pictured me as a bearded and tonsured writer. *Pascual López* was printed in the format of *Revista de España*, using the same plates. Typographically speaking, I have never seen an uglier book: long and flat like a fish, between smudged blue covers, and riddled with mistakes. To top it all, even the page numbers were incorrect. An irritable critic would demolish it, as they say, after merely looking at it. Despite this poor attire, fate looked kindly upon it. I felt the normal thrill of every author—although some will not confess it—when the first book is well received. One day it was a flattering letter from a respected mentor; another a handshake from a new colleague, an unexpected positive article, or a brief review, which is like the cry of a circus acrobat to cheer the other members of his team; or a momentary look of recognition from the absent-minded; or even the first scratch of envy, which sensitizes our skin and stimulates our hot bloodstream. All these things are joy, life!

When I remember the date when *Pascual López* appeared, I am surprised not at how quickly time flies, but at the mutations and renewal that art undergoes within short periods. Hardly five years have elapsed, and how different the Spanish literary scene looks!

The leading critic then was Don Manuel de la Revilla. He died shortly after the publication of my novel, to which he dedicated his last articles. Although he was already free of Krause's influence, his boldest aesthetic attempts never went beyond an occasional boast of positivism. A conservative in literature, an eclectic inclined to classicism by his tendency to order, he felt disoriented when he stumbled on what he called "temperament"—Echegaray's, for example—which could not be measured by the yardstick of good taste and good sense. I do not know what the distinguished critic would think of the current changes, but I suspect that he would never champion naturalism, or at least would reject many of its dogmas.

In 1879 and 1880 the generation born from the revolution of 1868 came to the foreground—I say "born" not because it supported the revolution unanimously, but because its talent and goals shaped themselves against the revolutionary background. German metaphysical thought gave way to French positivism and psycho-physics; the novel prepared to compete with drama and lyric poetry—the two favorite genres of romanticism—and to recover its place of honor in Spanish literature.

The fathers of this generation, from Mesonero [48] to Pereda, are so well known that there is no need to list them. Let us begin with more recent dates. In 1879 gentle winds of realism blew, not unlike the warm spring breeze of a February or March afternoon. No one spoke yet of naturalism, although Zola's novels, like obscene pictures or defamatory libels, were already objects of curiosity and scandal. The first that fell in my hands, *L'assomoir*, had an informal dedication written in it. After some complimentary opening remarks, the signer commented that he knew how fond I was of every novelty in every genre, and that this book in particular seemed to be in style among "aristocrats, bankers, literary bohemians, and other people of bad taste." If I mention this dedication it is because it expresses a dated viewpoint; today a cultivated person like the one who wrote it would not make so much of Zola.

The important thing about the Spanish novel of those years is not so much its penchant for realism as its explicit goal of restoring the Castilian language, ill-treated by the Krausists as well as comic opera writers, novelists writing in installments, translators of romances, and a host of political authors and journalists of the revolutionary period. This abuse provoked a purist and archaistic reaction, particularly in the narrative of Valera, the most refined and literary of our contemporary authors and, therefore, the most respectful of critical dictates; besides, he has a God-given ability to revive old forms and bring to light charming relics, forgotten terms and idioms, which his ingenuity renders fresh and free of pedantry. *Pascual López* did not escape this restoring zeal, and for this reason its style received much praise and I was affiliated with realism and connected to the picaresque tradition. Revilla, despite his hostility to female writers, was not the least of my novel's enthusiasts.

As praise makes me more self-critical than censure, I examined my novel as soon as this honeymoon ended. I had serious doubts regarding the obsolete prose of *Pascual López*. I remembered that sometimes, when I had tried to fit my modern ideas into the molds of Cervantes and Hurtado, form and content had refused to harmonize and had waged a furious war. I thought of how the heroes of my novel conversed, and how the people of Santiago really speak nowadays. No critic had raised this objection; I, however, found something false and artificial in my work. It is a good thing, I said to myself, to return to spoken language and to absorb at the same time as much of the classics as we can; but we must not forget the lesson of the fabulist:

> Since we are still moved to laughter
> by the notions of that foolish modern painter,
> how can we not laugh forever
> at the ancient phrases of a novel writer?
> Affectation he judges fine, indeed;
> he speaks with purity but no clarity,
> finding no word of our age unworthy
> if it was noble in the days of the Cid.

I promised myself to write no more period pieces. Despite my successful debut, a new literary project took my attention away from the novel. Whenever I traveled to Santiago, I contemplated at length the front door of the convent of Saint Francis, whose melancholy setting and secluded, austere air have for me a peculiar fascination. The hours I have spent there have been among the most pleasant and peaceful of my life. From the patio would come the clear and monotonous rumor of the fountain, punctuating the conversations of the monks. What did we talk about? Outside the world revolved, trains ran in a cloud of fire and smoke, laboratories were busy; the voices of orators, the sinister laughter of the world, the squeaks of machines, the explosion of dynamite—all resounded far, very far. The only noises that came to that door were the dripping of water, the pious tolling of the bell as it lingered in the quiet air, and the imperceptible rustle of the novice's sandals when he walked by, with his eyes down and his hands in the sleeves of his tunic. Time had stopped as if by magic: I was at the core of the Middle Ages. To complete the illusion, through the half-open door I saw a fragment of Gothic cloister like granite lace. We talked about the Patriarch, the *Florecillas* (Little flowers),[49] the five stigmata, and the whole wonderful legend, and a heavenly light purified my heart. I never tired of those fantastic colloquies. If I entered the convent sad and confused, I came out comforted, envious of the perfect peace and childlike candor that seemed to revive even in the souls of the most evil sinners.

At that time I began to write *San Francisco*. I would have finished it at one stroke of the pen had my health not failed—an unusual event, for my constitution is vigorous and strong. I was diagnosed with a hepatic ailment, whose first symptoms must have been the deep sorrow and gloomy thoughts that I had tried to forget at the convent's door. The doctor prescribed the waters of Vichy. I left for France in September 1880.

The bathers were already leaving the elegant spa. The hotel, with its lobby decorated with wild vine, ivy, and clematis, and its splendid walk of chestnuts and sycamores, belonged entirely to me. As is normal in such places I had plenty of time, and while the October breeze stirred the vine leaves I wrote the opening pages of *Viaje de novios* (The honeymoon), and for the first time read Balzac, Flaubert, Goncourt, and Daudet.[50] In the morning I walked into the library with my glass of *grande grille* and stuffed a book in my pocket; in the afternoon I savored it with that physical and intellectual happiness that convalescent people feel when their bodies relax and their souls wander freely.

At last I understood what worried me after the publication of *Pascual López*: it was the course of the modern novel, its importance and prominence in contemporary letters, its irresistible strength, and its duty as an epic genre to experience and reflect nature and society, without disguising the truth or replacing it with more or less beautiful literary fictions. I reached the conclusion that each country must cultivate its own novelistic tradition, particularly when it is as distinguished as in Spain; at the same time, it must accept modern methods based on rational principles appropriate for our concept of art, which has certainly changed since the seventeenth century. I did not believe that we should reject innovations in the narrative craft on account of their foreign origin. A quick historical survey indicates that Latin countries—Italy, France, and the Iberian Peninsula—have, since time immemorial, exchanged aesthetic ideas and reciprocated literary influences. We drew inspiration from the Romans and in turn, through our orators and poets, transmitted to them our bombastic style; Spain assimilated the French troubadours and, to even the score, implanted its drama in France. The list of loans from nation to nation is endless and will always remain so. It is a process of fecundation.

The results of my meditations linger in the prologue and text of *Viaje de novios*. As far as I know, the prologue was one of the earliest and perhaps most resounding echoes of French naturalism in Spain, comparing it, to its detriment, to Spanish realism. However, I do not claim any prophetic gift, and if I am mistaken it is up to those who know better to correct me. After all, as I had just come from Paris, there was no special merit in my initiative.

Before I go any further, I shall relate how I met the last glorious bastion of the romantic generation, Victor Hugo, when I stopped in Paris on my way back from the spa. The author of *Hernani* invited me to his coterie or, I should say, to his court, for he looked like a deposed king. His sumptuous living room was lighted by a glittery chandelier of Venetian crystal, dressed in silk, and decorated with splendid tapestries. Seated in double rows on both sides of the room were the last courtiers of the fallen monarch, tardy neophytes and stragglers of romanticism. While some of them remained quiet, others stood and talked softly to each other. Victor

Hugo gave me a seat by his side, and at once there was silence. General attention focused on us, as we initiated the dialogue of harmless questions and timid answers typical of such situations. I sought shelter behind a huge bunch of heliotropes that I was holding, in order to conceal my embarrassment through the interrogation and my veneration for that old representative of the past. But at one point Hugo, after professing to regard Spain as his second homeland, deplored its backwardness and added that he considered it inevitable, given the pitiless burning of writers and scholars by the Inquisition. With all due respect to Victor Hugo, I replied that the peaks of our literary splendor coincided with periods of the Inquisition, which neither interfered with Spanish letters nor had roasted a single writer or scholar, only adepts of Judaism, witches, and visionaries. He was not convinced, and I, carried away by my inveterate zeal to defend Spain from groundless accusations, plunged into a controversy with the elderly man! I did it, I hasten to say, in good form and a respectful, friendly style. When the poet stated that in 1824 autos-da-fé[51] were still performed in Spain, I refrained from telling him that he was committing a gross anachronism, and simply begged him to verify his information and see for himself that the Inquisition, officially suppressed in 1812, had actually ceased to function long before.[52] A lady who sat opposite me and acted as hostess—I believe her name was Madame Lockroy—asked me slyly if I "had studied history at a Dominican school."[53] As I inhaled the perfume of the heliotropes and played with my fan, I thought to myself that things had gone too far. So I answered that Michelet, Thiers, and other French historians had taught me a great deal about the dragonades and the massacre of Saint Bartholomew,[54] the Terror, and other episodes of French history that make the atrocities of the Inquisition pale by comparison. The Spanish Inquisition, I added, would not have persecuted Clément Marot[55] or executed André Chénier, because in Spain we pride ourselves on our respect for the muses, as my presence in that house proved. "Voilá bien l'espagnole,"[56] Victor Hugo whispered, half smiling; and he began to rhapsodize about Spain, which in his view was the most romantic country in Europe, and to ask me about our contemporary poets and writers, of whom he knew nothing.

The night passed in the twinkling of an eye. The disciples seemed to come out of their spell, for they moved and talked; in that royal room—a true poetic inquisition—only an unexpected accident like the arrival of a foreigner could generate a debate and break the ice of that almost hieratic respect. At midnight I said good-bye forever to Victor Hugo. He gave me autographed portraits of himself and his grandchildren and kissed me on the forehead. This is a French custom that I, true Spaniard that I am, sometimes find in poor taste; on that occasion, however, I was moved by this man in his eighties who bent under the weight of glory rather than age, even though the latter was already pushing him to the grave where he now sleeps. May his soul rest in peace.

To guarantee the success of my thermal treatment, throughout the first months back in Spain I did not work intensively. I limited myself to finishing *Viaje de novios*. Once I had fully recovered, I completed *San Francisco de Asís* during a summer at Granja de Meirás. The pleasant seclusion of country life greatly helped me to concentrate on a single idea and develop it throughout the chapters of the book.

After the publication of *San Francisco* in two volumes, I began to consider a *Historia de la literatura mística española*, a splendid and unexplored subject, which I found fascinating and worthy of a pen of gold and diamonds, rather than my modest one. The more I thought of it, the more I realized that I should expand my topic and cover Spanish letters in general, an enterprise that would be longer but not much more difficult. At the time I was taking advantage of a winter month in Santiago to research in the university library—not a very arduous task—with that zest of the initial stage of a project when we wish the day had forty-eight hours. The rector gallantly lent me his own office, and ordered that the books I might need be brought there. One afternoon there was a heavy snowfall, unusual for Santiago. The doorkeeper, freezing and with his nose as red as a beet, dutifully waited for me at the door, although he did not expect me to turn up. When he saw me, he exclaimed from the bottom of his heart: "If I had your income, miss, I certainly would not leave home today just for some books."

On those glacial afternoons, between entertaining readings of Masdeu and the *Cancionero de Baena* (Songs of Baena),[57] I drafted the articles of *La cuestión palpitante*, to be published weekly in the literary section of *La época*.[58] My purpose was to comment in a clear and pleasant style on naturalism and realism, which no one had analyzed systematically, although they were the subjects of intense but superficial discussions. I decided to contact the press and jump into the arena, with no other weapons than a thin shield of anecdotal erudition, light enough to attract the uninitiated without intimidating them and to allow me freedom of action. Success rose higher than hope. The extraordinary liveliness of that little book written off the cuff will always amaze me. The only calculated effect in it was its very unpremeditation and spontaneity, because I wanted it free of didactic pretensions. These light, combative, improvised articles have generated endless controversy, enthusiastic support, and considerable fuss and contradiction; they have been translated and seriously analyzed by the foreign press; and they have even induced Valera to take up his never-rusty pen after a long hiatus. Meanwhile I, who, thank God, am not easily blinded by my own achievements, see the book in all its insignificance, attribute its good fortune to its timely appearance, and apply to myself the truism that what matters is to be in the right place at the right time.

The power of events, in literature as in everything, is more decisive than the actions of the individual. Undoubtedly, even if I had not written *La cuestión*, French naturalism would still be known and its influence on Spanish literature important, just as French classicism and romanticism have been in the past.

La cuestión aroused the Spaniards as much as a literary issue can arouse a nation whose main topics of conversation are politics, bullfights, and women. There is no room here to repeat what has been said and written of my articles since I published them hardly four years ago; it would certainly provide material for a curious book, not devoid of advice for literary reformers. Neither shall I mention those writers who have more or less explicitly taken my side; it would appear that I claim them as devotees of mine, when in truth many could be my mentors and all have pursued their own ideas. On the other hand, I am willing to talk about my adversaries. Among the first to object to or altogether disapprove of my arguments were Núñez de Arce, Alarcón, and Campoamor; Valera formulates his opinions in a series of articles published in *Revista de España* under the title *Apuntes sobre el arte nuevo de hacer novelas* (Notes on the new art of the novel), and judging from what he has written so far, his criticism is reduced to a protest, as courteous as befits such a confirmed gentleman, in the name of classicism and good taste, although he recognizes my independence from Zola's aesthetic theories. Alarcón maintained a kind of epistolary debate with me on naturalism shortly before his unsettling diatribe at the Academy, in which he dubbed this literary school "the dirty hand of literature" without making the slightest distinctions. Though in my letters and *La cuestión* I treated him with the respect that his talent deserves, he has become annoyed and has taken offense, when it is actually he who has offended others: in recent writings he has complained that the naturalists deny him "water and fire." Well, he denies them water and soap!

In Campoamor and Núñez de Arce critics have already observed a certain tendency to realism hindered, particularly in Campoamor, by the peculiar nature of their poetic geniuses. Neither of them opposes Zola's innovations completely, although Campoamor in his philosophical-aesthetic-humorous pieces interprets the issue quite differently from the naturalists. When *La cuestión palpitante* came out, Campoamor had a mind—so he wrote to me—to contest it. I wish he had, for he would have done it with the best humor in the world!

The tide of reaction came foaming furiously, as it usually does after an innovation, with a hoarse and angry uproar. In general, the things said earlier about romanticism were repeated about naturalism, with the addition of many new insults. The most indignant were those who confessed that they neither had read nor intended to read the execrable novels in question, and discussed the evil doctrines advocated in *La cuestión* without having even leafed through it. As I write, a speech by Señor Guillermo Estrada, president of the Catholic Youth of Oviedo, lies on my table; it deals with the novel and its current influence and also with Leopoldo Alas's *La regenta*.[59] I know Señor Estrada personally; perhaps he recalls how we met: it was at the coterie of a distinguished lady in Pau. I regard him as a cultivated, serious, well-meaning person, incapable, in sum, of joining the legion of vilifiers. How can I not be surprised when I hear him say of me that "I got the notion to champion naturalism," as if he said that I got the notion to throw stones? It is true that two lines down he speaks of my "sincere desire to remain loyal to my religious principles," which always sounds fine to me, particularly on Señor Estrada's lips; but had he read *La cuestión*, it is to be hoped that he would have added that I do not embrace Zola's views as a whole or follow passively in the wake of foreign nations, as he thinks our novel does now. I examine naturalistic aesthetics in the light of theology, extracting and rejecting its heretic, deterministic, and fatalistic elements as well as its tendency to utilitarian didacticism, while striving for a syncretism that leaves faith intact. I do not claim to have succeeded, but it is only fair that Señor Estrada and those who feel as he does acknowledge my attempt.

Neither the high priest of the French school, Emile Zola, nor the numerous foreign critics who have reviewed the excellent translation of *La cuestión* published in Paris by Alberto Savine deny it its independence and originality; they add that it is legitimate for a Spanish writer to base a new Catholic naturalism on the literary tradition of her country. God knows that as I hurriedly jotted down a few pages in the cold office of the University of Santiago, nothing was further from my intention than to create a manifesto, a school, or anything similar; but it is equally true—as anyone who reads my book will admit—that I did not limit myself to translating French naturalism for the Spanish public. I selected from it what I deemed sensible and advisable, and systematically attacked the rest. Just as I protest today, with the encouragement of foreign opinion, I protested in the course of a debate with Luis Alfonso[60] in *La época* in 1884. "I can't get over my surprise," I said, "to see that they are trying to make a female Zola out of me, or at least an active disciple of the French revolutionary. Where I radically depart from Zola is in his philosophical concept. As you know, a year ago in *La cuestión* I hastened to analyze his deterministic, fatalistic, and pessimistic beliefs, concluding that no Catholic could follow him along those paths." Needless to say, the philosophy of a system is its basis and its backbone.

I am as opposed as anybody to the exclusive nature of intellectual schools, and I suggest that the term *school* be replaced with *method*. By method we must understand the critical axioms and aesthetic principles on which artists of a given generation concur. To me, it is unquestionable that these principles change within brief periods of time; only in this sense do I sometimes speak of a *new school* or *renewal,* to follow the current expression. Well, I have noticed that the few people abroad acquainted with our present literature detect in the best modern Spanish novelists a common denominator, that *something* that identifies a new literary movement. At the same time, they admit that Spanish naturalism, verism, realism, or whatever we may call it, for this is no time for such distinctions, differs as much from French naturalism as the latter does from its Russian counterpart. And yet over here they continue to repeat, with the obstinacy of the willfully deaf, that servile imitation of the French novel has ruined our narrative.

To some extent, the essence of these accusations is to be found in Señor Estrada's last statement, in which, following a dictum of Saint Francis of Sales,[61] he compares novels to mushrooms in that the best is not worth a cent. If he had said this in the first place, we would have saved ink, saliva, and pointless arguing. A person summoned by God to spiritual life and the conquest of the kingdom of heaven, who says with rigorous logic, "Since I am not saintly, I must be mad," can apply the mushroom principle to infinite intellectual and artistic products; he may think the same of drama, poetry, statues, paintings, gardens of delight, comfortable rich furniture, parties, sweet music, a great tenor voice, ladies' dresses, or physical and even moral beauty, which may and sometimes does arouse spiritual infatuation and concupiscence. However, we must not get our genres mixed up: this is not literary criticism.

Traditionalists and conservatives, so divided on other issues, generally concur on their hostility to both French and Spanish naturalism, without differentiating one from the other as they ought to. In *Ciencia cristiana,* the knowledgeable and elegant writer Señor Díaz Carmona has condemned them, and so has Señor Cánovas del Castillo in his book *El solitario.* In fact, his chapter on this topic is the only disappointment in a work otherwise rich and valuable to modern literary history. *La época* continues to avenge the wrongs committed against idealism even after the antinatural-istic campaign of Luis Alfonso, who represents the official position of this elitist newspaper. In these circles the word *naturalism* is distasteful and shocking; in the academies it is a bomb.

Menéndez y Pelayo, who after all is a contemporary of the young generation, sympathizes with many of the modern doc-trines, with the exceptions stated in his prologue to the second edi-tion of my *San Francisco*. He deplores, I must add, the importation of French aesthetic notions as if they were fashion designs; more-over, his strong sense of national identity impairs his judgment of French novels, the best of which he has not read and I doubt if he could appreciate, despite his lucid intelligence and admirable understanding, because of his repugnance toward *modernism*. It is a matter of temperament. Nothing gives him more pleasure than to discover in some seventeenth- or eighteenth-century Spanish aesthete the principles formulated today by Zola or Goncourt; and to demonstrate that Father Arteaga[62] knew everything about these disputes between idealism and naturalism, our unfamiliarity with Spanish authors being the reason why nowadays such debates seem new. I do not imply that Menéndez y Pelayo, whose intelligence feeds on Horace and Plato, will follow Zola any more than the rest of us; but I believe that his independent mind will sooner or later approach these questions without bias. In his last works he has come such a long way that I, who shall tirelessly insist on my independence from any school, sometimes find myself only a hair's breadth apart from him.

From what has been said it might be inferred that only con-servatives look with misgivings upon the modern novel. Not at all. Here is Montalvo, the remarkable prose writer from Ecuador, author of *Siete tratados* (Seven treaties) and *Mercurial eclesiástica*, who opposes it. When Señor Calcaño dubbed us "pirates," in order to exterminate us he requested Pi y Margall's help; in fact, realism should expect nothing from a thinker so saturated with Hegel and Proudhon.[63]

There is an explanation for this phenomenon, if we consider that the goal of contemporary novelists is to make faithful portraits without revealing the point of view of the painter. Those who share the beliefs of a novelist would applaud until they skinned the palms of their hands if he systematically advocated their ideas, a method that produces books like *Bororquia o la víctima de la Inquisición*. To wit: a freethinker, something that three-fourths of the people most of us know today are, enters the scene; the thing is to vilify him, to suppose him capable of every vice and crime, and give him a fit punishment on the last page. Then I depict a poor village priest of meager means who lives among peasants and is a child of peasants himself; I endow him with the knowledge of Father Secchi and the virtue and leadership ability of Saint Vicente Ferrer, thus creating an angelic candidate for sainthood. If, on the other hand, I ignore these formulas and tell things as they happen, I am a heretic and a turncoat, I am on the side of *the others*. Let us now reverse our hypothesis. *The others,* in order to take me to their bosom, require that I present them as so many Gracchuses[64] and victims of a brutal persecution by the theocracy, personified by a priest capable of eating children raw or something to that effect. What I have done so far is, as Pereda would say, "to state the case"; what follows is based on experience.

Anyone who walks the road to my hometown at dusk will meet numerous groups of women leaving the tobacco factory after work. Whenever I saw them I used to think: could there be a novel under these cotton dresses and threadbare shawls? Yes, my intuition responded, wherever there are four thousand women, no doubt there are four thousand novels; it is a matter of finding them. One day it struck me that those dark, strong women with a resolute air had been the most devoted partisans of federalism in the revolutionary years. Then I became interested in the study of a political conviction rooted in a female who is at once a Catholic and a demagogue, simple by nature, yet doomed to evil by the hardships of factory life. My third novel, *La tribuna*, probably was born from these thoughts.

For two months I went to the factory every morning and afternoon to listen to conversations, sketch characters, and catch words and feelings in the air. I acquired local newspapers from the federal period, which were already scarce; I summoned memories, described La Coruña of my childhood, which has improved considerably since, and reconstructed the days of the famous Pact,[65] an important chapter in the history of Galicia. The book had no satirical pretensions at all. Far from developing the comic potential of the subject, I would say that I underplayed it, as some papers that I still keep can easily prove; such events, when they take place on a small stage, always offer, by the law of contrast, both a comic and a tragic side. Nevertheless, *La tribuna* offended Tyrians and Trojans alike. The Republicans imagined themselves caricatured, while delicate conservative sensibilities were hurt by the frank descriptions of working-class life. A book, in order not to scandalize anyone, must carefully mix imagination, rhetoric, and truth; in *La tribuna*, the amount of truth is out of proportion to that of rhetoric. Its French translator, Carlos Waternau, told me this year in Paris that he had found the novel an interesting document of the Spanish revolution, treated with the impartiality of the artist and without partisan exaggerations. How different was the verdict of many people on this side of the border!

Spanish industrial sites have been little studied, either because they are rare or because country life is indeed more poetic and appealing. The shacks of our peasants, wretched hovels invaded by cold and wind, in which calves and children sleep together, make nonetheless a comfortable impression. We must pity the child trapped in an urban shanty more than the one who daily basks in sun and rain and who, lacking meat, eats oxygen. The factory is the true social inferno open to the novelist, the modern Dante who writes the cantos of the human comedy; in it the lowest of the condemned is turned into a wheel, a cylinder, an automaton. Poor woman workers of the factory in La Coruña! I shall never forget their inherent goodness, their natural honesty and spontaneous generosity. They are capable of giving away everything they own when they see what they call "a pity."

I retained another memory that now seems particularly vivid. When I witnessed the all-female saturnalia described in *La tribuna* under the title "Carnaval de cigarreras" (Carnival of women at the tobacco factory), a charming, graceful girl caught my eye. About twenty years old and dressed as a student of the *tuna*, [66] she danced on top of a narrow table, playing a broken tambourine. She was slim, olive-skinned, extremely light. Her sweet, large black eyes glittered with the excitement of the dance, her hair flowed in ebony locks that came loose under the three-cornered hat, and her arm often rose with a youthful movement to keep a flower in place behind her ear. With her fresh voice she sang improvised couplets, addressing humorous compliments to me; and displaying a row of teeth like almonds, she joined in my hearty laughter, winked, and admitted her inexperience in poetry: "I got myself in a pretty pickle!"

Time passed and I learned that "a factory girl" had committed suicide because of some unreciprocated love. It was the merry little student, the dancer of the radiant smile who looked like a bird. She had saved enough to buy a gun, pretending in the store that it was a gift for a cousin of hers. The storekeeper had had some misgivings at first, but when he noticed the festive expression and lively smile habitual on the girl's face, he sold her the weapon. She shot herself in the heart. The poor body, soft and pure in form under the student's costume, was laid out on the autopsy table. Never before had I seen a country girl capable of an act like this; a deficient factory-worker's education, nervous tension, weakening of the blood, and constant unhealthy contact with the city have created a new woman, more complex and therefore more miserable than the peasant.

La tribuna was already at the publisher's but not yet in print when the steam engine covered for the first time the distance between Madrid and La Coruña. I had the pleasure of personally meeting many journalists from Madrid, among them several distinguished writers, and thanking them for the kindness they had always done me. In Spain the press as a whole concentrates on two topics that occupy the minds of the Spaniards, namely, politics and bullfights; however, it also counts on a powerful literary element, and although newspapers speak mainly of bullfights and politics and banish literature to the background, their pages are filled with talent and wit.

After *La tribuna* I wrote another novel, *El cisne de Vilamorta* (The swan of Vilamorta), which, together with a collection of novellas entitled *La dama joven* (The young lady), I sent to the publisher before leaving for France for the winter of 1885. The framework of *El cisne* and *Bucólica*, which in my view is the strongest of the short novels, differed from that of *La tribuna*. Having been absent for years from the province where the action takes place, I had to resort to memories, always vaguer than the immediate description of reality. This is also the case with *Los pazos de Ulloa* and *La madre naturaleza* (Mother Nature).

People often ask me why I change the names of the real settings of my novels. Since we are in the vein of novelistic and biographical confidences, I shall explain my reasons. The first one is to prevent objections against possible factual inaccuracies; for example, locating the fair of Cebre at the entrance of the village when it is actually a mile away, or something of this sort. The second, to rid myself of servile realism, which I abhor as much as I worship the heartfelt truth deduced from an overall impression rather than from trivial particulars. The third, to have more *freedom* to create characters, for surprising as this may seem, I have not *copied* any of the characters of my novels. Not only is copying seldom legitimate or delicate, it is never artistic.

What I am saying may be difficult to believe, but I shall try to illustrate it with a recent practical case. Not long ago I found out in Paris that Zola does not copy either, and I learned how he managed to design Souvarine, the interesting Russian nihilist in *Germinal*. Zola was careful not to choose any of the nihilists who live in Paris, track him down, or take notes on his appearance, habits, and actions. Instead, he studied tendencies and ideas common among nihilists, asked his Russian acquaintances, collected information about the situation of the Slavic race, listened to a story one day, and looked at a face the next; and gathering all these beams of diffuse light, he proceeded as an artist to create the unforgettable type of the demented socialist.

I know that Zola's method presents difficulties, and that if this path led the great author of *Germinal* to the violent symbolism of *La obra* (The work), how can it not lead lesser artists like me astray? As long as we are cautious, however, I prefer it to the supposedly systematic naturalistic approach, which is to write what we see to the last detail and recreate the age, figure, speech, and life events of such and such an existing person. No matter how curious we may find an anecdote we heard yesterday, how comic or dramatic the story of someone we know, in which we have participated as witnesses or actors, if we commit it to writing with rigorous accuracy it will turn out to be a tepid biography or an inane account. A chronicle may be no more than a faithful, exact narrative of real events; as I understand it, this is not sufficient either for history or for the novel. Neither of these two genres allows falsehood; all the elements in them must be real. But the truth shines more brightly when it is free, meaningful, and created by art.

This theory applies in particular to the characters, which give the author more initiative because human life is shaped by free will and fatality, whereas nature is shaped by fatality alone. The environment prevails, and to this prevalence we owe the mountains of Pereda's Santander, the mores of Galdós's Madrid, the Asturias of Armando Palacio and Leopoldo Alas, the Catalan villages and second capital of Spain of Oller.[67] By a natural impulse every novelist maps his own territory, be it his birthplace or his habitual residence.

I have focused on the Galician region, whose romantic beauty, varied aspects, picturesque customs and traditions, and ancient heritage deserve a better pen. In *Pascual López* I tried to portray academic life and the old medieval Galicia, represented by Santiago; in *La tribuna*, the young industrial Galicia where I was born. In *El cisne* I studied a small town, with its intrigues and petty politics; in *Bucólica* a poor ignorant peasant girl, the precursor of Graziella, at the mercy of her instincts; in *Los pazos de Ulloa*, the Galician mountains, feudalism, and the decadence of an aristocratic family. In *La madre naturaleza* I indulged in my fondness for the country, my homeland, and the landscape. In fact, I love the country so much that some day I would like to write a novel in which all the characters were peasants; but I stumble on the problem of dialogue, a problem that, according to a newspaper I have just read, Zola, the most daring of novelists, avoids in his last novel, *La tierra* (The earth) by making the peasants speak French instead of patois. Genius is omnipotent, and therefore Zola will skirt these obstacles, but I feel that the graphic, timely, malicious sayings of our peasants are inseparable from the old romance language they speak; and that a hybrid novel half in Galician and half in Castilian would be an ugly monster, which in no way could reflect the beauty of those wholly Galician poems enriched by peasant expressions.

To this day I have not written a single line in Galician. I think that it is precisely because I have no pretensions in this respect that I enjoy Galician literature so much, particularly poetry. I do not scrutinize its spelling and syntax, and I prefer those poems that are closer to peasant speech, thought, and sensibility. Last year the Society of Craftsmen of my hometown did me the honor of asking me to preside over a solemn act in memory of our greatest regional poetess, Rosalía de Castro. In order to praise her poetry in dialect,[68] all I had to do was collect my impressions and cast them into a speech. Although composing it was a relatively simple task, the prospect of reading it in a large hall to an audience of three thousand people intimidated me; I was afraid not of "going blank," as they say, but of not having a powerful enough voice. On that occasion I doubled the debt I had contracted in June to Emilio Castelar,[69] when he and other distinguished writers and friends held a banquet in my honor. The famous orator, invited by the society, arrived in La Coruña a few days before the event. I took this opportunity to read my speech to him and disclose my fear that my voice might not carry beyond the table. I cannot say how kindly and generously he gave me strength and advice, how benevolently he assessed the speech, how supportive he was. On the eve of the designated day, Castelar, sitting in the chair of my study, brooded over whether I should or should not hold my notes in my hand as I read. A born artist, he was concerned with the choreographic aspect of the performance, and I suspect that he would have gladly watched me practice gestures before the mirror. Posture did not seem so important to me; what worried me was that on that same evening Castelar was going to speak in La

Coruña for the first time, and the audience would surely be ill-disposed toward those who delayed this pleasure. And yet, if I had to preside, I could not possibly save my speech for the end.

The theater was so packed that there was no room for a pin, and every resonance was drowned in the midst of the compact crowd. To make space for extra seats the presidential table and the judges' seats had to be moved to the back of the stage, where even the actors would have to strain their voices in order to be heard. This heavy attendance encouraged rather than intimidated me; dramatic actors are as energized by the electricity that a large audience communicates as they are enervated by a half-deserted house. My only fear was that my larynx would fail. I rose to my feet, for finally we had decided that I would stand. I cannot say how weak, erratic, and hard my voice sounded amid the imposing sudden silence of thousands of people in an atmosphere pregnant with human warmth and breath, where one could hear a fly. This sensation oppressed my throat. But when I had hardly finished the first paragraph, I heard on my right the voice of Castelar, pleasantly surprised and enthusiastic, repeating: "Very good, very good! This is the right tone, stay with it!" I breathed. My throat had warmed up, my utterance was easier and stronger every moment. The audience, far from growing impatient, granted me attention and approval, which I, whose only ambition was to avoid a total fiasco, deeply appreciated. I shall always believe that I owe most of my good fortune to Castelar and his excitement, which was neither frivolous nor calculated, but full of conviction and kindness. When he finished his splendid tirade he pressed my hand, while hurrahs and applause roared in the theater; and giving free reign to his Greco-Latin temperament, artistic above all, with his bulging eyes shining joyfully, his face drenched in sweat, and his lips still half open from the stream of words, he told me: "We must be happy,

Emilia. We have made possible a pure and lofty aesthetic pleasure. So let's be happy!"

Now that I have discussed most of my writings, including some still unpublished and others that are only projects, I would like to mention that this year I have undertaken a task I had never dreamed of: I am a translator of French, which is a fairly modest job. For the last two winters nearly every Sunday I have visited Edmond Goncourt's attic in Paris. I used to tell the old master about the difficulties of translating his work, owing to the infinite subtleties, innovations, boldnesses, shades, delicacies, and frills of his highly refined style. He had no hope of ever being translated in Spain, but then he heard that in Barcelona there was a Spanish version of *La fille Elisa* (Young Elisa) and asked me to get him a copy. I passed his request to Narciso Oller, and in a few days the horrible creature reached my hands and those of the victim. What an expression on Goncourt's face when he saw his novel expanded by an appendix on studies of the penitentiary system, and translated and printed in a way I dare not describe! Goncourt's nervousness and refinement rendered the episode comic. Had he understood Spanish, I would have quoted Iriarte's [70] fable:

> Some translate very fine works
> and turn swords into spikes;
> others translate the worst,
> and then sell spikes for swords.

In sum, I decided to translate *Les frères Zemganno* (The Zemganno brothers), not only to find out if I could do it without depriving Goncourt of his glory or the Castilian language of its honor, but also out of personal affinity with and admiration for the exquisite artist.

His charming attic remains one of my best Parisian memories. Gathered there are the princes of the modern French novel: Zola, Goncourt, Daudet, and other promising "youths," as they say in Paris: Huysmanns, Rod, Maupassant, Alexis. I listen to them curled up on a Turkish sofa, close to the host. When I occasionally take part in the discussion, it is to remind those victorious Gauls that Spain exists and produces novels, and that good novelists are no less numerous there than in France. They call this habit of remembering and praising the homeland "Calvinism." One day Goncourt asked me if on the other side of the border idealism and naturalism fought each other; I answered that there was no fight to speak of because, to our regret and to the detriment of art, the idealists had stopped writing altogether. "Over there you don't have a Georges Ohnet[71] either?" "None," I replied. He turned to his guests with his mildly ironic, peculiar smile, and exclaimed: "Do you realize how lucky the Spaniards are? They don't have Ohnet!"

I shall not continue to talk of Paris because my recollections are so recent and numerous that they would fill many pages. Nor shall I dwell any longer on the novel, whose present state you, reader, know better than anyone—you who, unconcerned with the animosity of some critics, the scandal of naturalism, and the distinctions of Scholasticism, appreciate and enjoy works of merit. Little by little, guided by instinct alone, you select the healthy national nourishment served on fine china, and discard the indigestible food that they used to put on your table: heavy socialist dishes à la Eugène Suë, banquets of Arabs and Christians, historical cakes Dumas-style, moralistic and edifying confections, circumvoluted and stupefying cotton-candy yarns from England, and last but not least, the never sufficiently eulogized novel in installments, this lively genre that still squirms among other rubbish in the wastepaper basket. And perchance you will protest indignantly, like the donkey of the fable:

> . . . I eat
> whatever you feed me: but you are unjust
> if you think straw is what I like most.
> Give me grain, and watch how I eat it.

If I were sure to have contributed in some way to this relative prosperity of the Spanish novel, I would not regret the hours spent with pen and paper in the cell of the old Granja de Meirás, in a corner of Mariñas. Here I feel the fever of artistic creation most intensely. Not that La Granja has a Gothic appearance, or resembles a Scottish castle or one of these modern palaces that a conspiracy of money and bad taste has strung along the roads of San Sebastián and Biarritz. La Granja is so rustic that it even lacks a coat of arms; it was removed from the facade by my grandfather, a flaming liberal of the hottest variety, that is to say, a Mason. On all sides vegetation covers and devours the house, low and irregular but large. When I get up and open my bedroom window I see a scene worthy of Watteau, a temptation for a watercolor painter. The smooth sky has that lovely hue of good cigar ashes peculiar to Galicia, for English skies are usually darker and colder. The foliage of the tree of love— hibiscus in botanical terminology—fades against this background like a pale green veil spattered with pink flowers, which resemble playful touches of a whimsical brush on a landscape of soft colors. When I want fresh air after work I go to the nearby wood, whose steep, grassy trails run between aralias, paulownias, chestnut trees, and fragrant broom. A little farther down, in the middle of the property, there is a fountain. The stone drinking trough drips onto the smooth surface of the water, on which there always drift yellow leaves fallen from the bushes or a miniature boat capsized, a wreck from the Battle of Trafalgar, which Jaime has been recreating ever since he read *Episodios nacionales*. In the garden and around the fountain the magnolias half open their urns of alabaster, the grenades their flowers of curly coral; the vines climb up the arbor

to the windows, between whose glass panes sometimes a stem of
fuchsia or a shoot of passion flower is caught. Beyond the garden
the brook, flanked by fresh watercress, disappears down the vast,
sloping meadow. The long course of the wall is a garland of trees,
which, bent by the weight of their fruits, lure the passers-by with
the amber distillate of their pears, apples, and peaches. How can I
fail to recall the well-known lines of the contemplative poet:

> The air through the orchard moves
> offering our senses a thousand smells.
> The trees shiver
> and their soft whisper
> makes us forget gold and scepter.[72]

"A thousand smells" is hardly a hyperbole. I believe that in the
garden of La Granja all the flowers and plants of the world are
represented, from the cedar to the hyssop; and on those clear
nights that Friar Luis liked so much, when the sky is sprinkled
with stars and the wind subsides, and all the sounds of the country
cease, a mysterious symphony of aromas seems to fill the silence.[73]
Some of them are common and familiar, like the scents of honey-
suckle, morning glories, heliotropes, lilies, verbena, cloves, sweet
peas, and roses. Others are exotic and reminiscent of the Orient, of
sunny lands, carpeted rooms, splendid balls: the faint ilang-ilang,
the aristocratic gardenias, the brooding magnolias, datura, which
is like an amphora full of nard perfume, the dreamy white helio-
trope, passion flowers that reek of honey, Cuban peas with their
aroma of vanilla, yellow roses, and wistarias, whose perfume is as
faint as a vague memory.

The cell in which I write overlooks not the garden but the courtyard. On my left there stand the immense granary and the dovecote; not long ago thousands of pigeons came to drink and bathe
in the big pond, to the chagrin of the red and silver fish that swim

in it. On the right, the wall and the fertile fig tree; a couple of billy goats, so white and shiny that they are worthy of being sacrificed at the altar of the god Pan, munch its new shoots. Across from my room I see the gate through which cattle, their melodious bells tinkling, pass to go to the mountain. In the middle of the courtyard there is a haystack of straw, a huge heap of dry, plush, pale gold inviting one to plunge in it and take a nap when the heat burns. The courtyard smells not of flowers but of fresh-cut herbs drying in the granary: mint, gentian, fennel, and other wild plants found sticking out of the bales of grain. It smells of eucalyptus gum, bread cooking in the oven, and smoke—yes, smoke, so pleasant and light when it blends with the air. And then there is the smell of the stables, which breathes new life into sickly lungs and swells healthy ones.

In the afternoon the horizon recedes to the wide row of camellia bushes that runs across the entire valley, and to Lake Sada, caught between two mountains like a fragment of a broken mirror. Beautiful melancholy landscape at night, when the moon rises behind the dark chestnut trees like a fireball; bright in the daytime, when among the camellias and yuccas one spots the precipitous flight of a squadron of ducks, still dripping from a splash in the fountain; or the passing of a four-year-old child, a creature of light and joy, flesh of dark milk and rose petals and dressed in an open white shirt: bare arms, even lovelier since the sun tinted them the color of agate, knees in the air, a straw hat on his head, his chestnut hair flowing in loose curls, a dimple on each cheek, and laughter playing on all his features.

From this oasis I write to you, reader, my unknown friend, who so patiently have heard me narrate my *memories of the new age*. God be with you.

Emilia Pardo Bazán

Granja de Meirás,[74] September 1886

Notes

1. André Chénier (1762–94): French poet guillotined during the French Revolution.

2. Philarète Chasles (1789–1873): French writer, critic, and historian.

3. Throughout the nineteenth and early twentieth centuries the Spanish government waged wars with its African colonies. In this case Pardo Bazán refers to Leopoldo O'Donnell's expedition to Morocco in 1860, which ended with the conquest of Tetuán.

4. Juan Prim (1814–70): Spanish general and politician, leader of the liberal revolution of 1868 mentioned in *The House of Ulloa*; General Ros de Olano (1808–86) also supported the revolution; Bernard and Roland: celebrated heroes of medieval epics.

5. The Basque country has a long tradition of self-rule and struggle for independence. In the nineteenth century the ultraconservative Carlist party embodied Basque separatism; today the most radical advocate of separatism is the terrorist group ETA.

6. *Quintillas:* poems of five verses.

7. Jean de La Fontaine (1621–95): famous French fabulist whose works have been translated into English by Marianne Moore, among others.

8. Louis Barthélemy: French abbot (1750–1815), author of didactic works, a biography, and a novel; Cesar Cantú (1804–95): Italian writer and historian, author of a popular *Universal History*.

9. The Jacobins and the Girondists were, respectively, the radical and moderate parties of the French Revolution. Madame Roland, a distinguished member of the latter, was guillotined in 1793.

The Temple of Paris was originally a medieval church built by the Templars and later transformed into a prison. During the Revolution the royal family was locked in the Temple, where the young prince spent the last three days of his life.

10. Pigault-Lebrun (1753–1835): French novelist and playwright. The Spanish title that appears in the text is probably a translation of *Le garçon sans souci*.

11. Juan Ruiz, archpriest of Hita: fourteenth-century Spanish poet, author of the *Book of Good Love*, a classic of medieval literature; Francisco Delicado: fourteenth-century Spanish author of picaresque novels; Pierre de Bourdeilles, Lord Brantôme (1535–1614): French historian.

12. Here we miss the pun in Pardo Bazán's original sentence, for in Spanish *malo* means *bad*.

13. Alonso de Ercilla (1533–94): Spanish poet and soldier who participated in the conquest of Chile and narrated it in his epic poem *La Araucana* (The Araucanian); Jean Baptiste Racine (1636–99): French poet and dramatist considered,

with Corneille, one of the two greatest authors of French tragedy of the seventeenth century; José Zorrilla (1817–93): romantic Spanish poet and dramatist, author of the popular *Don Juan Tenorio*.

14. Bartolomé (1562–1633) and Lupercio (1563–1613) Argensola: Spanish poets who were brothers.

15. Pardo Bazán probably refers to Ignacio Hermosilla y Sandoval, a member of the Spanish Academies of Language and of History who died in Madrid in 1802.

16. Francisco de Quevedo (1580–1645): together with Luis de Góngora, the most prominent Spanish poet of the seventeenth century. He was also a brilliant prose writer.

17. *The Wandering Jew* is one of the best-known novels of Eugène Sue (1804–57).

18. Fernán Caballero: pen name of Cecilia Böhl de Faber (1770–1836), foremost representative of the Spanish romantic novel.

19. Gaspar Núñez de Arce (1834–1903): poet and politician; José Echegaray (1833–1916): politician, poet, and playwright who won the Nobel Prize for literature in 1904; Manuel Tamayo y Baus (1829–98): dramatist; Cándido Nocedal (1821–85): writer and leader of the Carlist party, which he abandoned shortly before his death. The literary reputation of these Spanish authors rose and fell with their political careers.

20. The traditional alliance of the Spanish Catholic church with conservative forces—the aristocracy and the army—has brought frequent outbreaks of anticlericalism. In the nineteenth century the liberals were a minority and had to rely on the support of extremist elements that were always on the verge of violence. In this case, anticlerical disturbances were partly a reaction against the conspicuous presence of the church in Isabella II's court. On the other hand, the conservatives were equally violent in their repression of the liberal movement. Similar events preceded the civil war of 1936.

21. Amadeo I was an Italian prince who reigned in Spain between 1871 and 1873. He was succeeded by the Republic.

22. Victor Alfieri (1749–1803), Hugo Foscolo (1778–1827), and Silvio Pellico (1788–1854) were some of the leading Italian poets and dramatists of this period. Foscolo, however, is best known for his novel *Ultimi lettere di Jacopo Ortis* (Last letters of Jacob Ortis), which Pardo Bazán mentions later.

23. Karl Krause (1781–1832): German philosopher who had a profound influence in Spain in the second half of the nineteenth century. His ideology attempts to reconcile the scientific positivism of his age with a kind of pantheistic spiritualism.

24. Cartagena: city in southeastern Spain that in 1875 fought for its independence and was bombed by the central government.

25. *The Abodes:* one of the most celebrated mystic works of Saint Theresa (1515–82).

26. Friar Luis de Granada (1504–88): Spanish writer and orator who belonged to the order of the Dominicans.

27. Immanuel Kant (1724–1804) held that the content of knowledge comes after sense perception, but that its form is determined by categories that exist a priori in the mind. He also believed that God, freedom, and immortality cannot be proved but are rationally implied.

28. Friedrich Hegel (1770–1831) held that every idea and fact (thesis) belongs to an all-embracing mind, in which it evokes its opposite (antithesis); these two result in a unified whole (synthesis), which in turn becomes a new thesis.

29. Johann Wolfgang von Goethe (1749–1832), poet, dramatist, and novelist; Friedrich Schiller (1759–1805), dramatist and poet; Gottfried Bürger (1748–94), poet; and Heinrich Heine (1797–1856), poet and essayist, were all major figures of the German classic and romantic periods.

30. Friedrich Wilhelm Joseph von Schelling (1775–1854): German philosopher who wrote several studies on Kant and Fichte and became the leading thinker of the romantic school and a prominent figure of the movement generally known as German philosophy; Johann Gottlieb Fichte (1762–1814): German philosopher strongly influenced by Kant, on whom he wrote several works.

31. Benito Pérez Galdós (1843–1920), José M. Pereda (1833–1906), Juan Valera (1824–1905), and Pedro Antonio de Alarcón (1833–91) were major figures of the realistic Spanish novel. *Episodios nacionales*, which Pardo Bazán mentions a few lines further on, is a collection of more than fifty short historical novels by Pérez Galdós. Some of his best works—*Fortunata and Jacinta* and *Torquemada*—have been translated into English.

32. Simonides (556–467 B.C.): Greek poet who wrote epigrams, elegies, and odes.

33. Juan Pantoja (1551–1608): court painter of Philip II and Philip III, famous for his portraits of the royal family.

34. Marcelino Menéndez y Pelayo (1856–1912): Spanish humanist, critic, and politician whose opinions were highly regarded in his time. He wrote important historical, political, and literary essays.

35. Antonio Cánovas del Castillo: leader of the conservative party in power between 1878 and 1881, mentioned in *The House of Ulloa*.

36. Ramón de Campoamor (1817–1901): Spanish poet and politician.

37. Francisco Giner de los Ríos (1839–1915): Spanish writer and philosopher of Krausist and liberal tendencies. He was an innovative pedagogue and a key figure in the intellectual life of Spain.

38. Benito Jerónimo Feijóo (1676–1764): writer, critic, and theologian who was one of the chief representatives of the Spanish Enlightenment. Pardo Bazán admired his feminist views.

39. Concepción Arenal (1820–93): Spanish journalist, novelist, and philanthropist who was one of the most prominent female figures in the nineteenth century.

40. Duns Scotus (1265?–1308): Scholastic philosopher and theologian who separated philosophy from theology and interpreted God's reason as an expression of divine will; William of Ockham (1300?–1349?): English philosopher; Roger Bacon (1214?–94?): English philosopher and scientist.

41. This whole passage refers to the debate between faith and science, a central issue of Scholasticism.

42. Alessandro Manzoni (1785–1873): Italian poet and novelist. *The Betrothed* is his novelistic masterpiece. For *Cartas de Jacobo Ortis*, see n. 22.

43. Bulwer-Lytton, Edward George Earle Lytton (1803–73): English novelist and playwright popular in his day.

44. John William Draper (1811–82): American scientist who made valuable contributions in photochemistry and photography. In 1840 he took the first photograph of the moon.

45. Angel Secchi (1818–78): Italian Jesuit and astronomer, author of important works on the topography and physical structure of the planets; Ernst Heinrich Haeckel (1834–1919): German biologist and philosopher.

46. *Pepita Jiménez* is Valera's masterpiece; *The Three-cornered Hat* is one of Alarcón's best novels.

47. Diego Hurtado de Mendoza (1503–75): Spanish writer to whom some critics attribute the greatest picaresque novel of Spain, *Lazarillo de Tormes*. Vicente Espinel (1551–1634) wrote another classic of the picaresque genre, *Marcos de Obregón*.

48. Ramón de Mesonero Romanos (1803–82): popular author of articles and humorous, picturesque sketches of Madrid life.

49. *Little Flowers of Saint Francis:* account of episodes in Saint Francis's life attributed to Friar Hugolino de Montefeltro.

50. Honoré de Balzac (1799–1850), Gustave Flaubert (1821–80), Edmond (1822–96) and Jules (1830–70) de Goncourt, and Alphonse Daudet (1840–97) were among the masters of the realistic French novel.

51. Autos-da-fé: public punishments, especially the burning of heretics, carried out by the Inquisition.

52. Pardo Bazán's apology for the Inquisition may well be partisan and emotional. In fact, on numerous occasions in history the Inquisition banished books and imprisoned their authors. Leaving aside her own prejudice, however, her data are more accurate than Hugo's. As far as is known, the Inquisition did not execute writers and lost most of its power after the seventeenth century; it was abolished by the Constitution of 1812.

53. The Dominican order is known for its political and religious conservatism.

54. Massacre of Saint Bartholomew: killing of Protestants ordered by Charles IX of France on the eve of Saint Bartholomew's day (August 24) in 1572. "Dragonades" refers to the persecution of French Protestants in general.

55. Clément Marot (1496–1544): French poet who was accused of heresy and had to flee to Italy.

56. "Good for the Spaniard!"

57. Juan Francisco Masdeu (1744–1817): Spanish Jesuit and historian; *Cancionero de Baena:* collection of medieval Spanish poetry published in 1445.

58. *La época:* prestigious newspaper of Pardo Bazán's time.

59. *La regenta:* masterpiece of Leopoldo Alas, published in 1885, and a classic Spanish novel of all times. It is currently available in English under the same title.

60. Luis Alfonso (1845–92): writer and critic who contributed regularly to the main newspapers and journals published in Madrid.

61. Saint Francis of Sales (1567–1622): ascetic French writer.

62. Friar Hortensio Félix Paravicino y Arteaga (1580–1632): Spanish poet and theologian, well versed in secular and religious literature.

63. Eduardo Calcaño (1831–1904): Venezuelan politician and writer who in his article "Carta literaria" (*La ilustración española y americana*, February 29, 1884), launched a violent attack against the naturalists, likening them to pirates of literature beginning to wave their black flag in Spain; Francesc Pi i Margall (1824–1901): Spanish philosopher, historian, and politician who formulated Spanish federalism; Pierre Joseph Proudhon (1809–65): socialist French writer.

64. Gracchus: Roman tribune known for his civic and democratic principles. The people delivered him to his enemies, and for this reason he has become an archetypical victim of popular ingratitude.

65. Probably Pardo Bazán refers to the pact of Vergara, signed on August 31, 1839, at the end of the First Carlist War.

66. *Tuna:* group of students who serenade girls in the streets. They wear black hats and cloaks with bright ribbons. It is an old Spanish tradition.

67. Armando Palacio Valdés (1853–1938): Spanish novelist who set his fiction in his native province of Asturias, in northern Spain, which is also the setting of Leopoldo Alas's novels; Narcís Oller (1846–1930): realistic novelist who described Barcelona, which Pardo Bazán calls the "second capital of Spain."

68. Galician is actually not a dialect but one of the four languages of Spain, although perhaps the least spoken today. The other three are Castilian, also called Spanish because it is the official language, Basque, and Catalan.

69. Emilio Castelar (1832–99): Spanish writer and politician known for his powerful oratory.

70. Tomás de Iriarte (1750–91): famous Spanish fabulist.

71. Georges Ohnet (1848–1918): French author of romances very popular in their day, both in France and in Spain.

72. Lines from Friar Luis de León (1527–91), one of the great poets of the Spanish Renaissance.

73. In this passage Pardo Bazán paraphrases other fragments from Friar Luis de León's poems.

74. Clearly, Pardo Bazán's sensual description of Granja de Meirás—the house, the landscape, the child, even the Masonic grandfather—is evocative of the house of Ulloa. The city of La Coruña, where Pardo Bazán was born in 1851, purchased Granja de Meirás in 1939, at the end of the civil war, and gave it to Franco. Granja de Meirás became Franco's summer residence, and many of Pardo Bazán's manuscripts and other valuable materials were lost.